DIRTY LITTLE SECRET

Also by Jennifer Ryan

JENNIFER RYAN

DIRTY LITTLE SECRET

Wild Rose Ranch

AVONBOOKS

An Imprint of HarperCollinsPublishers

Excerpt from *Restless Rancher* copyright © 2019 by Jennifer Ryan.

DIRTY LITTLE SECRET. Copyright © 2018 by Jennifer Ryan. All rights reserved. Printed in the United States of America. No part of this book may be used or reproduced in any manner whatsoever without written permission except in the case of brief quotations embodied in critical articles and reviews. For information, address HarperCollins Publishers, 195 Broadway, New York, NY 10007.

First Avon Books mass market printing: January 2019
First Avon Books special mass market printing: January 2019
First Avon Books hardcover printing: December 2018

Print Edition ISBN: 978-0-06-289066-5
Digital Edition ISBN: 978-0-06-264532-6

Avon, Avon & logo, and Avon Books & logo are registered trademarks of HarperCollins Publishers in the United States of America and other countries.

HarperCollins is a registered trademark of HarperCollins Publishers in the United States of America and other countries.

FIRST EDITION

18 19 20 21 22 LSC 10 9 8 7 6 5 4 3 2 1

For you, Mom.
Thanks for all your support, pride, love, and faith
in me. It means everything. I love you.

DIRTY LITTLE SECRET

Prologue

Six years ago
Clark County Fair and Rodeo, Nevada

Roxy leaped off her horse, landed in the dirt, and tried to contain the smile that spread across her face for the man sitting in the stands staring right at her. His smile, the pride in his eyes, made her heart simultaneously swell with joy and drown in sorrow.

John came, but he wouldn't speak to her. Not here, where others could see them together and possibly connect the dots that she was his daughter. A child no one knew about. A child he'd never expected and didn't want.

Her mother made sure of that.

Roxy was doomed to be an outcast before she was ever born.

John came today to watch her barrel race on one of the horses he secretly sent to her. It's why she practiced every day and rode so hard in competition. The little girl inside her wanted to make him proud. She wanted him to like and admire her.

She wanted him to stand up and say, "That's my girl!"

But in eighteen years, he'd never even come close to admitting that to anyone.

These little glimpses of him and what could have been broke her heart. As much as Roxy wanted her father to love her enough to keep her, she wanted him to stay away.

"You won!" Sonya wrapped her in a hug.

"Again!" Juliana scrunched her mouth into a pretty pout. As much as she wanted Roxy to win, she wanted to beat her, too. Little sisters were like that.

Adria hugged her, then held her at arm's length. "He came." She glanced over at John. "And so did your sexy brother."

"He's not my brother." Technically he was her stepbrother by marriage. John had raised him as his own after Noah's mother suddenly died.

The son he always wanted.

Noah, the man sitting beside him, who got to call him Dad, who knew John as a good and decent man, knew nothing about her. Noah and Annabelle, his adopted children, got his love and devotion every day. They grew up with the life she could have had if only John had fought for her and revealed his dirty little secret.

"Noah's got the best ass in denim in this whole damn place."

"Don't swear," Roxy scolded Juliana, though she couldn't disagree with the statement.

The girl was growing up way too fast. At fifteen, she looked twenty-one. And men noticed.

Here, everyone stared at the notorious Wild Rose girls. If they hadn't entered their first rodeo in Nevada and won in spectacular fashion, maybe no one would have linked them to the infamous Wild Rose Ranch brothel located in a little town outside of Las Vegas—where prostitution was legal and their mothers worked.

It didn't matter that Roxy and her sisters *didn't* work there.

When Roxy and her sisters showed up at a rodeo, every eye in the place turned to them. The buzz of whispers spread, letting everyone know the girls from the Wild Rose Ranch had arrived to ride.

Many a cowboy had mistaken *what* they came to ride.

When they went to a rodeo, it was for the competition and winning.

It didn't seem to matter that they were in their teens. Their Wild Rose Ranch—*We Ride Hard* T-shirts sparked all kinds of cowboy fantasies.

Yes, they used the provocative name. They wanted to make it their own and be proud of it. They wanted where they came from to mean something more.

They wanted their little legitimate piece of the Ranch.

They were the best. She and her sisters had proven that again today. After all, Roxy may have just won the grand prize, but her sisters were in second, third, and fourth place right behind her.

They dominated.

A man whistled out to them. No matter how many wins, they were still perceived as *those* girls from the Wild Rose Ranch.

Which is why her father remained in the stands, a safe distance from her and any chance of rumors.

"Why don't you just walk up to Noah and tell him who you are?" Juliana nudged her with her elbow.

"He stares at you just like your father," Adria pointed out.

"Noah stares because he thinks we're prostitutes."

Sonya laid her hand on Roxy's shoulder. "Introduce yourself. Not as John's daughter, but just you."

"Why? What will that change? 'Hi, I'm Roxy.' Then what?"

"See what happens." Adria smiled. "Ask about him. You know you want to know what his life is like living with your father."

"I know what his life is like with John. Everything my life wasn't." John always sent the checks, but when she was really young her mother used the money to support her habit before she remembered to take care of Roxy.

She bet Noah was never ridiculed for being on the free lunch program at school. She bet he never had to root through trash in the cafeteria to scrounge up extra food for the weekend because there was no food in the house. He didn't grow up with cocaine dusting the table where he did his homework, or have to step over trash and used needles to get to the couch that smelled of stale cigarette smoke and pot. He probably never had to wear shoes a size too small and pants three inches too short because there wasn't any money for new clothes.

Noah didn't know what it was like to hide in a cupboard or closet when strange men came over. He didn't know how creepy and scary it was to have a strange man grab you and make you sit on his lap, his hold too tight, his face too close.

No, he didn't know that kind of fear.

He didn't know how it felt to have a mother named Candy, who had a body made for sin and used it to make a living. Only Roxy's sisters knew how it felt for people to look at you and think the worst because of who and what your mother was, because their mothers worked at the Wild Rose Ranch, too.

Noah didn't know anything. He lived his perfect life free of scandal and ostracism.

And that's how John wanted to keep it.

"It's time to go. Let's collect our prize money, load up the horses, and get the hell out of here."

Roxy led her horse away and kept her back to her father and Noah. She didn't want to think about what might have been anymore. She'd spent countless hours and sleepless nights doing that.

Her life hadn't been all that bad the last ten years. Not since Candy moved them out of the last grungy apartment to the Wild Rose Ranch.

Roxy liked the cozy house away from the big mansion.

She didn't mind being on her own with the girls who had become her sisters.

She didn't mind being alone in the world.

She didn't, she told herself again.

But just once she'd like one of her parents to choose her.

She'd like someone to choose her.

Chapter One

Six years later
Speckled Horse Ranch, Whitefall, Montana

John Cordero slumped in the saddle, fell off his horse, and landed in a heap in the dirt and tall grass as the horse danced away.

Shocked, Noah jumped off his horse and kneeled beside his stepdad. "John? John, are you okay?"

John moaned and rolled to his side. A fine sheen of sweat covered his rugged face, now sickly pale. His unfocused eyes filled with pain. "I have to tell you . . ."

"Is anything broken? Where do you hurt?"

John grabbed Noah's arm. "I'm okay. Need to tell you . . ." John closed his eyes and tried to catch his breath.

Noah tamped down his panic and worries. A moment ago, they'd been sitting atop their horses on the overlook staring at the long expanse of Speckled Horse Ranch spread out before them. Now, Noah grabbed John's hands and pulled him up to sitting, hoping the weakness he felt in John didn't mean something serious. "I need to get you home and to a hospital." Noah's mind went to a stroke or heart attack, neither of which he wanted to be true.

John's limbs remained limp, his body unsteady. Noah went around to John's back, squatted, wrapped his arms around John's middle, and lifted him up to his feet. "Come on, old man, help me out."

John reached for the saddle pommel.

Noah held him in place with his shoulder, reached down, grabbed his jean-clad leg, and helped him put his boot in the stirrup. It took all Noah's strength to lift and push John into the saddle. Before John could topple down again, Noah swung up behind him.

Lucky for him, the horse took their combined weight without throwing them both off.

Noah grabbed the reins and hooked one hand around John to keep him steady. "You okay?"

"This is damn embarrassing."

"You'll get over it." Noah nudged the horse to head home and kept their pace brisk, even though he wanted to gallop. "Hold tight. We'll be there soon."

John placed his hand over Noah's on his stomach. "You run this place well." A man of few words, John didn't say things he didn't mean.

The praise stunned Noah. "I learned from the best." Noah tried to pull John up, but John slumped forward again.

"I'm a difficult man, set in my ways. Rode you harder than any of the ranch hands."

That he did. No sense arguing the truth.

Noah had resented John's relentless drive when he was young. He had more than a few moments where he believed John thought he couldn't do anything right. But John sprinkled just enough praise and encouragement along the way to remind Noah that John wanted him to be the best and a partner he could count on.

Noah owed John so much, so he'd worked hard to earn his place on Speckled Horse Ranch at John's side.

"Your mother was a good woman. She loved you. Loved me, even though I never made it easy."

"She was happy here." Thinking about his mother always made him sad. She had married John when Noah was two. Four years later, she died from complications due to an ectopic pregnancy. "I don't remember her well, but I still miss her." The admission didn't come easy.

John's big body trembled with the effort to stay upright in the saddle.

His skin turned a sickly gray. Noah wondered if all this talk about the ranch and his mother meant John wanted to join her in heaven.

The thought stopped his heart. They couldn't cover the ride down the hill and across the wide pasture fast enough.

"Beth was happy here. I was happy with her," John confided.

When Noah's mother died, John sat him down in his study and told him straight out that no matter what, he'd stay on the ranch. From that day on, even though he was only a boy of six, John had taught him how to run the ranch, working day in and day out side by side. Noah had no other family. He couldn't lose the only father he'd ever known.

"After I lost Beth . . . well, no one could replace her. I tried but never found that kind of connection. So I settled. Lisa played to my ego. She made me feel young and alive again. But that all changed almost the minute we got married."

Noah hadn't liked Lisa the second he'd met her. The feel of the house changed the instant she moved in, and he never got that sense of his mother and home back. Lisa's presence, the way she changed this and redecorated that, sucked out the last reminders of Noah's mom.

She wanted the place to feel like her home, too, but the callous way she went about it stung.

He also resented Lisa for the way she treated John and their marriage, leaving him when times got tough. It left John even more closed off and disheartened.

Noah still didn't understand why they had married when they both carried on a string of affairs neither of them spoke about and tried to hide despite the other knowing.

Noah would never forget the look in John's eyes when they stood outside the hospital nursery window looking in at Annabelle. He'd never seen anyone look so disappointed, and even more unbelievable, hurt. John never let it show that anything got through his thick skin, but seeing that squalling blond-haired, blue-eyed baby put that hurt in his golden eyes like Noah had never seen. To this day, although John always treated Annabelle with nothing but kindness, Noah sometimes caught him looking at her with that same hurt in his eyes.

Noah, young and uncertain about having a stepsister, hadn't understood the look until days later when they brought Annabelle home and he'd overheard John and Lisa's heated argument in their room that night. One look at Annabelle's bright blond hair and blue eyes had told John what all of Lisa's protests to the contrary didn't. Annabelle wasn't his daughter, but the product of one of the many affairs Lisa kept quiet, but hadn't managed to keep secret.

While John accepted Annabelle, even loved her in his own way, he'd never forgiven Lisa. Not for the affair, but the undeniable proof that he'd been unable to get her pregnant himself after years of trying.

Noah remained silent on the subject. He focused on the ride, wishing for one of the guys from the stables to come out, see them coming, and help him with John.

"I don't know why I married her. After your mother and the baby . . ." John ran his hand over his black hair that had grown more salt and pepper these last years. "I wanted another child." John squeezed his hand hard. "Don't get me wrong, you were a good son. I'm the only son to parents who had little family when I was born. Don't know if any of them are still around. I just wanted my name, my blood, to be here long after I'm gone."

Noah, still reeling from hearing John say he was a good son, high praise from a man who doled out very few compliments or niceties, understood the man's need for a legacy.

At thirty-one, Noah had been contemplating his lonely-looking future and wondering if it wasn't time to find a wife, have some kids, and make a family of his own. Without any good examples of a happy marriage and with a string of flings under his belt, he often wondered if he could make a relationship work.

Hell, who was he kidding, he'd learned from John, never let a woman get under your skin. He ended his last relationship because Cheryl wanted more than he was willing to give. Judging by the number of voicemails and text messages Cheryl left on his cell phone, she wasn't ready to give up on him.

John expected some kind of answer, so Noah said, "I understand. You took care of me, sent me to college, and gave me a job and a life here on the ranch, even though I'm not your son. I appreciate everything you've done. A lot of men, my father included, would have dumped an unwanted child." He knew little about his own father, who cheated on his mother while she was pregnant with him. She divorced him and his father took his freedom and never looked back.

"You were never unwanted," John replied, his voice gruff. "No matter my shortcomings as a parent, never think I didn't want you here. You reminded me of myself at your age. You love ranching, the horses, the life. I enjoyed teaching you, seeing you discover new things. You wanted to follow in my footsteps. You put that college degree to work, changed things here and there, and helped make this place what it is today."

A lump formed in Noah's throat.

John broke the silence that settled between them. "I'm not proud of some of the things I've done. Most you know about, but some, well, I've kept a few things to myself. I have lots of regrets. One that is too late to make right. I hurt her because I was a coward, concerned about my reputation instead of protecting her."

Noah had no idea who or what John was talking about.

"Listen, son, what I'm trying to say is that soon this will belong to you."

Noah's heart sank. He hoped that day wasn't today, but feared John's heavy weight against his chest meant something dire.

"I have things I want to say." John sucked in several quick breaths. "Things. I. Need to tell you." He struggled to get the words out.

"John, please, stop talking. We're almost there. I'll get you to a doctor."

John winced in pain and leaned heavily to the side. It was all Noah could do to hold him up and against his chest.

"I need to get this out. You run this ranch, but you don't know . . . everything. Promise you'll take care of her. She's never had anyone."

"I promise. Annabelle will be fine."

John's head bobbed forward and up several times. "No. I need to tell you about . . ." John's words trailed off and his whole body went lax.

Noah swore. Hoping he was close enough to the stables for someone to hear him, he whistled. The high-pitched sound carried and Robby rushed out and spotted them. Noah reined in next to the ranch foreman.

"What happened?"

"He collapsed. Help me get him in the truck."

Robby took John by the shoulders. Noah swung down from the horse and caught John's legs.

Annabelle ran out of the house. "Oh my God!"

"Get the truck door, Sprite."

Noah and Robby muscled John into the front seat and buckled him in. No time to wait for an ambulance to drive all the way out here, they'd drive him to the hospital and get him the help he needed.

Noah hoped they were in time.

THE HOSPITAL WAITING room walls closed in on Noah as he paced, his long stride eating up the stained carpet. He rolled his shoulders, but nothing eased the ache that had taken hold and wouldn't let go. Wild thoughts raced through his mind.

He hung on to only one: John Cordero was the strongest, most stubborn man he'd ever met. He wouldn't dare die of something as stupid as falling off his horse.

But John hadn't been in the saddle in more than two months. He'd made excuses and complained of getting old and aching joints and too much damn paperwork.

The usual John complaints Noah heard so often, he didn't think anything of it.

"Mr. Cordero?"

The doctor's voice brought back the panic he'd felt seeing John unconscious in the truck.

"Yes. It's just Noah. How is he?"

Annabelle stood and wrapped her arms around Noah's middle. He hugged her close, needing her support as much as she needed his.

"Your father is in the ICU. He's critical."

"What happened?" Tears streaked down Annabelle's pale cheeks.

"I've been treating Mr. Cordero for the past eight months. He asked me to come and explain his condition. He has a rare brain tumor."

"The trip to Chicago two months ago." Noah put the pieces together.

"I sent him for some specialized treatment in hopes of shrinking the tumor and prolonging his life. Unfortunately, it wasn't as successful as we hoped. Frankly, it was a long shot, but Mr. Cordero was willing to tolerate the treatment."

"He's been so tired lately." Annabelle pressed closer to Noah's side. At fifteen, she'd endured enough loss in her short life. Lisa, fed up with raising a baby and John's increasing disinterest in anything his wife did, walked out when Annabelle was just three, granting custody to her ex-husband.

Again, John lost the woman, but kept the child. John had done his best raising Annabelle on his own.

"Last I saw him a week ago, he was having difficulty with his balance, his vision was blurry, and his motor functions were deteriorating."

If Noah had known he'd have never let John on a horse. The thought of what could have happened if he'd fallen while they galloped across the fields shuddered through Noah's body.

"The tumor has caused some bleeding deep in the brain. It's only a matter of time."

"Are you saying he's dying?" Annabelle couldn't seem to comprehend the doctor's implausible words.

"I'm sorry, miss, but yes."

"How long?" A strange gruffness filled his voice, and Noah choked back the emotions welling up inside him.

"Hours. Maybe a day or two." The doctor waited a moment while they absorbed the devastating news.

Annabelle's nails dug into his side, her grip tightening along with the band around his chest, but he didn't feel the pain. Everything inside him went numb.

"Mr. Cordero left instructions detailing his wishes. I've contacted his lawyer, letting him know we've invoked the living will. We've made John comfortable. He slips in and out of consciousness with varying degrees of alertness. This may continue for a while. You're welcome to stay with him in the room. If there is anyone you need to contact, I suggest you do it immediately."

"Mary, our housekeeper, and Robby, our foreman, are at the house. They'll want to come and say goodbye," Annabelle stammered. "What about Mom?" she asked, uncertain.

"You can call her on my cell, Sprite."

"She probably won't care."

Probably not, Noah agreed, but didn't voice his opinion. "Call her. No matter what she says or does, at least you know you tried." He dug his cell out of his dusty jeans pocket and handed it to her.

He waited for her to take a seat in the corner before he spoke to the doctor again. "Is there anything you need me to do? Decisions have to be made."

The doctor clapped a hand on Noah's shoulder and squeezed, offering what little comfort he could under the circumstances. "Eight months ago, I told Mr. Cordero to get his affairs in order. The living will he set up takes care of all the decisions needed in this situation. Spend time with him. Say goodbye."

The doctor left with that damn sympathetic look on his face. Noah turned to Annabelle, worried about the call to her rattlesnake of a mother. Not surprising, Annabelle looked worse for talking to her instead of better.

"She's not coming," his sister mumbled and dropped the phone in his hand.

He bent in front of her and put his hands on her knees. "I'm sorry, Sprite. You tried."

"Fat lot of good it did me. She hates me."

"She doesn't hate you. She doesn't even know you."

"Isn't that worse?" Sometimes Annabelle was too damn smart for her own good.

Noah cocked up one side of his mouth. "Do you think she'll ever change?"

Annabelle folded her arms over her chest. "No."

"Then quit expecting her to do what you *hope* she'll do, instead of the thing you *know* she'll do."

Annabelle's head fell forward. "What's going to happen to me?"

"What do you mean, Sprite?" He brushed a strand of wet hair off her tear-stained cheek. He wasn't prone to tender gestures, but her eyes were still bright with unshed tears, the blue depths filled with nothing but sadness and a fear he understood all too well. No one liked to be left behind.

"I'm a minor. If Dad dies, I'll have to go stay with my mother. She doesn't want me. She'll leave me again and I'll be alone."

"Never." Absolute certainty filled his voice, though he wasn't sure he spoke the truth. If John died and Lisa wanted Annabelle, he'd have a hell of a time gaining custody. "I'll never let her take you."

He hoped Lisa didn't get some wild bug up her ass and make him a liar.

If the doctor was right and John had prepared for this day, Noah hoped John had figured this out with his lawyer.

"Can we see him now?"

He held his hand out to her. "Come on, Sprite. Stop worrying. No matter what, it's you and me."

"You swear?"

Noah understood her fear. Where she still held hope that her mother would come around and want to be with her again, Noah had erected a shield to keep people out and his feelings in.

Much like John, he'd learned that no one could hurt you if they didn't know you cared.

"I swear. No one will ever come between us."

Chapter Two

Roxy sat bolt upright when her phone rang. She swiped the back of her hand over her mouth, wiped away the embarrassing drool, and picked up her phone expecting one of her sisters. She'd fallen asleep at the kitchen table after working all night and morning. She checked the time and caller ID. The number on the screen didn't register. Could be a cable system customer.

"Hello."

"Miss Cordero?"

"Yes, this is Roxy."

"You don't know me. This is Tom Nelson. I'm the lawyer who represents your father, John Cordero."

"I know who my father is."

Tom paused at her sharp tone.

Her sisters Sonya, Adria, and Juliana were left to wonder about their fathers. Those guys probably didn't even know they had daughters.

"Um, yes, well, he's in the hospital."

Roxy sat up straighter, but couldn't find any words. Everything inside her went still.

"The doctor believes he won't make it through the night." Her ears buzzed with the rush of adrenaline and denial that shot through her system. She barely heard Tom's next words over the hum in her head. "I took the liberty of booking you a flight. It leaves in two hours. You'll need to hurry to make it."

The shocking news took her by surprise. She didn't know how to feel. Sad. Worried. Angry. Scared. Emotions swirled in her heart.

"Roxy, your father is asking for you."

Her heart had grown cold the last many years her father stayed out of her life. She wanted to feel indifferent, but couldn't, not when her heart broke thinking that if she didn't hurry, she'd miss her chance to make things right.

She rattled off her email address. "Send me the flight information and where to find him. I'm on my way."

She hung up, unable to talk any longer like her world hadn't just been turned upside down. Again.

The little girl inside her loved her daddy. The adult harbored resentments that he hadn't been the perfect father to her that he was to Noah and Annabelle. Understanding why didn't appease the sad little girl part of her.

Adria walked up beside her and placed a steaming mug of coffee and a warm slice of apple cinnamon coffee cake on the table. Roxy jumped, startled anyone was home. She thought at least Adria would be attending her classes at UNLV. Juliana wasn't always so conscientious about school or work.

"Have you seen her?"

Roxy shook her head, knowing Adria meant her twin, Juliana. Identical DNA didn't mean they had the same personalities. While Adria worked hard in culinary school and her business classes, Juliana ran off to find any kind of trouble she could on the strip, ditching classes for fun and leaving real life to worry about later. Just like Juliana and Adria's mother. Just like Roxy's.

Roxy took care of everyone, but right now she didn't have it in her to worry about Adria and whatever Juliana had done to make her worry.

"What's wrong?"

Roxy stared out the window of her little ranch house she shared with her sisters at the three-story Wild Rose Ranch mansion where her mother lived. From here, she could see part of the lush backyard garden that surrounded the large pool and two spas. At this time of the morning, most of the red velvet drapes were drawn in the upstairs bedroom windows.

Few clients stayed the night, but a few stragglers were probably passed out with one or two hookers draped over them.

Her mother might be one of them.

Ugh! She wiped that yucky thought out of her mind and focused on her father and their strange relationship. "My father is dying."

Adria's eyes went wide. "What?"

"His lawyer just called. John's in the hospital. It's only a matter of time. Hours it seems."

And here she sat wasting time. But would being there change anything?

"What are you going to do?"

Her phone dinged with an email. She held up the phone. "All the arrangements have been made."

Adria took her hand and pulled her up out of her seat. "Come on. I'll help you."

That's what they did. They may not be blood, but they were family. Her father might be family, but he was a stranger, a ghost in Roxy's turbulent life.

Adria tugged her by the hand into Roxy's room. "You get dressed. I'll start packing. How long will you be gone?"

"His lawyer said he won't last the night."

Adria's frown matched Roxy's irritation. "And he notified you at the very last second?"

Roxy had been an afterthought in her father's life. It didn't surprise her she was the last to know. It surprised her she was notified at all.

"Are you going to tell Candy?"

"Hell no." The last thing Roxy needed was Candy's interference, or worse, her wanting to go with Roxy. One look at Candy standing over his deathbed would certainly kill her father on the spot. Candy would probably shake him down for more money. She wouldn't put it past Candy to pull out his IV line and jab it into her own arm just for the high-octane pain meds.

Candy didn't care about John. She only cared about what she could get from him.

"I don't blame you. Candy's not exactly the compassionate sort."

No. She'd probably flirt with and seduce every doctor in the place. She liked a man with money to burn. On her.

Roxy shuddered. Just when you thought a situation couldn't get worse, Candy found a way to muck it up even more.

Adria packed. Roxy stripped off her leggings and T-shirt and found something comfortable to travel in and appropriate to see her father.

Efficient as ever, Adria closed up the small suitcase she'd pulled out of the closet and stuffed with more clothes than Roxy thought she needed, shoes, the makeup bag from her bathroom, along with the other essentials she'd need. "All set."

Roxy finished brushing out her long hair. "I don't need all that. I'll probably be back in the morning."

"You never know. Come on, I'll drive you to the airport."

Roxy followed Adria out to the car wondering if this was a good idea or not. Maybe some things were better left in the past.

Chapter Three

Noah saw her sneak into John's hospital room. Damn. Roxy hoped to slip in and out unnoticed by the family. The last thing she wanted to do was intrude upon their bedside vigil. Still, John was her father and she deserved a few minutes to work her way through the muddled mess of emotions his imminent death invoked.

She deserved to say her piece.

She always thought there'd be time enough to meet again, have that awkward talk about why he'd left her with Candy. Why, after years, the calls and visits became few and far between. Ask him why their relationship dwindled to nothing but a check in the mail every month. That he did so without fail, even to this day when her eighteenth birthday had long since passed, gave her some hope that he was taking care of her in his own small way.

Maybe he didn't know how to approach her and felt as she did; the chasm between them was so wide, they didn't know how to bridge it.

Stepping into his room, seeing him lying so still, much thinner than she remembered, and deathly pale settled the old anger and hurt and brought forth a longing for more time.

"He's been in and out of consciousness most of the day," the doctor explained. "I'm sorry to say, he hasn't been lucid for many hours. I'm not sure he'll wake up again. His condition is rapidly deteriorating. I don't expect him to linger much longer."

"I appreciate your honesty. I'm sure his family wants to remain here with him. I won't stay long."

"As long as you need. Tom informed me of the special circumstances. We'll run interference while you're here."

"I appreciate it. They have enough to deal with right now."

The doctor nodded, patted her shoulder, and left her alone in the room with her father.

He always seemed so big. Now, with him in bed, he seemed so small, his life so fragile, a shadow of the strong and confident, overbearing and arrogant man she remembered.

John looked terrible lying in that bed, his bronze complexion waxy and pale. Dark circles marred his eyes. She'd never seen him in anything but a black cowboy hat, denim, and pearl button plaid shirts. The smell of disinfectant overshadowed her memory of his woodsy, earthy scent. The smell of the outdoors, horses, and hard work.

In the too-few short visits they shared over the years, she held on to a lot of memories. Hoarded them and pulled them out whenever she needed to remind herself that even strong, good, decent people made mistakes and took the easy way out when it was offered.

No doubt, when John realized dealing with her mother was nothing short of banging his head against a wall, he'd decided to stop the madness and go his own way. It explained why every time he popped into her life, he avoided Candy at all costs and asked her to keep their visit a secret.

Standing in front of him now, her anger wasn't only for his leaving her behind, but for being stronger than her and walking away from Candy. Something Roxy to this day still couldn't bring herself to do for fear Candy would self-destruct.

Roxy couldn't handle the guilt or shame that life without Candy would be better.

Roxy took the seat beside John. She reached for his hand, pulled away before she ever touched him and felt foolish for fearing his rejection.

Timid, she laid her hand over his on the bed and gave him a soft squeeze. "Hey, Dad, it's me, Roxy." Touching him brought her back to being nine years old. She remembered running to him, screaming,

"Daddy," and leaping into his open arms. His bright smile died when he saw the bruises on her cheek and arm. He hugged her close, felt her tense when he hurt her bruised back. He ordered her to wait outside the dismal one-room apartment while he talked to Candy. The loud argument drew neighbors' interest. Not long after the yelling started, John walked out the door again. He stopped in front of her, told her to be a good girl, go to school every day, learn as much as she could, so she never ended up like her mother, and he left.

"It's been a long time. Years, this last time." How did the time go by so fast? When did she stop waiting for him to show up? Minutes passed in silence before she could speak again. "Why'd you do it, Dad? Why did you leave me there? Why didn't you take me from her?"

"I always wanted you."

Startled by the whispered words, she jerked her head and stared at him, hoping beyond hope he'd pull through even though she knew that to be a fantasy.

Golden hazel eyes opened and met her identical ones. Surprisingly, a tear slid down John's cheek.

Tears welled in her eyes. "I missed you," she confessed. "I prayed you'd come back for me."

"Tried."

"Right. No one knows better than me how Candy can make you wish you never met her." She didn't have to imagine her mother testing John's patience to the point he broke and gave up.

"So proud of you." His eyes drifted closed, despite the effort he put into keeping them open. "Loved. You. Always."

"I love you, too." Like always, her love was all mixed up with anger and hurt. She wondered if she'd ever love someone and feel nothing else but happiness.

Not likely. Not in her life.

She felt the difference in him, heard the slowing of his heart monitor and knew he'd fallen back into a deep sleep. She gave herself a few minutes to watch him, study every line and curve of his face. She turned his hand in hers and traced the rough calluses on his fingers and palm. A working man's hands.

She remembered the feel of his rough thumb brushing over the bruise on her cheek and how soft that caress was despite the size and strength of him. She remembered how he took up the space in a restaurant booth the few times he came to town and whisked her away for a few hours of strained conversation over a meal she could barely choke down. Her emotions flowing and ebbing inside from rage to extreme happiness at seeing him again. The swirl of emotions choked off her ability to speak. The only thing that saved her from screaming in frustration each time was the fact he looked just as uncomfortable as her.

Time ticked away. She didn't know what she was waiting for, but it never came. She still felt troubled. They had been and were doomed to forever remain acquaintances.

This visit didn't settle anything between them. Just like all their other visits. They would never have the chance to talk about the past, put it to rest, and find a way to have a new kind of relationship now.

She pressed her face into his hand and felt the brush of his fingers on her face. She kissed his palm, held his hand against her skin for a moment longer, then stood with his hand still held in hers. "I have to go. Your children will be back to stay with you."

His hand contracted in hers. Something inside her eased, hoping that his attempt to hold her there meant he wanted her to stay, too. It was enough. Her heart full, she leaned down and kissed his cheek, pressed her nose into the crook of his neck and inhaled his scent. His hand contracted in hers again.

She let him go, stood on her own two feet like she'd always done, and did the hardest thing she'd had to do in a long time. "Goodbye, Dad. Maybe you'll look in on me from time to time like you used to."

Comforted by the crook of one side of his mouth into a semblance of a grin, she patted his hand and left the room to let the doctor know she was done.

Time to head back to the Ranch, her job, and the only family she had left, her mother.

Not a great enticement for going home.

But she still had three sisters she'd collected.

She wished she'd get a chance to see her father's ranch.

Not in the cards. It belonged to his children, a testament to the life he shared with them. Not her.

She scolded herself for the petty thoughts.

The doctor stood by the nurses' station. "I'm all done. Thank you for letting me see him. Um, if you wouldn't mind, please call me with updates on his condition."

"Of course."

"And when he . . ."

The doctor touched her shoulder again. "I'll let you know." He pulled a slip of paper from his clipboard. "Tom left this for you."

"Thank you."

She opened the slip of paper and read the hotel name and address, date and time of the funeral, and her return flight information. She hadn't planned on staying for the service.

She had so many other regrets, she didn't want to miss attending her father's funeral.

She rode the elevator down to the lobby, the silence deafening in the wake of realizing she'd never hear her father's voice again. She walked across the parking lot and sat in her rental car, loneliness and grief her only companions amongst the rows of empty vehicles. Her heart felt too heavy to hold in her chest. Tears pricked her eyes and stung the back of her throat.

She would never see her father alive again.

She'd carry the longing for more time with him for the rest of her days. She'd regret all the things she'd wished to have with him and not making the most of the time they did spend together.

And for all the unfulfilled wishes, lost time, and missing her father, she let the tears fall in a torrent because no matter what, she loved him. Her daddy. Maybe not the best one, but hers.

Chapter Four

Noah stood on the driveway in the bright sun, tipped his Stetson back, and let the warm rays settle on his face. Eyes closed, he focused on the heat on his skin and blocked out all thoughts. Just for a moment, he set aside the reason for the ache in his chest. Most of all, he preferred the quiet of the outdoors to the somber mood in the house.

Lost in thought, he didn't hear the car drive up and park behind him. A pair of soft, small hands settled over his eyes and startled him out of the first moment of peace he'd had in the two long days since John died.

Cheryl stepped around him. He remembered her sweet perfume from better days and hot nights. Her simple black dress clung to her soft curves and showed a lot of tempting skin. When she caught him looking, a smile spread across her lips but didn't brighten her eyes. "Miss me?"

Lust and a good healthy dose of male ego got him tangled up with Cheryl. Beautiful, outgoing, she drew him in, and he'd wanted her. Then he got to know her and a great body didn't hold up to the fact they had little in common.

Cheryl was nice. She just wasn't for him. He wanted someone different.

"It's been a while." He broke things off with her four months ago.

"Too long."

He wanted to agree, but found he couldn't.

He didn't miss *her* but what he wanted with a woman. Someone in his bed each night, a partner by his side every day.

"I'm so sorry about John. You two were so close. I came to stay with you. You shouldn't be alone at a time like this."

He didn't want to go down that particular potholed road again. "I have my sister. I promised her we'd do this together. As a family."

Cheryl scrunched her mouth into a lopsided frown. "She's not really your sister, you know."

Noah fisted his hands and backed Cheryl up a step and got in her face. "Say that again, and I'll toss you off this ranch." He'd lost his mother and John. Annabelle was the only family he had left in this world. And today of all days, he refused to let anyone tell him Annabelle and he weren't family.

Cheryl held her hands out to her sides. "I didn't mean anything by it."

"Then why say it?" He stepped away, giving her space and him a moment to rein in his anger.

Cheryl appeared lost for words.

"I suggest you head for the church. All of John's friends will pack the place in no time. Annabelle and I will be there soon."

Cheryl tried to reach him again. "Everyone loved him."

Noah grinned and shook his head. "People respected his talent with horses and admired his business skills. Loved that cantankerous man? Some of them. The ones who knew him well."

Annabelle stepped down the stone entrance to the house, stood by his side, and gave Cheryl an appraising gaze. "So, you're back."

Three words that conveyed how much Annabelle disliked Cheryl.

Noah shook his head. "Sprite, Cheryl just came by to offer her condolences. That's all."

Cheryl tried to say something, but Annabelle cut her off. "It's time to go. You promised. Today, you and me."

"You and me, Sprite. Always," he swore, knowing she needed the reassurance.

Cheryl hooked her arm through his and prompted him to escort her to her car. "Whatever you need, Noah, I'm here for you." She rubbed her hand over his chest and smiled invitingly up at him.

"Um, thanks." He didn't acknowledge the underlying offer in her words.

Annabelle climbed into the waiting limo taking them to the service. He followed her a moment later. The driver closed the door, leaving them in the plush interior.

He dreaded today and tried not to think or feel.

But faded memories of his mother flooded his mind. He wished he could remember her smile and the sound of her laugh. Soon, he'd forget the sound of John's voice and the twinkle that came into his eyes when he appreciated a beautiful woman walking by.

"You're quiet, Noah. Are you thinking about Dad?"

"Remembering all the times he spotted a pretty girl." He gave her a halfhearted smile, trying to keep things light. He didn't want today weighed down with somber thoughts and talk.

John would want them to remember the good times, revel in life and not drown in death.

"He'd get that sappy smile and his eyes would light up." She grinned, knowing as Noah did that John never set out to hurt any of those women. He just appreciated their many attributes and took what comfort they offered to soothe his troubled heart.

"I'm going to miss it. Him. I don't think I'll ever go to a rodeo again and not anticipate one of his elbow jabs to check out one of the riders."

Annabelle grabbed his arm. "Remember how he'd drag you over to the barrel races? God, how he loved to watch those women ride."

Noah remembered.

Reading his thoughts, she added with a backhanded slap against his chest, "He liked the girls from the Wild Rose Ranch the best." Her grin spread from ear to ear and her eyes shone with mischief. "You know what they say about those girls," she coaxed, her smile infectious.

"What do you know about *those* girls?" he asked, knowing full well she'd heard the rumors the women worked for the illustrious Nevada whorehouse.

"I'm not a kid anymore, you know. I've heard things."

"You just close your ears to things like that."

"Don't tell me Dad had to drag you kicking and screaming to watch them ride."

Lucky for him, he didn't have to answer that loaded question. They pulled up to the entrance of the church and the driver opened the door for them.

A small crowd gathered outside the doors leading into the church.

"It's time to say goodbye, Sprite."

"I'd rather stay right here and talk about . . ."

He slapped his hand over her mouth, something he'd done since she was a kid when she tried to rile him with her outrageous outbursts. "Let's go." Her lips vibrated against his hand with her giggles.

The trip down memory lane and her infectious laugh eased his heart. Something he didn't think possible today. He loved her for it. He didn't care what blood or a piece of paper said, she was his sister in his heart.

He stepped out of the limo and held his hand out to help her exit.

When she stood with him and saw the people gathering in front of the church, she hesitated, then stared up at him, her eyes earnest. "Do you think he was happy?"

"I think he was like most of us. Happy with many aspects of his life, but wishing things could have gone better in others. Being a father and working the ranch made him happy."

"He never found his true love," she said sadly.

"I like to think he loved my mother, and after she died, he couldn't find anything close to what he had with her." Was it wishful thinking to hope John and his mother found happiness and love together?

Before he and John had that last talk up on the ridge, he might not have thought so, but now he thought that's what John was trying to tell him in his own way.

"I hope so. I'd hate to think he never felt true love before he died."

Noah hugged her close. "Whether he did or not, he loved you, Sprite. Let's go in there, thank him for all he did for us, and give him a proper goodbye. After, we'll go home, gather our friends and neighbors around us and celebrate his life."

"Cowboy style." Annabelle found her smile again.

"A couple of the guys stayed behind to fire up the smoker and grill." He wrapped his arm around her shoulders and walked with her to greet their friends. Every step closer to the church erased their earlier good humor and the weight of the reason for their being here settled heavily in their hearts.

"She came," Annabelle sputtered out.

Noah hated surprises.

This one put a stone in his gut. Annabelle's mother, Lisa, stood on the church steps with Cheryl. They both locked eyes on him and smiled.

The two of them together added up to trouble in his mind.

"Noah."

He turned and found his best friend.

"Sorry about John. He was a good man." Austin's bloodshot eyes, underscored by dark circles, and his haggard expression hinted that he might quite possibly still be drunk from last night. Austin spent too many nights brooding and drinking these days.

"Yes, he was. The best," Noah replied.

"How are you holding up, Sprite?" As close as brothers, they'd both called Annabelle by that nickname since she was holding on to their jeans and toddling next to them.

Annabelle hugged Austin, then stepped back to Noah's side. "I'm doing okay. You haven't been to the ranch lately. We miss your visits."

Where had the years gone that Noah stood beside his sister, now a poised young woman who spoke like an adult? John would be proud of her for holding up so well, carrying on, despite her grief and uncertainty about her future. She impressed the hell out of him.

"Family should stick together." Hurt and anger flashed in Austin's eyes. He was still reeling from his father's betrayal. "I saw Lisa a few minutes ago. If she causes you any trouble, Sprite, you let me know. Noah and I'll take care of it."

Annabelle gave a slight nod.

Out of nowhere Cheryl appeared, pressed into his chest, and wrapped her arms around his neck. Noah instinctively grabbed her waist. Big mistake. She snuggled closer.

"It's going to be okay, Noah."

Austin cocked his head and stared dumbfounded at Cheryl wrapped around him. "You two got back together?" Surprise with a touch of what-the-fuck-were-you-thinking filled Austin's voice.

Noah reached up, took Cheryl's forearms, and extricated himself. He answered Austin, but stared down at Cheryl. "No. We are not back together."

Cheryl smiled sweetly up at him, then turned her gaze to Austin. "I'm here to help a friend through a difficult time."

Austin read the situation and slapped Noah on the shoulder. "No need, honey, I'm here."

"Austin, Annabelle and I will take a moment with John before the service begins. Come in with us," Noah offered.

Austin planted his hand on Noah's shoulder and gave him a long look, appreciation that none of Austin's recent misbehavior had damaged their friendship. Austin was hurting himself. Noah hated it and had offered his help, but Austin had his pride and wallowed in it.

They walked in together, Noah and Austin flanking Annabelle. Noah felt better having his friend's support.

Like John, Noah wasn't a particularly religious man. He didn't attend church unless dragged. If he wanted to commune with God, he did so in his saddle out in nature. Whenever he had a problem, something to think through, a need to be quiet and alone, he rode, found a pretty spot to stop and enjoy the outdoors and let the peace envelop him.

The priest greeted them just inside the church doors. "Noah, Annabelle, my deepest condolences on your loss. If there is anything you need, guidance during this difficult time, please don't hesitate to call on me."

"Thank you, Father Patrick." Annabelle took the lead. "We appreciate all your help setting up the service. I'm sure it's going to be wonderful and just what John would have wanted."

"He was a good man. Everything is ready inside the church. Please, come with me and I'll take you to him."

Chapter Five

Mottled colors splashed against the quiet, peaceful church walls from the sparkling stained-glass windows. With a heavy heart, Roxy walked alone to the front as Jesus stared down at her from a cross hung on the wall. He'd never answered any of her prayers. She didn't offer up any now. She'd gotten the point long ago: you're on your own.

Thanks for nothing.

She wished her sisters were here.

Standing in front of John's casket, she felt as alone as she'd ever been.

"Hello again, Dad. I'm sorry this is the way things end between us."

Now that he was gone, she didn't know what to say, so she went with the first thing that popped into her mind. "I hoped I'd see you in a suit on my wedding day. This isn't exactly what I had in mind." She pressed her hand to his chest and smoothed it over the lapel of his navy blue suit. "You look very handsome."

She plucked a white rosebud from the bouquet on top of the casket and fit it into his lapel.

She stood in silence. Her thoughts scattered and confused. Sometimes she felt the anger rise over the injustices she felt John had allowed her to suffer because of his absence and indifference. Her thoughts turned to unfulfilled wishes and hopes, and back to the overwhelming sadness that he was gone.

Unsettled, she spent her time trying to sort out her mind and heart, only to come to one conclusion. She'd lost John too soon and needed to remember the old adage: life is short, live it now.

Funny how that thought made her think of her mother and all the time she wasted trying to make Candy be something she wasn't and do the right thing. Her choices were her own. Roxy needed to stop trying to change Candy and live her own life. How many times had she thought it would be best to move away from the Ranch, her mother, and make a new life for herself?

Easier said than done.

"Roxy," Tom called from behind her.

She jumped and turned to face him, her hand pressed to her racing heart.

"Sorry. I didn't mean to scare you." His eyes took a little too long to rise from her chest to meet her eyes. "The limo just pulled up outside. The priest will buy us a few minutes before Noah and Annabelle come in to have a few minutes alone with John before the service."

"I've said my goodbye." Not much to say in this one-sided conversation.

"I'm glad you stayed for the service. John wanted all his kids here."

She pressed her lips together. "I'm not so sure about that. They don't know about me."

"They'll meet you at the reading of the will."

"I'm sorry, what?" After the funeral she planned to go back to her hotel for another night of movies and too much quiet before her morning flight.

"We'll meet with Noah and Annabelle at the ranch to go over the will."

"Surely I don't need to stay for that."

Tom's eyes strayed back to her chest. She had the urge to bend her knees and shrink down until his eye line was back on her face. Wasted effort. She knew men like Tom. Their eyes glassed over and the little boy inside them jumped up and down screaming, "Boobies!" She also knew it was only a matter of time before he got all grabby hands and forgot his good sense.

Men.

"We'll do the deed after the barbecue up at the ranch tonight at eight."

Was that a double entendre? *Do the deed.* She resisted rolling her eyes. *That's what you think.*

He closed the distance between them, standing too close, and reached up and cupped her shoulder in his hand. "I was surprised to learn about you."

She took a step back, making his hand fall away, and met his lust-filled gaze with a cold stare of her own. "John's and my relationship is . . . was complicated." She feared John had told this letch all about her and Candy.

Voices rose in the back of the church and the doors began to open, saving her from having to answer any awkward questions Tom's statement alluded to.

"You need to be there." Tom stared her down, then turned to the back of the church.

"Fine." With a last look at John, she turned just as the priest stepped in, Noah and Annabelle behind him. Roxy resisted the urge to turn and stare at the pair. As mixed-up as her emotions were over John's death, they were even more convoluted when it came to John's children.

The children he raised, loved, and kept with him when he'd abandoned her.

Chapter Six

Noah followed the Father into the church and spotted Tom and, if he wasn't mistaken, the same dark-haired woman he'd seen at the hospital two nights ago. Without looking their way, she rushed away and disappeared through the side door.

"Who was that?" Annabelle asked.

"I'm not sure," Father Patrick responded. "Tom asked me to allow her in before anyone else arrived."

Noah walked ahead and met Tom near the dozens of bouquets of flowers outlining the coffin and spread out around the raised stage. As if a flower garden exploded in the church, their rich scent filled the room.

"Who is she?" he demanded.

Tom cocked one eyebrow at Noah's tone. "There isn't time to explain now. It's complicated. Like everybody, John had a few secrets."

Noah wanted to knock the smug look that went along with that cryptic statement right off Tom's face.

Secrets. He hated them as much as surprises.

Annabelle pulled on his hand and dragged him away from Tom toward John's open casket. Austin and Tom walked back down the aisle.

Annabelle nudged his arm. "Maybe she was Dad's girlfriend."

For some reason, Noah didn't like the idea. "I didn't get a good look at her, but I think she was too young to be his girlfriend."

"My mother is twenty years younger than Dad."

"That woman had to be in her early twenties, Sprite. Not much older than you."

"Oh." Annabelle scrunched her lips. "Have you noticed how secretive Tom seems the last several days? Ever since Dad went into the hospital, he's been acting strange." Annabelle might be young, but she didn't miss much.

Noah didn't like Tom's smug attitude. He'd get his answers soon. "Forget Tom. This day is hard enough without him creating more drama."

"My mother brings enough into our lives. Why do things have to be so complicated?" Annabelle's gaze fixed on John, her thoughts in the past.

"Relationships are complicated, Sprite."

"Why can't we have had a mother and a father who loved us? A real family?"

Noah wished a thousand times that his mother hadn't died and he'd lived with her and John on the ranch, one big, happy family. But then, he wouldn't have Annabelle. "I wanted that, too. But you can have it, Sprite. You're just going to have to make it for your kids when you're older. Much, much older," he teased, and bumped his elbow into her shoulder.

"You're old," she teased back. "Why don't you have a wife and kids, yet?" Annabelle smiled up at him. "I think it'd be cool to be an aunt."

"Enjoy thinking about it, because it ain't going to happen anytime soon."

"You never know," she teased.

Annabelle's gaze settled on John's casket. Noah wrapped his arm around her shoulders and drew her the last two steps up to John's open coffin.

"He looks nice in his suit, but he probably would have been more comfortable in his jeans and cowboy shirt." Annabelle burst into tears.

"Ah, honey, don't do that again." Noah handed her his handkerchief and awkwardly patted her on the back. Giving in to his emotions, his eyes filled with tears. John's death had hit him hard at the hospital, but seeing Annabelle break down and the sight of John in the coffin was too much. He choked back the tears and wrapped Annabelle in his arms. Her head pressed to his chest, her fists clutched the back of his suit jacket, and he laid his cheek on top of her head and held her close.

People filed in and he sucked in a deep breath and led Annabelle to their seats in the first pew.

Austin stood and wrapped him in a bear hug after Annabelle took her seat. His friend gave him a hard squeeze, slapped him on the back, and sat next to Annabelle. Noah sat on her other side and barely remembered any of the specifics as one after another of John's friends stood and gave eulogies. Noah let the kind words, jokes, crazy stories, and gentle rebukes about John's stern countenance fill him up, until he thought he'd burst with missing the only father he'd ever known.

After the priest gave the last blessing, Noah, Austin, Robby, their ranch foreman, and three of John's closest friends served as pallbearers, taking John out to the waiting hearse.

From there, everything went by in a blur, from the drive to the cemetery and the graveside ceremony that ended with him and Annabelle watching the casket lower into the grave and both of them tossing a white rose and a handful of dirt onto the casket.

Through it all, he couldn't seem to shake one thought. Although John had friends and him and Annabelle, where was the loving wife, the life partner, the best friend who stood by him through thick and thin?

For the first time, Noah truly wanted a wife and children. He didn't want to find himself at the end of his life, sitting atop that hill overlooking the ranch and not have the woman he loved beside him.

Annabelle squeezed his hand. "Noah, everyone left for the ranch. Whenever you're ready, we should go, too."

He shook free of his thoughts. "You ready?"

She hesitated. "Not really. Everything is going to change tomorrow."

"Everything John left behind will still be there."

"It won't be the same," she said with a petulant tone.

He gave in to her childish outburst and conceded, "It won't be the same." It seemed to make her feel better.

She sighed and plucked a white rose from one of the many bouquets spread out before them. She brought the bloom to her nose.

How utterly feminine a gesture.

Why did John have to leave him now when Annabelle appeared to be blooming before his eyes?

Next thing he knew, she'd want to start dating. With her long blond hair, blue eyes, and slim, but rounding five-foot-four figure, she was very pretty. In another couple years, she'd be a knockout, and he'd be knee-deep in sex-crazed teenage boys.

"Let's go, Sprite. People are waiting on us."

She walked with him to the car, her arm tucked through his. He settled her inside and turned back to the quiet cemetery and the freshly dug grave.

"Rest in peace, John."

He slid in beside Annabelle. She leaned her head on his shoulder. The limo turned right toward the cemetery entrance and he stared out the window, back at John's grave.

Annabelle must have been doing the same, because she blurted out, "There she is again."

Noah saw her. No one would miss the beautiful woman walking past the headstones straight for John's grave.

The woman swiped at her cheek and wiped away tears. He didn't know how he knew that, but he felt it. She stood beside John's grave, crying, her shoulders slumped, head bowed. Her grief weighed her down. He read it in her, because he felt it in himself.

"Let's stop and see who she is," Annabelle suggested.

"Whatever her reasons, she's made a point to only see him when they're alone. I'll ask Tom about her again at the barbecue."

He'd let her grieve in her way and have this time with John, but if it was the last thing he did, he'd discover the identity of John's mystery woman.

Chapter Seven

Friends, neighbors, ranch hands crowded the stone patio. Cheryl and Lisa topped his list of people he wished had stayed away. Cheryl clung to him. Lisa acted like she owned the place. Tom made Noah's list of people he'd like to throw out. The arrogant, sneaky lawyer evaded his questions with cryptic statements about the mystery woman and surprises in John's will.

Noah wanted to find Tom's father and demand he come out of retirement and work for them again so he didn't have to deal with Tom anymore.

He downed the rest of his beer and tossed the bottle into the recycle bin. He wanted to go down to the stables, saddle a horse, and ride out for a few hours. Maybe up to the overlook.

Mary stepped up beside him.

Before he gave in to that desire, he needed to focus on unfinished business. "It's almost time for the reading of the will. Mind coaxing the few lingering guests to go home?"

"You might have some trouble getting rid of Cheryl." Mary gave him a toothy smile. "She's barely left your side. Will we have company for breakfast?" Mary's bland tone conveyed how little she wanted to add another place at the table.

Noah felt like squirming under her stern gaze, but stood firm. He'd never brought a woman home to the ranch. He wasn't about to start now with an ex. "We aren't together anymore."

Mary jabbed him in the gut with the back of her hand. "Have you told her that?"

"Several times." He didn't know how to make it any clearer. "She doesn't hear me."

"She's a woman who wants something."

"It isn't me." That wife and family seemed even further out of reach.

"You were always such a smart boy." She patted his cheek and moved away, walking through the dwindling crowd to hint that people should go home and give the family their privacy.

Noah grabbed a cold beer, slipped away, and headed for John's study, unable to accept another sad condolence.

Raw inside, he sank into the corner of the sofa, unable to bring himself to take John's seat behind the desk. Thoughts of John and what was to come swamped his mind. He twisted off the top on his beer, tossed the cap on the coffee table, took a swig from the bottle, leaned his head back against the couch, and rubbed his thumb and index finger over his brow, trying to ease the aching throb building behind his eyes.

Despite his words to Annabelle to the contrary, he sat in the quiet room, John's ghost everywhere, and waited for the reading of the will and the inevitable changes in his life.

He cringed when Annabelle walked in followed by Lisa, Cheryl, and Tom, interrupting his momentary solitude. He didn't need this. Not now, when his emotions were raw.

"Sulking and drinking alone." Lisa tsk-tsked him with a shake of one pink painted fingertip.

He downed the last of his beer and seriously considered pouring himself a double whiskey at the bar by the bookcases where Tom helped himself to a splash of bourbon over ice.

Noah refrained. "I wanted some peace and quiet after that crowd we had here today."

"John had a lot of good friends." Cheryl settled on the couch next to him, her thigh pressed to his. She patted his knee. The buzz he felt wasn't from having a woman next to him, cozying up to his neglected body, but from the four beers he'd consumed, one after the other. Scrunched into the corner of the sofa, he had no room to move away.

Some mindless sex would take the edge off, but his inner voice warned him to beware. He'd hate himself in the morning for using her when she clearly hoped they'd get back together.

Nope. Not going there.

"Cheryl, thank you for coming today, but I think it's time you went home." And gave him his space.

"Oh, come on, Noah. Let her stay," Lisa coaxed. "Everyone knows John left everything to you and Annabelle. There are no big secrets here."

John died. Didn't that matter?

Yes, Noah and Annabelle would carry on the ranch, but they'd both give it all up to have John back.

Didn't anyone else feel the same?

"You're lucky I let you in this house. Being Annabelle's mother doesn't give you the right to decide who stays and who goes."

"Noah, honey." Cheryl's palm rubbed up and down his thigh, making him uncomfortable, and not in a good way. "You shouldn't go through this alone."

He stopped her hand by placing his over hers, removing it, and putting it on her own lap. "Thank you for your concern, but—"

Cheryl surprised him by leaning in and planting her mouth softly over his in a coaxing kiss that was warm and tempting. For a second, he gave in to the memories, the moment, and let go of the anger, frustration, and grief he'd been carrying all day.

But reason and reality returned when he realized she was taking advantage.

He came to his senses and pulled away.

He took her forearms and pulled her hands from his shoulders. "This is not happening. It's time for you to leave."

Embarrassment mixed with anger filled her eyes and pinked her cheeks. She stood, gave Lisa a long look, then left the room, slamming the door behind her.

Lisa gave him that disapproving look she walked in with again. "She just wants to help."

"Annabelle and I want to do this alone."

"If you think I'm leaving, you're nuts." Lisa planted herself in a chair beside the other sofa where Annabelle sat with her hands on her knees, head down between her shoulders.

"Tom, perhaps we can start with custody of Annabelle," Noah suggested, trying to move this along.

"She's coming home with me," Lisa said matter-of-factly.

Annabelle's head shot up and the color drained from her face.

Noah leaned forward and pointed at Lisa. "The hell she is. She belongs with me, here on the ranch."

"I'm her mother."

"This is her home. The place you left her without a second thought when she was three."

"Stop." Tom held up his hands. "John already decided what happens next."

"Then read the will and tell her she's not taking Annabelle from this ranch."

All he wanted to do was kick Lisa and Tom out and have a moment with Annabelle to find a way to let go of the grief and get on with their lives.

Tom gave Noah another of those cryptic looks, then blew his mind. "I'll read the will as soon as John's daughter arrives."

Chapter Eight

Roxy followed the curve of the road in her rental car to a long straight-away that revealed her father's home. Glorious, the expanse of green pastures, old shade trees, and well-maintained barns, outbuildings, and a large covered training ring spread out before her. Even in the fading light, the house was magnificent. Gray stone walls and gleaming glass windows enclosed the first floor. The windows and doors trimmed in a bright white against the shades of gray. The second floor was cedar shingles, silvered from time and weather, with the same white trim on the windows, decks, and railings. Well-maintained gardens flowered in white, pink, red, and purple. The bushes bloomed in profusion. She loved the many shades of greens with the bright colors. The landscaping drew her in and gave her a sense of peace. Being here, on the ranch her father loved, amidst the bountiful gardens and grasses, brought to mind how much she disliked the hot, arid, sparse desert.

She tamped down thoughts that this could have been her life.

So many horses. They gathered together in some of the pastures. Others stood sentry at the fence rails, or grazed on the lush wildflower-dappled grass in the fields. The ranch and her father were well-known for the quarter horses and Appaloosas. Beautiful sorrels, gorgeous palominos, and dozens of spotted Appaloosas as far as the eye could see.

Her anger might have gotten the better of her most of the time, but in her quiet moments, usually atop a horse from this ranch, she reminded herself that he may have never sent her a birthday or Christmas present wrapped in pretty paper, but he'd given her something infinitely more valuable and necessary in her life. Why couldn't she see that when she was a teenager, sucked up her pride, set aside her anger, and come here and demanded he acknowledge her in some other way than with a check and a horse?

She put everything she had into caring for and loving them and it had made a difference in her life. Without them, who's to say she wouldn't have ended up just like her mother?

A woman in an Accord peeled out of her father's driveway and sped past her. When she pulled in, only a few cars sat parked near the four-car garage. She wondered who they belonged to, and hoped she could avoid a scene in front of the family's company.

She spotted the white extended cab truck with Speckled Horse Ranch emblazoned on the door arching over a brown-and-white Appaloosa. Her father's truck.

Sometime between the moment when she first spotted the ranch house on the rise and coming down the hill, the front porch and garden lights had come on, illuminating the stone path to the entry. The house and lights looked welcoming, but her nerves kicked in, sent a battalion of butterflies fluttering in her belly, and she hesitated to get out of the car.

"I don't belong here."

This place belonged to Noah and Annabelle. John had made that clear by never inviting her to visit.

She should have ignored Tom's request for her to come for the reading of the will. Her father had done his part paying child support. She didn't expect that he'd left her anything. But there was one thing she wanted. If Noah and Annabelle would allow her one small memento.

Never one to put unpleasant things off, she stepped from the car, and with only a slight hesitation, walked to the front door.

It wasn't lost on her that she had to knock on her father's door, instead of walking in like she was welcome.

Roxy tapped the brass horse head knocker a couple of times and held her breath, not knowing what to expect.

A petite woman answered the door wearing a black peasant skirt and sweater. She wiped her hands on a white towel, her deep brown eyes rising to Roxy's face. "Oh my God!" The woman wrung the towel in her hands and stared with wide eyes. "Who are you? You must be family. A cousin?"

"No, ma'am. I'm Roxy Cordero. John's daughter." She'd never said that to anyone. Neither had John.

The woman gasped. All the color drained from her face.

Roxy rushed forward and grabbed her by the arms to steady her. "I'm sorry I startled you. Tom asked me to stop by."

The woman pressed the towel to her chest. "He never told me, anyone, about you."

"I know."

John didn't want anyone to know he'd fathered a child with a drugged-out hooker.

At the time, he had an orphaned son to raise and a standing in the community that meant more to him than admitting he was a flawed man.

"May I come in?" The butterflies swirled in her stomach with the fear that she'd be denied entry to her father's home.

Why didn't she turn around and leave? If this was the reaction she got from this woman, what would John's children do?

"Yes, yes, come in." The woman used the towel to wave her inside. "I'm Mary. I've worked for John for over thirty years. I'm the house-keeper and cook."

"Thirty years, sounds more like family to me."

A new kind of shock crossed her eyes before they softened and Mary smiled. "Thank you. I'll show you to John's study, where everyone has gathered, and introduce you. Ah, will you be staying here tonight? I can have one of the guest rooms ready for you in no time at all."

Roxy shook her head. "That's not necessary. I've been staying at a hotel in town for the last few days."

"Then, you saw him before he passed?"

"I did."

Mary's eyes shone with relief that came out in her expressive sigh. Mary cared deeply for John. It mattered to her that they saw each other before he died.

The house was a blur as she followed Mary through the entry toward the closed double doors. But her steps faltered when she spotted the silver framed photos on the mantel above the stone fireplace in the other room.

John. Noah. Annabelle. Various ages. Together. Separate. The family.

A family she'd been denied.

He wanted them. Not her. Not really.

"This difficult day has been made more trying with the arrival of Annabelle's mother, Lisa." Mary broke the awkward silence.

"John's second wife. His first passed away, if I'm not mistaken." Candy fell somewhere between John's two wives.

"That's right."

John filled their awkward silences during his visits with stories about his life and kids, unaware they made her feel less like his and more the unwanted outsider.

Mary stopped in front of the closed solid oak double doors, her hand on the brass door handle. "I don't know anything about your relationship with John, but Noah and Annabelle . . . they're grieving." Mary obviously wanted to ask about her, but held back.

Roxy put her hand on the woman's shoulder to stop her attempt to explain, and in a way warn Roxy not to hurt Noah and Annabelle. Two people she probably considered her children as much as John's after thirty years in this home.

"I only came to say goodbye to my father. Nothing more. I leave on the first flight home tomorrow morning." John hadn't offered her any part of this place during his life. She didn't expect anything from him after his death. The only thing she'd ever wanted was answers. Now that he was gone, so was her chance to ask for them.

Roxy wasn't sure how to read Mary's relief that turned into concerned lines on her face.

Mary opened the door. Before Roxy stepped in, she had the overwhelming urge to run, knowing if she stepped into that room, everything in her life would change forever.

Chapter Nine

Roxy's first glimpse of Noah up close confirmed two things. Her attraction to the handsome stranger hadn't dimmed from her rodeo days. The rattle of awareness and need she always felt when she saw him was nothing compared to the jolt that shook her body now. And she still resented the hell out of him for being the son John wanted more than his own flesh and blood.

"John's daughter?" Noah asked Tom, who nodded toward her.

Noah's gaze snapped to hers and narrowed on her face, connecting with her eyes, studying them. Recognition raced through his eyes and then something like surprise and rage filled them before he turned his head to glare at Tom.

"Hi, I'm Roxy." She paused before spilling the rest of the surprise. "Cordero."

"No way," the blonde in the chair blurted out. Annabelle's mother, Lisa, she guessed. "John didn't have any children of his own."

"You're wrong." To prove John did have a family, she walked to Annabelle.

Tears spilled down the young girl's downturned face. "You must be John's daughter, Annabelle. From the way he spoke about you, it was clear he adored you." Roxy held out her hand and waited.

The girl took a second to finally look up at her. With slow deliberation, she reached out and took her hand. "Roxy?"

"That's right." Roxy covered Annabelle's cold hand with both of hers. "I'm so sorry about your dad." Roxy had to choke back her own tears seeing the girl cry for their father.

"Um, thank you," she managed in her dazed state. "Are you really his daughter?"

"Flesh and blood."

Noah swore behind her and she glanced sideways and caught him running a hand over his brow. "The monthly checks to Nevada." He fell back into the sofa.

"Yes," she confirmed, and gave Annabelle's hand a squeeze and placed it back in her lap.

She turned to the man on the other sofa and took the few steps to him and held out her hand. "Noah, his son."

He refused her hand, so she let it drop to her side. Rejected by her father and his son. She shouldn't be surprised, but it hurt.

Before she stepped away, Noah grabbed her hand. The streak of heat that raced up her hand and arm startled her. From the look in his eyes, he felt it, too.

"Why didn't you introduce yourself at the hospital or funeral?"

She tried to tug her hand free so she could focus on anything else but him, but he didn't let her go. "I didn't want to intrude on the family."

"I thought *you* were family." Lisa bit out the words with her disbelief.

"I'm his daughter." She understood that distinction, even if Lisa didn't.

Noah's eyes told her he understood. She caught a touch of sympathy before the anger returned.

"You have his eyes." He stared, looking for something in the depths of her gaze.

She pulled a lock of hair from over her shoulder. "Same complexion and hair color, too." She let her hair fall over her chest and down to her waist. A strand landed on Noah's hand holding hers. The heat in his eyes intensified.

She needed some space, so she slipped her hand free of his. This time, he let her. She turned to face everyone else in the room, leaving Noah on her left and just out of her line of sight.

"Where have you been all this time?" Annabelle asked. "You've never come to the ranch."

"I was never invited." A cold, hard truth that left a lump in her throat.

Noah sat forward, rested his forearms on his knees, and stared up at her, his eyes narrowed. "What the hell do you mean, you weren't invited?"

"I haven't seen or spoken to my father since I was eighteen. Even then, I'd only seen him a few times since I was nine. Before that, he came around several times a year."

"Then what the hell are you doing here now?" Lisa demanded.

"Tom invited her." Mary glared at Lisa.

"You weren't invited to this meeting," Lisa shot back.

"Neither were you," Noah snapped at Lisa.

"I'll give you your privacy." Mary nodded to Noah, letting him know she appreciated his support and walked out.

Roxy turned to the man who'd brought her here. "Tom, thank you for inviting me to my father's home. I've wanted to see it and meet Annabelle and Noah a long time, but I have an early flight and should get going, especially if you have family business to discuss."

She took one long look around the room and took in the tall windows, wall of books, the watercolor paintings, and John's solid wood desk. Big and sturdy, just like him.

"If it's okay, I'd like his hat." Everyone stared at her.

"His hat?" Noah asked.

"Black Stetson. He wore it every time he came to see me."

"She's just playing coy. She came here for her piece of the pie." Lisa held Roxy in her narrowed gaze.

One side of Noah's mouth drew back. "Why do you want it?"

She couldn't believe Noah begrudged her something so small. He got everything. "Why do you care? It's just a hat. You got to live here with John. Can't I have this one thing?" She reined in her emotions and glared at Noah.

"Fine. Take it. I don't care."

Roxy read the lie in his eyes. He cared very much and resented the fact she wanted anything of John's.

John lied to him. Noah couldn't take out his hurt and anger on John, so he directed it at her.

Finally, Tom stepped forward. "Listen, Noah, Annabelle, I know you're surprised to find out John had a daughter."

"I'm not convinced she is his daughter," Lisa interrupted. "I was married to the man for six years and he never said anything to me about her."

Roxy didn't offer up an answer, even though they all stared at her waiting for one. She didn't owe them any explanations. John didn't want them to know about her. He didn't feel the need to explain, why should she?

"I only found out about her when John was admitted to the hospital," Tom confessed. "My father handled the will. When he retired and I took over, the only business I did for John pertained to the ranch, not his personal file. She is his daughter, a DNA test proved that long ago."

"He actually confirmed it with a test?" Roxy asked, surprised.

"You didn't think he took your mother's word for it, did you?"

Roxy frowned. "I suppose not."

Tom knew the truth. That revelation and his demeanor unsettled her.

He glared at Tom. "Why didn't you say anything when you found out?"

"I had to protect John's privacy. His living will and instructions for what to do if he was incapacitated or dying included Roxy's contact information. Only then did I take a look at John's will."

"What does this mean?" Fear filled Annabelle's words. "Do we have to leave?"

Chapter Ten

Annabelle's question echoed through the silent room. Her fear became Noah's. What if John left everything to Roxy, his biological child? The child he'd talked about on their last ride wanting to carry on his legacy here at the ranch.

Noah had worked his ass off since he was a kid. John groomed him to take over. But what if John simply wanted him to continue to run the place for his real daughter?

No fucking way he worked for her. He'd take Annabelle and . . .

It hit Noah then. John would never toss him and Annabelle off the ranch. He'd never take their home from them. He loved them. He raised them like they were his own.

So why had he treated Roxy like an outsider? If he longed for his own child, why hadn't he ever invited Roxy to the ranch? Why tell her about them but never say a word about her? It didn't make sense. Not when John had been honest with Annabelle about her not being his biological child, but he loved her as if she were anyway.

"Why did John keep you a secret?"

Tom's smile confirmed he knew why. "There's a story there."

"And not yours to tell." Roxy held Tom's gaze. Hers held a demand for silence.

Tom's smile never wavered. "Sit at the desk. We'll get started."

Roxy complied and ran her hand over the wood.

Noah fisted his hands, holding back the anger at seeing her taking John's seat like she already owned the place.

Tom opened his briefcase in front of Roxy on the desk. "Let's let John answer your questions." He pulled a stack of papers from his briefcase and handed a thick manila envelope to Roxy. "Don't open that until I'm finished reading the will. What's inside is separate from the ranch and John's other assets. Okay?"

"Um. Fine." Fear and uncertainty washed over Roxy's face and flashed in her eyes before she pulled herself together again.

Tom walked over and handed him an envelope. "That's for Mary and Robby. I thought you might like to tell them John left each a fifty-thousand-dollar bonus and the small bungalow property they live in."

"I will." Noah smiled, happy John did right by them, rewarding them for their hard work and years of loyalty. It made him wonder if he'd do the same for all the years Noah worked side by side with him.

Tom leaned back against the desk and addressed everyone in the room. "We don't need to read the entire will. Noah, Annabelle, I'll leave a copy for you. Roxy, you've got a copy in the envelope."

His gaze went to Roxy, who sat quietly taking in everything and everyone in the room. Unlike Lisa, she didn't have a predatory, expectant look in her eyes as she waited for Tom to read the rest of the will.

Did she expect her due?

If she got it, would she kick him and Annabelle out of their home? Or simply make it unbearable to stay?

Noah's earlier fatigue turned to tense anxiety and dread. He anticipated the inevitable changes when John died, but he never expected things to be this unknown and complicated. It unsettled him in a way that shook the foundation of everything he believed about John and his place in John's life and his future on the ranch.

"'To my three children,'" Tom read. Like Annabelle's, Noah's gaze shot to Roxy. John considered her one of them. Noah held his breath as Tom continued. "'I leave you all my assets, including Speckled Horse Ranch. Annabelle, you will receive twenty percent.'"

"What! That's not fair," Lisa protested.

Tom didn't acknowledge her outburst, but read on. "'Noah, I'm sorry if this disappoints you, but I think you'll understand. You receive thirty percent.'"

"No fucking way." He fell back into the sofa and rubbed his hands over his face.

"'Roxy, you'll receive the remaining fifty percent.'"

Tom's words, John's really, echoed through his head.

"'But there's a catch.'"

Noah sat forward again. "What catch?"

Tom turned to Roxy and read on. "'I'm going to ask you to do something, I have no right to ask at all. I let you down. I had my reasons, but what do they matter when you suffered because of them. Given time, I hope you'll understand, and maybe find a way to forgive me. In order for you to keep your share in Speckled Horse Ranch, you have to move into the house and stay until Annabelle graduates high school and turns eighteen.'"

"Are you kidding me?" Noah raged. "He never says one word about her to us, and now he wants her to live here?"

Tom sighed. "Noah, let me finish." Tom turned back to Roxy, who sat there with nothing to say. "'You've taken care of your mother all these years. I hope you'll find it in your heart to stay and help take care of my daughter, Annabelle.'"

Tom turned back to him. "'Noah, you and I have tried to raise Annabelle the best we knew how. Annabelle is a teenager, and I feel she needs a woman's hand in guiding her through the next few years of her life.'"

Noah pinned Roxy in his gaze. "We didn't need any help then. I don't need your help raising my sister now."

Lisa pointed her finger at him. "That's because she's coming home with me."

"No way in hell I let you take her."

Tom interrupted whatever comeback Lisa clamped her jaw down on when he ordered, "Let me finish." Tom eyed both of them and continued. "'I'm confident Roxy can guide her with a young woman's perspective and, with Roxy's background, the experience and wisdom she's gained in her own life. For these reasons, I've named Roxy and Noah as Annabelle's legal guardians.'" Tom locked eyes with him. "'You will both oversee her care and inheritance.'"

"He can't do that." Lisa lashed out. "She's my daughter. It's up to me to oversee her inheritance." Lisa really meant she wanted her share.

"You signed over sole custody to John as part of the divorce," Tom pointed out.

"Yes, but now he's gone. It's up to me to make sure everything he left her is taken care of properly."

"I'll make sure of it because there's no way in hell I'm letting you touch it." Noah tried to contain the rage, but it got the better of him. "I'll protect Annabelle and all that's hers. *I* run this ranch. I've been here with her from day one."

"The paperwork is in order, signed by a judge," Tom added.

For the first time, Roxy spoke up. "What happens if I refuse to move to the ranch?"

Everything in him went still. He never considered she wouldn't want her piece of the ranch.

Part of him wanted her to walk away.

Buried under his anger, he conceded she was entitled to claim what belonged to her by blood.

"Noah and Annabelle will split your share. Noah will be granted sole guardianship of Annabelle."

Lisa glared at Tom. "That's ridiculous. She's fifteen. She can't live with a grown man who isn't even related to her."

Tom cleared his throat. "John felt Annabelle would be better off with two adults in her life, a man and a woman raising her. A judge agreed."

The hard truth sank in. In the eyes of the law, Annabelle was his sister. However, if Lisa pulled out a DNA test, the courts would know that Annabelle wasn't John's child either. John must have suspected that Lisa would try to take Annabelle back to get control of her inheritance, and if Noah had to go up against Annabelle's mother alone, he'd have a harder time convincing a judge to let him, a bachelor with no kids and no blood relationship with her, be her guardian. Not when her mother was around. But John's adopted son and his daughter fighting for custody of their sister all with their father's blessing . . . They stood a chance.

"Annabelle, may I have a word with you in the other room?" Roxy asked.

Noah leaned forward. "Roxy, you have no idea of the circumstances . . ."

Roxy held up her hand to stop his next words. "I have a very good idea of the circumstances. After all, I know what it feels like to be abandoned by a parent."

That shut Noah up and canceled out some of his anger. He really had no idea what happened to make John stay away from his own daughter all these years.

"You don't know anything," Lisa spat out as Roxy walked out of the room without commenting.

Chapter Eleven

Roxy stood in the living room, waiting for Annabelle to follow her out, and took in the garish burgundy-and-gold-patterned sofa. The chairs, covered in some expensive silk fabric, made her eyes hurt. Nothing in the room looked comfortable. In fact, the room appeared unused. Too bad, it had a beautiful marble fireplace. Large windows overlooked the side yard garden and fountain. Though the crystal lamps were beautiful and cast a soft glow over the room, the wall color looked like putty, tan with a tinge of green. Yuck.

"Um, you wanted to talk to me." Annabelle stepped into the room, her hands clasped in front of her.

"I do. You're very pretty," Roxy said to break the ice.

Annabelle's black dress was simple with cap sleeves, fitted over her softly rounded breasts and down her torso to her waist, where the skirt flared out and dropped to just below midthigh. The perfect dress for someone so young. Her blond hair hung to the middle of her back. Rhinestone clips held the sides away from her peaches-and-cream face. She wore the barest amount of makeup with a swipe of clear lip gloss on her lips. The resemblance to her mother ended with the attributes she couldn't change.

Lisa's makeup was overdone, her lipstick a deep wine to accentuate her full lips. Her hair was curled and tousled, cut short to just below her chin. Roxy guessed she was going for the sexy "just tumbled out of bed" look. Her too-tight clothes and ostentatious jewels simply said, *I'm try-*

ing too hard to show you I've got money to burn. I want every man after me and every woman to wish she could be me. Again, Roxy knew the type all too well.

"Thanks," Annabelle responded, but not like she really cared one way or the other.

"You look like your mother."

"I'm nothing like her." Annabelle's direct gaze dared her to contradict that defensive statement.

Roxy laughed, enjoying Annabelle's spirit. "I know what you mean. It still pisses me off when people assume that because I look like my mother, I must be just like her."

For the first time since entering the room, Annabelle relaxed her rigid shoulders. They faced off over the gold-leaf-metal-and-marble coffee table. "I don't know what your mother looks like, but to me, you look like John. It's the eyes. That same strange golden color."

"The eyes, skin, and hair color are him. The rest"—she swept her hand down her lush curves that many men and women coveted—"pure Candy."

"Your mother's name is Candy?"

"It's been Candy since she was sixteen years old, ran away from home, and moved to Vegas. But that's not what I want to talk to you about. I'm going to ask you something and I want an honest answer. Not what you think I want to hear, or what you think Noah expects you to say, but the truth."

"Okay." Annabelle's wariness returned.

"Do you want to live with your mother?"

Annabelle's mouth scrunched. "John left me a lot of money, didn't he? I mean, I know we've lived a good life—there never seemed to be any kind of financial issues. The ranch does really well from what I've heard."

"None of that answers my question." Roxy waited for the girl to get to the point.

Annabelle turned to the six-foot-tall windows and stared out.

Roxy gave in to the girl's need to talk out her thoughts. "I don't know the financial situation with the ranch. I'll go over the accounts when I have time. Based on what I've seen and the money John sent to me over the years, I'd say you'll probably never have to worry about money."

Annabelle glanced over her shoulder. "Even though I only got twenty percent?"

"Yes." Roxy didn't hear any disappointment in Annabelle's voice, so answered the question directly and didn't ask if she felt cheated.

"My mother wants to control that money. If I go with her, she'll probably spend it all before my eighteenth birthday."

"While a judge might grant your mother custody, it's unlikely he'd give her control of your inheritance because it's tied to the ranch, which Noah and I will run. But if she did gain control of the money, she can't spend it all. Most of the money is probably tied up in this house, the property and buildings, and the horses. I don't know if John owned any-thing else, but your mother can't spend what isn't liquid."

Annabelle's eyebrow shot up. "Huh?"

"Cash. She can't make Noah and me sell the house or other assets to get more cash. So even if she burned through your cash, you'd still have other assets to your name."

"Um, okay. So, if I stay here, you and Noah will be my guardians?"

"Yes."

Annabelle turned and faced her again, studying Roxy intently. "You'll have to move here and live with us."

"Yes."

"If you don't, Noah will be my only guardian and my mother will have a better chance of taking me away from him." An unspoken question underscored Annabelle's statement.

"Yes." Roxy didn't offer any other information. This had to be Anna-belle's decision. "You still haven't answered my question."

Annabelle asked her own. "Do you even want to live here with us?"

I don't know. She'd always wanted John to want her to live with him. This wasn't what she had in mind. She had her own life, and now that he was gone, he gave her what she'd always wanted but not the way she wanted it. She didn't want it to be like this. "If I want my inheritance, I have to."

"That didn't answer *my* question," Annabelle shot back.

Roxy smiled. Annabelle reminded her of herself when she was much younger. At fifteen, Annabelle didn't have half the life experience Roxy had at that age, but she did have a good head on her shoulders and was capable of something most teenagers couldn't accomplish—she thought about someone other than herself.

"I will live here on the ranch." The certainty in her words surprised her. Roxy hadn't really had time to think about John's request and what it would mean to her life. But she wouldn't leave Annabelle if she didn't want to go with her mother. Not like John left her with a mother she didn't want to live with.

"Listen, Annabelle, as guardian, I'll expect you to go to school and get good grades. I'll oversee your life like a parent. I'll be responsible for the things you do and the choices you make. If I think you're not making good choices, you'll hear about it. If I think you're being a snotty brat, you'll hear about it. You don't know me, but take this to heart, I won't put up with any BS."

"So you're a hard-ass, who's going to ride me unmercifully, like Noah."

"I don't know Noah, or anything about the relationship you two share. All I can say is, you do the right thing, and I'll back you one hundred percent. When you do well, I'll be there to cheer you on. Screw up, and I'll be all over you."

"Sounds just like Noah." Annabelle expressively rolled her eyes with her arms folded across her chest.

"Then you know what to expect. Let's go back inside and you can tell Noah it's settled."

"I never answered your question."

"Yes, you did." Roxy closed the distance and stood close.

"I want to stay with Noah. This is my home. My mother can make things really hard, and she'd make Noah's life a living hell to get her way." It sounded just like her and John's relationship with Candy. Which is why John wanted her to protect Annabelle.

"So for Noah's sake, you'd go with her, even though you'd regret it and you hate her."

An immediate rush of denial filled Annabelle's eyes, but Annabelle held her tongue.

"Don't worry, it's not a mortal sin to hate your mother. Believe me, I know. Remember one thing," Roxy began.

"What?"

"Don't ever put someone else's happiness before your own. Making yourself miserable won't necessarily make the other person happy. If you went to live with your mother to save Noah the trouble of fighting for you, how do you think that would make him feel?"

"Angry. Maybe sad."

"Right, so you'd be unhappy, he'd be angry and sad, and the only person who'd be happy is your mother as she tries to get her hands on your inheritance. Think about the decisions you make and how they affect you and the people around you. Make good choices for you."

"What if there are only bad choices?"

"Make the best choice of the bad and work to find something better. This is your life, Annabelle. If you don't stand up for yourself and ask for what you need, who will do it for you?"

Annabelle shrugged, but Roxy had made her think. In this case, Annabelle had made the right decision. Roxy hoped when faced with another difficult choice, she would do so again.

"Who decorated this room?" she asked to ease the tension and move to a less intense line of discussion.

"It's hideous."

"Let me guess, your mother?"

"John changed a few of the other rooms. This one is pretty bad, but it's not as bad as my room."

"Good lord, is it possible to decorate worse than this?"

Annabelle laughed and knocked shoulders with her.

Roxy remained unsure of how she'd manage moving to the ranch, keeping or losing her job, and harder still, dealing with Candy when she found out John left Roxy half his estate—and a teenager.

Chapter Twelve

Noah ignored Lisa's stare and leaned forward, planting his elbows on his knees and running a hand through his hair in frustration. He expected John to name him guardian of Annabelle. Noah accepted the responsibility wholeheartedly. But John had gone and thrown Roxy in the mix and complicated things.

Would she stay?

His protective instinct flared to life in his chest.

She had to say yes. She'd be out of her mind to give up 50 percent share in the ranch.

Then again, maybe he was crazy for wanting her to stay. For Annabelle's sake.

Yeah, right.

The thought of her under the same roof sent a thrill through his system that temporarily overrode his anger and surprised him with the force of it. No denying she was stunning. He still felt the zing of electricity that shot up his arm when they shook hands. The dress she wore covered her from shoulders to knees, but did nothing to hide her curvy figure.

Tom noticed, too. The man hadn't taken his eyes off her chest, since she arrived.

Noah doubted any man could walk by Roxy and not want her.

She was going to be trouble with a capital *T* with so many men working on the ranch.

Great, just what he needed. Someone else to babysit besides Annabelle.

But damnit, if she refused to live on the ranch, he'd end up in court fighting a nasty battle with Lisa.

He hoped it didn't come to that.

Frustrated, his thoughts all over the place, Noah ground the heel of his hand into his left eye and tried to massage out the headache pounding along with his heart.

"I can't believe John would do this to you and Annabelle." Since attacking him didn't work, Lisa attempted to make him an ally. "This place should be yours, and he just leaves it to that woman. No one knows her. You've run this ranch with John since you were a boy. You can't let her get away with this."

He agreed with most of what she said, but he also understood John's wishes.

God, he didn't know if he could work with her day in and day out and not touch her. Hell, he didn't know if he could work with her at all. The last thing he needed was another woman coming into his home and changing things, disrupting his life, and telling him how to run his ranch.

"John didn't leave me a choice. He wanted her to live here. He gave her part of the ranch. And didn't say a damn word to me about it."

"He left her *half*. For god's sake, Noah, the man was out of his ever-loving mind. We don't know anything about her, and she gets half."

Noah didn't hear anything in that tirade that said Lisa was concerned about Roxy being legally responsible for the care of her daughter. No. Lisa didn't want Annabelle to lose out on a bigger piece of the ranch. A piece Lisa would do everything possible to control.

"John wanted it this way," Noah said by way of explanation. "It's that simple." And damn complicated for him, Annabelle, and Roxy. They were the ones who had to live with John's decisions.

"Contest the will. He was sick longer than anyone knew. Obviously, he wasn't thinking clearly."

"Actually," Tom interrupted. "She's been named in the will since she was born. John's updated it several times over the years, like when Annabelle was born. I've seen all the versions my father completed. Originally, everything went to Noah. When Roxy was born, they shared the ranch sixty-forty. When Annabelle was born, John changed it to the current split."

"I don't care what the DNA test says, maybe we can prove she isn't his daughter." Lisa tried to come up with anything to change the unchangeable. John was named as the father on Annabelle's birth certificate, but one DNA test would prove otherwise. DNA didn't lie.

Maybe he should just pay Lisa and send her away and out of Annabelle's life again. He could afford it. But could he afford the headache? Give Lisa an inch, she'd keep coming back until she got the whole damn mile.

"There's a reason John didn't want her."

Noah's heart squeezed with that statement. Lisa hadn't wanted Annabelle. Not really. His biological father hadn't wanted him. Not enough to be faithful to his pregnant wife, to stay and work it out after he was born, or to find Noah now for an adult relationship. Not even to have a beer and say he was sorry for not being there Noah's whole life.

John wasn't like that. He cared enough to leave Roxy half the ranch as some sort of apology for whatever happened between them.

"Doesn't matter," Tom stated. "Noah and Annabelle aren't his blood relations. Roxy is."

Lisa opened her mouth to protest further, but Tom stopped her. "As his biological daughter, contesting the will would open the door for her to make a case against Noah and Annabelle."

"Why would I do that?" Roxy entered the room with Annabelle. "Aside from the fact that John raised them, and this is their home, it's just stupid. They are his family. I don't care what the DNA says about them or me. DNA tells you where you come from, but it doesn't say who you are."

Noah sat back surprised by her comments. She was right, and he should remember John felt that very same way.

Roxy looked him in the eye. "Annabelle and I talked. We've come to terms with the whole guardianship, and she understands I take that responsibility seriously. She wants to stay with us on the ranch."

Noah didn't know how he felt about that *us*. "I never thought she wanted to leave."

"I asked her what she wanted. As someone not given a choice where I live, I thought she might like her say."

Noah understood her implied reprimand. John demanded she stay here to get her inheritance. More than that, he'd never asked her if she wanted to live here.

Noah should have asked Annabelle and not assumed she'd want to stay. Lisa might be a class-A bitch, but she was still Annabelle's mother. So he gave Annabelle a choice. "Annabelle, honey, do you want to live with your mom?"

Annabelle's eyes went wide. He hated to put her on the spot and conceded that Roxy asking her to leave the room for the private talk was a much better solution. But he needed to hear her say it.

Her eyes darted to her mother, but never really settled on her. She bit her bottom lip, and said, "I want to stay here."

"Let's make that happen," Tom interjected, and pulled out the papers. "Noah, Roxy, if you'll sign here taking over guardianship, we'll make it official."

"Wait a damn minute." Lisa stood and planted her hands on her hips. "Don't I get a say in this?"

"No," Noah answered for Tom.

"Hey, I gave birth to her."

"You were an incubator," Noah shot back.

"Enough." Roxy handed him the papers along with a pen. "Lisa, your daughter made her decision. This is her home, she's got school and friends. She needs time to grieve John's death. Uprooting her now isn't a good idea. She needs stability. Noah and I can give her that."

"And I can't."

Noah signed the papers and handed them to Tom. "Luckily, you won't get the chance to prove the only thing you really want to do is control Annabelle's inheritance."

"Even if she gained custody, John named Noah and Roxy to oversee her inheritance. It's paid out to her in increments on her eighteenth, twenty-first, and twenty-fifth birthdays. At that time, she'll control her inheritance on her own," Tom explained.

Lisa's face turned red with rage.

Noah knew exactly what was coming next and hated the flash of misery he saw cross Annabelle's face when her mother stood up in a huff. "This is ludicrous. She's my daughter and I have absolutely no say."

"You have no say because you've proven the only person you think about is yourself," Roxy commented, her voice cool and controlled.

"You don't know me, or anything about my relationship with my daughter."

"I knew since the moment I saw the two of you together that you have absolutely no concern for your daughter's well-being. Not once have you offered her any words of comfort, held her hand, hugged her close and re-assured her everything was going to be all right." Roxy shook her head. "She lost her father, and the only thing you're worried about is how much he left her and how fast you can get your hands on it." The words came out thick with emotion.

"Easy for you to say since you got the bulk of the estate and control of my daughter's portion, too."

Roxy didn't respond to the insinuation. "Noah loves his sister. He'll do everything he can to make sure she's raised right and her inheritance is protected."

"You don't even know him," Lisa shot back.

"I know he held her hand through the church ceremony. He wrapped her in his arms at the cemetery and let her cry out her grief. I saw the way he bent to her ear and offered her the words and sentiments she needed to look up at him and smile. They have a bond. Something you don't share with her. I know by the way he looked at me when he found out I was named guardian that if he doesn't like the way I treat Annabelle, he'll make damn sure I know it and he'll get a judge to remove me from that position. Not because he wants control of her twenty percent, but because he loves her and wants the best for her. I wish, for Annabelle's sake, you felt the same."

Roxy sighed, gave Annabelle a commiserative look, then turned back to Lisa and pinned her in her steady golden gaze. "You don't know me, but if you did, you'd take this to heart. Mother or not, if you think for one second I'll stand by and let you hurt that girl, you better think twice.

The operative word in guardian is *guard*. Believe it when I say, I take that very seriously. Especially, when it comes to you."

Impressed, Noah sat back and smiled at the indignant look on Lisa's face. He'd never seen her speechless.

Annabelle stared up at Roxy, her mouth open in shock. A smile spread across her face and her eyes lit up with awe.

Noah and John had stood between Annabelle and Lisa, but neither of them had really stood up for her. Not like Roxy just did. Everyone understood that Annabelle would stay with John, and Lisa accepted that and took the money and never really made trouble. With John out of the way, Lisa saw Annabelle as an easy mark. Not so with Noah by her side, but Roxy had just added another barrier to Lisa's schemes.

Annabelle schooled her features again. Never one to draw her mother's attention, he wondered how long she'd waited to actually hear someone put her mother in her place. More, she needed to hear someone stick up for her. He and John had done so in subtle ways, but it obviously hadn't been enough. Annabelle needed Roxy's blunt announcement that she meant to guard Annabelle from her own mother.

Maybe John had a good idea. Mary was like a mother to them, but Roxy was younger, and Annabelle might respond better to her direct approach. Mary tended to coddle Annabelle. Roxy seemed more inclined to expect more from Annabelle and demand she give it.

Maybe Roxy was exactly what Annabelle needed.

She intrigued him.

Yes, he wanted to know about her mysterious background and relationship with John, but he also wanted to know who she was and what made her tick. What happened to her to give her that stubborn tilt to her chin, challenge in her words, and the confidence to stand up for Annabelle and mean it with every fiber of her being?

Chapter Thirteen

Roxy turned her back on Lisa and her pathetic attempts to finagle her way back into Annabelle's life with the sole purpose of robbing her blind. Roxy knew how it felt to have a mother who cared nothing for you, unless she could act the part to get something from you.

"I've had enough. I'm leaving." Indignation tinged Lisa's voice, but the only thing she was mad about was not getting her way. She walked to the study doors without a backward glance.

Roxy couldn't help striking one more jab. "Not even a goodbye for your daughter?"

Lisa let out a very unladylike grunt, turned on her three-hundred-dollar stilettos, and walked out. The front door slammed shut a moment later.

Roxy went to Annabelle and placed a hand on her shoulder. "Don't worry, Annabelle. Believe me, it's better she ignores you. Nothing worse than having your own mother kiss and hug you in some overblown show of fake emotion."

"I wish she'd stay away. When she's gone, I don't have to think about it."

"When she's here, she makes you confront the anger and hurt you always feel, but can numb while she's away," Roxy added.

"Exactly," Annabelle said on a sigh.

Noah looked from Annabelle to Roxy and back again. "Let's just be happy she's gone. Knowing her, she'll lick her wounds, spend a fortune to soothe her ruffled feathers, and be back at the most inopportune moment possible."

Annabelle frowned, and Roxy took it that Noah's words had come true on numerous occasions.

"How do you think she'll react when she finds out her alimony payments stop now that John's dead?" Tom grinned, enjoying stirring the pot.

Noah groaned and rolled his eyes to the ceiling. Annabelle looked disturbed.

"I'll send her a letter," Tom suggested.

"Fine," Noah agreed. "Make sure she understands that going after custody of Annabelle, so she can get child support, isn't going to work either."

"I will." Tom made a note in his day planner.

"Tom, what else do I need to know about John's plans for me?" Roxy didn't hide her irritation that her father, after all these years, pushed her into a corner and made her do what he wanted. And he used her weakness to make her do it: a sister.

When John visited, he asked about her life, which for her revolved around her sisters. He knew how much her sisters meant to her. How she'd die for any one of them. And now she had another to raise.

"You can work out the details for running the ranch with Noah. You'll both sign on the accounts jointly. As you heard, the terms for your inheritance state you have to live here until Annabelle turns eighteen. You have one week to move into the house. After that, you can't be gone from the ranch more than five days a month."

"What? I have a home, friends, a job. You expect me to change my whole life in a week."

"Those are John's terms. Do you know what fifty percent of John's estate is worth?"

"That is beside the point. I haven't seen or heard from him in years and he leaves me a ranch to run, a child to raise, and expects me to change my entire life at the drop of a hat."

"Don't forget the envelope," Tom reminded her.

Roxy glared at the innocuous item. John had already turned her life upside down. What else did he want from her?

Not one to put off unpleasant tasks, she opened the envelope and pulled out the contents. On top was her copy of the will. Underneath, a sealed envelope with her name scrawled across it. Beneath that she read the property deed and felt every ounce of blood drain from her face.

She placed both hands on the desk and stared down at the name on the deed.

The Wild Rose Ranch.

"Roxy, are you okay?" Noah asked.

No. She was not okay. This couldn't be right. He couldn't own 80 percent of that place.

She flipped pages and found the business contract.

Fuck me.

John had made her the Madam of one of the most well-known brothels in all of Nevada—and her mother's boss.

Dirty, rotten, son of a bitch.

Here she thought John was finally offering her a way out of Nevada and the life her mother chose over her daughter at every turn. Instead, he'd been supporting that lifestyle.

Now he expected her to run it.

What did that say about what he thought of her?

Probably the same thing everyone else thought when they discovered she lived at the Wild Rose Ranch.

The same thing Tom obviously thought judging by his lascivious gaze.

She tried to give the Wild Rose Ranch another kind of reputation through her horse training and rodeo competitions. Still, the stain of her mother's life never washed off.

"Roxy, just so you understand, the contents of that envelope are yours alone. Noah and Annabelle do not share in that part of John's estate."

"Let me guess," she replied to Tom's statement, "they know nothing about this."

"It only pertains to you," Tom confirmed, the grin saying more than anything that he thought this a juicy little secret.

"God forbid he taint this ranch, his children, and his reputation by admitting how he got his daughter."

"I think you misunderstand," Tom said, giving John the benefit of the doubt when Roxy wanted to rage. "He named you as guardian for

Annabelle. He gave you half his assets here. I can only say he kept that separate because it's your life."

"Right." She pointed to the papers. "You think this is my life."

Tom's eyes filled with confusion. "He included a note. Perhaps it explains things better."

"No explanation necessary. He's made himself quite clear. He's made me responsible for her. Just like he did when he left me with her."

But now she was responsible for all the women who worked there. And the whole damn place.

Roxy stuffed the contents back into the envelope and ignored Noah's and Annabelle's stares.

Noah didn't even try to hide his curiosity and asked her point-blank, "What's in the envelope?"

"The answer to years of wondering why my father didn't want me." The words held a lifetime of scorn.

"Whatever is in that envelope, I can't imagine John meant it in a spiteful way. He wasn't like that." Noah tried to soothe her.

She appreciated the sentiment, but the truth remained. "The father you knew, who loved you and cared for both of you all these years, is not the same man I knew."

Noah didn't give up defending John. "I don't think he meant to insult you. By the look on your face, that's exactly how you took it."

"Noah, you have no idea what you're talking about, and if you did, you wouldn't be offering me any kind words." She went to the bar, poured a dollop of whiskey into a shot glass, and downed it. The sting burned down her throat, but didn't stop her from thinking. "If that's all, I'm leaving."

"I'll walk you out," Tom offered.

She picked up her envelope and followed him to the door. Noah and Annabelle remained seated, looking tired and overwhelmed.

Noah stood. "I guess we'll see you in a week."

The halfhearted smiles and nods goodbye told her they both needed time to absorb the changes in their lives.

She knew how they felt. Only they had all the time in the world.

She had to get home, settle things at the ranch, talk to her employer about keeping her job, pack, and move to a new place where she had no friends.

And she had to run a ranch with a man who clearly didn't want or need her help.

She let out a big sigh at the daunting thoughts.

Tom stopped short in the entry before the front door and she ran into the back of him. He spun around and grabbed her by the shoulders to steady her. Or so it seemed until his hands glided down her arms and the back of his fingertips grazed her breasts. She went still and raised her gaze to meet his lust-filled eyes.

"You're not what I expected." His gaze swept down and up her. "When I found out John left you the Wild Rose Ranch . . ." He shook his head, the disbelief quickly turning back to desire. "I was astounded to discover he owned such a place, but to know his daughter lived there. Well, I couldn't wait to meet you."

"Is that right?" She dropped her voice an octave, baiting him.

Tom responded to the husky tone. They all did. This wasn't the first time she'd dealt with someone like Tom, who made assumptions about her because of where she lived and how she looked.

Tom rubbed his thumb over her arm, taking the shiver of disgust as a sign of interest. "I admit, I've never been to a place like that, but now that you're here, I'm thinking all kinds of wild thoughts. You'll be living here. So close. I hope we can come to an arrangement."

He stepped closer.

It was all she could do not to cringe from his touch as his hand slid over her side and rested on her hip.

"What sort of arrangement did you have in mind?"

"You're so beautiful and sexy. It'll be hard to wait for your return. I'll call you when I'd like to meet. Unless you'll get your own place nearby to work, I've got a place picked out. The Mountainside Motel off Highway Nine. Not too far away, yet discreet enough to keep the arrangement just between us."

"You've thought of everything. Except you neglected to consider one thing."

"Oh, of course, the fee." He gripped her hip tighter. "I'm sure we can come up with something that works for both of us."

"Now see, that's where you're wrong."

He traced his finger along the side of her face, pushing her hair back over her shoulder. "I'm sorry, I don't understand what you mean."

"I would *never* agree to be with you, you fool." She kneed him in the balls.

He fell to the floor and onto his side, clutching his junk and wailing like a baby. "You bitch."

"That part you got right." She stared down her nose at him. "Listen good, because I am only going to say this once. Keep your damn hands off me. I am not a prostitute." She opened the door and walked out without closing it, leaving Tom writhing in pain in the marble entry.

A few steps from her rental car, Noah caught up to her, grabbed her arm, and spun her around. "Hey, why the hell did you do that to Tom?"

"He mistook me for a whore. He won't make that mistake again."

Noah's eyes went wide as he tried to process what she said. "I'm sorry, he what?"

She shook her head. She didn't have it in her to explain. "Never mind."

"Hell no. What did he say to you?"

"He was just thinking with the wrong head. I incapacitated the one doing the thinking, so he'll remember to use the one on his shoulders the next time he sees me."

"If he did something inappropriate, maybe he needs a lesson in manners." Noah turned to get some answers from Tom, and maybe get his own shot in, too, but Roxy grabbed his arm and stopped him.

In Tom's impaired state, he might say something he shouldn't about the Wild Rose Ranch.

John didn't want Noah or Annabelle to know anything about it.

If they found out, she wouldn't be welcome here.

Not that Noah wanted her here in the first place.

Well, that might not be exactly true. Because the moment she touched his arm, their eyes met, and neither of them acknowledged the electricity snapping between them.

She dropped her hand and rubbed it down her thigh, trying to erase the tingle, but nothing would diminish something that powerful.

"Did you want something?"

Noah stuffed his hands in his pockets. He glanced back at the house, Tom's moans drifting out the open door, and turned back to her looking uncertain. "Are you sure you want to do this?"

She cocked her hip and stared up at him. "Trying to dissuade me from moving in and living up to the terms of the inheritance?"

He glared, his mouth drawn in a tight line. "It's my job to take care of Annabelle."

"Our job," she corrected.

"Annabelle doesn't need anyone else in her life who uses her to get what they want."

"Let's get one thing straight, you and me, right here and now. This is *our* ranch. *We* run it together now. Annabelle is *our* responsibility. We make decisions together for her sake. It's going to be difficult enough for me to come into your home and disrupt the life the two of you have shared all these years. Let's not make this harder than it has to be by squabbling over who got how much, or who's known who longer. As far as I'm concerned, this is a fifty-fifty deal between us as far as decisions go. If you're not on board with that, it's only going to make things harder for all of us, but especially Annabelle."

"Fine. We'll try it your way. For now."

"Great. One last thing to clear the air. I know you're pissed about the way things got split. I wasn't part of John's life, yet he left me the bigger share. You want to be pissed at me, fine. I can take it. But when it comes to making decisions for her, we do it with her welfare in mind, not any grievances we have with each other."

"That sounds good, but I don't know a damn thing about you, yet John and you expect me to trust you with this ranch and my sister. You want me to work my ass off every day and hand over half of everything this ranch makes because you share some DNA with him. You want things equal between us, but they're not."

"No, they aren't. You got damn near every day with *my father*! You grew up here, happy and loved, while he left me with a mother who is a thousand times worse than Lisa could ever hope to be. I barely got a phone call two or three times a year, never got a letter, a birthday party, or Christmas by the tree with hot chocolate and gifts. In the end, he left me half this place and"—she held up the envelope—"made me the one thing I spent my whole life trying to avoid becoming after being raised by my mother."

Saying it, knowing it, made her heart hurt even more. "You've got reason to be pissed, but believe me, he didn't do half as much to you as he's done to me."

Chapter Fourteen

Roxy scanned the boxes and suitcases spread over her room and sighed. It had taken three days to sort, discard, donate, and pack her remaining belongings, change her mailing address at the post office, add her name to all the Wild Rose accounts at the bank, and buy a car over the phone in Whitefall. Why not? She had the money. This way she could leave her truck here for the five days a month she was allowed to come home, check on her beloved horses and sisters and deal with the business she didn't want to think about, let alone own.

Her sisters surprised her this morning by staying home from their respective jobs and school to help her finish packing.

"Spill it. What's bothering you? The fight you had with Noah before you left?" Sonya asked.

She could tell her sisters anything, so she shared her thoughts, however mixed-up they were at the moment. "He's not what I expected. His love for Annabelle comes through so clear. The grief I saw in him over John's death . . ." She didn't know how to explain that kind of depth of feeling.

Sonya, ever the skeptic, asked, "You mean he isn't the spoiled 'everything should be mine because I'm John's son' kind of guy?"

"Noah is protective of his sister, his ranch, everything he cares about. I don't know if he'll ever get past what John did and work with me without all the hostility."

"Admit it—you want him to like you," Juliana coaxed.

"I don't want him to hate me."

"Because you think he's hot." Juliana had a one-track mind sometimes.

"My feelings are all mixed-up. Yes, I'm attracted to him." The man was gorgeous. That dark, thick hair. The smile that mostly came out only for his sister. The intensity in his eyes when he looked at her. His loyalty and devotion to his sister. "I even like him. But I resent the fact John chose him. We *have to* work together, but I'd like us to be friends."

"You want to be more than friends." Juliana didn't know when to shut up. Even when she was right.

"I have a hard time with that part of relationships."

"We all do," Sonya admitted. She smiled and added, "Well, except for Juliana."

"Can I help it if I like to have fun and you guys drag your baggage around like some apology you owe the world because some asshole fucked our mothers for a price? The men, our mothers, they got what they wanted, so why are we carrying around the guilt of that bargain when neither our mothers nor those men feel any remorse?"

None of them had an answer. They all dealt with their backgrounds and upbringing in their own way. Juliana simply ignored the stares, the whispers, and outright speculation and advances from men and lived her life with a carefree attitude, doing as she pleased. One of these days, her tendencies toward partying and playing like her mother were going to get her into trouble. Of all of them, Juliana was the most likely to end up like their mothers, or worse, dead from too much drinking, drugging, and living on the wild side.

Roxy feared Juliana counted too much on all of them to set her straight when she let her wild ways get away from her. Now, with Roxy moving to Speckled Horse Ranch, Sonya mired in work at the financial firm, and Adria finishing her degree at the university, Roxy feared Juliana would stumble and fall without them there every moment, ready to catch her.

"The point is, it's going to be hard enough dealing with each other about the business and Annabelle. Mix in the charge that pulls us together when we're close and it's a recipe for disaster."

"Maybe not." Adria cocked her head to the side, the way she did when she turned serious. "Give it a chance. In such close quarters, either your anger or lust will explode. I'm thinking he might try to wring your neck, then change his mind and use his hands for something entirely different." Adria wiggled her eyebrows.

Roxy hit her sister in the face with a sweater.

They all laughed and it felt good to let loose with her sisters. But one thing still weighed on her heart. Roxy sucked in a big breath and let the words fall. "John owned the Wild Rose Ranch. He left it to me."

Silence filled her small bedroom more than all four of them in there together. The tension grew so thick, she felt like a piece of fruit trapped in a Jell-O mold.

"He what?" Sonya asked.

"He left me . . ."

"I heard what you said," Sonya snapped. "All this time, you never told us," she accused.

"I just found out." Roxy tried to make them understand what her inheritance meant. For all of them. "The point is, I think we should all benefit from that place. Adria and Juliana, gather up all your bills. Credit cards. School loans. Everything. Give them to Sonya."

"Why me?"

"You're my new financial advisor. I'll pay off yours, Juliana's, and Adria's debts. Next semester, I'll pay for their classes. I'll also pay you a monthly salary to oversee whatever investments you'd like to suggest or I make on my own. I'd also like you to take a look at the Wild Rose books, make sure everything is on the up-and-up."

"You're serious?" Sonya asked.

"Your talent with numbers is being wasted at that firm. I know you've worked your ass off to get where you are, but they're dragging their heels in promoting you."

Sonya nodded with agreement and a self-deprecating smile.

"If I can't use the money from that place to help my sisters, what good is it?"

"This place, our home, the horses," Sonya pointed out, "the four of us together made a difference. Who knows what would have happened to us if we hadn't ended up here, with Roxy, together."

Roxy opened her arms. "Group hug." Her sisters practically tackled her, but Roxy didn't care. She held on tight, already missing them. They'd never been apart more than a day or two. Now she wouldn't be back for another month.

Sonya tugged a lock of her hair. "Go feed the horses. We'll finish up in here. Then we'll go out for dinner."

Adria pointed at her. "Your treat."

Roxy loved her sisters for making this transition easier on her. She'd miss them over the next days and weeks as she settled into her father's ranch and Noah's and Annabelle's lives. Not that they really wanted her there. Like her, they didn't have a choice.

Chapter Fifteen

Roxy left her room and headed for the barn. The letter with her name on it sat on the kitchen table. The damn thing mocked her. She refused to open her father's letter and see what he wanted to tell her after his death that he couldn't find the time to say to her face. Her sisters had all coaxed her to read it, but she'd held firm.

Not now.

Not yet.

She closed the front door and stood at the covered porch railing, the sun beating down on her, and looked at the cactus and plants growing in the yard. Nothing like the gorgeous colorful gardens surrounding the house in Whitefall.

She stared across the pastures to the grand white mansion, red and pink wild roses circling the sprawling house, defiant in the blazing heat. She couldn't see it, but out front was the tall arching sign that read, Wild Rose Ranch.

The brothel represented everything bad in her life.

Not exactly the stock of fillies she kept in her stables. No, the mansion held some of the most beautiful high-priced prostitutes in the state.

How could John do this to her?

Stepping off the porch, she walked along the gravel path to the back.

Candy preferred the extravagant big house.

Roxy preferred her privacy and the solitude of the three-bedroom, two-bath cottage. Though a pasture separated the two structures, it seemed the brothel would always cast a shadow over her life.

But she wouldn't let it consume her life. She pulled her ringing phone from her pocket. *Please tell me I still have a job.*

"Hello, Greg."

"Roxy, I got your email. Sorry to hear about your dad."

She leaned against the barn wall. "Thanks. I know this is short notice and we're really busy . . ."

"Don't worry about it. You're one of my best designers. I understand your predicament, and I've spoken to the big boss. Your solution will work out great for you and us. We lost Nancy six months ago when she went on maternity leave. I can't believe we never thought to make this a telecommuting position. As you pointed out, all you need is email and your computer."

"I won't forget you stuck your neck out for me."

"Thanks, but this is a good decision for you and the company."

Roxy's stomach fluttered with joy. "Well, thank you anyway."

"You're welcome. We'll talk soon." They ended with goodbyes and her promise to get in touch once she settled in at the ranch.

Roxy danced a jig to the barn door, kicking up dust. For Annabelle, she'd change her life and move to Montana, but that didn't mean she had to give up everything. She'd worked hard to earn her spot and reputation at the company. She might have money now, but she still needed something that was hers. Something that gave her a sense of accomplishment and achievement.

She slid the door open and stepped into the slightly cooler interior. Vinny was the first to stick his big head over his stall door and nicker at her, blowing out his nostrils into her hair when she came near.

"Hello, baby. How's my big man?" Vinny rubbed his fuzzy nose against her cheek and nibbled at her hair.

Her mind went to thoughts of Noah. It did often these last few days.

What would he do if he found out she owned the Wild Rose Ranch?

She tried not to let the fear overwhelm her and set thoughts like those aside. Much easier to think about the six-foot cowboy with the dark hair and amazing whiskey-brown eyes. The way he looked in his black suit, charcoal-gray tie, and polished cowboy boots. The width of his shoulders and the way his crisp shirt spread across his wide chest. She'd wanted to . . .

"I know that look," her mother said from the barn door. The sun highlighted her golden hair, hanging down to cover her full breasts in waves of curls. The hot pink tank top barely covered her nipples. If she leaned forward, she'd spill right out of it. The Daisy Duke shorts barely covered anything. Her long golden legs went on for days.

Who wears four-inch spike heels to a horse barn? Her mother.

Despite the tiny lines at the corner of her eyes and around her lips, she still looked fifteen years younger than her forty-six years with the body of a teenager and the me, me, me attitude to match. Overdone pink eye shadow, a thick layer of black mascara, and pink lip gloss. If her mother kissed her with that slick goop, she'd cringe.

Not that her mother had ever been that affectionate with her.

How did men put up with that stuff?

Her mother walked to join her, hips swinging, boobs bouncing, lace peeking out of the tank top. Yep. Men are stupid. They'd kiss that gloss-slicked mouth to get Candy naked and under them. Or on top of them. On a bed, or on the floor. Standing up, or lying down.

This was starting to sound like some pornographic Dr. Seuss book.

"What are you doing here?" Resentment laced her words. Her mother always intruded at the worst moments.

"You were thinking about a man."

Right up until you walked in and reminded me he'll find out about you and assume the worst of me.

It happened too many times to count. The disappointment and hurt still stung, despite her thick coat of armor. Roxy had a feeling with Noah there'd be no protection. He'd somehow strip her of all her shields and leave her vulnerable because he was John's favorite. And if she hadn't been good enough for John, she wouldn't be good enough for Noah.

"What do you want?"

"Oh, we aren't talking about him. Must be a real good guy," she said, fishing for information. Candy twined a lock of hair around her finger. Flirting and seduction were second nature even when no one was around to play with her. "I stopped by the house. John left you the bulk of his estate."

Leave it to Candy to walk right into her place, plop herself down, and start reading documents that didn't belong to her.

"What else did you go through?" She feared this visit was because her mother found out she owned the brothel. *Please, no.* The last thing she needed was a hooker who thought she had power. Candy would make everyone at the Wild Rose Ranch miserable and Roxy irate because she'd have to clean up Candy's mess.

"Why didn't you open the letter from John?"

"None of your business."

"He's your father." Candy's voice dropped like she cared. She didn't.

Roxy learned a long time ago never to believe anything Candy said or did, especially if it appeared selfless. Candy didn't know the meaning of the word, or give in to sentimentality.

"He made sure to get the DNA test to prove it."

Candy shrugged, her head tipping to the side, but not an ounce of regret or remorse crossed her lovely face that her father could have been one of half a dozen given the week she was conceived. "I never pretended or lied. He knew exactly who and what I am when he slept with me."

"Always make them pay up front." She recited one of her mother's many lessons on dealing with men.

"Damn right, sweetie."

"Why did John stop coming around?"

"Maybe the man on your mind is that Noah who got thirty percent of your inheritance."

It didn't surprise her that her mother changed the subject to one of her favorites—men. "Noah is John's son. Of course, he got a share. The question is why he left me anything."

"You're his one and only daughter."

"Annabelle is his daughter. Noah, his son. I'm the one he threw away."

"Not true. He's supported you since you were born."

"Yep. Sent me money every month. Sent you money every month until I turned eighteen. A pretty good deal for you, since you have no obligation to John and can have a new man every hour on the hour."

Candy's eyes lit with amusement along with the playful smile. "And I do. When it suits me."

Truer words were never spoken.

The ache in Roxy's heart throbbed and pulsed. Her throat went tight and she choked back the tears she hated to admit came so easily when she allowed herself to wish her mother was different, that her childhood had been different. Didn't do her a damn bit of good and only made her angry.

In a rare show of concern, her mother said, her voice soft, "But that's not you. Tell me about Noah."

"Nothing to tell."

Candy's smile died because Roxy wouldn't play her game. "You were never a good liar."

"That's your forte." Her mother didn't deny it. "How about we try the truth? John came to see me when I was nine, you two fought, and he never came back and stayed like he did before that day. What happened?"

"Let it go."

"Not this time. I want the truth."

"He left you a fortune. You want to blame me for something, blame me for that," Candy defended herself. "I did that for you. You'll never have to work a day in your life. Not the way I did."

"Bullshit. As inexplicable as it is, you love what you do. It's like some kind of high when men come on to you, pay you top dollar for your favors."

"Favors. Aren't you the old-fashioned one. They pay to fuck me, darlin'. Plain and simple. For that short time, they want me, love me even. I'm beautiful and sexy and wild. Their dream come true. My father thought I'd be nothing. He called me stupid and ugly and a hell of a lot worse. He tried to beat it into me. But look what I've accomplished. I make more money in a year than he made his whole miserable life."

Roxy knew very little about her mother's family. It surprised her Candy mentioned them at all. When she was young, Candy made it clear they only had each other. Not a comforting thought when her mother downed another shot and did another line and sank further into oblivion, forgetting she even had a daughter for days on end.

"You make money on your back."

"And on my knees. On all fours. Who cares how I make it? I'll never have to scrape by on food stamps and public assistance checks. That's the life he doomed my mother to, and I picked myself up at sixteen and left them behind and all their misery. We may have had it rough in the beginning, you and me, but you never went without a meal. You had the best clothes. You went to a good school and even graduated college."

Just like Candy to gloss over the bad and misappropriate the good times to suit her version of events. "You left out the years before we came to the Ranch, when you spent the money John sent on drugs instead of food. We lived in our car, cheap motel rooms, apartments that should have been condemned. Every day I wondered where we'd end up next. My belly hurt from hunger. My clothes were never clean, and neither was I." Kids at school could be so cruel about such things.

Candy made her life hell.

But then, when she was ten, John bought the Wild Rose Ranch, Big Mama found her mother and offered her a job, and Roxy had a safe place all her own, nice clothes, a stocked fridge and bursting cupboards. She went to school every day. She didn't have to stay home and take care of her drugged-out mother. She went to college.

Though she didn't know it at the time, John gave her those things and renewed her sense of security.

Another piece of her resentment fell away. He cared, even if he took the coward's way out and didn't acknowledge her or take her away from this place and Candy because he didn't want to ruin his perfect life in Montana.

He didn't want people to know his dirty little secret.

"Stop being so dramatic. We were poor and I did what I had to do for us to survive. Now look at us."

"We were poor because for a good long time the only thing you remembered how to do was drink and drug and whore. I put you to bed, made sure you ate, and took care of you when you couldn't even stand, let alone walk straight. Do you have any idea how scary it was for me when you overdosed? Twice. To watch some guy pounding on your chest to make your heart beat again. To see you dumped into a cold shower to wake you up as you threw up all over yourself. To worry that you might die and leave me there all alone." Roxy's voice shook with emotion.

For a split second, Candy's eyes filled with understanding and remorse. "Those days are long behind us." Of course Candy wanted to move on from the past, leave it behind them, and never look back. Candy could do that because, let's face it, she couldn't remember most of that time.

Roxy remembered it all, right down to the echo of fear.

"Since we moved here, we've been living the good life, sweetie. I always wanted to be rich, have men and champagne and everything I ever wanted at my fingertips." Candy's priorities were men, booze, drugs, money, and extravagance in any and all combinations possible. And to excess. Once in a great long while Roxy made the list. Not always. Certainly not often enough.

Candy had a knack for forgetting the unpleasant and focusing on the shiny, sparkly parts of her life she loved so much. "This life has kept you here with your horses. Lord knows, they're the only things you love."

"John gave us this life."

Her mother's head cocked and one perfectly arched eyebrow shot up. "What do you mean?"

Since the reading of the will and learning she inherited the Wild Rose Ranch, Roxy had put a lot of thought into figuring out what her father had done for her over the years. She played out the timeline of her life, filling in the pieces where John fit and then disappeared.

"When I was very little, John came around three or four times a year. He discovered you beat me. You and John fought."

Candy's lips pressed together, but she didn't comment about how volatile she used to get when she was high.

"He said goodbye and never came back. Several months later, we moved here."

"So," her mother said, getting that petulant tone that reminded Roxy of a grumpy child. "Don't think I didn't know he came to see you once in a while."

Roxy sucked it up and revealed John's secret. "Did you know he owned this place?"

That got Candy's attention. "What? No he didn't. Big Mama owns and runs this place."

She'd regret this, but she wanted to put Candy in her place for once. "Big Mama owns a small portion, but John bought the bulk of the business and the twenty acres surrounding us to put you someplace he could keep an eye on you and me."

Candy clasped her hands together at her chest, bounced up and down from her knees, and squealed, "And now we own it!" The exuberant smile spread across her beautiful face.

Sometimes, it was hard to look at her mother, see how beautiful she was, and know how rotten she was at the core.

"Not *we*. Me! I'm the Madam of a brothel." The pain threatened to overwhelm her. How could this happen? She'd studied hard, made good grades, went to college, earned her degree, and found a good, honest job.

Now this.

Dragged back into the muck of her mother's life.

"Big Mama runs this place."

"That doesn't make it any better." Rage filled every word.

Candy rolled her eyes. "How did I raise such a prude for a daughter?"

"I raised myself," Roxy snapped. "I want an answer. Why did he leave?"

"How should I know? He was rich, lived in another state. He was a good honest man who didn't want anyone to know he'd fucked a whore and knocked her up." Candy shrugged the whole thing off with a pouty frown. "He didn't want us."

The instant sting of those words hurt, but not as much as the thoughts she'd harbored for so many years. But maybe she'd been wrong. Maybe the truth was closer to: he didn't want anyone back home to know about them, but he did love Roxy and wanted to take care of her and keep her safe. He did so the best he could, even though keeping his secret meant more to him than giving her the life he gave Noah and Annabelle.

"What did you do?" Roxy backed her mother into the stall door, using her body to block Candy's escape.

"Back off," Candy demanded.

Roxy didn't back down. "What. Did. You. Do?"

"He threatened to take you away from me."

"You didn't want me. You've made that clear more times than I can count."

Candy twirled another lock of hair, looking all innocent. "You were mine."

"I was a paycheck. Back then, you needed his money for your next bottle and fix."

"That's not fair." But the truth. The pouty frown returned.

"I'm the first one to say, no, it's not fair. It sucks to know your own mother took away a good and decent childhood, so she could keep cashing in."

"You don't understand. I was desperate then. It wasn't like it is now."

"No. It's not. John knew you'd never be anything but what you are, so he found a place for you."

"You got your cottage and ranch, so don't think he didn't give you something, too." Candy took a breath. "You're right. All that moving around was rough. A few times, we moved so he couldn't take you from me."

"You hid me from him!"

"He always found us again. Sometimes using a PI and other times I came up short and needed money."

"You're a real piece of work."

"You know, not everything is my fault."

"Really? That's hard to believe."

"Fine. You want to know. When he saw the bruises on you . . ." Her mother frowned. "You know I didn't mean it. It was the drugs that made me do it." Of course Candy blamed the drugs instead of taking responsibility for abusing Roxy. "You're my girl. I couldn't let him take you."

There was some sentiment in Candy's convoluted thinking, but Roxy wouldn't be swayed from getting the answers she wanted.

"For once, tell me the truth, not your version of prettying up the mess you made."

The pout on her mother's lips made many men jump to please her and tease that hurt look off her face. It never worked on Roxy. She saw right through the false emotion. To this day, she wasn't sure her mother actually felt anything, but walked through her life numb, trying desperately to find anything—booze, drugs, men—that made her feel something.

"I used his life against him. He had a pregnant wife at home. How was he going to explain a little girl he didn't tell her or anyone about? How was he going to tell her he'd been coming to visit you and fucking me at the same time?"

Lisa had been having affairs, too. Annabelle had been proof of that.

"He didn't want to lose his wife. He thought that baby was going to give him the happy little family he always wanted. Do you think that woman would have wanted to take a hooker's child and raise you along with her little girl?"

Lisa didn't even want Annabelle.

"When I pointed out what he had to lose, he left."

"Not good enough. John wanted to keep you from hurting me. His relationship with Lisa was rocky at best. There had to be more."

Candy planted her hands on her hips. "You really think I'm low."

"Spill it!"

"You can be a real bitch. Fine. I told him to go ahead and take you home. I'd love to visit you, maybe move there and start over. There had to be a lot of lonely men looking for a warm woman to see them through the long winter nights. Maybe I'd find a job at a bar and do what I do best."

Oh God, John would have had two women in town sleeping around. One for fun. One for profit. No wonder her father abandoned all hope of bringing her to the ranch.

"John knew I'd do it. I would never let you go. The checks kept coming. I guess, yeah, he sent Big Mama to make me the offer to work here and separate you from me." Candy shrugged. "We were both happier."

The sad reality of their relationship.

"He left angry. I figured we'd go back to the way things had always been. I don't know why he stopped coming. I guess he was happy with his family." This time her mother wasn't trying to be callous. She really didn't know what happened to her father.

Roxy shook her head. "That baby he thought would change everything turned out not to be his. Lisa is a royal bitch. John divorced her. I'm not sure what happened with Noah's mother, but I think it wore on him."

"A man can only take so much."

"You and Lisa gave him a run for his money. Literally. That's all you wanted from him when he had so much more to give. He poured everything into trying to keep Lisa happy those first three years of Annabelle's life. Which left little time for him to sneak away and see me. I think he wanted to give Annabelle everything he never had the chance to give me. But it fell apart anyway. Time passed. My resentment built and we grew apart. So he did everything he could to make Noah and Annabelle happy and build his ranch. He needed those things to work in his life. Maybe, like me, he thought there'd come a time when we could lay it all out in the open and forgive our shortcomings. Maybe he thought when Annabelle was grown, he'd tell them about me. As adults, we could find a way to be, if not family, then friends."

"What difference does it make now? Because of me, you're rich. You've got a lucrative horse ranch and own the best brothel in the state." Pride lit Candy's eyes.

"Because of you, I lost touch with my father. If you'd let me go with him, I could have grown up loved like Noah and Annabelle."

"That bitch of a wife of his probably would have sent you back."

Probably. "Or maybe John would have divorced her sooner and still raised his kids on his own."

"He could have come back for you after he divorced Lisa. He didn't. He made his choice and left you here with me."

"You threatened to prostitute yourself out in the community where everyone knew him and would know I was your daughter."

John couldn't live with that. Not that John deserved the benefit of the doubt, but by that time, Roxy was living with her sisters, doing well in school, competing with her horses, and generally happy in her new life. Maybe he didn't want to take her away from the one place she'd finally settled into and found a normal life. Well as normal as possible with a mother like Candy.

"What will you do with the brothel?" Of course her mother cared more about that than what Roxy was going through.

"Burn it to the ground," she suggested.

"With the money it makes, you'll never have to work a day in your life ever again." Her mother's eyes lit up. She was surprised the blue didn't turn to money-green.

Roxy had enough. "Go back to the mansion. We're done."

"You should thank me for what I did for you."

"You used who you are to keep John away and hurt me. So remember you have a roof over your head because he put one there, and I allow you to stay. The money spilling out your bra and thong every night is because of the job I allow you to keep. So behave, because I won't be here to pick your drunk ass up off the floor anymore."

Candy huffed out her anger. "Careful, little girl. What would people think back in Whitefall if they knew you owned this place? This little town knows everyone who works here, or like you and the girls, who's associated with it. The brothel brings money into this dinky town but that doesn't mean people accept us."

"Like you care."

"I don't care what anyone thinks of me."

Too many times people she thought were friends had turned on her. In high school, a couple of boys she liked pretended to like her. When it became clear they only wanted one thing and were willing to pay for it, she stopped giving boys the benefit of the doubt that they actually wanted her. A very hard lesson to learn at such a young age.

"You better make sure Noah never finds out. You'll lose your piece of the ranch. He won't want you raising his kid sister."

"No one but the lawyer knows I own the ranch."

"You better hope it stays that way. All the lawyers I've met . . . not a decent man among them. They're all out for themselves. The only person you can rely on is yourself."

"You've taught me that well," she countered. "I don't need anyone else to show me what I already know. Now get out. I have work to do."

Roxy waited for her mother to leave before she let the tears fall. She didn't know why she cried. For the little girl who could have had a father if only his life hadn't been so heartbreaking and complicated? If only he'd cared more about her than his reputation.

No. For the first time, she really let herself feel the loss of her father.

He loved her.

She held on to that and forgave him for letting time, distance, and pride keep them apart.

Chapter Sixteen

Roxy sucked in a deep breath, stared up at the red lights beside the front door of the Wild Rose Ranch, and wondered what the hell she was doing going in this way, instead of through the back.

Tonight, she wanted to see this place with new eyes.

As a guest would.

As the owner.

Roxy knew the brothel's basic routine and inner workings, but she'd never paid close attention to how the business side ran. Her mind always went right to the scantily clad women, the men who came to fulfill their fantasies, or whatever debauched itch they wanted to scratch, and the exchange of money for something she thought should include more than greed and lust.

She rang the buzzer and waited for Big Mama or security to buzz her in after checking her out on the surveillance cameras. The huge glass-paned wood doors with the carved vine of wild roses opened. Big Mama stood before her, arms outstretched, one hand on each door. Framed in the light, her red hair glowed like fire. The black bustier lifted her ample bosom. With a red rose in her hair, a black velvet choker with a blood-red ruby at her neck, and a full black skirt encasing her wide and round bottom, she looked the picture of an old-time Madam. Seeing Big Mama dressed for the night always made her think of dance hall girls, gunslingers, poker, and some guy at the piano playing a bawdy tune.

"Big Mama."

"Miss Cordero. Welcome."

Leave it to Big Mama to know exactly why she was here and coming through the front door. She'd made it her business to know exactly what everyone coming through her door wanted.

Most repeat clients made appointments. Many even left special instructions. Big Mama kept track of client's preferences and ensured that when they arrived the girls catered to their every need without them having to ask.

"Thank you for understanding."

Big Mama smiled and closed the doors behind her. Roxy stood in the huge white marble foyer and surveyed the lovely red velvet sofas, subdued lighting, and erotic art displayed in ornate gilded frames. These paintings were suggestive, but not lewd. Inside the main house, the art was much more graphic, but exceptionally well-done and expensive.

"It's different to walk in as the boss. Shines a whole new light on things."

"I think I've seen things clear enough for years."

"Now, honey, you know you've only seen this place as your mother's vile playground and the reason she deserted you. For a second there, you looked around and thought of it as a business. You're not a child anymore. John left you this place, knowing how much you hated it, but also knowing you'd do right by these women and me. The way he tried to do right by you."

"It doesn't change the fact I can't keep this place, Big Mama. This isn't the life I wanted, and I worked damn hard to become something different."

"Different, you said—not better. Some of these women are your friends. You'd never turn your back on a friend. Besides, John made it clear you can't sell this place for five years. He may not have raised you, but to his dying day, he provided for you. This place will do that now that he's gone."

Roxy's education about her father just kept coming. "You fed him information about me. That's how he knew when I got my driver's license, that I got accepted to college, so many other things, I can't even think of them right now."

Big Mama held her hands together in front of her. "He loved you, honey. He knew he did you wrong and tried in his own way to make things good for you. Your mother made that difficult at every turn."

"She makes everything difficult," Roxy confirmed.

"Let's take the tour and I'll buy you a drink, honey. Looks like you need one."

"I certainly will after this."

"Put your boss's hat back on. We run a clean, honest, and lucrative business. The men who come here expect a certain standard—privacy, class, and elegance. When they enter the house, it's part of the fantasy. Old and elegant—even the furnishings play a role as the men meet the girls."

Big Mama opened the next set of doors and they entered another large area, the grand staircase leading up to the girls' rooms. The ground floor had a few specially appointed rooms for more diverse tastes. Some men wanted to be dominated. Others wanted to be treated like babies. Literally, in some cases. Whatever the fantasy or need, Wild Rose Ranch accommodated its clients, be they men or women. It wasn't unheard of to have women visit alone, or with their spouse or lover.

Big Mama nodded to one of the many men scattered throughout the house as security for the girls. He pressed a button discreetly hidden behind a drapery. Roxy knew that a bell rang upstairs in all the ladies' rooms and in the main rooms and bar downstairs. If the women weren't already with a client, they were expected to come and line the staircase to be picked over by the next client.

"This is the beginning of the dance," Big Mama began. "The client gets a look at all the girls. He makes his selection, or selections, and the lady will take him into the bar or one of the parlors for a drink and some conversation to break the ice."

"They'll flirt and warm the guy up for the negotiation," Roxy added.

"Exactly. It gives the customer a chance to settle in and relax."

The ladies lined the staircase. All dressed in gorgeous cocktail dresses. Silk and satin, beads and rhinestones. Some, simple and elegant. Women any man would want on his arm at an important event. Everyone's boobs were displayed to draw a man's eyes, whether by the deep dip of silk, or encased in a bustier. Gorgeous legs went up from high heels revealed by high slits or short skirts. Some were skinny with lithe figures, others fulsome and curvy, a couple even plump and round. Everyone posed to show off their best assets. Whatever a man's tastes, here it was lined up and waiting for him to crook his finger to bring it to him.

Roxy sighed out her relief that her mother wasn't among the women called to the stairs. It unsettled her to think her mother was otherwise engaged in one of the rooms upstairs. Although Candy would love to look down at her with a smug smile, knowing Roxy was here to discuss business with Big Mama.

"She's tending bar right now." Big Mama read her mind. "Since you're leaving tomorrow, I figured you'd be in tonight. She's become a little unpredictable and snotty since she learned you own the place."

"Candy?" The note of shock to her voice emphasized her sarcasm. "You have my permission to remind her that her place here is subject to the same rules you issue to all the girls."

"She's just acting out a bit, feeling out this new arrangement, seeing how far she can push."

"Push back. She's not to be treated any different than the other women."

"Is it true, Big Mama? Does Roxy own this place?" A blonde called out the question.

Roxy and Big Mama had kept their voices down, so the others didn't hear them discussing Candy.

"Roxy does own the majority share in the business, but Big Mama runs this joint, just like I've always done." Big Mama gave her a sideways look, letting her know nothing had really changed.

Roxy didn't have any argument. Even if she did, Big Mama looked ready to put her in her place. It eased the tightness in her chest, knowing that if she wanted, she could stand back, collect her money, and never step foot in this place again because Big Mama ran the show.

Roxy backed up Big Mama's statement. "That's right. I came tonight to take a look around, get the feel of the place, but I'm leaving for Montana and Big Mama will remain in charge."

Most of the girls looked relieved, others remained skeptical. It was no secret how much Roxy hated this place. They might think she'd sell it. No telling what another owner might do, or how he'd treat them. The thought left her sick inside.

And that's when it hit her. Roxy had no intention of selling. She couldn't take the chance another owner would treat them like property or worse. Because of the personal nature of their job, they needed to be protected and respected. Big Mama looked after them like her children. She made sure they were happy here and scolded them when they got out of line. When necessary, she reminded them that they were employees in this playhouse and could be fired.

"Okay, ladies, we've got a bachelor party coming in about twenty minutes. Be ready to entertain." Big Mama waved her arm and the women dispersed.

Roxy felt sorry for the bride-to-be whose fiancé wanted one last wild night with another woman. Roxy hoped it was the last. Any guy who'd go to a whorehouse before getting married probably wasn't the staying kind. More the straying kind.

They walked to the next dimly lit room. Her mother stood behind the curved wood bar, a mirror behind her, bottles lined up like soldiers. Candy poured and flirted with the men lining the bar with girls draped over them or sitting in their laps. Six lined up at the bar, several more men sat on the sofas and chairs scattered about the room.

Amy whispered to the impeccably dressed man beside her. He gave her an indulgent smile, cupped her face in his big hands, and kissed her softly on the forehead. She stood and rushed over. Her black silk gown was held together with clasps at her shoulders. The material draped over her breasts and down to her waist in a deep V. A band of material circled her waist; another just below her hips secured the material in front and back, but down the sides, she was left completely bare, giving everyone just a glimpse of her hidden curves. Sexy.

The man who'd sat with her watched with loving eyes as Amy flew into Roxy's arms. Roxy found his expression odd. In fact, it looked like he was quite taken with Amy.

"Roxy, you're here. I'd hoped to see you while I was in, but I haven't been able to catch up with you." Amy spoke softly so as not to disrupt the other couples.

Roxy held her friend at arm's length and scanned the pretty gown up close. "You look wonderful." At seventeen, Amy had been wildly in love with a cowboy for two years. They planned to get married, start a family, and live happily ever after. Amy turned up pregnant and the cowboy got cold feet and disappeared on the rodeo circuit, taking up with a new cowgirl at every new town. Amy, devastated and alone, got kicked out of her religious parents' house for being an unwed mother. She needed a way to keep her head above water and support her child. Desperate, she somehow ended up on the Ranch. Big Mama took her in, gave her a job, and Amy and Will were set for life with the money she made here.

"How's my favorite little boy?"

"Will is wonderful. He's with the sitter." Amy lived four hours away and drove in one week a month to work. "So, you're really going to move to your father's ranch?" she asked.

Word traveled fast. "Annabelle needs me," Roxy said by way of explanation.

"That's your sister?" Amy asked.

"No, not really. She's Noah's sister." At the mention of Noah's name, Amy and Big Mama gave each other a knowing look. Was she that transparent? First her sisters and then her mother detected something about the way she said Noah's name, and now these two.

So she found him intriguing. The man was definitely gorgeous, well built, and his smile could fell even an eighty-year-old woman into his bed. Crap. Even now, she felt the ripple of awareness they shared echo through her system.

"I'm her guardian," she finished lamely.

"I might have to bring Will to see his aunt and meet your Noah." She paused, then added, "And Annabelle. See how you're doing in this new life."

"I'd love it if you came." Roxy meant it, too. She and Amy had been close over the last few years. Amy was only two years younger than her and often hung out with her and her sisters and went riding. They'd ridden together in several rodeos.

Amy was a good mother, and if her profession ensured her son's future, who was Roxy to judge? But judge she had, and it needed to stop. Live and let live. That would be her new motto where the Wild Rose Ranch women were concerned.

That included her mother. It had taken her a long time to get to this place, but she was done banging her head against the wall. Candy was going to do what she was going to do and Roxy was done hoping she'd somehow miraculously turn into a kind and loving mother with a nurturing heart.

"Roxy," Amy snapped.

"What? Sorry. I got lost in thought."

"I'm so glad I got to see you before you left. I've got to get back."

"Give Will a big kiss from his auntie. I'll send him his birthday gift next month."

"I love that boy," Amy gushed, and Roxy could see the love all over her face.

Roxy turned to her mother, who leered at her over the bar. Great. Candy in a snit—never a good thing.

Amy returned to her customer. Roxy and Big Mama took a seat in the corner at a small table with a vase of fresh wild roses and a candle burning in the center. "Who's the man with Amy?" she asked, curious.

"Judge Bettencourt. He's actually an old friend of your father's."

"Really?"

"Judge Bettencourt and your father's lawyer were the only two people in Whitefall who knew about this place. Your father knew how unhappy the judge was in his personal life and suggested he come here. He visits four or five times a year to see Amy."

Roxy's eyebrow shot up. "He's a regular."

"We have many who come and form relationships with the girls. Amy's regulars tend to be men looking for a sweet, loving woman who will pamper and care for them."

"She is that type of person. Even in this."

"Not all men who come to a whorehouse are looking for fun and games. Some come because they need something the women in their lives don't provide. In Judge Bettencourt's case, he's married to a cold woman who denies him what he craves. A lot of men who come here just want to fuck and be done. With Amy, Judge Bettencourt wants to make love, slow and leisurely. He takes his time with her, indulges his need for romance and closeness. When he's done, he stays for hours and holds her in bed, their bodies pressed close. In the morning, he'll kiss her on the forehead and be off to work again, like a husband leaving his wife for the day."

"Too bad he doesn't marry her and have her always."

"That would spoil the fantasy they play out. He doesn't love her any more than she loves him, but here, for a few hours, they can play the part. She's the wife he wishes he had."

Roxy propped her elbow on the table and planted her chin in her hand and stared at the couple talking intimately on the sofa.

"It's kind of sad," Roxy admitted.

"This job is about indulging, but it doesn't have to be all about sex."

Big Mama eyed her. "When are you going to let a man into your life, if for nothing else, to feel close to someone?"

"It's not been easy for me. People find out about my mother and assume . . ."

"You never take the time to change their minds," Big Mama accused, hitting the mark.

"I never found anyone worth changing his mind."

"I hope you find him soon, honey, before you waste your life away and end up alone, lonely, and more bitter than you are right now."

"I'm not bitter," she defended.

"You certainly aren't sweet. All I'm saying is stop worrying so much about the sex and focus on the closeness. Build a relationship with someone."

"Easier said than done when you've got my life."

"Your life is what you make it, honey." Big Mama's warm hand covered hers.

Roxy appreciated the gesture so much, she put her hand over Big Mama's.

"How about that drink?" she boomed.

Roxy glanced at Candy leaning over the bar, showing off her ample cleavage to a very interested twenty-something guy in jeans, a T-shirt, and work boots. Candy's gaze collided with hers and her smile notched up seeing Roxy uncomfortable with watching her mother work. "Let's finish this in your office."

"Don't let her poke at your open wounds," Big Mama advised.

"They're only open because she refuses to let them heal."

"You allow her to hurt you."

Roxy hated to admit she did let Candy get to her.

Big Mama wrapped her arm around Roxy's shoulders and herded her out of the bar and down a long hallway. They passed through one room with more than a dozen TV monitors stacked on a wall. A man watched the screens that showed every room in the house. If she didn't know where she was, she'd think he was watching every porn channel on the satellite service. Instead, the displays showed the girls in the bar, parlors, and having sex in the rooms. If anything got out of hand, the security guard would notify one of the men posted upstairs in the hall outside the girls' rooms.

"Just a precaution to make sure the ladies are protected," Big Mama reminded her.

"They don't mind the cameras?"

"After all this time, they probably don't even think about them anymore. As for the customers, they're informed up front that they are under surveillance."

"The women make them forget all about it," Roxy guessed.

"That they do," Big Mama answered with a smile and pointed to one of the monitors where a blonde bobbed her head up and down over a man's lap. His head thrown back, eyes closed, his hand buried in her hair, he guided her to move faster over his swollen flesh.

Big Mama cleared her throat and Roxy jumped, startled out of her transfixed state. "Sorry."

Big Mama only smiled. "Remember when you were fourteen and we had the talk?" She led Roxy through another door into her office.

Roxy couldn't forget and rolled her eyes. "You should teach sex-ed classes. We didn't so much talk as watch the monitors and you explained what was going on."

"Best way to learn something is to do it. Seeing it is the next best thing. I made sure you knew exactly what you were in for when you chose to take that step. It's more than my mother did for me. The only thing she told me was to lie there and shut up until he was done, that it was a duty to be performed, but not enjoyed. Let's just say, I learned different from doing."

Big Mama laughed out loud, and Roxy couldn't help but join in.

"God, my life is weird." Roxy shook her head, trying to wrap her head around how different her life was from most everyone else's.

The room looked like any other office. Thick beige carpet covered the floor. A desk with a leather chair behind and two comfortable club chairs in front. The pictures on the wall were of the desert sunset and various rock formations. *Just an office*, she thought, *but not for just any kind of business.*

Roxy fell onto the sofa in the small seating area off to the left and let her head fall on the back. She closed her eyes and sighed heavily.

"Feeling a little at sea." Big Mama guessed her mood.

Roxy opened her eyes and stared into Big Mama's emerald-green ones. Surprisingly, they were soft and full of compassion. Roxy did something she didn't often do and opened up. "This is my mother's life. I feel like I've been stuck in it so long, it's like a swamp, pulling at me and dragging me down no matter how hard I try to trudge my way out of it. Now my father wants me to live on his ranch and take over his life with the horses and his kids. He wants me to finish raising his daughter."

"You didn't turn out so bad. You raised yourself and your sisters. Despite the fact Sonya is older, she took her cues from you. You're the strong one. He knows you'll do everything you can to teach Annabelle about life and raise her up to be a good woman. You're a good woman," Big Mama said and patted her knee.

"I feel like I'm just playing a part in everyone else's life. When I graduated college and got my job, I thought I'd finally found my way. Things were just starting to come together for me."

"Have you ever really thought about what you want, honey? You've spent the better part of your life taking care of your mother and sisters. Oh, Joe and I checked up on you guys every day, took you where you needed to go, made sure you had what you needed to get by. The other girls' moms stopped by regularly. But you didn't really need us. You've been independent and strong and smart your whole life. You use your head in everything you do, except when it comes to your horses. There, the love comes out. Stop thinking about what your life is or isn't and start thinking of your future with your heart."

Big Mama glanced away, then back at her. "Your father told me when you were ready I should tell you why he left you this place."

"He knew I'd never leave Candy alone to destroy her life. I'm the one who's been standing between her and a grave for years."

"That's very nearly exactly his words."

Roxy tapped her temple with her index finger. "I'm always thinking."

"It's more than that. You may not believe this, but I think Candy held on so tight to you, because you're the only thing that truly belongs to her. Through everything, you've stuck by her side, pulled her out of many tough spots, despite her behavior and lifestyle. In some strange way, I think she knows that without you, she'll die."

"She almost did a few times." An ominous shiver ripped through her as the memories from the past rose up to haunt her.

"John gave you the Speckled Horse Ranch because it's where he was the happiest. He wanted you to know him through the place he built and worked his whole life. He's forcing you to leave here because he knew you'd never leave Candy otherwise. He hoped that time away, time in a place he hoped you'd fall in love with as much as he did, would help you put some distance between you and Candy. You can't spend your life as her safety net. He didn't want that for you and tried many times to get you away from her, though you may not realize that.

"He was so proud of you and everything you've accomplished. Don't think he didn't know how hard it was for you. How everything you did, right or wrong, you did on your own without him. It killed him to stay away."

Roxy cocked her head and really took in Big Mama's words and the soft expression in her eyes and on her face. "You really liked him."

"I respected him," she admitted. "He was in a very bad situation. Annabelle needed him. Through experience, you'd learned to take care of yourself. He couldn't let what happened with you and Candy repeat itself with Annabelle and Lisa. He saw how it affected you. So he made sure you were safe and kept Annabelle away from her mother."

"I guess, where Candy is concerned, that's the best he could have hoped for me. To be safe," she clarified.

"He hoped for so much more for you. I wish you could have seen the look on his face when he watched you accept your diploma from high school and college."

"You were both there?" Tears stung her eyes and fell down her cheeks. She'd wanted him to see her, to know she'd done it—grew up to be something different than her mother.

"I always thought of you as my girl," Big Mama admitted. "I never had a child, but you've brought me so much joy. I loved our shopping trips and movie nights."

"You were more like a mother to me than Candy ever was."

Big Mama rose and went to the small bar in the corner and poured two shots of whiskey. She handed Roxy one and sat beside her again. "Take some motherly advice. Leave this place behind when you go to your father's ranch. Put it out of your mind and don't think about Candy and what she's doing, or not doing that she should. Settle into your father's life. Let yourself be there and away from here. Stop thinking with your head and open your heart."

"Right now, I'm feeling numb." At Big Mama's cocked eyebrow, she added, "I'll try."

"That's my girl."

They clinked glasses and downed their shots. Roxy left an hour later not knowing how she should feel. Big Mama went over the books with her. Roxy was astounded at how much the women and the brothel made. She'd seen the balances in the accounts her father left her, but she'd never put it together with the Ranch in that way. In between talking about the business, Big Mama peppered in stories about John and the times he'd come to visit and the many calls he shared with Big Mama.

Roxy knew a few new things. Big Mama shared a very close friendship with her father, and despite his absence in Roxy's life, he always checked up on her in one way or another. It was comforting to know he'd never truly been out of her life, only standing on the sidelines keeping watch. If she'd ever truly needed him, he'd have been there. Knowing that eased some of her anger.

He knew she had enough of him inside her to stand on her own.

For the first time since finding out she had to move to the ranch, she felt hopeful about starting her new life. She still worried about her mother, but knew her father had been right. She had to leave this place and not live her life as Candy's daughter.

She'd done that for far too long.

She walked the path back to her cottage, the moon big and round in the star-studded sky. She thought of her father's ranch, the gardens surrounding the house and the green pastures. She thought of Noah.

He intruded on her thoughts far too often.

Would he be happy to see her?

Or hate her for coming to live on his ranch?

Could they find a way to work together?

She'd find out when she arrived tomorrow.

Chapter Seventeen

N oah raced across the pasture, his horse galloping at top speed, and still the damn ornery gelding that escaped his stall and jumped three fences and made a run for it outpaced him. The gelding jumped a fallen tree and ran into a narrower pasture, slowing as he approached yet another fence line. Noah breathed a sigh of relief that the gelding had finally spent his burst of energy before Noah's poor horse gave up the chase and Noah lost the gelding, or it got hurt taking one jump too many and tragedy struck.

Rope in hand, Noah dismounted and approached the skittish horse, slow and easy. He swung the rope left, but Houdini danced right. The rope caught on the fence. Houdini backed off, raking his hoof in the dirt and snorting out his disgust at Noah's failed attempt to catch him.

The damn horse mocked him.

Lasso unhooked from the fence, Noah threw again, hooking the horse around the neck. Houdini reared up, hooves punching the air before he landed on all fours again, backed up, and pulled Noah along until he muscled the horse into submission.

Tired, dirty, sweaty, hungry, he still had several hours of work ahead of him. Since John's death and the reading of the will, worries and frustrations had piled up and weighed him down.

Roxy drove off leaving Noah with no way to contact her, no idea where she lived, and completely in the dark about when she'd return. If ever.

Tom ignored his requests for Roxy's phone number and information about his elusive partner. Vindictive ass held a grudge after Roxy kneed him in the nuts.

Noah didn't have time for that kind of bullshit.

Not when he had a grieving teenager to deal with.

Annabelle stayed in her room for days, barely eating, refusing to talk to anyone. Yesterday, she refused to get up on time to go to school. He'd practically had to drag her out of bed and make her. He hated to yell at her, but she refused to see reason. If he backed down now, she'd walk all over him.

This morning had been marginally better, but it still took a concerted effort to get her out the door.

One hell of a day, and there he stood in the pasture, breathing hard and out of patience.

Who the hell was Roxy anyway?

John didn't want her in his life, so why the hell did he leave practically everything to her?

And what was in that envelope that pissed her off so bad?

It wasn't the angry look in her eyes that made him think about her so often. It was the intense hurt beneath it.

Why would John insist she come live here and do something to hurt her so deeply that she might not agree?

He couldn't believe John could be so cruel. Especially to his own daughter.

So what the hell was really going on?

He couldn't figure it out.

Decisions had to be made. He couldn't sign a damn check without her.

Noah set all that aside and got back to work. He soothed and calmed Houdini, then led him over to Noah's patient and obedient horse. Noah rode back to the stables leading Houdini at a much slower pace than he'd gone after him. Both horses were tired by the time he reached the ranch.

He rode into the yard just as Harry walked out of the stables.

"I fixed the stall gate. Want me to take the pest?"

Noah handed off the rope. "Cool him down and get him some water before you brush and feed him. Make sure he's locked up tight before you leave for the night."

"You got it, boss." Harry patted Houdini's nose. "Any word on when your new sister arrives?"

"She's not my sister." He didn't think of her that way. They didn't share blood or even a roof over their heads growing up. They were strangers.

Still, something nagged at him. Like he'd seen her somewhere.

He'd searched for her on Facebook and Twitter. Not that he used either of those. He didn't find her. He Googled her and got a jumble of other Roxys, mostly porn stars, none of them as sexy as his Roxy. Which only invoked more fantasies about her because, damn, that body of hers was made for dreaming about.

But that's not all that drew him to her. The compassion she showed Annabelle stuck with him.

"Robby said she's a dead ringer for John all wrapped up in a gorgeous package."

Noah raised a brow, not believing that's how Robby put it. "Is that what he said?"

"He said she could be a model."

"What she is, is your boss."

"Let's hope she doesn't go changing things."

Everyone who worked on the ranch worried about her coming in and throwing a wrench in the operation.

Noah had the same concerns. She might own the lion's share, but he and Annabelle still had a say. Noah wasn't about to roll over and let her muck up what he'd worked damn hard to put in place here. The business ran on budget and made a more than decent profit.

What the hell did she know about ranching anyway?

He had no idea, which was why he'd give her the paperwork and keep her away from the horses.

And he'd watch every move she made.

Everything, including Noah's life, felt like it was on hold, waiting for her return.

Noah scanned the ranch and surrounding land. The sun dipped lower, about to reach the crest of the hills. Once it fell behind them, it would be dark in no time. He turned his attention back to the main house and driveway. No car. No Roxy.

Noah dismounted and walked his horse into the barn behind Harry and Houdini. An hour spent unsaddling his horse, brushing him down, feeding and checking all the horses in the stables helped work out his tight muscles.

He could think of another way to work off some stress, but the only woman on his mind and invading his dreams he barely knew and needed to stay in the strictly hands-off column if they were going to find a way to live and work together.

If she showed up.

He headed up to the house for dinner and to do what he'd been doing every day since Roxy left—waiting for her to come back.

Noah went in through the side door to check the messages on the office phone. He settled into John's chair behind the desk. A wave of grief hit him. He tried to keep busy these last few days, but at moments like this, when things were quiet, he missed John. He missed going over the accounts, talking about how training the horses went, discussing decisions that needed to be made. When Noah allowed himself to think about the last few months, he realized John had slowly been giving up control and letting Noah handle things. It had been subtle. John didn't want Noah to know the end was near, but John knew what was coming and slowly stepped back and let Noah take the lead.

The phone rang, bringing him out of his thoughts.

"Speckled Horse Ranch. Noah."

"Hey, it's Tom. Is Roxy there?"

Noah glanced out the window at the darkening sky. "Not yet. Have you heard from her?"

"Not a word. I tried to call her before I called you, but got her voice mail. Maybe she's on the way."

"I hope so. Give me her number. I'll call her."

"I'll keep trying. If she's not back by midnight, she forfeits everything."

Code for Tom refused to be lenient after the way she'd introduced her knee to his balls.

"With what she got, she doesn't need the horse ranch."

That got Noah's attention. "What do you mean by that?" No money had been taken out of the ranch or house accounts. So what had John owned and given to her that Noah didn't know about? Some secret account? He didn't see how when he saw all the balance sheets for the ranch.

"Nothing. I'm not supposed to talk about it. Listen, let me know when she arrives. You never know, maybe she won't show. A woman like her, she can't be trusted to do the right thing."

"What the hell does that mean?"

"Nothing. Forget I said it."

As if he could.

Noah liked Tom's father, who had a long history with John and the ranch. He'd been skeptical when Tom took over this past year, and Noah's trust in the attorney eroded with every slip of Tom's loose tongue about Roxy's secret leaking out. As much as Noah wanted to know what John left Roxy, if this kept up, Noah would have no choice but to fire Tom.

"Call me when she gets there so I know she fulfilled the terms." Tom nearly tripped over all those words and hung up, leaving Noah more confused and without Roxy's number yet again.

Based on the conversation Annabelle told him about, Roxy agreed to move for her sake. The inheritance was a nice bonus, but Annabelle and Lisa's relationship sparked some kind of protective instinct in Roxy. The comments she made about her own mother, the way she'd stood up to Lisa and called her on her shit straight-out spoke of a woman who'd had to deal with something very similar. Roxy wanted something better for Annabelle. If that meant uprooting her entire life and moving to the ranch to make it happen, she had the guts to do it.

Roxy knew he and Annabelle were raised as brother and sister, they'd stand together.

She was the outsider.

Still, she agreed to come.

So why the hell wasn't she here yet?

Unable to solve the Roxy puzzle, he rose and followed his nose to the kitchen and the smell of melted cheese, peppers, and spices that made his stomach grumble. Noah walked into the kitchen just as Mary pulled a casserole out of the oven. His empty stomach rumbled again. Mary laughed and set the hot dish on the stove to cool before she put it on the table.

Mary glanced at his face, reading him like a book. "Don't worry, she'll be here."

He intentionally misunderstood her. "I thought Annabelle was upstairs in her room."

Mary frowned and shook her head, not believing him for a second. "You know who I'm talking about."

"Is the room ready?"

"I cleaned and moved all your father's clothes to a guest room. I thought she might like to go through them."

"Why?" Noah asked, wondering what a woman would want with men's clothes.

"Well, she wanted his hat. Who's to say she doesn't want something else?"

"I still don't get the hat thing." Noah washed his hands and arms at the sink for dinner. He should probably go upstairs, shower, and change out of his dusty clothes, but he was too hungry to take the time.

"It means something to her. Why wouldn't you want her to have it?"

"It's not that. I just don't understand why she wants it."

"Ask her."

He shrugged and wiped his hands on a towel, stole a tomato from the salad Mary took out of the fridge, and popped it into his mouth. "I would if she were here, but she's not," he grumbled.

"I left the hat on the dresser for her. The new mattresses arrived yesterday. They're on the bed, but I'll have to get her some new sheets and a spread more suited for her. I hoped to do so today, but I never got a chance to head into town. Truthfully, I'm not sure what she'd like."

"Let her get whatever she wants." Just thinking about her laid out on a bed, naked, set his system on fire. All that golden skin, those curves, against crisp white sheets.

Stop thinking about her like that. She's your partner.

He needed to keep reminding himself.

"Don't we have anything to put on the bed tonight?" he asked.

"We do, but it's all pretty ugly. The last person to buy bedding for the rooms was Lisa."

"No wonder none of us likes our rooms."

"Why didn't you say anything?" Mary gave him a nudge in the belly with her elbow.

"It's not high on my priority list. Annabelle's is the worst." Noah gave a shiver at the thought of sleeping in all the pink ruffles.

Mary laughed. "It is pretty bad. She's not a pink and frilly kind of girl. I guess I should have done something about it before now."

"Not your job. You're busy enough keeping us fed and the house clean. Maybe next weekend I'll take Annabelle shopping and we'll both fix up our rooms. Something new to start this next part of our lives."

"She'd like that." Mary handed him the oven mitts and picked up the salad and basket of fragrant garlic bread. "Grab the casserole and bring it in. Call your sister to the table. Robby will be here any minute and we'll eat." She pushed the kitchen door open with her plump rump, went through the door, and looked back at him over her shoulder. "She'll be here," she said again.

Noah laughed. Not much got past Mary. Either that, or he was that transparent. He hoped she only guessed he was worried for Annabelle's sake. If she had any idea about the dreams that kept him up at night, he'd never be able to eat dinner across from her again.

As worried as he was about Roxy, Annabelle's silence worried him more.

She and Robby joined them at the table moments after Mary finished setting out the food. No one spoke as they passed the dishes.

Annabelle moved her food around her plate, but didn't really eat. Her pale skin and the dark circles under her eyes told him he wasn't the only one not sleeping.

"What did you do today, Sprite?"

"Nothing."

"I thought you'd have some friends over, maybe go riding for a while."

She shrugged, speared a cucumber, and dragged it though the creamy dressing, but never ate it.

"I know you miss John, but you can't close yourself up in this house. You need to get out, do the things you like, live your life. It's what John would want."

Her gaze shot up to his. "Why isn't she here?" Annabelle slammed her hands on the table and made her plate jump. "She said she'd be here."

"And she will," he assured her.

If Roxy made a liar out of him, he'd kill her. Annabelle needed reassurance. He never realized how much.

Annabelle's eyes glassed over. "If she doesn't show up, will my mother take me from you?"

Noah leaned forward and put his hand over hers on the table. "She can try, but I'll never let that happen."

Annabelle rose from her seat and turned to go back to her room, but not before he saw the tears slipping down her cheeks.

"All you can do is reassure her," Mary said.

"It doesn't do me any good. Roxy made it clear that she'd stand with me between Annabelle and her mother. Where the hell is she?" He slammed his hand down on the table and the dishes rattled again. He never realized how much alike he and Annabelle were when they were mad. It made him smile.

Robby pointed his fork at Noah. "The girl had to pick up and move her entire life in a week. Think about what it would take if you had to do the same."

Those words echoed his own thoughts. "Yeah, well, she can only leave the ranch for five days a month."

"John put a short leash on her. Makes you wonder what he was thinking." Robby looked to Noah for answers only John knew.

Noah glanced at his watch, John's watch, and noted the time. "She's got less than five hours to get her ass through the door."

"It's a real fine ass," Robby acknowledged and saluted him with his glass of milk.

Unable to help himself, Noah laughed, picked up his iced tea, and clinked it with Robby's glass. "I'll second that."

"Men." Mary rolled her eyes and stacked plates. "The girl's got a pretty face, but . . ."

"She's got one hell of a body to go with that face," Robby added.

Just to rile Mary, they clinked glasses again. Noah tried to hide the smile, but failed miserably.

"But, I'd think two good and decent men—notwithstanding your antics tonight—would remember that girl stood up for Annabelle to Lisa, laid Tom out for being rude to her, and is changing her whole life to take care of a child that isn't hers and she's never met until a week ago. Beneath that pretty package is a good heart and a hell of a lot of pain and hurt. John left her. He never went to see her for years. Why?"

"I don't know, Mary." Ashamed for being distracted by her looks and forgetting, even for a moment, that he didn't really know her, or what she'd been through, he sobered. He knew the kind of hurt she must feel being left by a parent. He could only imagine what kind of life she had when she said her mother was worse than Lisa. He shivered at the thought.

"I think I'll go watch the ball game I recorded on the DVR. Want to join me, Robby?"

"He's going to help me with the dishes," Mary interjected before Robby could say a word.

"You had to know you were going to pay for the comment about Roxy's ass," Noah joked.

Robby shrugged and gave Mary a wicked grin, smacking her on the bottom. "I'll be making up for it real soon," he teased his wife of more than twenty-five years.

Noah rolled his eyes and cringed. Mary and Robby were dear friends, more like family than anyone else in his life. Thinking of them together in bed gave him the willies.

"I'll leave you to it." Noah walked out of the room, Mary giggling like a schoolgirl at something Robby said in his deep voice.

Noah settled on the couch in front of the big screen TV and lost himself in the game. With the score tied, he thought about Mary and Robby and their long and happy marriage. He envied them. They shared a deep love and a friendship that kept them laughing, talking, and sharing their time together with a kind of joy Noah could only hope to have with a woman. John had often nudged him in the ribs and pointed to Mary and Robby and said, "Now there's a marriage."

Noah shook off his thoughts of couples and relationships and tried to focus on the ball game, but all he listened for was the sound of a car coming down the drive.

Annabelle slid onto the couch beside him around ten. She stuffed a pillow at his side and lay down. He brushed his hand over her head and rested it on her arm.

"How you doing, Sprite?"

"I miss Dad."

He squeezed her arm and tamped down the sadness that hit him at odd times. "I miss him, too. Especially when I'm out riding. One of the mares gave birth and I turned to tell John the new foal was a beauty and realized he wasn't there."

"He used to stop by my room every morning before school, poke his head in, and say, 'Get a move on, girl. Time to learn something.'"

They fell silent, lost in their memories. Annabelle broke into his thoughts of John always pushing him to be the best. "It's late."

"She'll be here," he assured her, knowing very well how she felt. Their lives had already changed so much with the loss of John. Annabelle was counting on Roxy to be an added barrier between her and her mother. Noah hated to admit he stood a better chance of keeping Annabelle with Roxy beside him. They could provide a stable home as two parental figures. At least, he hoped the courts would see it that way if Lisa challenged them. If Roxy didn't show, Annabelle would take it as a personal hit. She'd worry about when her mother was going to strike.

The game ended with his team losing in the last inning. He watched the news, surprised by his relief at not seeing Roxy's picture after some accident or other tragedy. Stupid to worry about her like this, but he couldn't seem to help himself. He had a lot of questions about her, her life, and the mysterious way John had treated her. Like a complex puzzle, he knew he'd spend far too much time trying to figure her out when he should be seeing to the ranch and Annabelle.

Seven minutes into a late-night show, the comedian's monologue unable to make him laugh, despite the clever jokes, he heard it. A car rumbled down the driveway, stopped, and the engine shut down. A wave of relief hit him like a sledgehammer.

Chapter Eighteen

Noah waited for the sound of the front door, but it never came. Annabelle stirred beside him. She'd fallen asleep shortly after their talk. He didn't want to wake her if the visitor wasn't Roxy, so he turned the volume down on the TV and got up, careful not to jar her.

At the front of the house, he looked out the living room window and spotted the brand-new black Camaro parked in the driveway.

Eleven forty-two. She'd cut it close. Too close for his comfort.

She didn't get out of the car, so he went out to get her. When he came around to the driver's side door, he saw her, head back against the seat, eyes closed.

Noah opened the door, expecting her to greet him in some way and surprised to see that only after a few minutes home, she'd fallen asleep. With her head tilted toward the center of the car, the dome light spilled over her face and highlighted the dark circles under her eyes. Drawn to her, so peaceful and sweet, he reached out and traced his fingertips over her soft cheek. He might have kept touching her soft, warm skin, but she came awake with a start, her eyes wide on him.

"Hey. You planning on sleeping in your car all night?"

"I don't have a key to the house." She yawned, but never took her eyes off him.

Noah hadn't thought of that. Come to think of it, he hadn't put a lot of thought into the details of her living here.

"We'll take care of that in the morning. I guess we've got a lot of things to work out. First things first." He took out his cell phone and dialed Tom. "She's here," he said when the attorney answered with a gruff hello.

"She cut it close," he responded.

"Doesn't matter. She made it."

"Let me talk to her."

Noah took exception to the hostile order. "You don't trust me?"

"A woman like her could get a man to lie for her."

Pissed off by Tom's unspoken accusation, he spit out, "Not me." He handed Roxy the phone, noticing she could barely keep her eyes open.

"I'm here," she stated. No hello or pleasantries included.

Noah couldn't hear Tom's side of the conversation. He only had to guess when Roxy responded, "I'd watch my mouth if I were you. Threats like that can get you into trouble. I've read the terms of the will. I know them to the letter. You might remember you work for me. For now." She hung up. "Asshole. God, I am so tired."

"You look it, but you're still gorgeous." At her cocked-up eyebrow and the tilt of her lips from the smile she tried and failed to hide, he held his hands out. "What? I can be a nice guy. Sometimes."

"I think that 'sometimes' is really an almost always."

He smiled. "Are you flirting with me?" he asked, only half teasing.

She laughed at his audaciousness. "Let's just say I read people well."

"The way you read Tom."

"Men like him can't hide who they are. They let their impulses guide them. Will you be mad if I fire him?"

"Not if he deserves it."

Tom seemed to be working on pissing both of them off, which seemed like a bad idea to do with a good client.

She yawned and closed her eyes again, resting her head back against the seat, looking like she was content to sleep in her car for the night.

"Did I pay for this car?" He wondered, not for the first time, if they were going to go at it every time she wanted to spend money on unnecessary things, like new cars.

Maybe he was just being a jerk and spoiling for a fight because of the resentments John created when he kept Roxy a secret.

"Nope," she answered without looking at him. "I have my own money. Want to see the receipt?" Not a single trace of anger resonated in her husky voice.

He dropped the subject. She needed a car living this far out of town. If she paid for it herself, it was none of his business.

"Come inside. There's a bed with your name on it."

She didn't open her eyes, but one dark eyebrow shot up. "Let me guess, yours?"

"When I invite you into my bed, you'll know it."

Her eyes opened and her mouth dipped into a frown. "You said when."

He shrugged, not in the mood to play games, so he went with the truth. "The moment we met, something sparked."

He waited for her to deny it, but she didn't and swung a leg out of the car. "Back up, big guy. I'm too tired to dance around this thing with you right now."

He held out his hand. She eyed it and him warily, but in the end, took it. Her warm fingers glided over his skin and he took hold and pulled her out of the packed car. "Did you drive the whole way?"

"No. I paid the airlines a fortune for the extra bags. The truck with some of my stuff will arrive tomorrow. My flight landed late. I took a taxi van to pick up the car and had to transfer all this stuff, so it took longer than I anticipated."

"Want me to bring it in?"

"Leave it. I'm too tired to do anything but crawl into bed."

His grip tightened on her hand. He had a witty innuendo to go with her statement, but held it back. Her sluggish walk and multiple yawns spoke the truth. The woman was exhausted.

"How did things go back home?"

"As expected," she answered without answering.

He planned to find out what things were really like for her wherever she came from. He had a sinking feeling his perception of John would deteriorate the more he got to know Roxy.

They entered the house. She tried to pull free of his hand, but he held tight, pulling her toward the family room. "Annabelle tried to wait up for you, but fell asleep on the couch."

"She thought I bailed on her," Roxy guessed.

"She hasn't been herself the last week."

"She misses her father, her mother is plotting to make her miserable, and I'm late getting back."

"She takes things to heart."

"I should have called her. No one ever cared about my coming or going."

"I think she's hoping you're going to kick her mother's ass."

"I will if that woman even thinks about taking her from the only home she's ever known."

Noah felt something ease inside him. Sharing the worry, knowing Roxy would stand with him against Lisa to protect Annabelle made it that much easier to carry the burden.

Reluctantly, he let go of Roxy to lean over the couch and nudge Annabelle awake. "Sprite, wake up. She's here."

Annabelle rubbed her eyes, turned, and stared up at them. "Hey," she mumbled still half-asleep.

"It's late. Shouldn't you be in bed?" Roxy sounded concerned.

Annabelle bolted upright and grabbed his hand, turning it so she could read his watch. The sigh of relief whooshed out of her. "You made it."

Roxy leaned against the top of the couch on her forearms close to Annabelle. "I'm sorry you worried. I had a lot to do and not a lot of time to do it. Next time, I'll call. Now, as your guardian, I'm telling you to go to bed and get some sleep."

"Bossy."

To Noah's amazement, Roxy laughed. "I've been called a lot worse. You'll get used to me. After all, I'm going to be here for a while."

"Planning your escape already?" A line formed between Annabelle's eyes as she glared.

"Just stating the facts. I wasn't asked to come, but now that I'm here, I'm committed to seeing you graduate and go off to college."

"All righty then. That's my cue to go to bed."

Noah laughed and explained Annabelle's eye roll and hasty departure. "John and I have been riding her for the last year to really think about what she wants to do with her life, so we can pick the right college."

Roxy cocked up one side of her full lips. "I'll join forces with you. She might change her mind later, but she needs a direction."

"Agreed. And you're going to bed before you fall asleep on your feet."

"You mentioned there is a bed for me."

"A whole room," he teased. "You'll take John's room. The guest rooms are nice, but they share a bathroom between. John's room has a connected bath and a walk-in closet. Mary cleaned out John's clothes and we ordered new mattresses for the antique bed. As much as it pains me that John is gone, this is your house now, too."

"Thank you, Noah. I'm sure it's been a hell of a week, getting used to this place without him."

"Yeah, and you pissed me off, leaving without giving me your number or answers to the questions I have about you and John."

"With John gone, I don't think we'll get the answers we want." She yawned again. "I'm too tired for twenty questions tonight."

"You'll learn I don't give up easily."

"Neither do I," she countered.

"Come on, let's get you into bed."

That eyebrow shot up again, and he gave her a cocky smile. "After you." He gestured with his hand toward the hallway and stairs. They reached the top and stopped on the landing. "Your room is to the left. Mine, in case you're wondering, is two doors down to the right."

"Annabelle's?"

"First door on the right. Two guest rooms across the hall from our rooms."

"This is a huge place."

"Over six thousand square feet. Half of which are yours."

She gave him a side-eyed glance. "Which also pisses you off."

"Absolutely."

She folded her arms under her breasts. "Is that why you left that stack of bills, mail, and other papers on John's desk for me to handle?"

"I work my ass off on this ranch. You should do your share."

"A little passive-aggressive, wouldn't you say?"

"I don't hit girls." Unfazed, Noah let her know he was still working through his anger.

She unfolded her arms and set her shoulders. "I hit back."

"I know. Tom knows."

She headed down the hall away from him, soft light from the windows silhouetting her hourglass shape against the pale walls.

They reached her room and he flipped on the lights. The chandelier in the middle of the room went on, revealing the naked bed. "Oops. I guess Mary forgot about the bed after dinner."

He knew exactly why she'd forgotten, since Robby probably took her back to their place to make up for his comments at dinner about Roxy.

She shrugged, trudged to the bed, and flopped down on top of it on her stomach. She barely scooted herself up onto the bare mattress before closing her eyes. "Good night, Noah. I'm sure you know your way out."

He chuckled, walked to her side, and grabbed her ankle. He worked off her sneaker and did the same with her other foot.

"Thanks," she mumbled. "I'll do the paperwork tomorrow."

"Bet your ass, you will." To prove his point and just to be ornery, he smacked her bottom.

He walked to the doorway and turned off the lights. He stopped short at her words.

"Noah, things are complicated right now. They're only going to get worse over the next few weeks while we try to find a way to work together. It's daunting to deal with your anger and lust. Dial it down. I don't sleep around for sport."

"Neither do I."

Yes, she was a damn sexy woman and he wanted her badly. After seeing her in tight jeans and the curve-hugging purple top, his dreams would be hotter than ever.

But he got what she meant. They had a lot of unsettled business between them. They needed to work and live together under the same roof.

If he wasn't careful, she could use his attraction to her to manipulate him and possibly get what she wanted. He didn't want that kind of relationship with her, or anyone.

He hoped John knew what he was doing bringing her here.

Right now, Noah didn't know her well enough to trust her.

After how he acted tonight, he didn't know if he could trust himself around her.

Chapter Nineteen

Roxy opened one eye and took in her surroundings. The unfamiliar furnishings and room took a minute for her to place. Her father's home. His room. A new life.

The thought made the butterflies in her belly flutter with nervous anticipation. She didn't know what to expect from this new life. She'd barely had time to pack and move, let alone think about what would happen once she got here.

She rolled onto her back and stared up at the black wrought-iron chandelier with candle flame lightbulbs. The new mattress beneath her was soft, firm, and comfortable. She liked a good bed. It would come in handy now that she had three jobs to oversee and knew she'd be spending a lot of long hours trying to keep up with the demands of all of them.

She gathered the soft blanket Noah must have draped over her last night and clutched it to her chest. A familiar smell drifted over her. Noah. Not a good sign that she already recognized his scent. She needed to stick to business.

Annabelle needed them to be responsible adults, not horny teenagers looking for a hookup.

But her heart melted thinking of him coming back last night and covering her with a blanket from his bed after she fell asleep.

Sweet.

She could handle a man in a temper, filled with lust, mean, and even distant. But sweet. She didn't know what to do with that.

In her world, a man who knew how to be kind seemed like a four-leaf clover. You knew they existed, but you had to go looking for them.

"Time to start my new life." She rolled up and bounced off the bed fully intending to go out and unload her car. To her surprise, all her bags were lined up next to what she assumed were the closet doors.

"Well damn, the blanket wasn't enough, you dragged all my gear in the house and up the stairs, too." That warm feeling in her heart spread.

Roxy walked into the bathroom expecting it to be as barren as the bedroom, only to be pleasantly surprised. A vase filled with fresh pink roses sat between the double sinks on the white marble countertop. Dark wood cabinets contrasted with the white marble floor. Deep blue towels were folded neatly by the sink and hanging on the bars. A glass-enclosed shower stood in the corner, sparkling clean. A huge Jacuzzi tub sat beneath a glass block window. She liked the simplicity.

Curious, she pulled open a few drawers and cupboards and found most empty, except for cleaning supplies, first aid necessities, wrapped bars of soap, and spare towels.

She returned to the bedroom, found her bathroom supplies, and brought them back with her. She turned on the shower spray, peeled off her clothes, grabbed her soap, shampoo, and conditioner, stepped into the big stall, and set them down. The hot water sluiced over her hair and face and down her body. Nice and hard. She leaned forward and let the water work on her tired back muscles.

It took nearly every hour of the last seven days to put her life in order back at the Ranch and move herself here. She still had some loose ends to tie up, but for the most part, this was day one of her new life.

Soaped, shampooed, and rinsed clean, she stepped from the shower and wrapped herself in one of the thick towels. Steam fogged the mirrors above the sinks. She found the switch for the overhead fan and flicked it on. Should have done that first, she thought, trying to get used to her new surroundings.

While she waited for the mirror to clear, she emptied the duffel bag with her hair dryer, curling irons, hair spray, perfumes, makeup, and other miscellaneous stuff. She put everything away where she wanted it and left her brush and perfume bottles on the counter. She plugged in the dryer and flipped her hair over her head. Bending at the waist, her hair hanging almost to the floor, she dried the long strands and used her brush to help speed it along. Once nearly dry, she stood and flipped her hair back over her head and finished drying it. Done, she used a little spray to hold the waving curls in place.

She stood in the bathroom doorway surveying the bedroom. Some-one, probably Mary, had polished all the antique wood furniture. The crystal lamps next to the bed sparkled. She walked to the stone fireplace and picked up the single framed photo on the mantel. Her father stood beside one of the fences, a huge white-and-black-spotted horse beside him with his head over John's shoulder. John had his arm hooked under the horse's head, and he smiled at the camera, his golden eyes bright and happy.

It made her sad she didn't know the side of her father who loved this place and his horses. She never got to see him at home, where he was happiest.

She didn't have a single photo of them together.

"I'm here, Dad. Now what?"

She turned to her bags. "Might as well unpack and make myself at home, right?"

Before she put her clothes away, she walked to the dresser and picked up her father's hat. She caught her reflection in the mirror and slipped the hat on her head. Not such a bad fit. She smelled him. A mix of the outdoors, aftershave, hay, and horses. Her eyes shone bright with unshed tears and she held them back as she thought about Big Mama's words.

John may not have been brave enough in life to bring her here, but in death he'd found a way to take her from Candy and not suffer the consequences.

She set the hat back on the dresser and went to her bags, emptied them, and filled the drawers and closet.

Dressed in jeans and a black T-shirt, her hair long and loose, she made her way downstairs over an hour later. Nervous, she found her way to the kitchen. The smell of fresh coffee washed over her when she entered. Relieved to find only Mary in the room, she skirted the breakfast bar and entered the spacious cooking area.

"Mind if I steal a cup of coffee?"

Mary jumped, spilling eggs over the side of a pan onto the stove.

Roxy frowned. "Sorry."

"No problem. I spaced out, thinking about the day ahead. And John. I apologize. I left last night without making up the bed. I'm so sorry."

"No trouble. I've lived on my own for a long time. I don't expect you to wait on me. Uh, maybe you should tell me what it is you do for the family, so I don't unintentionally step on your toes."

"That's very thoughtful." Mary beamed. "I cook all the meals and do the grocery shopping. Anything you want, please add it to the list on the front of the fridge. I also clean the house. I'm usually off on weekends, but Noah asked me to stay on last weekend and this one, since John passed, to make sure Annabelle isn't alone too much.

"I used to do John's room and laundry on Monday. If you don't mind, I'd like to keep that schedule. If not, I can switch you with Annabelle's Thursday."

"Monday is fine, but I don't expect you to clean my room and do my laundry. If you show me where the laundry room is and the cleaning supplies, I can do it myself."

"Nonsense. You pay me to take care of the house."

"I do?"

Mary laughed. "You and Noah and Annabelle. There's a house account I use for the groceries and John paid my salary, along with all the others out of the ranch account. You'll learn everything once you dive into that pile of paperwork."

"Noticed that, did you? Noah's passive-aggressive when it comes to being angry at women." If she was a guy he'd probably be more assertive.

"You got that right," Mary confirmed. "I expect he'll be off-kilter for a while longer until he settles into his new role, too. It's Annabelle I'm worried about."

"Kid's taking things hard. Lots of changes and her dad's gone. Her mom's a real piece of work."

"Lisa's not done yet. You can bet on that."

"I don't bet against a sure thing," Roxy replied. "Where is Annabelle?"

"Brooding in her room, I imagine. She hasn't come down. Noah and Robby will be in soon for breakfast. I've got eggs, bacon, and hash browns warming in the oven. If you'd like something else, I can make it for you."

"I'm good with coffee. About the bed," she began.

"The last time anyone bought new sheets and spreads, Lisa was married to John."

"She's responsible for that horrible living room," Roxy remembered.

"And a whole lot more," Mary confirmed. "Annabelle's room is a pink palace. Noah told me he hates his room, as well."

"Perfect," Roxy answered, and got a strange look from Mary. "I need a way in with Annabelle. I'll take her shopping. We'll bond over retail therapy."

"I'm here with her a lot, but I don't always have time to do the things I think she'd like to do." Mary had a job and although she loved Annabelle and would probably do anything for her, she wasn't her mother.

Roxy put her hand on Mary's shoulder and gave her a reassuring squeeze. "Don't worry. Both Annabelle and Noah love you very much. I've seen it in the way they treat you. I'll admit, I'm a bit of a closet decorator. I redid my cottage two years ago after I spent four months combing through magazines and swatches. A couple of bedrooms and that hideous living room will be fun. It'll give me a chance to make this place feel a bit like mine and not so much theirs."

"Only half this place is yours." Noah walked into the room from a mudroom off the back of the kitchen.

Roxy took a deep sip of coffee and gazed at Noah's irritated whiskey-colored eyes over her mug. Not so sweet and nice this morning.

"Noah!" Mary reprimanded with just his name.

"What? Am I wrong?"

"Not at all." Big mistake for Roxy to back down now or show any kind of weakness. Noah would take advantage. If she didn't stand up for herself, he'd walk all over her. He was pushing to see just how much control she was trying to exert over him. This would probably go on for a few weeks until they stopped dancing around each other and discovered just how the other one worked. Well, he was going to learn that she wasn't a pushover.

"Since half the house is mine, I'm taking the living room. Got a problem with that?"

Noah shrugged. "Take it. It's hands down the ugliest room in the house. Well, maybe Annabelle's room comes close."

"I'm going to fix that today."

"You are?" Surprise filled his voice and narrowed his gaze. He moved closer and took the coffeepot from beside her, pouring himself a mug. She stood her ground and leaned against the counter. When his arm brushed hers, she ignored the zing of awareness that shot through her. He smelled of hay and horses and fresh-cut grass.

God, did he have to smell so good all the time?

"I'm taking her shopping for new bedding."

"It's going to take more than that to fix her room." Noah stared down at her, standing entirely too close. "This some kind of girlie bonding thing?"

"It's my way of getting to know her. You two are close. I walked into her house a week ago and became legally responsible for her, which gives me the right to tell her what to do and how to act. I'm not her mother, or her sister. I'm not trying to be. I want to be her friend, someone she can trust and count on."

"You think a shopping spree is going to accomplish that?"

"It's a start, since I was never allowed to even visit my father and be part of your lives," she shot back.

Noah's hostility evaporated, so she dialed back her anger.

"Don't you think she'd like to redo her room? Or maybe you think she doesn't want to spend time with me?" Maybe Noah thought she was trying to take Annabelle from him, or at least get her on Roxy's side. Then again, last night he'd made sure she saw Annabelle and reassured her that she'd arrived on time.

"I just don't see how shopping is going to make her trust you."

"You must not spend a lot of time around women," she retorted, only half joking with him. She wanted to needle him for his condescending attitude.

"Oh, honey, I've spent plenty of time with women."

"Yes, but have you actually talked to any of them, or just tumbled them into bed, and then shoved them out?"

Mary gasped and spun around to stare at them.

Roxy kept an innocent look on her face, but noted the anger in Noah's eyes. He didn't like what she implied. Score another one in the nice-guy column, along with him covering her up last night, bringing up her bags this morning, and the way he loved his sister.

"I don't treat women like plastic utensils."

As in, *use them once and dump them in the trash when I'm done.*

The intensity of his voice shook her. The blazing anger in his eyes shot fire into her soul. She hadn't meant to hurt his feelings.

"I'm sorry, Noah. That was unfair and uncalled-for. I've had a hell of a week and I took it out on you."

Everything about him changed in an instant. His eyes softened and a slow smile spread over his face. He was so handsome, she could only stare. The longer she did, the bigger his smile. "You sleep like the dead," he blurted out.

Taken off guard, she took a sip of coffee to steady herself. "Yeah, well, a week wasn't a whole lot of time to clean out my office and tend to some other business. I had to get the horses settled and say my good-byes."

"Horses?" Noah asked.

She didn't want to lie, but she held back some of the truth. "I live on a ranch in a small town outside of Las Vegas. John sent me several horses over the years."

"Really? How many?"

"Twelve. Out of them, I bred four more."

"So, you ride."

She dismissed the skepticism in his voice that she was any good at it. "Practically every day," she confirmed.

"Maybe you won't be useless around the ranch after all." He tried to rile her again.

She didn't take the bait. "I bet I can outride you."

"Anytime you want to put your ass in a saddle against me, I'm ready."

"Not today, cowboy. I'm taking your sister shopping."

Noah cocked his hip. "You know we actually do real work around here. You've got a job to do."

She hadn't forgotten the pile of papers in the office. "I know." She walked out of the kitchen. The mail and paperwork on the desk in the study seemed to have grown overnight. Noah had dropped both her computer bags by the desk. Apparently, he really meant to assign her the paperwork and financials for the ranch and leave himself with the horses and breeding program. She'd give him his way for now. No doubt when he got his way, he'd start after her about doing some real labor around the ranch.

Isn't he lots of fun?

Chapter Twenty

Mary smacked him on the arm with a pot holder. "Noah! How could you speak to her that way?"

Noah had to admit, he'd nearly forgotten Mary was standing behind him. When Roxy was near, everything inside him focused on her.

"I don't know what John was thinking. *I* run this ranch. I don't need her coming here and changing things." He really should stop picking at her for what John did.

"Some things could use a change."

"She's been here less than twelve hours and it's already starting. Pretty soon, she'll be telling me how to raise horses and train them."

"Sounds like she might know a thing or two about both," Mary grumbled under her breath.

"Great. So John didn't think I could handle things on my own and brought her here."

"Noah, stop. He thought no such thing. Do you know why he wanted her here? I don't. Did you ever think it might have something to do with *her* life and taking *her* away from something John wished he'd saved her from long ago?"

"If he wanted to bring her here, why didn't he?"

"Yes, why didn't he?" Mary reiterated the question with a punch of anger behind it. "You might follow her lead and take some time to get to know her the way she's going to try to get to know Annabelle today."

"You want me to take her shopping?" he asked with mock horror, knowing she meant nothing of the sort.

"She rides. Take her for a tour of the ranch. Show her how you do things. Most of all, show her what John loved about this place. You had John practically your whole life. She can probably count on her fingers and toes the number of times he stepped into hers. She didn't ask to come here, or for any part of the ranch. She asked for his hat. I've thought about that. Something he wore every day of his life. That's all she wanted."

"It's easy to want something so small when he gave her so much anyway," he shot back, letting his anger slip the reins.

"What has gotten into you?"

"Her," he answered without thinking.

Mary gave him a knowing smile and it took everything in him not to squirm or shift under her matchmaking gaze.

"We don't know anything about her. Who's her mother? When and where did John meet her? Why didn't John tell us he had a daughter? Why didn't he bring her here if her mother is as bad as Roxy claims? She cleaned out an office. What does she do for a living? She's got a ranch with a dozen of our horses and more. Who's taking care of them?"

Noah didn't want to think about a boyfriend staying behind to care for the horses and Roxy leaving five days a month to shack up with him. Or worse, the guy showed up here to live with her. His hands fisted at his sides, and anger reigned over his thoughts and threatened to smother him.

"Noah." Mary's voice took on that soft and coaxing tone she used to calm him when he got worked up, but he didn't want to simmer down. He wanted to rage. "He loved you. You are his son. If he raised her here with you and Annabelle, would it have surprised you that he gave her half?"

"It just shows he thought more of her because she's his blood than he did for all the blood and sweat I put into this place."

"That's not true and you know it. I've never seen a man more proud of anyone as he was of you."

Noah sighed, knowing the words were true, but still feeling betrayed.

"Did you ever think he gave her the bigger split because he felt like he owed her and the only way he could pay her back for what he did to her was to give her half this place?"

"Why did he keep her a secret? Why didn't he trust me enough to give me the truth?"

Why the secret at all?

"He trusts in you to keep this ranch running. He trusts you to raise and care for Annabelle. He trusts you to do both with Roxy beside you. I don't know why he kept her a secret. John isn't here to tell you. Ask her."

"When John and I went riding that last day, he opened up. We talked about my mother. I think losing her and the baby really hurt him."

"He was never the same after your mother died," Mary confirmed. "For a while, he didn't seem to care about anything, except this ranch and you. He went from one woman to another. I think he was trying to fill the hole your mother's death left inside him."

"One of those women is Roxy's mother," Noah said, thinking out loud. "When Annabelle was born, I remember the look of deep disappointment on his face. He really wanted his own child."

"He was happy with you and Annabelle."

"I understood what he meant. I'd been thinking along the same lines myself lately."

"Really? You'd like a family? You'd make such a wonderful father," she complimented. "Oh God, please tell me that's not why Cheryl keeps calling."

"Hell no!"

"Thank God. The last thing we need around here is another woman, who . . . Oh, I'm sorry, Noah. You like her."

"We're over. The thing is, in one of the few lucid moments John had in the hospital, he asked me to take care of Roxy. He said she'd never had anyone else. He made me promise. At the time, I thought he meant Annabelle. But now . . ."

"You think he meant Roxy."

Noah shrugged, sure that's what John meant, but unwilling to admit it.

"You see. You said it yourself, he'd never been that open with you. He did trust you, Noah. He was trying to tell you about her. He never got the chance to finish."

Noah thought about it, and it did feel right. John had asked him to go for a ride; he wanted to be away from everyone where they'd have privacy. They'd ridden to their spot, where John had taken him countless times and instilled numerous lessons. They'd shared quiet talks and peaceful silences up in the hills overlooking the ranch. Yes, John had been trying to tell him about Roxy, but their conversation had been cut short.

Annabelle rushed into the kitchen, cutting off any further discussion about John, Roxy, and the fact that he'd inadvertently admitted he wanted to settle down with a wife and kids.

"What are you doing, Sprite?"

She looked up from digging through the junk drawer by the sink. "I need a tape measure for Roxy. She's taking me shopping."

The smile she beamed him melted his heart. It had been too long since he'd seen her this excited about anything.

"I heard. No more pink ruffles."

"Oh, it's more than that. She's going to paint my room and put up new curtains. She said she can make it look just like one of those pretty suites I saw in the commercial about that really expensive spa that opened up a few months back."

"I remember." Mary beamed. "That place was really beautiful."

"I showed her a picture online. Roxy said she could re-create it for me."

"I think we've got some painting supplies in the garage. I'll dig them out for you." Noah decided anything that put that smile on his sister's face he could get behind.

"Thank you, Noah." Annabelle bounced on her toes. "This is going to be so cool."

Mary grabbed the tape measure from Annabelle's hand. "I'll take this up to Roxy. You have something to eat before you go. You'll need your strength for all that shopping."

Annabelle didn't need to be asked twice. She grabbed the plate Mary had piled with food and rushed to the table. He hadn't seen her eat that enthusiastically in over a week. With a deep sigh, he took his plate and a seat at the table with Annabelle. No matter how jumbled his feelings about Roxy, he had to give her credit for bringing the smile back to Annabelle's face.

He wondered how many other surprises she had in store.

Chapter Twenty-One

Roxy stood on the stepladder, reached up, and put the curtain rod into the holder. She spread the curtains straight, then pushed them to the side to let the light and gentle breeze in.

"They're perfect, Roxy. He's going to love it," Annabelle said from behind her.

"The paint isn't quite dry, but I don't think it'll smear." Thanks to the two-in-one paint and primer, she'd been able to paint Annabelle's and Noah's rooms in no time.

Roxy stepped down to the floor and surveyed the room. "Not bad. You really think he'll like it?"

"He will. Thank you." Annabelle slammed into Roxy's chest and wrapped her arms around Roxy and hugged her tight. "This has been the best day. I can't believe how fast you changed everything."

"You were a huge help." Roxy gave the girl a squeeze before setting her away. She wasn't used to being hugged and touched.

Annabelle had no trouble showing her affection. In fact, she was enthusiastic and outgoing. From their conversations, she learned Annabelle had a lot of friends, was part of the popular crowd, and loved horses, chocolate shakes, and country music. She hated her mother, her pink room, Noah and John hounding her about school, college, boys, and just about everything else. Roxy understood the underlying need; Annabelle desperately wanted a woman in her life. She didn't so much as say how happy she was to finally have a woman besides Mary on the ranch, but it came through loud and clear.

Roxy surveyed the room and took stock of all the changes, trying not to notice all Noah's things. She'd learned a lot about him being in his room.

He left his change scattered on the dresser, along with two screwdrivers and a pair of pliers. Apparently, Noah had a habit of stuffing tools in his back pocket and forgetting to put them away before he came in from the barn. Thirty percent of the laundry he tossed toward the hamper hit the floor. He liked boxer briefs, which she decided he'd look entirely too good wearing. Based on the number of books on his nightstand and stacked on a shelf, he spent most nights deep in a mystery or FBI thriller.

She loved the old antique sleigh bed. She'd played off the rich wood colors in all the furniture and added a hunter green spread with cream rope piping along the edge. The reverse side had alternating green-and-brown pinstripes between wide bands of the same cream color. The same reversible pattern drapes hung from the windows. Roxy kept the green side up on the bed with about twelve inches of the pattern folded down at the pillows. She used the cream-banded pattern on the inside of the room for the drapes, but the valances showed the deep green and cream piping. To complement the decor, she'd painted over the plain white walls with a cream to match the curtains and spread. The room felt warm, cozy, and inviting.

Before it had been nothing but unrelieved brown and white, bare and uninteresting.

"Do you think he'll like the pillow and lamp?" Annabelle smoothed her hands over the new cream pillow she'd placed on Noah's brown leather chair by the fireplace.

"They're perfect. He can read by the fire without keeping the overhead lights on. Help me spread the new rug out."

They unrolled the cream-colored rug that had an old oak tree with deep green leaves and thick reaching brown branches spreading out wide across the rug. Neither of them could help but run their hands over the ultra-soft, thick pile.

"I can't believe how lucky we were to find this. It's nice to look at and so soft and plush. I want to take off my shoes and sink my feet into it." Annabelle smiled, digging her fingers into the threads.

"You and I make a great shopping team. You spotted the bronzed lamp that looks like tree branches. I think it's perfect for this room and Noah." Roxy gave Annabelle's shoulder a squeeze to let her know what a great job she'd done.

"I think I like the rug the best."

Roxy smiled. "Me, too. Makes this sitting area by the fireplace perfect."

Tired after a long day, Roxy gave in and flopped backward on the bed and stared up at the bronzed branch chandelier over the bed. "I'm taking a break. You take the stepladder and garbage out before Noah gets back. We want him to get the full effect when he first sees the room."

"Okay. I'll be right back."

Roxy shut her eyes for a moment and quieted her mind. She smiled, thinking about how nice a day she'd had with Annabelle, shopping, talking, laughing while they painted. Exactly like being with her sisters.

"If I'd known you were waiting in my bed with a welcoming smile, I'd have been back sooner." Noah stood in the doorway just looking at her.

God, she was gorgeous. He leaned against the frame, knowing if he took even a single step toward her, he'd be unable to stop himself from doing what he'd been dreaming day and night about doing with her.

The smile faded when her eyes flew open. She rolled up from the bed and stood before him. Uncertain, she bit her full bottom lip and eyed him warily.

"Sorry," she said automatically.

"No woman's ever been sorry for being in my bed. Give me an hour and I'll prove it to you."

Her golden eyes flashed fire, reminding him of the way John's used to when he said something stupid and John didn't approve. He wanted to take the words back.

"Wham bam, thank you, ma'am. Is that it? I told you . . ."

"You don't sleep with men for sport." He believed her.

Damn if thinking about her sleeping with some other guy didn't send his blood pressure through the roof and prod at his little jealous monster.

Still, a beautiful, desirable woman like her didn't spend many nights alone. The thought that she'd had a string of long-term relationships, men who got to spend night after night with her set his blood to boiling. He wanted to be the only one touching her, kissing her, sinking deep inside her.

"Listen, honey . . ."

"I am not your honey," she snapped.

Feeling surly himself, he planted his fists on his hips and glared. "Roxy. I'm tired, dirty, and my shoulder's been killing me all day. One of the damn horses jumped the corral fence and three more before I caught up with him again. It's the fourth time that brat has escaped and led me on a merry chase. I'm hungry and I want a shower and a shave." He rubbed his palm over the stubble across his jaw. Maybe he'd keep the scruff if she was going to keep watching him with those hungry golden eyes. His body stirred, but he tamped down his rampant lust and focused on her and the fact he'd offended her. "I need some food and sleep," he finished lamely.

A week in bed with you would do me a hell of a lot of good, too.

"I'll leave you to it then."

She walked toward him, but he didn't move out of the doorway, so she stopped a few feet away, waiting for him to move.

"I'm sorry about the smart remark. Your being here provokes something in me," he admitted.

"I've noticed." She crossed her arms under her breasts, making the sun-kissed mounds rise out of the deep V in her paint-splattered black T-shirt. His mouth watered. When he met her eyes again, she dropped her arms, knowing very well what he'd been staring at.

"Noah!" Annabelle shouted from behind him. "Do you love it? Isn't it perfect? Roxy did most of the work, but I helped her paint and put everything together."

For the first time, Noah looked around the room. Finding Roxy lying across his bed stole his focus from anything else. She seemed to do that no matter where he found her. "I . . ."

"You don't like it." Annabelle's vibrant smile fell into a deep frown. She scooted past him to stand next to Roxy.

Great, Roxy must think him a complete asshole for not saying one word about all the work they'd done on his room.

He noted the new bedding, curtains, the green-and-white-swirled glass bowl filled with his change and miscellaneous pocket stuff he always tossed on the dresser. A vase burst with white flowers on the table by the bed; his books were lined up and stacked on the shelf, his most recent one lying facedown on the table beside his leather chair. A new lamp and pillow making the space inviting. He loved the new rug in front of the hearth.

A fantasy blazed across his mind of Roxy laid out, naked, her arms outstretched, reaching for him. Flames waving in the fireplace, making light dance over her golden skin.

"I, um, can't believe you did this in one day. The place looks great," he mumbled, feeling like a complete idiot.

"Keep the windows open for a while to air out the paint smell. I put a couple extra sets of sheets in the linen cupboard in your bathroom," Roxy explained, looking uncomfortable. "Annabelle, I'll finish your room tomorrow. Excuse me, I've got some other things to do."

"Mary said dinner is almost ready."

"I'll grab something later. I need to make a call." She hesitated, then turned and wrapped Annabelle in a hug. "I had a great time with you today."

He'd never seen anyone exit a room so fast and look so out of sorts.

"Did the two of you have fun today?"

"It was awesome! She took me to this great bistro for lunch. We shopped several stores before we ended up in this really expensive high-end boutique. That's where we bought all the bedding and curtains and that amazing rug and lamp. Don't you love it, Noah?"

"I really do. You picked some great stuff."

"I didn't. She did." With a frown, she admitted, "Roxy did most of the work. I helped, but she's amazing. You should see what she bought for my room."

"How'd she pay for all this?"

"She used a credit card," Annabelle went on without a second thought to the money.

Noah wondered how she could afford a new car and all this without using money from the ranch account.

"It's going to be awesome. I can't wait until she finishes my room, too. We painted and got rid of all the pink and ruffles, but I wanted to get your room done, so we could surprise you." Frowning, her enthusiasm fading, she said, "You don't look very surprised or happy."

"I am, Sprite. I really like what you've done."

"Roxy did it, too. It would have been nice if you'd thanked her." Annabelle scrunched her lips. "You don't like her. That's what this is about. You don't want her here."

"I hardly know her. What did you two talk about at lunch?" Noah hoped to learn something about her.

"She asked about school and how I liked living here. We talked about Mom and a little about Dad, but it made me sad, so she asked me about my friends and what I like to do."

"Did she tell you anything about her and Dad?"

"No. She wanted to know if I did a lot of things with him. I told her how we used to go riding and camping and fishing. She seemed real interested."

"Did she tell you about her mother, or her life back in Vegas?"

"No." Annabelle tilted her head, lost in thought. "Actually, every time I asked about her, she changed the subject. I never really noticed. She wanted to know about me, so I did most of the talking."

Noah wrapped his arm around Annabelle's shoulders and pulled her close. "Don't worry about it, Sprite. You had a good time. Your room will look great, and you won't be embarrassed to have your friends over. You shared the day with Roxy and she got to know you. I'd say all in all, you had a great day." He rubbed his hand over her shoulder. "I need a shower. Tell Mary I'll be down for dinner in ten minutes." No time to shave.

He wondered if that look Roxy gave him when he touched his beard meant she really did like him unshaved. He wondered if she'd like the feel of his scruffy face against her round breasts. Or between her thighs.

Make that a cold shower.

He scooted Annabelle out of his freshly painted room.

Alone, he took in the space with one long sweep of his gaze. He hated to admit, he liked the changes—a lot. Roxy had done a great job and he couldn't wait to try out the new sheets. Preferably with her in them with him.

He didn't think he'd get the image of her lying on her back on his bed out of his head for a long time.

Still, he wanted answers to his questions. He wanted to know what made Roxy tick. He wanted her in his bed.

Hell, he just plain wanted her.

He had no idea for what or why, beyond satisfying his urgent need to get his hands on her perfect body.

Still, her courage, strength, confidence, and easy manner intrigued him. She pulled at him like no other woman ever had.

That had to be it. She was a mystery he needed to solve. He didn't know anything about her and that's what interested him. Not necessarily her, but the not knowing was what drove him.

You're lying to yourself.

He stared at his reflection in the mirror over the bathroom sink, peeled off his shirt, and tossed it toward the hamper. It hit the side and landed on the floor. What bugged him the most was that it was Roxy who stirred his feelings and made him burn in the night.

Her. John's daughter. Half owner of *his* ranch.

A woman who most of the time could barely look him in the eye and kept everything about herself a secret. But when she did look at him with a fire burning in her golden eyes before she banked it and turned away, he saw the potential for what they could have together.

But, like John, she didn't trust him with her secrets.

He worked off his boots; tore off his jeans, boxers, and socks; and stepped into the shower, turning on the water. The shock of cold soothed his overheated body. The water heated, and he called himself ten kinds of fool for thinking getting involved with his partner in the ranch was a good idea.

Since his body refused to give up having Roxy, he found some five-finger relief, stroking his hand up and down his hard length until his balls tightened and he came with a jerk that shook his whole body. The release was nothing compared to what he wanted to experience with Roxy, but it took the edge off.

When he headed down for dinner, his gut fluttered with anticipation—not for food, but another glimpse of her.

Chapter Twenty-Two

Noah stepped into the kitchen, the only light coming from over the cooktop and the open refrigerator door. Roxy stood in front of it, popping grapes into her mouth and staring at the contents on the shelves. The smell of coffee helped wake his mind, but Roxy's softly curved and rounded ass woke up the part of him that had kept him from sleep most of the night.

He'd come down last night expecting to see her at the dinner table. Instead, she'd entrenched herself in the office with the door closed. He wanted to make her come out, demand she answer all his questions, but Mary stopped him with a look and a soft reprimand to leave her be. She needed time to get used to them and living here.

"Morning," he grumbled, still waking up from another night of restless sleep. Four o'clock seemed an unholy hour to be up, even for him.

"Good night." She shut the fridge door and headed out the back way toward the stairs.

"Wait."

She stopped and turned to face him, her eyes tired with dark circles beneath.

"Are you just now going to bed?" He noted the smudge of yellow paint on her cheek. "Were you painting again?"

"The living room. I just finished."

"Why didn't you wait to do it today?"

"I got caught up on some work emails and passed that tired state where going to sleep is near impossible, so I did the living room. It happens to me a lot. My mind is still going, even though I'm tired. No sense going to bed just to lie there thinking for hours. I've discovered it's better to keep busy until I can sleep."

"You have a lot of sleepless nights?"

"More than I'd like."

"Me, too, lately," he remarked under his breath.

She turned to leave, but he stopped her. "Wait." She turned back again. Her eyes fell down his face to his bare chest and over his jean-clad legs. They shot back to his face and held his gaze. He could tell she didn't want him to see that lapse. No matter the pull of electricity between them, she seemed as reluctant as him to acknowledge it or give in to it.

"Noah . . ."

God, the way she said his name.

"It's late and I'm exhausted. Can this wait?"

"Ah, thank you. For my room. I, uh, really appreciate it." He ran a hand through his hair, uncomfortable under her penetrating gaze.

"How'd that taste coming out of your mouth? You thanking me for anything after John left me half of your ranch and home?"

"Like horseshit." Not really, because the thing was, she got it.

Despite the fact she had to be jealous as hell that he'd grown up here with John, she understood his anger and resentment. She had a side. He had a side. And she was willing to concede that his feelings mattered just as much as hers.

She laughed, and the sound went right to his belly and tied it in knots.

Unable to fight it any longer, he closed the distance between them and with one hand sliding to the back of her neck, his fingers buried in the thick mass of silky hair, he pulled her lips to his. She smelled of paint with a hint of flowers, like the ones she'd left by his bed. Their smell teased him all night and made him think of her.

His instinct was to devour, but he felt her tense and her eyes went wide. Watching her, he brushed his lips against hers. Once. Twice. With barely a touch, he tasted a hint of the sweet grapes she'd eaten.

She stood perfectly still; her breath washed over his mouth from her slightly parted lips. "I thought we agreed this wasn't a good idea."

"We both lied about that." He kissed her softly again, lingering over the sweet torment. He could take the kiss deeper, have her wrapped in his arms and begging for him to take her to bed. He saw the hunger to match his own in her eyes, but he also caught the slight hesitation and a trace of—not exactly fear, but doubt.

About what, he didn't know. He didn't believe Roxy was afraid of anything. She'd left her old life and moved to a stranger's house because a young girl needed her. That took guts, knowing her welcome wasn't exactly friendly, at least on his part.

Instead of taking what he wanted, he gave in to instinct and pressed his mouth to hers in a soft undemanding kiss that was warm and sweet and unrushed. He didn't pull her closer, but enjoyed the feel of her mouth against his, the way her eyes fluttered closed as she sank into the kiss and the moment with him, and the brush of the hard tips of her breasts barely skimming his chest as her breathing deepened. Time stopped.

He withdrew slowly and she leaned into him, her mouth following his until they broke the kiss.

Her eyes flew open and studied him.

"Thank you for putting the smile back on Annabelle's face."

"You're welcome. She's a great kid. I like her." The soft smile told him she meant it. "Good night, Noah." She stepped back and his hand slid out of her silky hair and across the soft skin along her neck.

"Night." He stood rooted to the floor and watched her leave. Aching to go after her, he turned to the coffeepot and poured himself a mug. Cup in hand, he walked to the living room to survey her late-night work and wondered what kept her awake.

He flipped the switch and the lights came on. It didn't take but a quick look to see that a soft pale yellow had transformed the once-ugly space. The white casings around the tall windows stood out and made them appear even larger. With the furniture draped in the tarps he'd found in the garage earlier, the room looked unfinished, but better for not having to look at the hideous sofas and chairs. Lisa had the worst taste, but Noah liked Roxy's. He hoped she got rid of the furniture and bought something that suited the house and was comfortable and nice to look at.

Noah turned and started up the stairs.

Did she know how deeply that kiss affected him? He had a hard time not going after her, crawling into her bed and making love to her until his body was sated and she wasn't his every waking thought. Maybe then she'd stop haunting his dreams.

Probably not.

Somehow he knew once with Roxy would never be enough. Like a drug, she'd worked her way into his system and he needed more.

The office was dark, except for the glow from both her laptops. He flipped the switch and walked to the big desk. The stack of mail and papers he'd left her had been sorted, but it didn't look like she'd done anything with them. Yet. If she didn't get to them soon, he'd have to have a word with her. She needed to pull her weight. He needed to be able to trust her to keep up with the accounts and orders.

He walked around to John's chair and stared down at the screens. No pictures of a boyfriend. He shoved the relief out of his mind. One screensaver showed a sorrel horse with a golden mane. The other displayed a profusion of blooms in an overgrown garden surrounding what appeared to be a gray stone castle. The colors were brilliant, and the scene, nothing short of breathtaking.

Annabelle's words came back to him—she hates the desert.

"Maybe John did bring you here for a reason. Did he want to pay you back for leaving you? Or did he want to take you away from something and this was the only way?"

NOAH THOUGHT ABOUT that off and on all day. He ran the brush over his horse, thinking about Roxy and the horse on her screensaver. One from this ranch?

How come he didn't know John sent them to her?

Some of the men working nearby stopped what they were doing and stared out the barn doors. The whispers and nudges started. Roxy must be on her way down. He'd heard the men speculating about her, talking trash, and taking bets who'd get the first date. He'd stayed out of it and let them have their fun. One thing he knew for certain, none of them was going to touch his woman.

The brush in his hand stopped midstroke and he stood tall and stared into nothing, completely taken off guard at that one simple, yet so complicated thought.

When the hell did she go from being a thorn in his side to his woman?

With a lick of his lips, he remembered the kiss, her taste, the way his insides melted with that simple press of lips. Something had shifted in him. Softened.

But did she feel the same way?

She'd warned him that giving in to their attraction would complicate things and potentially make it impossible to work together. But if she started dating someone on the ranch, he didn't know what he'd do, but it wouldn't be good.

As she passed several hands and they stood taller and smiled at her, he wanted to punch every single one of them in the face. He had an unreasonable need to fire them all.

He wanted to keep every other man away from her, so he could keep her for himself.

He wasn't a possessive guy. Until now. And he didn't like it. Because it made him feel irrational and on edge.

She walked up to him and he glared down at her, unsettled that she'd tied him in knots without doing a damn thing except walk into the stables.

If she knew how much he wanted her, thought of her, the effect she had on him, she didn't show any satisfaction at his torment. Instead, she matched his mood.

"What now?" She glared right back at him.

"Shouldn't you be up at the house doing the paperwork you keep putting off?"

Every man on the ranch had found a reason to be in the barn in the last two minutes. They had an audience, all of which had their eyes plastered to Roxy's ass as she stood in front of him, looking defiant and pissed. He had to admit, he loved it when her eyes flashed fire like that.

"Looks like the boss isn't happy about having to give over half the ranch to get a piece of that fine ass," someone whispered, but not low enough.

Roxy's eyes went cold.

She handed him a folder stuffed full of bills attached to checks she'd made out from the ranch account. He'd been so focused on her, he hadn't even seen the papers.

"Sign those. I'll send them out."

He took the folder and the pen she offered. While he stood by a cabinet, double-checking all her work and signing the checks, she took up the brush he set down and stroked his horse. Damn if the creature didn't nibble at her hair and nuzzle her neck when she came close.

I'm jealous of a horse.

"Want to go for a ride?" Harry asked, and even Noah heard the innuendo. The only thing Harry wanted Roxy to ride was him.

"She's got work to do up at the house." Noah gave Harry a look that had him backing off instantly.

Roxy didn't say a word and ignored them both and kept brushing the horse.

"Aw, come on, give a guy a chance."

Noah stepped away from the papers and stood in front of Harry, hands fisted at his sides so he didn't wrap them around the asshole's throat. "You'd do well to remember who she is."

"Oh, I know exactly *what* she is." Harry's wolfish grin matched the light of lust in his eyes. He stepped aside, rubbed his hands together, and stared at Roxy's backside. "I look forward to working with her."

The others looking on chuckled at Harry's blatant attempt to get Roxy's attention.

Noah caught the glare Roxy shot at the men over her shoulder.

All of the gathered guys laughed.

Something was going on here, but he had no idea what, which pissed him off more because he didn't like these guys making Roxy feel uncomfortable.

"Get back to work!" Everyone started and bumped into each other as they quickly cleared out.

Noah turned to Roxy. "I don't know what's gotten into them. I knew having you around might cause some trouble at first, but this was just . . . strange."

"Yeah." She rolled her eyes. "Strange. Just sign the checks. Don't worry about them. I can handle it."

"I guess you're used to guys hitting on you. But still, if anyone gives you a hard time, let me know. I'll take care of it."

"I can take care of myself."

John's words slammed into his mind. *"Take care of her. She's never had anyone."*

He took a step toward her and she stepped back. He kept moving and she retreated, until her back hit the stall door.

"I made a promise."

Her eyes went wide and watchful. "What promise?"

"A promise I intend to keep. If the guys get out of hand, you don't have to put up with it, or deal with it alone."

"Do you mean that? You'll be on my side?"

The intense look on her face and the trace of hope in her eyes had him answering with an earnest "Always."

He cupped her face in his hands and brushed his mouth against hers, like this morning. This time, he didn't hold back, but took the kiss deep when she opened to him. He swept his tongue inside, tasted the apple juice he knew she favored and her. God, she was so sweet. He kept the kiss slow, feeling the shyness he'd felt in her this morning, too, slowly evaporate. Her hands skimmed up his sides and around his back to his shoulders. She moved closer and sank into him.

He wrapped his arms around her and pulled her to him. Her breasts pressed to his chest, and he tried not to crush her, but he needed her closer. Their tongues tangled together and he traced her bottom lip. She sighed his name and he dived in for more. He slid his hands over her back, pressing her close. He found the hem of her shirt and slipped his hands beneath to her warm, smooth skin, dragging them up her spine.

Her hands pressed to his chest and she pushed him away, but he didn't let her go.

"Noah, stop." She shoved his hands off her sides and yanked her shirt down. "Enough."

He hadn't realized he was about to drag her shirt off over her head in the middle of the barn where anyone could see them. He stepped close and slid his hands over her sides and held her hips. "I'm sorry. I got carried away. My brain shuts off when I'm near you," he admitted.

"I noticed. This isn't the time or place." She turned her head to stare down the long aisle between the stalls. He followed her gaze and saw one of his men, Harry again, standing down a ways watching them. "Please, sign the checks."

Without another word, he stepped away and went through the checks, verifying them against the many bills and signing them. When he got to the feed store, he checked the bill twice before turning back to her. "The check is twenty-five percent less than the actual bill, but you've noted a change in the price on several of the items."

"They've been overcharging the ranch. I called and negotiated a new rate."

He tipped his head and narrowed his gaze. "I've haggled with the manager a dozen times and he never budged. How did you do this?"

"I told him that I could order the supplies online from a supplier in Vegas, who'd charge me the same as he's charging the ranch for the same supplies with shipping."

"You bluffed?" he asked astonished.

"Hell no. I buy the feed for my horses from a very reputable supplier. I've established a relationship with them. They'd not only supply my ranch, but this one and be happy to take my business."

"I'll bet," he said offhand, making her glare. "I just meant you're beautiful, and your voice . . . I bet old Mr. Cooper at the feed store kept you on the line just to listen to you."

Her lips pressed into an irritated line. "So I get my way because of the way I look and sound, not because I gave him a sound argument for giving us a fair price?"

"Um, I . . ." He didn't know what to say, because he'd jammed his whole foot in his mouth.

"Sign the damn checks."

Two things occurred to him. Whatever ground he'd gained in getting closer to her, he'd lost. And although she had to know how beautiful she was, this wasn't the first time someone attributed her accomplishments to her looks and not her smarts.

"Roxy, I'm sorry." He held up the updated bill. "I appreciate that you took the initiative and saved the ranch money. You did a really good job."

"I can't help the way I look." Her soft voice drifted off as if she were telling a secret to the wind.

No, she couldn't. And it made him think. She never dressed to show off. Her clothes fit her well, but they weren't revealing.

Roxy didn't put herself on display, yet she drew every man's eye because she was just naturally beautiful from her heart-shaped face down to her long, toned legs.

"You don't use your looks to your advantage. I'm sure in most situations you don't have to. You know I want you." His blunt statement made her cheeks pink with embarrassment. "Some women would take advantage of that and use their body to get me to fall in line. Not you. When I kiss you, you hesitate for a split second, and then it's like you give yourself permission to give in, let go, and you fall into me. It's sexy as hell and makes me want you even more."

Lost in thought, trying to put his words together to tell her how special those intimate moments between them felt, he didn't notice how still she went.

"There's confidence in the way you carry yourself. You know who you are and you don't apologize for it. You stand up for yourself and others. Look at the way you sized up Lisa and took on being Annabelle's guardian. I have no doubt you'll protect her from any threat, including any to her sweet heart. You took one look at Annabelle and saw yourself. I don't know what your life was like with your mother. I'd like to know everything about that and you. But whatever you've been through, it's made you strong and independent."

"Stop."

"I'm just getting started. I know those things about you, but there's so much more I have yet to discover. And I will, because you live here now. And you're right, we need to learn to work together and trust each other.

So I want you to know, I see more than the gorgeous package, Roxy. I see you."

Tears glistened in her eyes. "You say that now, but when you find out all those things you want to know and about my mother, you'll change your mind."

"Nothing will make me see you any different than I see you right now."

The look in her eyes was so raw and pleading and miserable. He read the resignation that despite his words to the contrary, there would come a time when he'd forget this moment and see her in a different light.

He didn't understand completely, but he knew she was hiding something and it had everything to do with her mother.

To seal his vow to remember this moment, he slipped his hand behind her head, drew her close, and brushed his lips over hers. He took the kiss deeper, trying to erase whatever it was that cast a shadow over her life and made her so unwilling to release control to the point that she had to consciously let her walls down and step into his arms.

He trailed kisses along her jaw, kissed her cheek, her nose, and her forehead. She stepped away, but kept her hands at his waist, gripped in his shirt. Progress. She didn't put more than a small space between them.

"Please, Noah. Sign the checks."

"Retreating," he teased to coax her out of her somber mood.

"Catching my breath. You're easy to deal with when you're running cold, but hot, you're a handful."

"Honey, I'm just warming up."

"Lord help me." The unshed tears washed away and she finally smiled.

He needed to see the light come back into her eyes, because seeing her near tears tore at him. If she actually cried, it might break him in two.

"Noah! He's about to jump," one of the men shouted from a nearby stall.

"Shit." Noah made a run for the stall door, grabbing a rope on his way. He ran through the stall to the outside corral just as his nemesis jumped the fence and made a run for it across the pasture. Before he could make another move, Roxy came flying out of the barn doors on his horse, riding bareback, a rope in one hand. She chased the beast down, jumping the next fence no more than five strides behind him. Before

Houdini made it to the next fence, she roped him in, an expert move that thoroughly impressed him and the men who'd gathered to watch her fly across the pasture, her black hair streaming out behind her like the horse's tail.

Damn, that woman can ride.

"She's one fine rider." Robby stepped up and echoed his thoughts.

"Bet she likes riding cowboys more than horses." Harry's comment made the other men laugh. Young, full of himself, and loose with his tongue to cover how awkward and fumbling he was with women—everyone for that matter—Harry tended to be outrageous to get attention.

"She favors the boss, but it won't be long before we're all getting some action."

That crossed the line. Noah moved without thinking and shoved Harry into the wall. "She's a partner in this ranch, and you'll treat her with the respect she deserves or you'll be out on your ass."

Harry's eyes danced with merriment.

Robby grabbed his shoulder. "He got the message."

Noah stepped back. Harry rushed over to the three other guys milling about watching Roxy ride back to the stables. They laughed and smacked Harry, like their kid brother who'd gotten scolded for acting out.

Robby waited for the men to walk off before saying, "You changed your tune about her."

"You saw me kiss her," Noah guessed.

"Looked intense."

Noah went silent for a minute, trying to gather his thoughts on what he felt, how she made him feel. "She's not what I expected. A woman who looks like that"—he cocked his head toward her—"you'd think she'd be more . . . outgoing," he said for lack of a better term.

"She's not a flirt and she doesn't use her considerable assets to get what she wants." Robby put it into better words than Noah had done.

"She's timid, unsure of herself when someone touches her. Annabelle hugged her and she didn't know what to do. Hold on, or just stand there until it was over. I kiss her and she hesitates, then follows my lead. I expected her to be more like Cheryl." Noah still felt like he hadn't made his point, unsure what he really felt or meant.

He couldn't figure Roxy out, but knew something significant lay behind her shy demeanor.

"You're a good-looking guy," Robby began, and Noah glared at him, making Robby laugh. "I'm not hitting on you. Just stating a fact. You've never had trouble getting a woman to notice you, or fall into your bed when you wanted. Cheryl, like many of the others you've dated, threw herself at you. Part of it was your looks and you're a nice guy. Part of it is your position on this ranch and the money you have . . . then and now.

"Roxy seems to have her own sense of self. She strikes me as the kind of woman who doesn't need a man to take care of her. She's been doing that her whole life I'd guess based on some of the things she's said and I've heard. I have a feeling she's like nothing and no one you've ever known. The way she stuck up for Annabelle, moved here to ensure her future—Roxy's a woman worth keeping. She's a woman who'd do damn near anything for a friend. Look what she did for a stranger."

"She came here because John left her half this place."

"If you believe that, you aren't looking close enough." Robby frowned like Noah had disappointed him.

The feeling didn't sit well. "I know why she came," he admitted. "It still rankles, what John did. I don't understand it, or her, really."

"Getting her into your bed will only allow you to get to know her so much. It leaves the most important parts of her hidden. You really want to know the woman, talk to her. Find out all those secrets she's keeping."

"You think she's hiding something, too?"

"Women like their secrets," Robby said with a smile. "But that one, you only have to look into her eyes to see she's carrying a heavy burden. If all you want is to get her into your bed, you'll only cause a rift between you that will make it near impossible to run this ranch together. Raising Annabelle will be pure misery for all of you if you two are at each other's throats. Get to know the woman, Noah, ease some of that burden she carries, and you might have a shot at a life with a real partner by your side." Robby took a step away, but turned back. "A woman as beautiful as that should smile more. Since she arrived, I've never heard her laugh. Makes you wonder why."

"Hello, Robby." Roxy stepped forward, leading the two horses.

"Miss Roxy." Robby tipped his hat to her. "That was a real fine show. Anytime you want to ride, you let me know and I'd be happy to saddle up a horse for you."

"Thank you. I appreciate that."

"I'll take these two off your hands." Robby took both horses, leaving Noah standing with Roxy.

"Can I have him?"

Noah tried to focus. "What?"

"Houdini. Can I have him?"

He smiled because that's the name he'd given the escape artist. "What do you want with him?"

"I'm going to turn him into a world-class jumper. I think I might even have a buyer for him."

That got his attention. "You do?"

"I know someone. He's got a natural talent for jumping. A few weeks of training and I'll have him far enough along for my friend to see his potential."

"You can train him to jump?" he asked, impressed, if still a bit skeptical.

She didn't offer any proof to her claim beyond her confident stare. "Can I have him?"

"He's yours. I'd like to see this."

"You don't think I can do it?" Her eyes flashed with hurt to anger in an instant. He didn't mind her anger, but he hated seeing the hurt.

"I think you can do whatever you set your mind to. Hell, you redecorated half the house in two days."

"That was easy. Nothing but shopping and paint. Houdini needs a lot of work."

"No doubt. You'll probably spend half your time chasing him down," Noah teased.

"He'll come around to my charms soon enough, like you're starting to," she teased back, but looked away, uncertain.

He wanted to draw her out even more, so kept things light. "You're a hard woman to stay angry at," he confirmed.

"You weren't really angry at me."

He hated to admit it, but . . . "It's not your fault John surprised all of us with you. I have a feeling whatever I dish out, you can take, because wherever you came from, you've had a lot to deal with in your life."

She took a step back and stared past his shoulder. "Um, I've got a lot of work left to do. I need to get back to it."

"I make you uncomfortable," he threw out.

"I'm not used to . . . Well, this," she admitted, not really telling him much. "I spend a lot of time alone."

"Don't you have close friends?"

"A few. You're right. Life hasn't been easy for me." The matter-of-fact tone didn't add up with her need for him to see the real her and her admitting she didn't have many friends.

She didn't expound on that topic; he wanted to know more, a lot more, so he asked, "Why?"

"Why all the questions?" Suspicion filled her golden gaze. She eyed him, looking for his angle.

It clued him in that she didn't let many people close, because she didn't know what they really wanted from her.

Why does she have to guard herself so closely?

"Whenever Annabelle or I ask about you, you change the subject. John never spoke of you. I'm trying to get to know you. So, I'm asking, why hasn't life been easy?"

Taken aback by his bluntness, she bit her bottom lip and looked around to see if anyone else was listening to them, witnessing their exchange. No one in sight, she faced him, opened her mouth to speak, and closed it again.

He held his hands out wide, then let them drop to his sides again. "You aren't going to give me anything. You can't trust me enough to know that whatever you say will remain between us if that's how you want it?"

"It's not that. I don't know what to say. My life is complicated. Anytime I've confided in someone about my past, about my mother, they've changed. They look at me different."

Which was why it affected her so deeply when he said he saw her.

"You don't know anything about me, except what you've learned from our interactions together. Your opinion is based on what you see right in front of you."

"And you really think telling me about your past is going to change all that?"

"I know it will based on my experience with other people. Oh, many have said it doesn't matter, but in the end, it always does. It's like an oil slick on water that spreads and coats everything in my life."

"Do you want to take a chance I'll find out some other way? Or do you want to tell me yourself?"

She put her hands on her hips. "Calling me out?"

"I'm asking you to take a chance on me." He'd never cared that a woman held things back from him. He didn't need to know everything about them to spend time together, sleep with them, and part when the time came.

Roxy was different. He wished he understood why it was so damn important to have her trust when it had never really mattered with anyone else.

Roxy inhaled deeply and let out the breath in a whoosh. Resigned, she folded her arms around her waist in more of a hug than a defiant stance. Once the words were out, she wouldn't be able to take them back. Trust didn't come easy for her, but Big Mama's words came back to her.

Stop thinking with your head and open your heart.

"John met my mother in Las Vegas. He was there for a rodeo and to sell some horses. He met my mother in the hotel bar."

"I take it from what you've said, your mother looks like you." He swept his gaze over her curves.

Roxy laughed, but without any real mirth. "Yes. And no. We're about the same height and build, but she's blonde, blue-eyed, outgoing, and up for any kind of fun."

"You're reserved and shy."

"Usually, yes. I've had my moments, but I'm careful and cautious, because I know all too well what happens when you're reckless."

Noah folded his arms at his chest and eyed her. "Intriguing. Go on. John. Your mother. A bar," he coaxed.

She took another deep breath and pressed on. "They spent that night together and the next. He was out for some frivolous fun."

Unable to look Noah in the eye and spit out the rest, she stared at his chest. "My mother is all for encouraging excitement and pleasure to the nth degree. She likes to drink, do drugs, and party. She likes men who want to join her in her wicked pursuits, and who have the money to pay for it." The silence after she got those words out stretched and made her even more uneasy.

"She took a shine to John, an obviously wealthy rancher. They had a couple of good nights together. He went home to his ranch, and she went about her partying, until she found out about me. She slowed down during her pregnancy, but mind you, that's relative in her world."

She sneaked a peek at Noah's frowning face. He didn't approve. Who would? But this was only the beginning. He still didn't know the whole ugly truth.

"When she gave birth to a raven-haired, golden-eyed child, she couldn't have been more pleased. She knew I belonged to John, but because of her lifestyle couldn't be sure until I was born."

Noah either missed or dismissed the part about the question of her paternity. "How long before she let John know about you?"

"Candy didn't wait long."

"Candy?" Noah asked, surprised like everyone else that she called her mother by that name.

"My mother. She goes by Candy. Has since she moved to Vegas at sixteen, a runaway."

"Damn, that had to be a hard life for her."

Roxy liked that he had the compassion to think about poor, young Candy. "It didn't help her natural tendencies toward addiction and over-indulgence in all things."

"So that's what you've been hiding. Your mother is an alcoholic and addict."

Roxy gave a short laugh. "Candy would never call herself those things. She doesn't apologize for the things she does or see anything wrong with her life." She raked her fingers through her hair, wondering if Noah would hold on to his empathy once he knew the whole truth. "Candy wanted her golden ticket, so she told John I was his. You can't believe a word that comes out of Candy's mouth, so John came to see me."

"He wanted the DNA test."

"I suppose so. My mother said he took one look at me and smiled."

Noah stared off into space. "He told me right before he went into the hospital he wanted to have a child of his flesh and blood, his name, run this ranch. I think he was trying to tell me about you."

"Maybe." She couldn't be sure of John's motives. She shook off the melancholy threatening to swamp her and pressed on. "Anyway, John didn't want anyone to know about Candy, so he gave her what she wanted."

"A steady income," Noah finished for her.

Roxy picked at imaginary lint on her thigh. "You can't domesticate Candy. The steady income kept Candy in booze and drugs. My mother wasn't picky back then about her surroundings, so we lived in some rotten dives. More often than not, food was an afterthought. She liked to party, but never alone, so men came and went, oftentimes daily. With the ups and downs that came with her addictions, she could be volatile."

"She hit you." The anger in Noah's words touched her, but she didn't let it get to her. Too many times she'd gotten to this part of the story only to have someone turn on her when she finished telling the rest of the tale.

"On one of John's visits, he found me a little worse for wear. I was nine. They fought. John left. I only saw him a handful of times and spoke to him by phone a dozen more times after that. It made me angry and bitter. I hated him for leaving me with her."

Noah shook his head. "That's what doesn't make any sense. The man I knew would never turn his back on a child who needed him. If he knew you were being hurt and you were in danger, he'd have brought you home. I don't get it."

"He had a new wife and a baby on the way."

Noah raked his fingers through his hair. "Lisa and Annabelle."

"Candy didn't want to let me go and lose her monthly income. She pointed out that if he brought me home, he'd have to explain where I came from and why no one knew about me. John had told Candy about Lisa, and she knew there was no way in hell Lisa would accept me. Since I met Lisa, I can see she was right."

"So John left you with an abusive mother to avoid an argument with Lisa?"

"No. He left me so he didn't have to admit to being with Candy and getting her pregnant. He didn't want Lisa to know he slept with my mother when he visited."

Noah frowned even deeper.

"Candy made it clear that if John brought me here, she'd follow and the lifestyle she had in Vegas would come with her. He didn't have the courage to face the embarrassment and humiliation. He wanted to keep his marriage to Lisa together and give Annabelle the life he couldn't give me."

"But Annabelle wasn't his, and he and Lisa divorced."

"By then, John got my mother and me to a safe place, and he didn't want anyone to know where that was either. In my eyes, he chose the son he always wanted and a daughter he didn't have to explain."

Noah raked his fingers through his hair. "He did."

She acknowledged that with a simple nod, though it still hurt her heart. "Our relationship became very strained."

"So John moved you to the ranch where he sent you the horses?"

"Yes. My mother lived in the big house, and I lived in the cottage by the stables nearby."

Noah cocked his head. His eyes drew together with concern. "You lived alone."

"Trust me, it was better that way. I preferred it."

"Roxy, you were just a kid."

"I hadn't been just a kid in a long time. Taking care of my mother when she was at her lowest points throughout the years, I learned to take care of myself. I learned how not to be her."

There in the barn, he reached out and stroked his big hand down her hair. The sympathy in his eyes made her heart ache with a need to reach out to him and accept all he wanted to offer.

"I can't believe John kept this to himself." Anger dripped from every word. "I had no idea about you, what you were going through . . ."

She appreciated the sentiment laced with the same frustration she felt much of her life. "After his nasty divorce, he committed himself to raising you and Annabelle and giving you a good life on this ranch."

"And forgot about you?" Disdain filled Noah's words.

"He'd sneak onto the Ranch to see me once or twice a year. On my twelfth birthday, John sent me two horses. Until then, I was lonely. More than the horses, he gave me such a gift in them. I spent all my time with them when I wasn't in school. Over the years, he sent me more horses and I became quite good at training them. John continued to support Candy and me, though he sent us separate checks to ensure I got the money and could buy what I needed. He paid for me to go to college."

"So he supported you, but he barely saw you." Noah frowned in disgust.

"I didn't make things easy. Candy made his life a misery."

"Sounds like she did the same to you."

"She's very good at it," Roxy confirmed in a teasing tone, but Noah wouldn't be coaxed into lightening the mood.

"I can't imagine your life. It's so hard to believe the way you grew up, living alone since you were ten, relying only on yourself and a check from John."

"I had a few people looking out for me. John hired someone to help with the horses. I had my sisters."

"You have sisters? How many?"

"Three. Like you and Annabelle, we're not blood, but chosen. Sonya, Adria, and Juliana. Their mothers work with mine. They checked in with us a lot more than my mother ever did."

"If John never wanted anyone to know he'd been with your mother and had you, why did he make you come here now? Why did he insist you stay here and forbid you to leave for more than a few days a month?"

"I suppose because I've always been Candy's daughter and I don't care what anyone thinks about that, but John did. Enough that in life he couldn't bring himself to admit it and stand up to the scrutiny. Instead of facing the inevitable talk and some people's scorn, he took the coward's way out and left it to me to tell you."

"Tell me what?"

"The one detail I've held back." And she couldn't hold it inside any longer. She wanted to tell him. She wanted him to understand. She wanted him to not disappoint her with his judgment or turn his back on her. She wanted someone, him, to finally, truly not judge her and find her guilty for her mother's sins.

"John understood better than I did that I was wasting my life trying to save Candy's. I couldn't admit to myself, until John forced me to come here, that I can't save her. No one can. Because she doesn't want to be saved. She's Candy, and she's going to do what she's going to do whether I approve or try to stop her."

"Mary was right. He was taking you away from a destructive life and giving you a better one."

"Yes, though it took me a couple days to see that myself." She looked him in the eye and hoped to ease his mind about what John had done to him. "Noah, he gave me half the ranch because he felt like he owed me. Not the money he left, but the life I could have had if he'd fought for me."

"He didn't fight for you." His anger showed in every word he bit out.

She appreciated it. "And I was angry for a long time that he didn't. I was his true child and I wanted him to choose me." She hated it when that childish thought filled Noah's eyes with hurt. "It took time and perspective to learn that blood doesn't make you more or less someone's child or mean they love you more or less because of it, Noah. You and Annabelle are his kids just as much as I am."

"You said it yourself, we got to have him every day. But that's because he stayed away from you."

"Well, dealing with Candy is like beating your head against a brick wall. You'll only end up bloody and with a raging headache. He chose to leave me in a life that I knew, rather than make your lives harder. In addition to not wanting to put his marriage in jeopardy and change your lives, John was a respected father and a rancher with wealth and prestige amongst the people of this town and in the rodeo and horse business. Bringing me here would have tarnished his good name—and all of yours. He couldn't bring himself to do it."

"Why?" Noah asked, taking a step toward her.

"Because," she began, and stepped around him to grab the file filled with bills and checks. She turned back, faced him head-on, and looked him dead in the eyes. "My mother is a prostitute."

Speechless, his mouth dropped open. His eyes left her face, focused on her size 34 double Ds and down her slim waist, flared hips, and toned legs before his gaze came back up to her face. The look in his eyes tore her heart to shreds.

She pointed at his face. "That look right there, that says *that body would make a lot of money. I wonder how many men she's been with and how much she charges.*" Roxy tried to speak though her chest had tightened to the point she could barely breathe. "I tell you *she's* a prostitute and you forget everything I told you about how I grew up, went to college, and made my own life. You go right back to the way I look. You can't help but think it. Question it. Her mother is a hooker. With a body like that and how she was raised, she must be, too."

It had been a long time since she allowed herself to hurt like this, but she couldn't put her crumbled walls back together when the pain grew with every beat of her broken heart.

Stupid. She thought he was different.

"All the comments the ranch hands have made are running through your mind. The innuendos they've thrown around for days. Tom's doing, no doubt." She spoke her suspicions out loud. "He's the only one who knows about my mother, thanks to John's will and that damn envelope he left me. Vindictive bastard that he is, Tom's getting back at me for kneeing him in the nuts. See, he looked at me like you just did, assumed I'm my mother's daughter, and propositioned me. It's not the first time it's happened. I'm sure it won't be the last. If your men know, I'm sure rumors about me being a prostitute are working their way through the entire town. You better have a talk with Annabelle before it hits the high school."

She tamped down the tears clogging her throat and pricking her eyes.

"Now you know the big secret. John was too embarrassed and ashamed to admit he knocked up a hooker. He didn't bring me here because God forbid Candy followed through on her threat, moved here, and set up shop. She's ruined my whole life. Now she's ruined my chance for a fresh start."

"Is that why you told me about your childhood and your mother? Because you knew Tom shot off his mouth, everyone knows, and I'd find out?"

"You said you wanted to know me. I don't give a fuck what anyone thinks of me. I told you because I wanted *you* to know the truth. I hoped *you* would understand, and not look at me like you just did. My mistake. I was wrong. Again."

She turned and walked away, her heart bleeding, her mind denying what she'd seen in Noah's eyes even though she'd seen the truth. Now that he knew, he changed the way he looked at her, the way he saw her.

She'd hoped for a new start, but this was just the same shit different place.

It crushed her because with one kiss she'd thought they might have something worth opening her heart.

Now she knew better.

She'd never make that mistake again.

Chapter Twenty-Three

Roxy slammed the office door and fell into the chair behind the desk. Tears filled her eyes and silently trailed down her cheeks. She swiped them away, not wanting to cry because she stupidly thought Noah really cared about her. Enough that he'd listen and understand that what her mother did had nothing to do with her.

But she'd been wrong. Again.

She brushed another tear from her cheek and tried to breathe through the heavy pain in her chest.

For a minute, she'd thought she'd finally found someone who wanted to have a real and honest relationship. Someone who truly wanted to get to know *her*. Someone who saw her beauty and flaws, understood her, and didn't turn away but stuck by her side.

It hurt. And made her incredibly sad because she really liked Noah. She'd seen the way he loved Annabelle and wanted some of that for herself.

Her gaze landed on the white envelope with her name scrawled across it propped against the pen holder on the desk. She'd put off reading her father's note too long. There was nothing he could say that would make her feel worse than she did right now.

She picked it up, slid her finger underneath the flap and across the envelope, and pulled the letter out.

My beautiful girl, you are and will always be the most precious gift I was given. I wish we'd had more time.

This is long overdue, but I want you to know, I'm sorry.

I wanted to be the father you deserved and the man you needed. Because of who you are, your strength and perseverance, you turned out to be an amazing woman. I am so proud of you and all you've accomplished. With your kind, generous heart, I know you'll help Annabelle navigate her way into womanhood and she will be better for having you in her life. I was.

I hope you find peace, love, and joy on the ranch. I had those things to overflowing every time I was with you. I wish I could be with you now and every day.

Maybe if I'd followed my mother's advice I wouldn't have made so many mistakes in my life . . . or with you.

Live with purpose. Love with your whole heart. Treat others with kindness and grace. Forgive yourself and others.

Find someone who loves you as much as I loved you, sweet girl, where every second without you is a misery and every moment with you is a memory that brings a smile.

If you have that, you have everything that matters.

Though I wish I'd been with you every day, I was always watching over you. Even now, I'm with you.

I love you,
Dad

The words blurred as a torrent of tears spilled down her cheeks. She cried out her grief and broken heart. As alone as she'd ever been, she felt her father's presence and a soft whisper that everything would be all right if she followed his advice and found a little grace and forgave Noah his reaction to her news and didn't give up so easily on something she wanted so badly.

Chapter Twenty-Four

gain? That one word and all it implied haunted Noah for three long days. He'd thought of nothing else but their conversation in the barn and that one word she said before walking out without a backward glance.

The look in her eyes; so much pain. A lifetime of people turning their backs and disappointing her. And she'd added him to the list.

After the moment they shared, that kiss that rocked his world, he'd wanted to get to know her. He'd wanted her to want to open up to him. For a brief time, he had her complete trust. But the second she told him the truth about what her mother did for a living and he'd looked at her like she was a prostitute, too, his betrayal shut out any hope she'd ever let him in again.

Three days and she still refused to be in his presence or even speak to him.

It ate at him day and night. His rampant thoughts kept him working like a demon to tire his body and mind so he could put her out of his every thought and dream, but nothing worked.

Tired of his own company and the quiet in the stable's office, he headed out, hoping to catch Roxy before dinner.

He walked down the breezeway and gave up all hope of getting to the house without getting even more pissed off.

It only took a day for his men to stop making rude remarks and comments within his earshot. All except the one with his back to Noah, his hands hanging over a stall door as he talked to one of the other ranch hands.

Harry. "She'll be headed to the practice ring soon. And after . . . I'd like to strip her bare, bend her over one of the saddles in the tack room, fill my hands with those big titties"—he held his hands up like claws— "and fuck her until she screams. I wonder what that will cost me?"

"Your fucking life." Noah went blind with rage, ran to Harry, and shoved him away from the gate and onto his ass. Noah tried to go after him, but Robby came out of nowhere and held him back.

Robby gripped his shirt in both hands and shook him. "Get it together." Robby leaned in close and whispered, "He's young and stupid and shooting off his big mouth. You beat the hell out of him, you'll only make matters worse and end up in jail."

If Robby hadn't stopped him, Noah would have killed Harry in a blind rage. He still didn't have his head on straight. The urge to go after him still simmered in his blood, but Harry ran for it when Robby intervened.

Noah needed some space and time to cool down, too, before he addressed the rampant rumors and talk among his men and put a stop to it once and for all.

He hated that everyone believed a lie. None of them cared to ask her the truth. They all just took one look at her and assumed it had to be true.

She'd tried her whole life to make people see her without looking through the lens of her mother's life but never had, it seemed, which made her wary of everyone.

No wonder she was so guarded, so isolated and alone.

He saw that now.

The last few days she'd locked herself away in John's office and never joined them for dinner.

She worked late every night, woke early every morning to see Annabelle off to school, then she closeted herself away in the office until he came in for dinner and she sneaked out to work with Houdini, the name everyone on the ranch now called the fence-jumping-escape-artist horse.

All so she didn't have to see him.

Noah forced himself to relax. Robby released him and Noah walked out of the stables without another word. He walked up to the house and entered through the dining room French doors just as the front door banged shut. "There she goes." His stomach tied into knots and his heart sank.

She went out of her way to avoid him, and it pained him something fierce. In hurting her, he'd hurt himself.

Robby saddled Houdini every night, left him tied in the covered practice ring, a dozen jumps set up, and came up to the house to have dinner with the family. That's why he'd been in the stables minutes ago and stopped Noah from doing something stupid. Like put his fist through Harry's smart mouth.

True to her word, Roxy trained Houdini to be a world-class jumper. The men watched, but from all the grumbling he overheard, she never spoke to any of them, but concentrated on her work. Robby said Houdini was coming along. He'd only escaped one other time from his corral, and that time he'd run to Roxy as she walked back from the practice ring.

"Noah, dinner's almost ready," Mary called from behind him.

He stood in the newly decorated living room. The bright, cheerful yellow walls contrasted with his dark mood. He found himself sprawled on the new, comfortable tan sofa last night watching the game on the new flat screen above the fireplace, because Annabelle had commandeered the TV in the family room to watch some teen vampire series. Really, he'd hoped to catch Roxy coming out of the office, so he could talk to her. He fell asleep on the sofa long before she came out. He did wake up with a blanket draped over him and knew she'd put it there before going off to her room sometime in the early morning hours.

He watched Roxy through the window cross the yard and head for the practice ring. "I'll be there in a minute," he called to Mary, never taking his eyes off Roxy. He only got this short glimpse of her each night and didn't want to shorten what little time he had to look at her.

Mary came up behind him. "People are talking, Noah. I was in town, doing the shopping, and several people stopped me to ask about her."

Noah turned then, glaring. "Did they come right out and ask if she's a whore?"

Mary gasped at his blunt question. "No. That wouldn't be civilized."

"But talking behind her back, spreading rumors, and telling lies is okay?"

"Did she talk to you? Did she tell you about all this before the rumors started?"

Noah sighed, glanced one last time out the window, disappointed she was already out of sight, then faced Mary again.

"I spoke to her on Monday evening, not knowing the rumors had already started."

"She was trying to head you off," Mary guessed.

"I thought that when the rumors ramped up these last few days, but no. I wanted to get to know her. At first, she avoided my questions, so I pushed."

"I've seen the way you look at her." Mary had a certain gleam in her eye. "And the way she looks at you when you're not looking. The two of you could set the house on fire."

"I don't think you'll have to worry about that. She won't even be in the same room with me anymore."

"Why? What happened?"

"She trusted me enough to tell me about her life with her mother and I let her down."

"Come now, it can't be all that bad."

"Her mother is an alcoholic and an addict who used to hit her. If that's not bad enough, imagine her life with her mother spending the checks John sent on drugs instead of using it for, oh, I don't know, food and rent. Roxy spent her childhood taking care of her mother, because she was in no shape to take care of herself most of the time." He raked his fingers over his head, thinking of the hell that kind of life must have been for her. "But Annabelle and I lived our happy lives here because John turned his back on her. He didn't want us or anyone else to know he'd paid for sex and knocked up a prostitute. But don't worry, Roxy completely understands John didn't want the scandal to touch his young children or ruin his marriage to Lisa."

Mary gasped, but that didn't stop the words from falling from his mouth.

"Roxy was used to that life, so he just moved her and her mother to some ranch and left Roxy there to fend for herself, ten years old, alone in some cottage. Well, she has three sisters—friends really, but they lived together as sisters."

"Where were their mothers?" Mary asked.

He shrugged, still unable to process how Roxy managed on her own. "Maybe the other girls' mothers were around. Roxy didn't say much about them. Candy lived in another house, away from Roxy, which apparently suited both of them just fine. At that point, John sent one check to her mother and another to Roxy to ensure Roxy's safety and make sure Roxy had the money she needed to live on." Noah planted his hands on his hips, hung his head, and sighed.

"That poor girl. What it must do to her to know her father sacrificed her for both of you and the ranch."

"He took the easy way out, and it pisses me off. I can only imagine the hurt and anger she's suffered. She says she's come to terms with it. Maybe, but I think it will always be there. Still, John left her in that tumultuous life with Candy."

At Mary's raised brow, Noah explained, "Her mother. I want to kill that bitch for everything she's done to Roxy. If John was still alive, I'd have a hard time looking him in the eye and not kicking his ass. He hurt her and gave us everything. Then I hurt her with just a look." The punch to the heart hit him again when he remembered the pain in her eyes. "She told me about her life, confided in me why John brought her here, and I did the one thing everyone does when they find out what her mother is. I looked at Roxy and thought she'd make one damn fine hooker and imagined men would line up for a chance to be with her."

From the sound of things in the stables, Harry wanted first dibs.

Over his dead body.

"Noah, you didn't."

"Isn't it funny? Before I knew what her mother is, I thought of Roxy as strong, independent, someone willing to do for others without asking anything for herself. Brave—she didn't blink when it came to moving here, or standing up to Lisa for Annabelle." He hung his head. "None of it mattered. As soon as she said her mother is a hooker, I looked at her and all I could think was that she'd make a million bucks with that body."

"Noah, don't do this to yourself. You might have thought that for a moment, but then . . ."

"That's just it. There is no *but then*. Not in her experience. It changes the way you look at her always. She warned me, but trusted I'd be different, that I'd remember the moment we shared minutes before she told me everything. I couldn't see her through the murkiness of her mother's life. Not Roxy's life. Her mother's." He slammed the side of his fist into his thigh. "Damnit, who cares who her mother is and what she's done? That isn't who Roxy is."

Mary put her hand on his arm, but he drew away, not wanting to be touched or consoled for his bad behavior.

"It was a natural reaction. One you couldn't control. You barely knew her before all this happened."

Didn't matter. Everything he actually did know about her never led him to believe *that* about her, but the thoughts still crept in and ruined everything.

"She never used her body to manipulate me. She never came on to me to stop my anger or bitter remarks about her getting half the ranch. She never flirted with me or any of the other men. She never made suggestive remarks, or flaunted herself in any way. She conducted herself with manners and a directness I admired, because she never complained or whined or made the argument worse." She wasn't like any other woman he knew. "When I kissed her, I felt her shyness and the momentary tentativeness that gave way to her settling into me. Not calculation. Not coyness. A real and true reaction to being close to me, a man. Something that was obviously new, or at least not habit.

"Robby told me that sleeping with a woman doesn't mean you know her. If I wanted to know the real woman, I'd have to get to know her. He was right and wrong. Having her in my arms, I discovered something very precious about her. Talking to her, I learned the truth, but still believed what I projected onto her."

"You're being too hard on yourself. Talk to her again. Straighten this out. She'll listen."

"Why would she? I showed her who I am, someone who hears the truth, but only sees what everyone else sees when they look at her."

"That's not true and you know it. Maybe you wondered for a second if she was like her mother, but that thought never took root and you remembered who she is and why she's here."

Noah turned and stared out the window again. "That second of doubt will haunt me the rest of my days. It is the single biggest regret of my life. I'll never top that one second. God help me if I do."

"You will regret it even more if you don't even try to fix things. If you care this deeply for her, it's worth fixing. Don't waste a chance at happiness because of a misunderstanding."

Noah shifted, folded his arms over his chest, and glanced at Mary. "It's more than a misunderstanding. I lost her trust, something she doesn't give lightly or at all. I asked her to open up to me, and I let everything she said be overshadowed by my own stupid thoughts."

"You'll just have to convince her that you don't think she's like her mother."

"Telling her that isn't going to change anything when my actions showed her otherwise."

"Then action is called for to change her mind," Mary suggested.

It took him a minute to understand what she meant. "I don't think seducing her is going to prove I don't think she's a whore."

"Not alone it's not. But putting action and words together might. Have you asked yourself why it matters so much to you that you have her trust, that she opens up to you, that she thinks well of you? When you admit your true feelings to yourself, you'll find a way to make this right."

He ached with every passing second she refused to be in his presence. If he didn't fix things with her, earn back her trust, and get his hands on her again, he'd spend the rest of his life in pain and misery.

Was it love to feel this torn up inside over hurting someone?

Probably. But how would he know for sure unless she gave him a chance to figure it out?

He no longer cared about his share and her share and how things were divided.

"I just want to make things right," he said to himself.

Mary heard and spoke her mind as usual. "Can't do that when you're in here and she's out there. Talk to her."

"I will. Later." He didn't want to go down to the practice ring and confront her in front of all the ranch workers who lingered to watch her ride. He wanted to do it when it was just the two of them. Alone.

Not used to groveling, he wanted privacy when he crawled, and begged, if necessary.

"You need to speak with Annabelle, Noah, before someone says something to her."

"I've put it off, but I can't wait any longer. I'll go up and speak to her before dinner."

He tried to move past Mary, but she grabbed his arm and stopped him. "I hope you work things out with Roxy. Just keep in mind, though Whitefall has grown over the years, it still has a small-town mentality. John's memory will be tarnished. Some people will only remember that John slept with a prostitute, had a child with her, and estranged himself from his daughter to keep his secret. Until people learn the truth about Roxy, people will shun her for who they think she is and that will reflect on you because they think you're allowing someone like that to live here."

"I lost two sales today. A horse and a shipment of alfalfa." It infuriated him to listen to his longtime alfalfa and hay buyer explain that he no longer wanted to do business with *that woman* John had left in charge and that Noah should do everything possible to get control of the ranch back as soon as possible. It was amoral to have someone like her living with good people.

"Because of Roxy."

"Because people are stupid and judgmental. I know the man John was and the woman Roxy is. Annabelle does, too. John brought Roxy here to give her a better life, the one she should have had instead of us. I'll never forget that he sacrificed her happiness for me and Annabelle." The guilt settled heavy in his heart. "I swore I'd take care of her. I won't break that promise to John, no matter how hard she makes it."

"Show her that your father raised you to be a better man than he could be for her."

Noah appreciated the sentiment but wasn't feeling like the man Roxy needed at the moment. But he'd find the courage and the words to apologize and see Roxy through this difficult time.

He left Mary in the living room and trudged up the stairs wondering how he was going to tell Annabelle that Roxy's mother was a prostitute and everyone in town and on this ranch thought Roxy was, too.

How the hell am I going to explain this to a fifteen-year-old without getting into a discussion about sex?

Chapter Twenty-Five

N oah knocked on Annabelle's bedroom door, but thanks to the ear-splitting country music coming from inside, she didn't hear him. He pounded twice with his fist and opened the door just as the music went silent.

"Hi, Noah. Dinner ready?"

He stood in the doorway unable to move. Since the redecorating last Sunday, he hadn't been in Annabelle's room. Spellbound, he stared at the transformation Roxy had completed from Annabelle's bubble-gum-pink palace into a young woman's retreat.

"Sprite, your room . . ."

"Is awesome," she finished for him. "I've been begging you to come see it, but you're always busy. Isn't it the best?"

"Totally." He used one of her favorite terms. "I really can't believe it."

"Don't you love the wall color? During the day, it looks light blue, but in the evening when the light is dim, the walls turn this soft pale green. The new drapes are so pretty. Simple. No frills," she added, making him remember the ruffles.

The gauzy white drapes allowed the lavender shades behind them to show through. The bed was covered in a white spread with a green vine weaving across it with little purple flowers. White pillows stood against the solid pine headboard and a pale green blanket draped over the end. Beneath the bed, a thick purple area rug covered a good portion of the hardwood floor.

"Please tell me she burned the Pepto pink shag carpet," Noah said with a smile.

"I seriously think she wanted to. What do you think of the study area she set up for me?"

In one corner of the room beneath a large window facing the front of the house, Roxy had placed a large round pale green area rug. A white slip-covered chair sat in the corner, a floor lamp with a lavender tulip-shaped shade next to it. Her pine desk was next to the chair, her laptop open, bubbles bouncing across the screen.

"It's great, Sprite."

"She's so amazing. I described the kind of room I wanted and she did it. It's everything I wanted and more. I come in here and I feel so grown-up. Jamie and Kendra are coming over this weekend to see."

At the mention of her friends, Noah knew he couldn't put off their talk any longer. Soon, she'd hear the rumors.

"Listen, Sprite, we need to talk."

"What happened between you and Roxy? She won't even eat dinner with us."

Time to admit the truth and have that talk. "I did something I'm not proud of when I found out about her past."

"Did you see her room?" Annabelle often changed the subject when she didn't want to hear something unpleasant. Usually, it had to do with her mother.

"No. I haven't."

"It's even better than I expected. She didn't buy much for herself, but when she added it to what Dad already had in his room, it's like a hotel suite."

"I'm sure it's great, but we need to talk about Roxy." He tried to move them back on track and not think about Roxy's bed and whether she slept nude or in some skimpy outfit.

"She's out riding. Come see. You'll love it."

Before he could refuse, she grabbed his hand and dragged him down the hall.

"Sprite, we really shouldn't be in her room without being invited."

Annabelle stopped in her tracks and looked back at him with a wide grin on her face. Nope. No hope of having a conversation about Roxy without having one about sex. That devilish smile said so much without her saying a word.

"This is Roxy's private space." He refused to acknowledge her smirk.

"She'll never know we were here."

Annabelle pushed the door open wide and they stood in the doorway, looking in at Roxy's bed. Noah stood stunned. The room hadn't changed all that much. The same deep blue drapes hung at the windows, crystal lamps on the side tables illuminated the new white spread and pillows with a deep blue blanket draped over the end of the bed. None of that held his attention. The dark green throw that belonged to his mother lay pooled in the middle of the bed. The same blanket he'd spread over her the first night she stayed at the house.

If he could believe his eyes, she'd been sleeping with his blanket every night since.

"Whatever you said, I don't think she's as mad as you think." Annabelle's soft voice and words eased his heart and sparked a glimmer of hope. "I think she's sad."

Me, too, without her.

"I did something stupid and hurt her feelings."

"I wasn't sure I wanted her here," Annabelle began, "but the last few days have been really great. Not only did she fix my room, but she wakes me up every morning when I know she's barely gone to bed herself. She helps me pick outfits and do my hair. She gives me tips on my makeup to make it look sophisticated, but not overdone. She listens when I talk to her. The best thing is every morning she walks me to the door and tells me to have a good day. Every afternoon, she comes out of the office when I arrive home and asks me if I had a good day. You and Dad were always here, and I love you both for everything you did for me. With her, it's different. She makes me feel like I matter."

Noah stared down at her. "Honey, you matter to me. More than anything."

"I know. It's just, she's different. I've never had anyone around who's close to my age and knows about makeup and hair and decorating and talks to me about boys without making it into a lecture. She helps me with my homework and tells me to brush my teeth before bed. She took away my soda yesterday and handed me a bottle of water and an apple and told me to eat better."

"She's the mother you never had." Noah finally understood what Annabelle was getting at.

"Mary has been great, but Roxy understands me without my having to say very much. She gets how I feel about my mom."

"Has she told you about her mother?" He hoped Roxy had already explained and saved him from an awkward conversation.

"Not really, just little things about how her mother is selfish and always put Roxy last, if she remembered her at all." The compassionate look in Annabelle's eyes said she understood that last horrible part all too well.

"She's been on her own a long time, since she was ten. Before that, she was more the caretaker for her mother than the other way around. After, she lived without her mother in a cottage on a ranch John bought her. He wanted her to have a safe place to live with her horses."

"Why didn't he bring her here to live with us?"

Noah sighed and ran a hand through his already-disheveled hair. Stalling, he scraped his palm over his rough jaw and realized he hadn't shaved in two days. He remembered the way Roxy's eyes devoured him when he'd done the same thing days ago.

Now she couldn't even look at him.

"It's complicated," Noah responded to her question, unsure how to start this conversation. Annabelle obviously held Roxy in high regard. He didn't want to tarnish her perception in any way. Not when Roxy had done nothing to warrant it.

He didn't want Annabelle to feel the way he did: guilty as hell that John kept them and turned his back on Roxy, then ordered Roxy to stay here and raise Annabelle because—now he could see it—Annabelle needed Roxy.

"It's complicated. Code for something you think I'm too young to understand. Noah, I'm fifteen, not five."

"I realize that." He chucked her under the chin and she smiled.

"Whatever it is, just tell me."

"Rumors are circulating around the ranch and town about Roxy. Rumors about her mother and how Roxy was raised."

"I'm not surprised." Annabelle made him think she'd already heard something. "Small towns. Everyone has to know everyone else's business. She's new, so everyone is interested. Nothing ever stays a secret in this town."

"Well, Tom said something about Roxy he learned from John's will."

"You mean from that envelope John left Roxy. I've wondered about it. She shut me down and said it was none of my business."

"Stop being nosy," he admonished. "Tom used that information and started a rumor."

"Now it's gone viral," Annabelle guessed. "Something small turned into something big." Noah winced and frowned, prompting Annabelle to add, "I'm in high school. I know how rumors work." She rolled her eyes expressively and he almost laughed, but this wasn't funny.

"The thing is, no one should have found out about this."

"You should fire Tom. He's our lawyer, and whatever information he leaked is privileged."

Startled, Noah agreed. Annabelle understood things very well.

At his surprise, Annabelle remarked, "I'm young, not stupid."

"I never thought you were, Sprite. I'm not explaining this very well," he admitted.

"Noah. Annabelle. Dinner is ready," Mary called up the stairs.

"We'll be right down," Annabelle answered. "I get it. Someone said something about Roxy that's not true. It's all over town. Like all rumors, I shouldn't believe it just because someone says it. The important thing here is that you need to fix things with Roxy. Whatever you did, she clearly wishes things between you two were better."

Noah followed her gaze to the blanket on the bed.

"It's complicated." He didn't know how to explain his feelings for Roxy. They were supposed to be Annabelle's guardians, her role models. If things between him and Roxy didn't work out, it could make things hard for all of them going forward. The last few days had been really rough on him.

"You know what I like about Roxy? She doesn't answer with lame excuses like it's complicated. She speaks her mind, tells the truth, and lays it out there no matter what anyone else thinks. So, here's what I think, Noah. It's not complicated. You did something wrong. Apologize. As for the rumor, I'm starting to think people in this town need something better to do with their time."

"That's for damn sure," Noah responded. "About Roxy and me . . ."

Annabelle put her hand on his shoulder and looked him in the eyes. "I think the two of you would make a great couple. I've never seen you look at anyone the way you look at her." Romanticizing things, like only a teenage girl can do, she added, "She's the one, Noah."

"How do you know?" he asked, unsure himself.

"It's in the air when you two are in the same room. It's the look on your face when you see her, even if you're only watching her out the window."

"You've seen me watching her?"

"It's sweet, actually. Apologize."

"It may not be enough." That truth ate away at him. It immobilized him because he wanted to find the perfect way to do it.

"Doing nothing gets you nothing."

Wise words from his surprisingly sage sister.

"Flowers might be nice. She likes flowers."

He'd never been one to do the whole flowers and gifts thing with women. Funny, he didn't mind the thought of doing it for Roxy. Maybe the fact that he wanted to please her really did mean she was the one.

"I'm starving. Let's eat." Annabelle dashed down the stairs with all the exuberance of a teen.

He wished he had her energy. The last few days brooding over Roxy and working himself to exhaustion hadn't done a damn bit of good. All it did was make him irritable and brought him no closer to fixing things with Roxy.

He tromped down the stairs, realizing he hadn't told Annabelle about Roxy and the rumors. She had a good head on her shoulders and understood the difference between rumor and reality. Still, this could really tarnish her relationship with Roxy.

He held back telling Annabelle for that very reason. He didn't want to hurt Roxy by telling Annabelle and having her look at Roxy differently.

He entered the dining room and Mary gave him a questioning look, silently asking if he'd told Annabelle. He shook his head no, making her frown.

If he put it off much longer, he risked Annabelle actually believing the rumors, despite her grown-up attitude about them.

Chapter Twenty-Six

Noah knocked off early to catch Annabelle where the school bus dropped her at the end of the long drive. He needed to finish their talk. After, he planned to hunt down Roxy and invite her to go for a ride, so they could be alone and he could apologize, and grovel if necessary.

Robby caught him by the barn doors. "Looks like Roxy's guests just arrived."

"Guests?"

"Mary said Roxy got a call this morning telling her some friends were coming. She asked me to get four stalls ready."

Noah looked up at the drive and noted the long horse trailer behind a huge silver truck heading for the house. A sign on the trailer caught his eye. Roses entwined in a vine with gold script over it. Wild Rose Ranch.

"Fuck me." Noah's anger flared.

She'd told him the truth, but not all of it. She'd left out some very important details. If the rumor about her wasn't bad enough, having *this* trailer with *that* name on it drive through town and onto his ranch would certainly stir things up.

Every ranch hand on the place had seen that name at one rodeo or another in the West.

By the end of the day, no one in town or on this ranch would believe Roxy an innocent.

"I thought I'd seen that girl before," Robby commented.

"What?" Noah didn't understand Robby's calm demeanor when all hell was about to break loose.

"She's a champion barrel racer. She's won more championships than any other woman on the circuit. I think she holds several records."

"Who the hell are you talking about?"

"Roxy. That's why John always insisted we watch the barrel racing competitions. He was watching his daughter ride. And win."

Noah let loose a string of curses. "Do you think she knows?"

"That John watched her ride? I'd think so. At the very least she'd know Speckled Horse Ranch attended the rodeos. Seems she avoided John as much as he avoided her. They probably had an unspoken rule about no one knowing about their relationship. Sad really," Robby remarked.

When he first saw Roxy, he could have sworn he'd seen her somewhere. Now he put the past together into a picture he didn't like at all. He remembered seeing her with some other women from the Wild Rose Ranch. Her hair was always braided down her back and she wore a black cowboy hat. They all did.

Black, the color for outlaws and outsiders. Roxy had probably felt that way her whole life, despite never doing anything to merit the title.

The shock from finding out she came from that particular ranch wore off quickly when he started thinking it wasn't that far-fetched after what she'd told him about her mother. It did shine a whole new light on her childhood. Not only had she grown up alone, she'd grown up at one of the most notorious and high-priced brothels in Nevada.

"No one is going to believe she isn't a prostitute now." Robby spoke Noah's worst fear aloud.

"I don't think she cares. She's fought it her whole life. It wouldn't matter if she screamed it at the top of her lungs, or put up a billboard in the middle of town. People will look at her, know about her mother, and assume the worst. The thing is, I finally understand how frustrating it must be for her to be one thing and have everyone think you're something else. The minute I saw the name on that trailer, I forgot all about how many times I saw those girls win and only remembered that all of them, except Roxy, were hookers. I'm guilty of doing what everyone else does to her," he admitted.

"The difference is, you know the kind of woman she is," Robby reminded him. "Go say hello to your guests."

"She's still not speaking to me."

"She can't when you're avoiding her as much as she's avoiding you." Robby watched him, but Noah still hesitated, giving himself a minute to think about what he needed to say. "Annabelle will be home any minute. One look at that trailer and she'll have questions."

Nothing could have gotten him moving faster. He hesitated halfway up to the drive when Roxy ran and threw herself into a man's arms. He lifted her off her feet and spun her around, making Roxy laugh and smile like he'd never seen her do. Ever. His gut went tight and his eyes narrowed on the tall man holding on to *his* woman. Within a few more strides, he recognized the man, someone he hadn't seen in years.

"Joe." Noah stepped forward to greet their old ranch hand, who'd left years ago.

Joe released Roxy and came forward, his hand out to shake. "Noah. You've grown. Not such a gangly kid anymore," the older man commented. Joe had at least ten years on him, but they'd been friends when Joe worked for John. Apparently, he'd been working for John all along, just on another ranch.

"Good to see you, man. I see you've been taking care of Roxy for John."

"Always," he answered with a wink to Roxy.

Roxy didn't say a word, but skirted the two men and went to the passenger door of the truck. Sonya stepped out and engulfed her in a hug.

"You came." Roxy held tight to her sister, needing Sonya when she felt so alone in this new place.

"I came to check out your new place." The look in Sonya's eyes told her she came to check out Noah, too. "Joe told me he was bringing your babies, so I hitched a ride."

"You know, I didn't believe the vile rumors, but it's true. You're a hooker." Annabelle waved her hand to the Wild Rose insignia.

Sonya's sweet face turned red with anger. She glared over Roxy's shoulder at the young girl behind them.

Roxy's heart hurt, hearing those words come out of Annabelle's mouth.

Roxy turned to face Annabelle and her accusations head-on, but Sonya spoke first.

"Honey, you don't know what you're talking about. She may own the place, but she's no whore."

Roxy heard Noah swear from somewhere off to her side. Sonya turned to her with an apologetic frown when she realized what she'd said, thinking to make things better, but making them worse.

"Annabelle, I'd like to introduce one of my sisters. This is Sonya. Like you and Noah, we're not blood, but we grew up together." Roxy pointed to her friend. "Joe works at the ranch with me, taking care of the horses. Before that, he worked for your father."

A fact that she hadn't really put together until Noah and Joe shook hands, exchanging a few words of remembrance about John.

Annabelle's fury wasn't quite spent, the distraction of introductions didn't deter her for long. "Don't you have anything to say? Aren't you even going to deny it? You can't, can you?" Anger and hurt made her words tremble.

"Annabelle Marie, that's enough," Noah scolded.

"I've got this, Noah." Roxy didn't look at him. She couldn't. She didn't want to see the same indictment Annabelle made in his eyes.

"First of all, young lady, you demanded an answer to a question you never asked. Remember what I told you the night we met and I promised I'd be your guardian? I told you when you did well, I'd back you up. Screw up, and I'll be all over you. Well, honey, this is a major fuckup in my book. You'll hand over your cell phone until the end of the month. You want to take a rumor and accuse people without substantiating the story, you'll pay for it by not having the means to gossip with your friends."

Annabelle sucked in a breath and turned to Noah for support.

He came forward to stand beside Roxy, surprising her by his show of solidarity.

"You heard her." He held out his hand for the phone.

Annabelle huffed out a breath, dug through her purse, and slapped the phone into Noah's hand.

"You want to be treated like an adult," Roxy went on, "I expect you to act like one. You want to know something about me, ask a question. This 'hooker'"—she made air quotes to prove her point—"spent the last week redecorating your room, spending time with you, helping you with your homework, was nothing but a friend to you, and this is how you return the kindness. You're better than this, Annabelle. I expect better of you, the one person I've spent more time with than anyone."

"She said you own the Wild Rose Ranch."

"Is that a question?" Roxy raised an eyebrow, waiting.

Annabelle huffed again in frustration, but asked, "Do you own it?"

"Yes. Unbeknownst to me, John bought into the business years ago and he left it to me when he died."

"Are you, or have you ever been, a prostitute?" Annabelle's voice shook. It wasn't easy for her to ask. She obviously didn't want to hear an affirmative answer.

Roxy liked her more for having the guts to ask the hard questions. "No. Never." With a sigh, Roxy added, "I've told you a little about my mother. What I never said is that she's an alcoholic, drug addict, and yes, a prostitute. When you look like me and people find out about her, they automatically assume I'm one, too, because I was raised in that life, so I must be part of that world."

"Roxy had it rougher than me and Adria and Juliana. She looks the part."

Roxy couldn't argue the point. In jeans and a pink top, Sonya wore her dark hair pulled back in a ponytail, her dark lashes outlining hazel eyes, deep red lips accentuating her perfect pale skin. Her figure was lithe with soft curves, nothing like Roxy's sexy figure. Sonya was the epitome of the fresh-faced, yoga-loving, twenty-somethings you saw in commercials and sitcoms.

"At least, that's what some people think." With that little gem hanging in the air, Sonya locked eyes with Noah, letting him know she'd heard about their talk in the barn.

Noah sighed and looked away, but not before Roxy caught the shame in his eyes.

Sonya wasn't done yet. "Annabelle, Roxy doesn't have anything to do with the Ranch. She lives a quiet life away from the mansion with her horses and her work. She's a good and decent person, who's been saddled with a mother who's selfish and hateful to the core. Her mother is everything Roxy could never be. It's just not in her."

Roxy reached out and tugged Sonya's ponytail. "Thank you for that, sister." She turned to Annabelle. "What Sonya and I are trying to tell you is that you can't judge someone based on what you think you know. I own the business. A legal business."

"She's not doing anything wrong, and anyone who says otherwise doesn't know her. She'd never hurt someone, or use them for her own gain," Sonya continued.

"Annabelle, you will not announce to anyone that I own the Wild Rose Ranch. You will not discuss me, my mother, or anything I tell you in confidence. You will not confirm or deny rumors, or be drawn into adding to those rumors. Open your mouth and I'll ground you for a month. Feed information to the masses and you'll not get your driver's license until you're eighteen. Have I made myself clear?" Roxy asked.

Annabelle's eyes filled with tears. They slipped past her lashes in rivulets down her cheeks.

Roxy waited to see if they were because of the threat of not getting her license, because Roxy was being mean, or from genuine remorse for her behavior. Roxy didn't like being so tough on Annabelle, but she needed to learn that gossip wasn't always harmless. Sometimes it hurt and had real consequences.

"I'm sorry, Roxy." Annabelle's lips trembled. "You've been nothing but nice to me since you got here. Noah tried to talk to me last night about a rumor circulating about you. I told him I'd never believe a rumor, and he never got the chance to explain. Everyone was talking at school. I saw the name on the trailer and I thought . . . I'm sorry. Please don't leave," she wailed, and covered her face with her hands.

Roxy went to her then and took her into her arms and held her close. "I'm not going anywhere, sweetie." Roxy hugged her harder. "It's okay. You were shocked and it took a minute for things to become clear again." She turned her head to look at Noah for the first time in days, letting him know her words were meant for him, too. The truth was, she'd realized she'd overreacted to his response when he found out about her mother. She should have expected the look and the thoughts and known Noah would come to the right conclusion. Apparently, he had. She couldn't avoid him, or this situation, forever.

Roxy gave Annabelle a squeeze and let her go, turning to Sonya. "Let's get my babies out."

"Show Annabelle your tricks. She'll get a kick out of them."

Roxy reached out and brushed her hand down Annabelle's arm. "Want to see Vinny dance?"

Still trying to rein in her emotions, Annabelle could only nod yes.

"Okay, let's see if he wants to play. He might be a little cranky after being cooped up in the trailer, so no promises." Roxy turned to see Joe, Noah, and Sonya following her to the back of the trailer. Joe opened the gates.

Noah whistled softly. "I remember him. He was a pain in the ass. Refused to do anything."

"Until Roxy got a hold of him," Joe commented, and backed Vinny out of the trailer.

Vinny saw her and stomped and neighed, happy to see her.

"Hello, my man." Roxy rubbed her hands up and down his big head, reaching up to scratch behind his ears. She took Vinny's lead rope and walked down the drive a ways so she could do some tricks while Joe unloaded the other three horses.

"Ready?" she asked Vinny and Annabelle. Vinny responded by nodding his big head up and down.

"Get the spider," Roxy coaxed.

Vinny stomped his front hoof down on the imaginary spider and dragged his hoof back, squashing the nonexistent bug.

"Give me a kiss." Vinny responded by nuzzling her offered cheek, tickling her, and making her laugh.

"Big scary monster," she said, and raised her arms and made a face to scare Vinny.

He reared and kicked his front hooves in the air to ward off the monster.

Annabelle smiled for the first time since she arrived home.

Vinny landed back on all fours and neighed, shaking his big head at her.

"I'm not playing anymore if you're going to whine," she teased Vinny, and walked away, swaying her hips in an exaggerated manner. Vinny walked behind her, his head moving back and forth as he watched her ass sway. She stopped and he shoved his nose into her bottom and pushed, sending her stumbling forward a few steps.

Noah laughed along with Annabelle. He loved her playfulness with the horse. Noah saw her in a whole new light, and he realized how much he still didn't know about her.

"Dance," Sonya called out.

Roxy turned and dipped into a deep curtsy. Vinny leaned his big body back, front legs outstretched, and lowered his head into a bow.

"She's amazing," Annabelle commented, hiccuping from her recent tears.

"I should have warned you last night," he whispered.

"She had every right to be mad at me. I'm just glad she wants to stay."

"Me, too. Talk to her like that again, and I'll ground you for a month," he advised.

"I'm sorry, Noah."

"I know you are. So does she. I have my own making up to do with her."

"Hey, Joe, how about a leg up?" Roxy called.

Noah handed the lead rope of the mare he'd taken out of the trailer to Joe and stepped forward to help Roxy up onto Vinny's back. He stood close and cupped his hands. Without a word, she gave him her foot and he boosted her up.

"Stand back," she advised.

He stepped away, wanting to say so much and still not knowing how to even start.

Roxy coaxed Vinny into a series of complicated steps and trots, making it appear that the horse was dancing. It took a lot of time and training to teach a horse to make those complicated moves. Roxy made it look easy. And she did it riding bareback.

Joe stood beside him, watching Roxy dance across the drive, cheered on by Sonya and Annabelle.

"Took her forever to get that horse to cooperate. Now he'll do anything she says."

"Who taught her how to train horses?"

"I taught her the barrel racing and roping. Jumping and dressage, she learned from visiting a few trainers and reading up on the subject. She's not real keen on dressage. She's only taught Vinny and another horse she sold to a young girl just starting out. Now, the jumpers. She's one of the best with them. She's got a keen eye for knowing if a horse will take to the jumps."

"She's already found one here. Houdini. He's my escape artist," Noah said, grinning about the animal for the first time. "She took one look at him jumping his corral and a pasture fence and asked me if she could train him. In a matter of days, she's got him jumping like a pro."

"That's my Roxy," Joe stated, matter-of-fact.

"No. That's my Roxy," Noah responded, noting the slight smile on Joe's face.

"So, it's like that, is it?"

"It's like that. Well, it will be if I can get her talking to me again."

"She's got a soft heart, she hides and protects well. The two people who should have loved and protected her let her down. John loved all you kids. He left her where she was because he knew she could take it. It's past time she had to take it anymore. I thought her coming here would mean a quiet, happy life. Guess that's not going to be the case based on your sister's reaction."

"Rumors are circulating."

"She can't hide from her past, but she shouldn't have to suffer for what her mother does."

"I'm hoping I can help there," Noah said, wondering if he could fill that tall order.

"Keep her away from her mother," Joe advised.

"She's that bad?"

"Worse."

"I'll keep that in mind." Noah couldn't imagine worse than what Roxy described. He didn't want to let his mind go there because he didn't want to think of Roxy getting hurt. Again and again. "Come on, let's take these guys down to their new home."

Sonya came over and linked her arm through his and stood with him watching Roxy ride away. "I'm thirsty," she said out of the blue. "Take me up to the house. We'll have a drink, and I'll answer your questions."

He hesitated for only a second, then walked with Sonya up to the house. They took a seat at the patio table and looked out across the backyard to where Roxy and Annabelle on one of Roxy's other horses rode in one of the pastures.

"You like my sister." Sonya shaded her eyes to watch the two in the field.

"I've never met anyone like her. She's . . . special. Amazing. Her resilience surprises and impresses me. After all her parents put her through, growing up alone . . ."

"She had us, me and our sisters, but I know what you mean. It's not the same as having a loving family. We don't know what that is or how it feels. What you've had here, it's so foreign to us. To her."

Noah acknowledged that with a nod. "I had the life she should have had." That single thought felt like a lead weight in his bleeding heart.

"I'm glad you understand. So, what do you want to know?"

He stared at Roxy draped over Vinny, hugging his neck, her smile bright and carefree. "Everything."

Chapter Twenty-Seven

I hope I won't see you at the Ranch anytime soon," Sonya said by way of goodbye.

Roxy laughed and gave her a hug. "Not until next month. I'm banished to this ranch until then," she teased.

"I like your Noah," Sonya whispered into her ear, because Noah stood five paces away saying goodbye to Joe.

"I like him, too." She had let go her anger and resentment over the misunderstanding. "But he's not my anything."

"I beg to differ." Sonya held Roxy's shoulders with her arms outstretched. "Despite the obvious tension between the two of you, he's hardly left your side this weekend. Marry that man, or I will."

Roxy laughed at the joke, then caught Sonya's eye and all the laughing stopped at her serious look. "Sonya, you can have that life. A husband and children, the house and the dog. Stop working so much and start living."

"Look who's talking. And you just added to my work." Sonya indicated the stack of files Roxy and she had gone over for all her various accounts. "When I find my Noah, I promise, I'll take the time. You're lucky. Hold on to him, the way he tries to hold on to you, though you keep slipping away from him. Stop running, or at least let him catch you," Sonya pleaded.

"I have a feeling he hasn't let me out of his sight because he intends to catch me as soon as you're gone."

"I'm off." Sonya gave her a wide grin, then snagged Noah around the neck and hugged him goodbye. She stepped back and held him at arm's length. "Thank you for a lovely weekend. You hurt my sister, I'll hurt you. Believe me, I know people." Sonya's teasing tone took some of the sting out of her truthful words.

Noah laughed and tapped her on the shoulder. "Get lost."

Sonya winked, hugged Roxy one last time, and climbed into the truck.

Joe came to her, wrapped his arms around her, lifted her off her feet, and hugged her tight. "Don't worry about your other babies. I'll take good care of them and check on your sisters, make sure they don't burn the place down while you're gone."

"Thank you for always taking care of me," she said, and hugged him tighter.

"Be happy, darlin'."

Joe set Roxy back on her feet, shook Noah's hand, and gave him a nod goodbye.

Roxy stood, watching her friends drive away feeling the loss of the companionship she'd missed since coming to the ranch. Her throat constricted, and she held back the tears and watched as the truck disappeared.

Noah clamped his hands down on her shoulders and leaned in close to her ear from behind. The warmth of his body set hers on fire. "I like your sister. She's really great."

"She's one of my best friends."

"I'm sorry, Roxy. More than I can say. I let you down, and that's the last thing I ever wanted to do. You've taught me to never look at someone and think I know them based on a few simple facts or rumors. Please tell me my one moment of stupidity won't cost me getting to know *you*."

His arms wrapped around her and draped across her chest. She rested her chin on his forearm along with both her hands. Strong muscles corded under her fingers. His body pressed against her back.

"Honey, please . . . forgive me." Noah pressed his forehead to her hair.

"I didn't give you a chance to work out what I told you and make up your mind. I'm sorry."

"I made up my mind when we were in the barn and you were ordering me to sign checks."

"I didn't order you to do anything. I asked. I even said please."

He nuzzled his nose along the curve of her ear. "Yeah, I guess you did. Then you tried to get away."

"I needed to catch my breath," she said, frustrated he wouldn't let her go, but held her closer. "You have a twisted way of remembering things."

He pressed his face into her hair. "I remember how you felt in my arms. Just the way you do now. I remember the way you smelled, like flowers in spring. The way you tasted, the softness of your lips, the feel of your tongue sliding against mine," he whispered at her ear.

She sank back into him, mesmerized by his deep voice and the warmth that spread through her and pooled in her belly and rippled out to the edges of her being.

"All you remember is kissing me."

"I remember the overwhelming urge to hunt your mother down and kill her for even thinking of harming one hair on your head. My chest hurts just thinking of you in a cottage, ten years old and all alone every night. How lonely that must have felt. I can't imagine what it took for someone so young to live the way you did with only yourself and your sisters, no older than you, to rely on.

"I remember the hurt and misery in your eyes when I looked at you and thought something that could never be true about you. I remember thinking I'd rather cut my heart out with a spoon than see that look in your eyes ever again." His arms tightened around her. "I'm sorry, sweetheart. I never meant to hurt you. I do remember that moment we shared, the closeness I've never felt with anyone else. I want that back," he whispered, his lips skimming her earlobe.

She shivered. Her body responded to the heat in his touch and she rubbed her bottom against his thick erection pressed against her backside. Noah sucked in a breath and squeezed her tight.

"Every time I think about you, every time I'm close to you, I want you with a passion I've never felt for anyone. Tell me we have a chance to explore this connection neither of us can ignore anymore."

Roxy turned in his arms and pressed both palms to his chest, her head straight ahead, her eyes on her hands covering that hard expanse of muscle. She felt them bunch and relax as he moved his hands to her back and held her close in the circle of his arms, unwilling to let her move even an inch away.

"Roxy, sweetheart, you said you've always been cautious and controlled. Let go. Take a chance on us. Be reckless with me."

Damn if he hadn't pegged her right. Never one to go halfway, she went all in. Sliding her hands up his chest and rising on tiptoe, she wrapped her hands around his neck and pressed her lips to his. This kiss was nothing like the others. She opened to him immediately, invited him in, and followed him into the fire. Fearless.

"You kept both the girls to yourself all weekend," Harry said from nearby, "and now you've gone and sent one away. At least, you kept the curvy one."

Noah went rigid in her arms. His mouth left hers and firmed into a tight line. His eyes narrowed, like an outlaw ready for a fight. "I finally get you alone for a minute and someone has to ruin it." The disappointment in his tone eased the last remnants of her trepidation even more.

"You had her all weekend, give a guy a chance. Stop hogging her," Harry pleaded.

Noah's eyes went cold. He shoved her behind him and went after Harry.

Roxy grabbed his arm before he swung his fist and laid the poor kid out in the dirt. "Noah, wait. Let's not turn this into some barroom brawl. This is a business. He's an employee. There are rules and laws for the workplace."

Noah stopped glaring at Harry and glanced down at her, an understanding forming between them. "You're right. I meant to do this last week but got distracted. So let's deal with this once and for all and have an employee meeting."

Harry backed up and eyed Noah as he advanced. "You can't fire me for talking."

"Actually, yes, I can. Get to the stables and I'll tell you and the others what else I can fire you for."

Roxy followed Noah and Harry, who had the good sense to keep several paces ahead of Noah and out of his reach. Roxy felt the restrained rage coming off Noah, but she respected him even more for handling this the right way and not punching Harry in his smart mouth even if he deserved it.

Noah whistled for the guys out in the pasture to join them in the stables. He picked up the CB and radioed the guys farther out on the property to drive back in. Roxy remained silent and watchful as Noah paced and waited for the entire crew to join them.

Satisfied that everyone had gathered, he turned to the men. "I think it's time we clear the air about Roxy."

Snickers and whispered comments went up among the men.

"Shut it!" Noah took a step toward everyone, getting their attention with his rigid frame and steely look. "I'm talking. You're listening." Noah waited to have everyone's full attention again. "First, you've all heard the rumors about Roxy's mother."

The men smirked and gave Roxy side-eye glances.

"Yes, it's true. She's a prostitute."

One guy slapped another on the chest and said, "Told you."

"Her mother is, but Roxy is not."

"Come on, man, you expect us to believe that? She owns the Wild Rose Ranch." Harry eyed Noah with a look that said they all knew the truth and Noah was just trying to hide it.

They expected the ranch hands to wonder about Roxy with her horses arriving from the Wild Rose Ranch, but not that they'd jump to a conclusion that Roxy owned it.

Noah and Roxy exchanged a look that clearly said they both knew who outed her as the owner. Tom.

Another problem that needed to be handled. Soon.

"Just because she owns it, doesn't mean she works there." Noah tilted his head back, took a few seconds, then tried again. "We all know someone, or have heard stories about people addicted to drugs, strung out, not caring about themselves or the people around them." Noah looked at all the men, some of whom nodded. "John knew Roxy's mother would never get clean, so he got Roxy and her mom off the streets and out of the shitholes they'd been living in. He set her mother up at the Wild Rose Ranch and Roxy lived alone at ten years old in the cottage on the property. Roxy raised herself, trained horses, and took care of her mother when the drugs and drinking took over her life. Far too often and each time more devastating for Roxy to handle on her own. For reasons I still don't fully understand and admittedly make me think less of John, he left her there instead of giving her the loving, safe home Annabelle and I had here.

"When John died, he ordered her here, away from her mother and a life that only brought her pain. He left her the Wild Rose Ranch, which neither she, nor I, knew he owned. He didn't give it to her because he thought she wanted any part of working there, but as a means for her to continue protecting her mother from herself.

"That is a small part of Roxy's story. You want to know more, then take the time to get to know her the way I know her. She's kind and strong and courageous. She's taken all your shit and never once complained about the lies you tell about her.

"It ends now. This is a business. *Our* business. Roxy and I are partners. We will not tolerate sexual harassment of any kind in the workplace. There will be no more jokes, rude comments, sexual innuendoes, or outright propositions from any of you from this moment forward. You're better than that."

Looks of shame and embarrassment crossed the men's faces for their locker room talk. No one looked her in the eye.

"This is a family business. You all have helped John and me watch over Annabelle since she was a toddler on her first pony. Do you want her to think this is how men behave? That it's okay to treat a woman so disrespectfully? That it's okay to treat her like she's beneath you and you can use her as you please without any thought to her feelings?

"Roxy changed her whole life to come here to protect Annabelle from a mother who is nowhere near as bad as her own, but worse than any of us ever experienced. You know Lisa. You know the damage she's capable of inflicting on Annabelle with just her words. Imagine the kind of life Roxy had, punctuated with drugs and abuse and no one to keep her safe.

"Roxy is a champion barrel racer. She's a better horse trainer than John. I don't say that lightly. You've seen what she's done with Houdini. She's raised, bred, and trained horses for years. She's got the skills. I expect you all to respect her decisions. I expect you to respect her.

"She spent her whole life feeling like she didn't belong to anyone or anyplace. That will not happen here. On her ranch. This is *her* home. *You* work here. You don't like the terms, you're free to leave. Step out of line again, like you all have been doing this past week, you're fired. Clear?"

"Clear," the men answered back, some with sharp replies, others less than enthusiastic.

"Then I suggest you find the time over the next couple days to introduce yourselves properly to Roxy. Until then, get back to work."

A few of the men tipped their cowboy hat or baseball cap to Roxy before they headed out. Others simply gave her a nod and went on their way.

Harry, head down, eyes on his big feet, shuffled over to her. He stopped a few feet away, scrunched up his lips, and tipped his head just enough to meet her gaze. "Sorry I got the wrong idea about you. I said some stuff . . . didn't mean it. I got an uncle. Mean sonofabitch when he drinks."

"I know the type." Roxy gave him a grin to let him know she accepted the apology.

"You're real pretty."

Noah sighed. "Didn't you hear anything I said?"

Noah's rising anger didn't deter Harry. "Did you get that scar on your lip from your mother?"

"She liked to pop me in the mouth with the back of her hand when I said something she didn't like. Which was just about everything I ever said."

Harry pointed to the faint scar across his cheek, arcing toward the corner of his mouth. "He used a broken beer bottle. My mom barely got me out of the way before he slit my throat. All because I stole a chip off his plate when I was seven." Harry turned and walked down the alley toward the stable doors.

Noah hooked his arm around her shoulders. "I had no idea about his uncle."

"People don't talk about abuse. They hide it. He wants people to like him. So he's outrageous and gets a laugh and thinks they do. I like him more for being honest."

"I think you made a friend today."

"Because of you." She leaned into his side. "What you said to them, Noah . . . you have no idea what it means to me. They respect you. I think most of them will listen to you."

"All of them will if they want to keep their jobs. They'll do it because now they know something real and personal about you. If they can't treat you with kindness after what I told them, I don't want them here. Annabelle is turning into a beautiful young woman before my eyes. One day soon, they'll start noticing. I don't want them to think they can treat her the way they treated you." He shook his head. "God, I'm sorry I didn't put a stop to it sooner."

She stepped away from his side and faced him. "Believe me, I'm used to it."

"If you're trying to make me feel better, you're failing miserably. I hate it that stuff like this, and worse, are a part of your life."

"You're sweet."

"At least you don't think I'm an asshole anymore."

"You more than made things up with the way you welcomed Sonya here this weekend."

"She's more than your friend, she's your family and a guest in our home. Your sisters are welcome anytime." Noah turned serious again. "About Annabelle and what she said to you on Friday . . ."

"Forgotten. All of it."

"She's still very quiet around you." Noah took her hand and walked with her back up to the driveway toward the house, quiet, lost in his thoughts.

"She's afraid she's damaged something between us that can't be repaired. Don't worry, I'll fix it. Starting this afternoon."

Noah glanced down at her. "What do you mean?"

"Did you know she's interested in becoming a vet?"

"She loves the horses, but I've never heard her say anything about becoming a vet."

"That's because you and John hounded her about school and college. Typical teenager, she rebelled against telling you what she's thinking about studying rather than shut you up with an actual answer."

Noah rolled his eyes.

"Anyway, I called Dr. Garcia and asked him to change his schedule. Instead of coming in the morning when we need him, he'll come in the afternoon. He's agreed to allow Annabelle to watch and assist. He's going to offer her a weekend job during school and some more days during the summer. It'll give her an opportunity to experience the job and make sure it's what she wants to do. She's old enough to take on a job and learn some responsibility and money management."

"You set this up?"

"It's my job to take care of her. That includes nurturing her interests."

"Who helped you with your interests?"

"Joe taught me about the horses, helped me find people to talk to about training them. Big Mama—she's the Madam at the Ranch—watched out for me. She got me through the awkward teenage years and made sure I went to college, though I was headed in that direction already."

"A ranch hand and a Madam," Noah said, shaking his head.

"It wasn't an ideal childhood," she admitted.

"No. Because John left you. I had the childhood you deserved, while you were sleeping alone."

She smiled. "It really bothers you that I grew up without parents."

"Annabelle is fifteen. I look at her and think of you."

"Noah, don't compare me to Annabelle. I was never like her at fifteen. She's got friends and shopping and having fun on the brain. I lived in a small town where everyone knew who worked at the Wild Rose because it was the most prosperous business in town. By the time I hit high school, everyone knew about my mom. Teens can be cruel. Especially boys who only want one thing and could care less about your feelings, because, hey, you're just like your mom and not worth getting to know. Not really. I learned to keep my head in my books and spent my free time with my horses. My fun was going to rodeos and winning championships. Through it all, I had my sisters."

"I saw you ride," Noah admitted. "John loved to watch the barrel racing competitions. Inevitably, we'd hear about the Wild Rose Ranch girls competing. You guys only ever used your first names."

"People know the Cordero name," Roxy pointed out. "I didn't want to call attention to John's and my relationship any more than he did."

"I always thought John wanted to see the pretty girls. He really wanted to see you," he finished with a grin. "He was proud of you. It thrilled him to watch you ride and win."

"On his horses," she added. "I saw you, too."

Noah frowned. "And kept your distance, so nothing would tarnish John's family or business."

She steered the conversation back to horses. Nothing they rehashed would change the past. "In one of the rare conversations I had with Dad, he told me how impressed he was that I trained the difficult horses he'd sent to me. He said I had a knack for seeing what a horse was capable of and willing to do."

"You turned Houdini's tendency for escape and freedom into something controlled and deliberate. It's not easy to teach a wild-at-heart horse to run a course in a purposeful way. You've got a real talent."

Overwhelmed by his praise, her heart did a flip-flop in her chest. She had a hard time meeting his steady gaze. "Thank you." Heat rose up her face and ears.

Noah squeezed her hand. "You haven't received very many compliments, have you?"

"Not ones that were sincere."

Noah stopped and tugged her arm so she came around to him. He cupped her cheek in his free hand and stared down at her. "All I want to do is make you smile." He leaned down and kissed her on the forehead. "I want you to be happy here."

She stared up into his sincere eyes. "It's getting better by the minute."

Noah closed the distance like a bee drawn to a flower. His lips settled over hers in a soft kiss that demanded nothing and promised everything. He ended it before the heat rose to an all-out fire, pressed his forehead to hers, and stared into her eyes. "I'm so glad you're here."

"Me, too." She wanted to spend the day doing nothing but hanging out with Noah. "But I have to get back to work." She started toward the house, and Noah kept pace with her.

"What do you do in there for hours upon hours?"

"I have three jobs, you know?"

"I hadn't really thought about it," Noah admitted. "This ranch, *the* Ranch, and what else keeps you up to all hours of the night?"

Noah took her hand as they walked. It felt so natural, their fingers linked, bodies close.

Roxy used her free hand to brush her hair away from her face. She sighed out some of her stress and met Noah's inquisitive gaze. "In the morning through the afternoon until Annabelle gets home, I do my real job. I'm a designer for a company that supplies equipment to cable companies."

"Like TV cable boxes?" Noah asked.

"No. The equipment the companies use to get the TV signal to your home. Transmitters and amplifiers and housings for the equipment. It's a little complicated to explain. Anyway, a customer, a cable company, puts in a request for one of their systems. Some are small, maybe servicing a few square miles. Others are huge, servicing a town or a city. I take their request and draw a schematic of our equipment and how it's placed along the fiber optic cable line. There's a lot of calculations for loss over distance and . . ."

"I get it. It's complicated," he said, smiling. "You like it."

"It's interesting and every design is the same, but different. It's like a puzzle to put all the equipment together, get the customer the best results I can, and keep the costs reasonable. I can do it from home, because all I need is email and my computer programs to do the work."

"What do you do after Annabelle gets home?"

"Oh, um, I help her with her homework if she needs it and catch up on the ranch paperwork. I'm reworking the database you set up to run more efficiently. I've added some programs to automate some of the calculations you normally do manually. I've got the sales, bank stuff, and expenses populating a spreadsheet that will help when it comes time to do taxes."

"You've done all that in a week?"

"I have a degree in computer science. I'm great with a computer and the horses, not so much with people."

"You're doing great with me." He gave her hand a squeeze and drew her closer.

They walked along the path through the garden to the back patio by the family room and kitchen entrance. She stopped by the pond and stared at the water and lush plants and pretty flowers. "My being here has really complicated your life."

Noah tugged on her hand to get her to look at him. "It was getting boring anyway. I needed someone to shake things up," he teased with a wide grin.

She loved the way his eyes danced and he fell back into his good humor so easily after confronting his entire workforce and laying down the law.

"I don't think I'm quite what you had in mind."

His eyes turned serious. "Sometimes the unexpected is exactly what we've been looking for all along. We just didn't know it."

"Noah . . ." She tried to back away, but he held her hand in his firm grip and prevented her from putting any more space between them.

"You're everything I didn't know I needed in my life."

"You don't need people talking about you behind your back. I appreciate what you said to the crew. I think things will be different here now. But soon the rumors running through town will turn into snubs directed at you and Annabelle. I'm used to it. I don't really know anyone here anyway."

"We've lost some business, but people will come around when the truth gets out there. The guys will be talking about what happened here today."

Roxy bowed her head. "I'm sorry I've cost us customers."

"We'll get by without them. I have a feeling with your training skills, we'll have even more customers."

"You're optimistic, but this is just the beginning, Noah. Whatever it is you think you feel for me will change once my past interferes in your life more than it already has."

"You're wrong. If the people who have known me my whole life don't accept my word and remember my reputation, then I don't need them in my life."

"Those people think you have a hooker living under your roof and helping you raise your sister."

"You're a good and decent person . . ."

"Who owns a notorious brothel. You want to know what I spend my nights doing? I'm on the phone with Big Mama, checking on the girls and the night's receipts. I'm going over the books and the reservations, making sure the weekly testing on the women all came back clean. She runs the show, but I still oversee everything."

"Sell it. It's obvious you don't want to own it and you hate being a part of it."

"I can't. John's will states I have to hold on to it for five years."

Noah's eyes narrowed. "Why would he do that?"

"Because he knows I'm stubborn and it'll take me that long to figure out that it's an extremely lucrative business—and legal. Despite my personal feelings, I'd be stupid to sell it. He also knows I'd never jeopardize the women who work there by selling to someone who's more interested in the profit than their well-being. Also, when the ranch has had some lean years, John used the money he made from the Wild Rose Ranch to keep this place afloat. Most of the money is sitting in an account, but I've checked the books and over the years, he's had to make some sizable contributions to Speckled Horse Ranch to keep it going."

Noah swore. "I didn't know that," he admitted.

"Why would you? He hasn't used the money from there for several years. He saved it all for me. You've kept this place profitable for some time now. I think he wanted me to take some time and not make decisions based on emotion, but good business sense."

"I don't know what to say. You're damned if you do and damned if you don't. You can't sell that place, yet you make an exceptional income from it even though you hate it. You live and work here, but everyone thinks you're something you're not. They'll find out you own that place, will assume the worst, and never realize what an amazing businesswoman you are. Your life is so damn complex. Everything in it is complicated by that place and your mother. None of it has anything to do with you, not really, yet you're the one responsible for that place, those women, and all you get for it is grief, accusations, and people's scorn."

"Life is complicated, Noah. I do the best I can with the hand I've been dealt. All I'm saying is that if you get too close, some of the mud slung at me will inevitably land on you."

"I thought you were taking a breath. Instead, you're pushing me away."

"I'm warning you about what's to come." With a deep sigh, she admitted, "This thing between us, I've never felt this way about anyone."

"Good. I'd hate to have to beat the competition to hell to have you." That sexy, easy smile came to his face.

She reached up and touched his lips with her fingertips. He kissed her fingers and took her hand and placed it on his cheek, leaning into her palm.

"You're not listening to me." She frowned when his smile didn't waver.

"Sweetheart, I've heard every word you said. The thing is, you don't get it."

"What?"

"Nothing and no one is going to change my mind about you. Saturday night. You and me. Whitefall Hall. About three times a year, all the local ranchers and business owners get together for dinner and dancing. One of the organizers picks a local charity and the attendees make donations. I'll wear a suit and you'll wear a dress. I'll get to see your outstanding legs." He stepped back and scanned her from her feet to her face. "And maybe the rest of you," he added with a wicked grin, his dimples making him all the more adorable.

"So you think taking me to this dinner, showing up with the 'whore,' will be a fun date? We'll eat and dance, and people will whisper and gossip about us all night. This is your plan to get me into bed?"

"It's my plan to show people that you're just like everyone else. Well, you're better looking than everyone else."

His warm, calloused hands swept down her arms and back up again. Inexplicably, their bodies moved closer, though Roxy couldn't remember stepping forward. His touch did that to her, made her stop thinking and just feel.

"My plan to get you into bed"—his voice dropped deep and low—"is to keep doing this." His mouth brushed hers, tasting of his morning coffee and mint. "Until you're begging me to make love to you."

She wanted him to take the kiss deeper, but he intended to leave her wanting and stepped back.

"Diabolical." She glared at his smug face.

"Did you want something, sweetheart?"

Two could play this game. "Nope. I've got work to do. I'll think about Saturday."

Roxy turned to go inside, but she only got two steps away before Noah spun her around, cupped her face in his big hands, and planted his mouth over hers. That familiar zing zipped through her and she gave in to it, grabbing his waist and pulling him closer. God, he made her feel so wanted, the way he settled into her, took his time, and gave her everything she needed.

They lost themselves in each other until someone cleared their throat to get their attention. Mary.

Noah broke the kiss, but continued to hold her face and stare deep into her eyes. "Say yes."

"Yes," she answered, unsure if she was saying yes to going to bed with him, or going to dinner. Didn't matter. At the moment, she'd do anything to keep him and this feeling.

"The thing starts at seven and dinner's at eight. We'll leave at six-thirty."

"'K."

"Your phone is ringing again," he said, smiling.

"Huh?"

She fell right into his dancing eyes. She loved how playful and carefree he always seemed to be. She'd spent her whole life afraid to let go and have fun, fearing people would see her and say, *See, she's just like her mother.*

What did it really matter how she acted, or which impulses she gave in to, when they said it anyway?

Why did she hold herself back for them when what she really wanted to do was follow Noah into pleasure and fun and delight in this wonderful feeling they shared with each other? She'd seen enough frivolous relationships between men and women to know this thing between them was special.

Would it last?

Not if she didn't give of herself the way Noah did so easily. He didn't have her baggage holding him back.

Maybe it was time to set aside her reservations and stop wondering what everyone would think of her starting a relationship with him. Why did she care anyway when she wanted him this way? They weren't looking for an hour or two of pleasure. She could see Noah as a husband and father.

Dangerous ground. I'm getting ahead of myself.

Wasn't the fact that she did dream of what might be between them show that she did hope for a future filled with something more than the loneliness she'd lived with for too long?

His mouth landed on hers again and she fell right back into the spell, where nothing but him and having him close mattered.

He ended the kiss with a series of small nibbles at her lips. With a deep groan, he let her go, taking a step away. He grabbed her phone from the table where Mary left it and them alone. "You better get this. It might be important." He glanced at the carton of yogurt Mary left her. "That's not a proper meal."

The man thought to seduce her one second and take care of her the next. More than anything else he did or said, him wanting her to eat better, take better care of herself, did what all the kissing hadn't. She gave up fighting the inevitable. She wanted him. She gave herself over to the need rising inside her. Not the one that wanted the physical release and utter satisfaction his body promised hers, but the temptation he offered in spending time with her, the friendship they were forging, and the caring he showed for her in the smallest of ways.

She loved him, because in that one simple statement he'd shown her how much he cared for her. He'd had her right where he wanted her, ready to slide into his bed, but he didn't push. In fact, he cared more about what she needed than what he wanted.

"Roxy, are you okay?"

Her phone stopped ringing. She couldn't do anything but stare up at him. So handsome and strong and kind and generous and amazingly sexy. She reached up and touched her fingers to his mouth and over his jaw, his beard rough against her skin. "You're a really good guy."

"Uh . . . Thanks. You're still going with me on Saturday," he told her, not giving her an out.

"Yes, I am. I'll be the one in the dress that stops your heart." She took her phone from Noah's hand, grabbed the yogurt off the table, and headed into the house, smiling over her shoulder at the look of pain on Noah's face as he watched her walk away.

His, "Ah God, I'm a dead man," made her laugh, but she kept walking straight to her office. She knew a thing or two about restraint and increasing the anticipation. They'd take the next few days to settle in and get to know each other better.

Saturday night, she was going to knock him on his ass.

She'd never wanted to impress a man. Even with her background, she wondered if she was up to seducing *him*.

Chapter Twenty-Eight

Noah walked into the office and took a minute to study Roxy and Annabelle unnoticed. Annabelle sat on the sofa, a math book opened on the seat, her notebook propped on her knees as she wrote, her mouth drawn in a line of concentration. Roxy stared at her computer. Her right hand on the mouse, moving it and clicking. She stopped and grabbed her calculator, punched a long series of buttons, then used the mouse to click on something on the screen before she typed something in.

"What are you two up to?" he asked, surprising both of them.

"Algebra," Annabelle answered.

"Logarithms," Roxy responded, punching more buttons on her calculator.

"I'm glad I left the ranch books to you," he said to Roxy.

She looked up and cocked up one side of her mouth. "You're not fooling anyone. You've got a degree in business as well as agriculture and animal science. You run this ranch with considerable skill and knowledge, which is why I can sit in here updating your spreadsheets while you're out there running nearly ten thousand acres of horses, cattle, timber, hay, and wheat."

"You've been busy."

She impressed him with how fast she'd come up to speed on the ranch activities. Most people thought Speckled Horse Ranch only raised and trained Appaloosa and quarter horses. They were famous for both. But the ranch also ran cattle and had large fields of rotating crops. They grew their own hay and sold the surplus. Every few years, they contracted with a timber company to cull out the dead trees and some old growth to make room for the new. John had been most interested in the horses and cattle, but Noah began the other enterprises about ten years ago and all were profitable.

"It took a week, but I finally worked my way through that stack of papers you left me."

"I checked out the upgrades you made to the spreadsheets and programs. Damn fine work. You've cut a couple of hours off some of the calculations and cross-referencing, and taxes aren't going to be murder this year. You've saved us costs on feed, and I don't know how you did it, but you negotiated a better price on hauling the cattle."

When she only shrugged, he frowned. No one could have accomplished what she'd done in such a short amount of time. And doing her other jobs at the same time. That she actually got their costs down with vendors he'd haggled with unsuccessfully was nothing short of a miracle. In the future, with them working together, the ranch would be stronger and more profitable. John had been a good partner, but Noah had to fight for every inch he'd gained in improving the ranch and expanding the operations.

When he found out Roxy would be his new partner, he'd balked and hated the idea that everything he did would benefit someone who had no idea the amount of hard work and dedication it took to keep the ranch profitable. With Roxy, he didn't have to worry. She got it.

It also didn't hurt his ego to see that she was impressed with him and what he'd done for the ranch.

"All in a day's work." She picked up a red folder, the same one she handed him every day at some point to sign checks. He took it and sat in the seat in front of her desk. She handed him a pen and he slid his fingers over hers as he took it.

"Is this how old people flirt?" Annabelle asked from the sofa. "You guys talk about spreadsheets and taxes and stare at each other."

Noah thought this the perfect time to see how Annabelle felt about him and Roxy and this thing between them. He didn't want to label it. Not yet. Not when it was so new.

She was a damn fine partner for the ranch, but he wanted more. He wanted a wife who loved him. He took the "till death" part of the wedding vows seriously. When he married, he wanted it for life. Kids. A family that stuck together.

"I'm taking Roxy to the rancher's dinner thing this Saturday," he announced.

Annabelle's head snapped up. "Are you sure that's a good idea?" Annabelle's eyes darted everywhere but to Roxy.

"Listen, Sprite. Roxy and I . . . we like each other." That didn't come close to how he felt about her. "I want to take her to dinner and see if there's something more between us than spreadsheets and taxes," he teased to keep things light.

Roxy didn't say a word, her eyes went from him to Annabelle, waiting to see where this went.

"I think you two make a great couple." Annabelle made that announcement with all the nonchalance of youth.

Noah relaxed. A weight lifted he hadn't realized he'd been carrying. If Annabelle was against him and Roxy getting together, he didn't know what he'd do. He wanted Annabelle to be happy, but more, he wanted to be happy with Roxy.

"I just think you're kidding yourself if you think taking her to that dinner will change people's minds. Seeing her with you will only stir things up more." Annabelle's brows drew together with concern.

"Sprite, I don't care what people say."

"You should," she shot back. "It could make things worse for her. It's bad enough she's trapped here—"

"She's not trapped here."

Annabelle glared at him. "Are you blind? Have you not noticed that since everyone found out about her she hasn't left the ranch? Mary picks up everything she wants from town. I've asked Roxy a dozen times to go for a girl's day but she always turns me down. She says she's got work, but I know she doesn't want to stir up more gossip."

Noah stared at Roxy. "Is that right?"

It took Roxy a few seconds to meet his gaze. "It's true, I have a lot of work. But I am also trying to minimize the effect of my reputation on you and Annabelle. The last thing I want to do is cause a scene, especially with Annabelle with me."

Annabelle held her hand out toward Roxy. "See. Everyone is talking about her. What if they're rude to her when she goes into town? It's one thing to do it behind her back, but to do it to her face." Annabelle shook her head, clearly distraught about anyone disrespecting Roxy, or being downright mean to her.

Annabelle turned to Roxy. "You don't know the people attending that dinner. They're the most influential families around. They can make things very difficult for you and Noah." Annabelle gave him a pleading look. "Tell her, Noah. You know how they can be when they want to cut someone out."

"If you're this upset about it," Roxy began, "perhaps it's better if I stay home and Noah goes alone."

"No." Noah stood and walked to Roxy, pulling her out of her chair. He wrapped his arm around her shoulders and she leaned into him without his having to pull her close. His body responded to her closeness, but he kept his mind on the problem at hand. "You're not staying home. You're not going to hole up on this ranch like you did in your cottage."

"Noah, it's fine." She placed her hand on his chest. "They're your friends and the people you work and do business with. Those relationships matter."

He cupped her face in his hands, rubbed his thumbs along her soft cheeks, and looked into her sincere eyes. "You matter. We're going. All anyone has to do is spend time with you to know you're nothing like what they've heard."

Roxy frowned, her eyes filled with trepidation. "You're putting a lot of faith in them. Maybe it's deserved. My experience is that people who hold a certain perception of me don't tend to look for anything beyond what they think they see." She swept a hand down to indicate her body. "I don't exactly look like Suzy Homemaker."

"More like a Victoria's Secret supermodel," Annabelle confirmed. "I think you're gorgeous. I wish I looked like you," she said honestly.

Roxy laughed. "It's not all it's cracked up to be. You're lovely, Annabelle, and smart, and funny. Your kind heart shines through. Based on the number of boys hanging around the house the last week, I don't think you've got anything to worry about."

"They're here trying to get a look at you," Noah added, seeing Annabelle's eyes turn away. "Isn't that right, Sprite?"

"Perhaps." She gave Roxy a sheepish grin. "Half those boys never even noticed me."

Roxy left him to sit on the coffee table facing Annabelle. "They're not worth knowing if all they want to do is use you."

Annabelle's gaze dipped to her entwined hands in her lap. "I know."

Roxy touched Annabelle's chin and made Annabelle look at her. "Some high school boys think sex is a sport. All they want is everyone else to pat them on the back and cheer for them because they've been with a girl. You don't want to be someone's participation trophy. Girls like you and me, we do things with our heart. Being with a boy means something. We've been let down by people close to us. Trust means something. It's important. If a boy just wants to be your friend so he can get something out of it, he's not really a friend. He's using you. You're smart, funny, kind, a good friend, and a great sister. Your worth isn't tied to some boy liking you. Don't let anyone treat you like you don't matter."

"That's right, Sprite. Stick up for yourself. Like Roxy will do at the dinner this Saturday." He turned his gaze to her. "We're going. You and I are partners in this ranch. In addition to the charity element of this thing, it's a chance to network with other ranchers in the area. We'll go, talk shop, people will hear you speak about the ranch and business, they'll get to know *you*. They'll see who you really are, and if they can't set aside their misconceptions, then screw them."

Roxy held her hand out toward Annabelle. "Language."

"She's heard worse. And I mean it."

"Noah, I don't know ranching the way you do. I might update the spreadsheets, but I couldn't begin to tell you anything about the price of wheat, how much it sells for and why, or anything to do with cattle."

"Then stick to what you know. You're a championship barrel racer. You hold more titles than anyone I've ever met. You know horses and training and breeding. Don't think I didn't notice you changed a few of my picks for the horses. Some of the pairings you made are interesting. I admit, I hadn't considered them."

She opened her mouth, then closed it, unsure what to say and it made him smile. She thought she could pull one over on him.

"I was going to discuss that with you," she mumbled.

"I'm sure you were, since the breeding program has been in my hands for the last couple of years. I think your choices were well thought-out and sound. Although, there is one or two I think you should reconsider. We'll discuss it later. The point is, you understand horses and the raising and training of them. That will shine through, as you put it with Annabelle. So will your other many fine attributes."

"It's hard to hide them," she said, looking down at her curves.

"While I love all your physical attributes," he teased, "it's your personality I'm talking about."

"I change my mind. You two should go together." Annabelle nodded her approval. "You might not be able to change people's minds, Roxy, but Noah will. All anyone has to do is see the way he looks at you and treats you, and they'll know you're someone worth knowing."

"Thank you, Sprite. It means a lot you think that highly of me."

"Everyone does. You're a nice guy and you treat people well. You don't put up with anyone who's mean or rude."

"Maybe we should take Annabelle with us as a kind of buffer," Roxy suggested.

"I'm not taking my sister on a date." Noah cringed at the thought. He wanted to be alone with Roxy. Well, after they faced everyone.

"You're right," Roxy agreed. "I don't want Annabelle there when someone brings up the whole hooker thing."

"You know, if we stop talking about 'the whole hooker thing,' everyone else might, too."

Annabelle and Roxy both looked skeptical.

"I'm not talking about this anymore." Noah just wanted to take her out, not start a debate about what everyone thought. "We're going on Saturday. Now, Mary sent me in here to get you for dinner. Let's eat."

Roxy grabbed his hand and stared at his watch. "Is that the time? I've got to get down to the practice ring. I'm working with one of the horses, doing some barrel racing."

"Not until you eat dinner," Noah responded, twisting his hand to grab her wrist before she walked away. "You never eat with us. Mary says you either eat at your desk or standing in the kitchen, snacking on something. She leaves a plate for you in the fridge, and God knows how late it is before you eat it. You're coming to dinner with us."

"Noah, I've got things to do."

"You need to eat. Have you had anything since that yogurt this morning?" She looked thoughtful, and he said, "If you can't remember, it's been too long since you ate something. Come on. The family eats together."

"I'm starving." Annabelle bumped her elbow into his side as she passed and went through the door, leaving him alone with Roxy.

Noah, frustrated and feeling surly, grabbed Roxy around the waist and turned her into him. He swooped in and took her mouth in a demanding kiss she didn't hesitate to accept and give back. Her tongue slid across his and her hands slipped beneath his shirt and rose up his back, her fingers digging into his sore muscles. After a long day of work, her hands were like magic.

He kissed his way along her jaw to her ear, and whispered, "You smell so good." He inhaled and bit into her lobe, sliding his tongue along the edge before moving on to her neck. Her hands slid down his bare back and out of his shirt. He wanted her to touch him more and she did, grabbing handfuls of his hair and holding his head to her. He obliged her silent command for more, raking his teeth against her collarbone and soothing the small hurt with a slide of his tongue and openmouthed kisses to the pulse point at her throat.

She sighed, "Noah."

He wanted more of those soft gasps and his name on her lips.

Her breasts were so full and round in his palms. He swept his thumbs over the hard peaks. He wanted to drag her to the ground and peel away the layers of clothes until she was naked and writhing below him. He wanted to sink so deep inside her, even their hearts would beat as one.

She dragged his mouth back up to hers, and he had no trouble gratifying whatever she wanted from him. Anything she asked or demanded, he was willing to give to have her in his arms like this.

Something chimed in the distance and Annabelle's, "Noah, get the door," rang out, but he barely noticed either with Roxy in his arms, her perfect breasts filling his hands. He wanted to kick the office door shut and keep the world out.

Roxy had other ideas, so he tried to stop her from leaving his embrace by sliding his hands around her back and pulling her closer. She planted her hands on his chest and nudged him away. Her laugh did the one thing her earlier halfhearted protests could not. He stood back and took her in.

"God, you're beautiful. You hardly ever laugh. You should do it more often."

"You make me laugh." She reached up and slid her hand over his cheek the way she'd done this morning. He was coming to realize it was a guilty pleasure she allowed herself rarely, but she was getting used to reaching out and touching him. "You make me feel and do a lot of things I never did before."

"Never?" he asked, searching her face, putting those timid and hesitant gestures together to form a very innocent picture of Roxy.

"Well, not never. But so rare, they're almost forgotten. Do you know what I mean?"

"Again," he said, remembering their time in the barn when she told him about her mother.

"I'm sorry, what?"

"You said you hoped I'd see you and understand you, but you were wrong. *Again*. I take that to mean you trusted someone once and they let you down like I did."

"There was someone else a very long time ago. I was young and foolish and believed he wanted me. What he wanted was the lie come to life in his bed. I learned one thing. A lie can only be made true if I make it so. I wouldn't play his whore, so I was of no use to him."

"He was a stupid asshole and you're better off without him."

"Better off to stay in school and get my degree and a good job and put men aside. A few good guys tried to turn my head."

"You never gave them a chance," he guessed by the look on her face and understanding what she was trying to tell him. "Until me."

She nodded with a slight smile on her face, confident he'd understood her. "I'll get the door."

He let her go, thinking about what she'd just told him. There'd only been one man to breach the walls around her heart and he'd broken it and made her shut herself away again. No, not a man. Some young, stupid guy. She was talking about late high school or early college.

Until him.

He joined Robby at the dining room table.

"You look deep in thought." Robby waited, but Noah didn't answer. "A woman will do that to a man. Tie him up inside and leave him speechless. When that woman looks like Roxy and has a giving heart the way she does, she'll tie a man in knots both physically and emotionally. Smart woman. Knows how easy it is to fall into bed with nothing between you but a moment of pleasure shared. She's got the right idea. It's the getting to know you and letting you know her that will make this thing between you last."

Yeah, it would be easy to seduce Roxy into his bed, have her beneath him, on top of him, around him, but would it satisfy the part of him that felt a piece of her was becoming a very real part of him? Would she open up and confess her inner secrets, let him see the real Roxy beneath the confidence and strength she projected so easily, even though it hid a world of hurt and pain and disappointments she was only just beginning to share?

Things he was sure she hadn't confided to anyone else. She hadn't shared her delectable body with anyone, since that asshole broke down her defenses and hurt her.

With him, she gave herself over to their connection and revealed some of the most painful moments of her life. She did it despite the underlying fear he sensed in her. And even when he'd made that mistake, looked at her the wrong way, she'd taken a chance, forgiven him, and moved forward, deeper into their relationship, instead of closing him out.

"Noah, man, everything all right? You look like someone ran over your dog."

"We don't have a dog," Noah pointed out, shaking off his thoughts. "I was just thinking that Roxy is so different from any woman I've ever met. She's strong, confident, unflappable on the outside, but there's so much more going on inside."

"Complex women. Difficult to get to know them. They don't trust easily. In Roxy's case, she's got a lot going on in her life. It can't be easy for her, but she holds up well."

"Yeah," Noah answered. "We're starting to find our footing."

"She's the kind of woman who'll stand beside you through thick and thin. She'll walk into hell with you if she knows you'll still be with her on the other side."

What Robby said was true. Roxy said it to him without words, but the underlying statement held true.

She was a forever kind of woman. Not someone you take to bed and leave in the morning.

She was exactly who and what he wanted.

Chapter Twenty-Nine

Roxy hadn't made it to the front door before it swung open and Lisa stepped into the foyer. Lisa's white tank top dipped low on her black-lace-covered breasts. The dark under the light an easy way to show off her assets. Tight jeans hugged her curves and disappeared into a very expensive pair of cowboy boots. She shook back her tousled hair and glared right back with her smoky enhanced eyes. Her wine-red-painted lips turned down into a frown.

"If Mary can't even make it to the door anymore, Noah should fire her." Such callous words, coming from a heartless woman.

"What are you doing here?" Roxy wanted this viper out of her house. Now.

"I need to talk to Noah."

Right. Lisa hadn't come to see Annabelle. "He just sat down to dinner . . ."

Lisa pushed past her and headed for the dining room. "This can't wait."

"Mom. Why are you here?" Annabelle stood on the stairs, her eyes filled with dread.

"I'm here to talk some sense into your brother."

"You came because you want money." Disappointment filled those words, because Lisa rejected Annabelle just by making it clear something else took precedence over seeing Annabelle.

Roxy pointed to the kitchen. "Annabelle, I've got this. Go help Mary bring dinner to the table."

"But Roxy . . ."

"Go," she snapped, not wanting to give Lisa another chance to break Annabelle's heart.

When they were alone again, she turned her attention back to Lisa, who went on the attack. "John had to be out of his mind bringing you here."

"Sometimes, I agree with that," Roxy admitted, though she doubted Lisa understood that Roxy would do anything to keep her past and people's perception of her from tainting Noah and Annabelle in any way. "I care about them. I'd never do anything to hurt them."

"Who and what you are, your being here hurts them."

"They want me here."

Lisa frowned at the lack of complete confidence Roxy had in that statement. "We'll see. Because this is only the beginning of what's about to happen because of you."

Roxy didn't know if that was a threat or simply the truth based on the gossip that had already resulted in lost sales for the ranch and people changing their opinions of Noah and Annabelle because of their association with her.

Lisa didn't waste any time getting to why she was here when she walked into the dining room.

"Seriously, Noah, save yourself the money and ridicule and get back together with Cheryl, someone people will actually believe is your girlfriend and not your whore."

Noah glared at Lisa, then stood and grabbed Roxy by the arm before she passed him. His hands cupped her face and he stared directly into her eyes. "I don't care what she or anyone else thinks, you are my girlfriend. The only one I want."

His lips brushed hers, then settled warm and soft. He kept the kiss short, but with a world of promise and feeling behind it. When he pulled away, he kept his face close, his eyes locked on hers. His thumbs swept across her cheeks in a soft caress. "Just let that settle in for a while."

"It went all the way to my toes," she said to describe the heat and thrill that shot through every cell in her body.

"I meant the girlfriend thing and you know it."

Roxy understood, but hesitated to really accept. It seemed so odd and unlikely, yet here she was, standing in the circle of his arms.

"You'll get used to it, sweetheart." Noah brushed his nose against hers and pressed a quick kiss to her lips. He let her go and turned to address their "guest."

Furious they ignored her, and Noah called Roxy his girlfriend, Lisa crossed her arms under her breasts and glared at Noah. "What is she still doing here? People are talking. You don't want to be associated with someone like her."

Noah understood her meaning all too well, but asked, "Someone like her?" just to see how far Lisa planned to take this.

"You know what she is. Even her own father refused to have anything to do with her."

Robby stood. "Excuse me. I'll let you handle this in private." He eyed Lisa and shook his head in dismay and disgust.

Roxy poured a glass of apple juice from the pitcher on the table and sat in one of the chairs facing him and Lisa, calm and content to watch this thing play out without participating one damn bit.

Noah looked Lisa in the eye. "You don't know Roxy, and everything you've heard is a lie."

Lisa rolled her eyes. "How can you be okay with Annabelle living under the same roof with that slut?"

Noah barely held his temper. "You'll remember this is *my* house. You call Roxy that, or anything else like it again, and I'll toss you out on your ass. And you're one to talk. You flaunted your affairs in front of me when I was Annabelle's age."

Lisa didn't have a comeback.

"Roxy is kind and generous and without guile. She speaks her mind and tells the truth no matter what. Unlike you, she thinks about others before herself. She saw a spark of interest in what Annabelle wants to do in the future and found a mentor and job for her to see if she really wants to pursue a career as a veterinarian. Does any of that sound like she's harming Annabelle?"

"She's a hooker." Lisa spit out her outrage.

Noah sucked in a deep breath and tried to rein in his anger at hearing someone call her that again. "She is a ranch manager, horse trainer, a businesswoman, and a cable systems designer."

"A what?" Lisa asked, completely thrown off.

"She has a job. A degree. You know, that thing you get when you attend college for four years. She works for a company and earns a paycheck. But no one wants to hear that and believe it." He turned to Roxy, who sat quietly listening, a touch of a smile tilting her lips. "God, your life is so damn frustrating to explain, because no one listens."

"It's a pain in the ass. You're doing very well. Very sweet of you to try," she added with a bright smile that made his heart leap. It faded to a firm line. "Just toss her out and be done with it. It's not worth explaining when she's set her mind to saving you from me, so she can ingratiate herself to you and you'll do whatever it is she really wants."

Determined to get at least one person to listen, he turned back to Lisa. "I'm not finished."

Lisa softened her tone. "Stop this. You only look like more of a fool for believing her lies."

"I am so damn tired of having to say this. She is not and has never been a prostitute."

Lisa gave him a sad smile that said, *You're stupid for believing it.*

"You want to know what she's taught me and Annabelle in the week she's been here?" God, had it only been a week, well, two since he'd met her. "She's taught us to see past gossip and find the truth. That being a friend means caring for someone because of who they are, not what they do, or what you can get from them." He raked his fingers over his head. "She wakes Annabelle every morning before school and helps her pick out clothes and does her makeup and hair. She makes sure she eats right and does her homework. She cares about Annabelle's interests and nurtures them. She looks out for Annabelle like *you* never did and treats her with kindness and respect, even when she's acting like a bratty teenager.

"I could go on, but what's the point? You're not here because of Roxy or even to see your daughter. So let's get to it. Tom actually did his job and notified you there will be no more alimony payments."

"We had an agreement that he'd pay me until Annabelle turned eighteen. I want what's owed."

"As Tom told you, and you should already know, your divorce agreement died with John. As I see it, you've been paid enough money over the last twelve years you've been divorced to make a decent life for yourself and have plenty in the bank."

"Reinstate the payments or I'll seek custody of Annabelle."

"Go ahead and try. All you'll do is use up whatever money you have left on lawyer's fees. Roxy and I together make better parents than you'll ever be. A judge won't take Annabelle from a stable home with two capable adults watching over her."

"I'm her mother."

"You signed away your rights to John. He said Roxy is what's best for Annabelle, not you. And I agree."

"She'll be fucking every ranch hand on the place behind your back. You'll see."

Noah didn't rise to that bait. "Now we're talking about you and what you did to John. You made sure he caught you with one of the guys. Young and dumb and believing you'd never want to get caught with him, he lost his job and livelihood because of your games. And because he didn't want any part of you, he signed those papers just as fast as you did. You want to go to a judge and cast accusations at Roxy, there's plenty of truths about you that make you look worse than Roxy's undeserved reputation. You don't want me to prove to a judge which one of you is the better woman. Roxy will win hands down."

"You've always been a vindictive asshole."

"I'm Annabelle's big brother and I will protect her with my life." He pointed to the door. "Get out and don't come back."

"This isn't over." Not a very inventive threat, but Lisa meant it because she never quit when it came to getting what she wanted.

Lisa huffed out a breath, spun on her heels, and left him alone with

Roxy. The front door slammed. A moment later, she gunned the engine on her car and drove away.

"That was fun." Roxy broke the silence with her false brightness.

"Loads." He raked his hand through his hair and dropped into the chair beside her. He took her hand and brought it to his mouth, kissing her palm. She immediately reached for his face and placed her hand on his jaw. He leaned into her touch, needing the closeness.

"You've got to stop trying to convince everyone I'm not who they think I am. You'll only frustrate yourself more."

"I hate what people think of you."

"I know. It's one of the things I love about you." She boldly dropped that four-letter word between them.

Noah leaned forward in his chair, planted his forearm on his thighs, and just stared at her. He wanted to ask if she meant it, but didn't have to, because Roxy didn't say things she didn't mean. In her own way, she was letting him know just how deep her feelings ran. It made him so damn happy. And scared. As sure as he was that he wanted her, he couldn't bring himself to say the words that would tie him to her forever.

So damn good at hiding her feelings, nothing flickered in her eyes. She didn't look away and didn't say anything. He couldn't read anything in her that said whether his silence hurt or disappointed her. He didn't want to do either.

He broke the silence and the tension by asking, "Is that the only thing you love about me?"

Taking his cue to lighten things up, she responded with, "Nope. You've got a really great ass and the most chiseled abs I've ever seen."

He laughed and brought her hand back to his lips, kissing it with tender slowness. "Admit it, you're dying to get your hands on me."

She gave him a sexy as hell grin. "You know I do." Her voice dropped an octave to that seductive tone he liked so much, but she was careful not to use. Most of the time.

"That's not what you love most about me though." He kissed her wrist. Her pulse raced under his lips.

"No? What do you think I love most?"

"That I make you laugh, for one thing." She gave him a nod, her eyes locked on his mouth as he kissed her wrist again. "But the most important thing to you is that I see the real you. You're more beautiful on the inside than anyone I know."

"Noah." She sighed his name. Her hands came up to cup his face. She leaned forward and kissed him, long and soft and warm, her lips over his, her eyes locked on him. "You're very sweet."

He spoke, his mouth a breath away from hers. "You love that about me, too."

"Yes, I do." Her mouth touched his and she fell into him, giving everything.

Those simple words were a promise and pledge rolled into one.

She meant them and sealed the bargain with her kiss. A kiss that made his head light and his heart stutter and slam against his chest.

Humbled by her words and still electrified from the kiss, he lost his grip on her when she stood and took a step back. "Where are you going?" His body pulsed with his need for her, even as his mind swirled with thoughts after Lisa's visit.

"You said we were having dinner as a family. The family is in the kitchen eating without us." Her fingers combed through his hair and she tipped his head back so he looked up at her. "I'll tell them you'll be there in a minute." She smoothed out the lines on his forehead and he relaxed at her touch. The plaintive look on her face didn't help ease his mind. "I said too much."

"No you didn't. As always, you said what you meant. I needed a minute to let it settle."

"Finished?" She kept a teasing tone in her words, even if her eyes said she was skeptical.

"Not yet." He gave her back the honesty she always gave him.

His feelings for her ran deep. Yes, he wanted her in his bed, but he was also content to wait, get to know her better, find out all the little things he didn't know about her, like how much she liked apple juice and peach yogurt. Her sentimental side when she wore John's Stetson every time she rode. The way she babied her horses and greeted them with sheer joy when she went into the barn and they neighed a hello to her. The way she stopped everything when Annabelle needed to speak to her.

He loved how he could just be himself around her. "I didn't think we'd get here this fast. My head is still catching up."

"Fair enough. Let's eat. I'm starving."

Leave it to Roxy to make things easy. She held her hand out to him and he stood and took it. Yep. Easy. No demands that he talk about his feelings, spill his guts, and say and do things he wasn't ready to admit or commit to.

She gave him a tap in the gut with her fist. He tightened his abs and took the hit, making her smile. "Suck it up, big guy. You can take it. Life's a gamble. If you never risk the bet, you'll never hold the winning hand. I made it clear from the beginning what I want."

She didn't sleep around for sport. She wanted a commitment.

"I think you want the same thing."

Yes, he did.

"So, I'm all in. It's up to you to decide if you're ready to play for keeps."

Chapter Thirty

Play for keeps. The damn woman left him with those words, a challenge that she'd anted up and he was still holding out. He spent the last four days thinking of nothing else but that conversation and her final say on the matter before all hell broke loose at her work. She'd closeted herself inside the office, some big project that had to be done immediately, worth hundreds of thousands of dollars. It required her to take one conference call after another and spend hours at her computer drawing and redrawing her designs.

He woke up this morning and found her gone with nothing but a note left on his bedside table telling him she'd meet him at the dinner tonight. He wanted to kick his own ass for sleeping through her coming into his room and standing next to his bed to deliver her message. He had such a vivid dream of her running her hand over his hair and down the side of his head and over his jaw.

He could still feel her mouth press to his in a soft kiss and taste her on his lips. The dream took a turn and she was under him. Her soft skin pressed against his as he sank deep inside her. Her mouth covering his as she sighed out her pleasure and his name. Her hands kneading the muscles in his back and sliding down to his hips and covering his ass, her fingers squeezing and pulling him close as he thrust hard and deep.

Startled out of his thoughts, he jumped when a hand clamped onto his shoulder and squeezed. He blinked and his eyes focused on the man standing beside him smiling wide.

"Is it possible to get stood up by a hooker?" Austin's wide grin accompanied the bad joke.

"If you weren't my best friend, I'd kill you." Noah shifted and stood chest to chest with Austin and glared into his friend's eyes. It pissed him off to see them dance with amusement at his expense. Noah kept his head enough to realize they were clear and not clouded by booze for a change.

"Where's your wild rose?" Austin teased again, coming dangerously close to getting decked.

"She's meeting me here. Some last-minute business trip."

Austin mocked him with an eyebrow raise.

Noah inhaled deep and let it out slow. "I'm only going to say this once. She is not and never was a prostitute. Make me repeat myself, and we'll step outside and I'll beat it into you. It's bad enough everyone else is gossiping. I expect better of you, since you know what it's like to have people talking behind your back about stuff they know nothing about."

Austin slapped him on the shoulder, a silent apology for talking out his ass.

"Tell me about her. People *are* talking. Your ex-lady-love paid me a visit and asked me to talk some sense into you before Roxy ruins your life even more than she already has. Cheryl said *that woman* has you turned upside down, you even had hookers staying at the house with Annabelle. Now, if that's the case, all I want to know is, why wasn't I invited?"

Noah downed the rest of his whiskey, the ice clinking against the glass when he thumped it down on the tray held by a passing waiter. He shoved his hands in his pockets and glared at his best friend.

"Cheryl's got no right to be telling tales."

"I heard your girl's knock-out gorgeous, able to fell men with a single knee to the family jewels." Austin elbowed him, attempting to put things back on a lighter note.

Noah laughed, responding to Austin and the easy way his friend dropped the hooker thing at his word.

"Tom propositioned her the same day we buried John and read the will. He had a hotel all set up for them to meet. She told me he was thinking with the wrong head, so she made sure he'd use the right one the next time he saw her."

Austin burst out laughing, drawing everyone's eyes from the crowd dispersed around them. "I see why you like her."

"She's not what you expect when you see her. You look at her and every thought turns to sex. Then, you talk to her, find out about her life, and all you think about is how someone with her background has such a kind, generous heart. You'll see." He nodded toward the ballroom double doors.

They stared down the aisle between the white-draped dinner tables to the beautiful woman standing alone, outshining everyone in the room.

"Damn." Austin's hand slammed down on Noah's shoulder and squeezed. "You were right, I've got her laid out on white sheets, all that black hair spread over the pillow, and she's . . ." Austin gasped and sucked in a quick breath when Noah's elbow connected with his gut.

"She's mine," Noah stated, never taking his eyes off Roxy.

She looked like a midnight dream in her black dress that sparkled silver in the light. He had no idea how it did that, but when she moved, it shimmered. The top draped and hugged her full breasts. The material met at the edge of her shoulders and the sleeves were slit down the outside, meeting at her wrists. Unlike the rest of the dress, he could see through the sleeves to her golden arms. The rest of the dress skimmed her curves and ended just above her knees, the see-through material going on to just below. His eyes skimmed down her gorgeous legs to her pretty feet in a pair of silver strapped high heels.

"You say she's yours," Austin challenged. "Let's see what she has to say."

Roxy scanned the crowd, searching for Noah. He caught her eye and her whole face lit up with her brilliant smile. The relief in her eyes made his heart soar.

"Take your best shot," Noah challenged. "She'll shoot you down." *Because she loves me.* His heart swelled with the absolute truth in that thought.

Chapter Thirty-One

Roxy hated being the center of attention, but the moment she stepped into the ballroom, everyone's eyes focused on her. She kept her head held high and reminded herself not to fidget.

Show no weakness.

Even though she expected the stares and whispers, it still unsettled her.

With Noah by her side, she could get through this evening. Hopefully, people would hold their tongues and Noah wouldn't end up punching someone.

Sweet, the way he stood up for her all the time.

Still, she didn't want it to become a habit he had to repeat the rest of his life.

Her heart soared the minute she saw him, standing with the blond man she'd seen him with at the funeral. Noah's eyes landed on her, scanned from head to foot, and even from this distance, she felt the heat in his gaze. He liked the dress. She smiled and started toward him, dodging a waiter and two couples involved in a boisterous conversation.

Instead of coming for her, Noah stood back and his friend walked toward her, a very intense look on his face. Serious blue eyes held hers. She stopped in front of him and waited.

"I planned to lead with the whole, 'Are you a hooker?' thing, but I've thought better of it."

"Refreshing." She kept an open mind and tried not to read anything into his intense stare.

"Thanks. I'd hate to be lumped in with everyone else you've met."

The smile caught her off guard. It changed everything about him, softened the intensity surrounding him, and made him less cold.

"You mean everyone in this town who's staring at us, wondering if we're coming to terms on a wild night of meaningless sex?"

He held out his hand and she accepted it without reservation. If he was important to Noah, she'd give him a chance. "Austin Hubbard."

"Roxy Cordero. Infamous non-hooker and John's secret daughter." She shook, then released his hand. "So, Austin, best friend and protector, here to check me out and see if I'm good enough to be with Noah, did I pass?"

"Not yet," he answered truthfully. "I want to know if you're running some game on him, or if you're the real deal."

"All I want is him. Clear enough?"

"I guess since you got the lion's share of the ranch, you don't need his money."

"Everything I need comes straight from his heart. If he decides I'm not worth that, I'll leave him be."

"Word is, you can't leave the ranch."

"It's a big place. Two people could live on that spread and never see each other. The thing is, I like seeing Noah every day. What I don't like is anyone thinking they can hurt him because of me, or what they think of me. I hate that people are talking behind his back and tarnishing his good name. I love the way he defends me, but despise the need for him to do so. I came here tonight so people could see me and make up their minds. What I didn't come here to do is stir up any more rumors, or give people cause to think I'm doing something I'm not. So, if you'll excuse me, the longer we stand here together, the more everyone is speculating about us. I'm going to join Noah."

She stepped away, but he grabbed her arm and held her still.

"Smile at me, like we're friends." When she hesitated, he added, "Please."

She smiled and held up her end of the show. "Noah and I have been friends since we had training wheels on our bikes. Noah said you're not what people expect. Even though I agree with him, I'd take his word over anyone else's on anything. Which is why, in this case, I had to make sure. I didn't know if he was seeing you the way he wants you to be, or seeing the real you."

"Noah is one of the few people who took the time to get to know me. For that reason and a thousand others, I'd do anything for him. Satisfied?"

"Completely. Sorry. You understand."

"Completely," she mimicked and made him laugh.

She snuck a glance at their avid audience. "I expected the stares. Why are so many pointed at you?"

"You're not the only one who can stir up gossip." He winked and held out his elbow for her to take his arm. She did, and he led her straight toward Noah. "Look at the way he looks at you. He's got it bad."

"He's not the only one," she answered his unspoken question.

A distinguished gentleman with silver hair and Austin's distinct blue eyes stepped in front of them and blocked their path. The muscles in Austin's arm stiffened beneath her hand. He shifted to go around, but the other man sidestepped and blocked them again.

"It's not bad enough you've become the town drunk, now you're cavorting with whores in front of family, friends, and business associates." Those were fighting words.

Roxy immediately disliked this man.

Austin's eyes narrowed. His jaw firmed, muscles ticked in his cheek. Everything about him went on the defensive like some wild animal alerted to a threat.

Austin sucked in an angry breath, gearing up for an argument, but she cut him off, hoping to avoid a scene. Only family could push your buttons like this.

"Mr. Hubbard, we haven't been introduced. I'm Roxy Cordero. Owner of the Speckled Horse Ranch."

"I make it my business to know the people of this community. And we all know the Wild Rose Ranch is where you really work."

"In this case, you've been grossly misinformed." Noah joined them and defended her. Again. "Roxy is a businesswoman, ranch owner, and championship barrel racer. You'll treat her with respect." Noah's hot glare could melt steel.

"There is nothing respectful about a place like that."

Roxy couldn't help herself and blurted out, "Been there, have you?" When his eyes went wide with shock and disgust, she knew he'd never debase his self-perceived untarnished character. Lisa and Cheryl contributed to the gossip, but one person had crossed a legal line. And a reckoning with him was coming. "No. Tom spilled all the dirty secrets to you and everyone else because I wouldn't sleep with him. Funny, you receive information from someone so willing to sell out his clients and their privacy and take him at his word. You accuse me of something I've never done, and dismiss me with disdain and no chance to prove you wrong."

"John should have kept you a secret instead of inviting you into his home and this community."

Noah took a menacing step forward, but she held him back with her hand on his arm.

"Secrets never stay hidden long. I wonder what secrets you're hiding."

He glared. "I'll not be one of those men whispering my secrets to you in bed."

"My standards are much too high."

He gasped and Noah and Austin smiled beside her.

"This is the company you keep?" Mr. Hubbard asked Austin.

"Yeah, I have better friends than family. I've only known her ten minutes and already I like her more than I ever liked you."

Mr. Hubbard glared at her again. "He doesn't have a penny to his name. No job. No prospects. Nothing but a piece of land he's too stubborn to sell for his own good."

Roxy caught the undercurrent and the spark of something in the old man's eyes. "A piece of land you covet," she guessed.

His eyes went wide with surprise, but he masked it and glared at Austin. "One day you'll give up."

Austin puffed out his chest. "I'll never sell it to you."

"Stubborn . . ."

"Pot and kettle," she addressed both of them. "Austin, I'm interested in this land. Sounds like there's a story I'd like to hear."

Mr. Hubbard scoffed. "Like you're interested in a plot of dirt."

She smiled sweetly. "I'm interested in why *you* are interested in this particular plot of dirt."

"It's family land." Something didn't ring true.

"Family lives on it," she pointed out.

"It's none of your concern."

She held Austin's arm and leaned into him. "Austin is my new friend. I'm making it my business."

Mr. Hubbard's ears burned red with rage. "It's not worth buying."

She gave Austin an assessing look, wondering if he agreed. He shrugged, not wanting to be drawn into the scene further.

"Maybe I do want to buy it. Help a friend out, and all that, when he's down on his luck."

"That land is worth far more than you'll ever make on your back."

This time she had to plant her hand on Noah's chest to hold him back.

"You're dangerously close to leaving in an ambulance tonight," Noah warned.

The crude remark stung, but she laughed it off, so others around them thought he'd made a joke. "Well, I do have more money than the collective bank accounts of everyone in this room." She leaned in close. "Including yours."

She guessed at his wealth by the cut of his suit and the diamond ring and Rolex watch he wore. The boots alone probably cost him several hundred dollars. Aside from all that, she recognized the man's arrogance. She'd seen men like him come and go from the Ranch, taking what pleasures they wanted because they felt entitled.

This man liked hurting Austin and lording whatever secret he held about the land over Austin's head. Beating his son meant more than family bonds and loyalty.

"Interesting that you state the land isn't worth buying, but is worth a lot of money."

Mr. Hubbard took a step closer and practically growled out, "This is family business. If you know what's good for you, stay out of it."

"Moved on from degrading me to threatening women," Austin said. "Pathetic."

"Yes, you are," his father shot back.

"I'd take Austin over a man who turns his back on family any day." Roxy's heart took a hit because she'd been on the receiving end of cruel cut-downs by her mother. Usually when she was drunk or stoned.

Austin's father glared down his nose at her. "You'll regret crossing me."

She pressed her lips together and shook her head. "If Tom was willing to spill my secrets, I wonder what it will cost me to get him to spill yours."

Outraged, Mr. Hubbard huffed out his outrage and rushed away.

She'd guessed right about Tom being his lawyer, too. "I want to know everything about this land and why he's so hell-bent on getting it back from you."

Austin shrugged. "My grandfather willed the land to me when he died last year. My father wanted to add it to his acreage. I refused to sell because the land is from my mother's family. I wanted something of my own, something that was a part of her. He's pissed I won't sell it to him, so he fired me from the family business and cut me off. That's all."

"Bullshit." She didn't believe for a minute this was all about bad blood because the land passed to Austin and not his father.

Roxy reached out for Noah's hand. "Do you have any idea why Austin's father wants that land so bad?"

Noah linked his fingers with hers. "Because he's a vindictive asshole. No offense, Austin."

Austin stuffed his hands in his pockets. "It's the truth."

"I think there's something more there." She squeezed Noah's hand. "It's time to fire Tom."

"He deserves a hell of a lot worse for what he's done. He should be disbarred." Noah walked her toward a group of men who appeared very interested in them. "Ready to work the room, dispel the rumors, and schmooze the people who hold the money and influence in this town?"

"Sounds like fun," she groaned out.

Austin offered encouragement. "Just like my asshole father, these people are looking for anything they can use to peg you for who they think you are. Be yourself, and you'll do fine."

Noah squeezed her hand, addressed her, but raised his voice so the others overheard. "How was your business trip? Did you sort out the cable system requirements for your project?" Noah gave her an opening to discuss what she really did for a living in front of the expectant men.

She took his lead and went with it. "It was a very successful trip. We won the bid based on several of my designs and my overall proposal."

"What's this about a cable system?" one of the men asked, directing his question to Noah.

Still, it was a start.

"Roxy is a designer. She works for a company that makes the equipment cable systems use to get their services into people's homes. She designs the layout of the equipment across a town or part of a city to feed those customer's homes. I can't really speak to all of it. It's quite complicated, but Roxy makes it look easy. She works long hours and comes up with some complicated solutions."

All the men stared at her and she spent the next few minutes talking about her work and answering their questions before walking to the next group.

Noah and Austin made a great team, ushering her around to all the people they knew, introducing her and always working her job into the conversation. When they met other ranchers, not only did they bring up her job, but Noah, and Austin once he caught on, brought up her horse training and championship wins. Any time someone even hinted at asking about the rumors, or her mother, Noah or Austin changed the subject with hardly anyone noticing. By the time dinner rolled around, she'd spoken to half the room of guests, but everyone was talking about her.

In a different way now.

Noah was careful never to be overly affectionate. When men showed any kind of interest, Noah kept his hand at her waist, her body tucked close to his, but never too close. He remained attentive, but not demonstrative.

"I'm impressed." Austin leaned in close to her ear at the table. "You really are nothing like what I expected, or what a man thinks when he first looks at you."

"No, I'm not. But never forget I can drink you under this table, and if I turn on the sexpot, I can have you begging on your knees."

"If I'm on my knees, you'll be begging for mercy."

"Stop flirting with my girlfriend," Noah scolded Austin with a good-natured smile.

"I can't help myself," Austin replied with an easy grin. "She's so damn good to look at."

"Keep it to looking, or I'll break whatever part of you touches her."

To show Noah she only wanted him, she gave in to her overwhelming need to touch him, reached up and slid her hand over his clean-shaven jaw, leaned in close, and whispered. "I missed you today."

"Not as much as I missed you. I wanted to drive you here tonight, have you to myself for a while before we walked in together. Don't ever leave the ranch without telling me."

"I left you a note."

"I'd rather you have woken me up and told me."

Austin leaned into her other side. "Oh God, you two are too sweet. I think I'm getting a toothache," Austin complained with a silly grin.

"Dance with me." She leaned close and squeezed Noah's thigh.

His nostrils flared and his eyes locked with hers.

Austin stood and smacked Noah on the back. "You two have a good night. I'm out of here."

"I want to talk more about your land," she called after Austin.

He kept walking away, but held up a hand and waved to let her know he'd heard her, even if he was dismissive about it.

Noah stood, held his hand out to her, helped her up, and walked her to the dance floor. She went into his strong arms, kept a respectable distance between them, and smiled up at him as they swayed to the beautiful slow song.

"Why are you pushing Austin on this?"

"I want to help him get back on his feet."

"Why?"

She tilted her head, reading the jealousy in his eyes. "First, he's your best friend. Second, I don't like family turning on family over something as stupid as a piece of land. Third, I know men like Mr. Hubbard. If he wants that land, it's for a reason. If it's really worth something, Austin should benefit from it."

"Let's forget about Austin for now. He wouldn't accept my help. I doubt he'll accept yours."

She rubbed her hand up and down his chest and smiled up at him. "I can be very persuasive."

Noah stared down at her. "You were right about the dress. It's killing me not to peel if off you." He pulled her in close and rested his cheek against her forehead. "You smell amazing. You feel even better." He glanced around the room at all the men staring at her. "Why do you have to be so beautiful?"

She leaned back and stared up at him, hoping he saw in her eyes how much she wanted him. "Tonight, just for you." She took a small step back, took his hand, and tugged him toward the door. "Let's go home."

Chapter Thirty-Two

Noah held Roxy's hand the whole way home. It had been a long day for her. First, she'd had to fly back and forth for her unexpected business meeting in San Francisco. Then, she attended the intense dinner. Now, she relaxed and stared out the car window at the night sky. No need to fill the silence. He enjoyed sitting beside her, rubbing his thumb over the back of her soft hand, and enjoying the closeness as one after another country love song softly poured out of the speakers. Roxy relaxed in a way she'd never done since moving to the ranch.

He thought about the dance they shared.

Let's go home, she'd said.

"Do you miss living with your sisters?"

"I don't miss Juliana leaving her stuff everywhere and never washing a dish, or Adria clunking around the kitchen at four in the morning because she's been up all night studying. Sonya tends to worry about everything, which amps my own need to make everything in our lives perfect." She turned her head to look at him. "I miss the quiet mornings in the barn with the horses, our Friday night pizza and movies, and talking to someone who knows me inside and out and accepts me no matter what."

"You've got the horses at Speckled Horse Ranch. You and Annabelle seem close as sisters now. I'd like nothing better than a standing pizza and movie Friday night with you. Any night, really."

A soft smile spread across her beautiful face. "Tonight went better than I expected. The best part, dancing with you."

"Is the ranch home now?" That's what he really wanted to know.

"It's starting to feel that way. The office is a great space to work. I love training the horses. After your talk with the ranch hands, most of them have stopped looking at me like some Playboy pinup. At least when I can see them."

"I'm glad they're behaving themselves. I for one understand how hard it is not to look at you."

She reached out and cupped his cheek. Her amused smile made him grin. He turned and kissed her palm before she pulled her hand free.

"I knew it would take time to settle in and get people to accept me. I love the relationship you have with Annabelle and the way you two are so close to Mary and Robby. You're a family. And you've made me part of that. I'll have to go back to Wild Rose soon, but it's easier to go back knowing I've got you to come home to now. I hope that eases your mind and doesn't make you uncomfortable."

Noah pulled into the driveway and stared up at the dark house. "Why would you think that unsettles me?"

"You've been very careful lately, moving this relationship forward slow and easy. While I appreciate it, I feel you holding back. I know it's to give me time because of our misunderstanding, but it's also starting to feel like you can't do or say what you want around me. I don't like that. Tonight around all those people, you were so careful not to touch me in a way that was too familiar. Even when we're alone, you're so cautious."

"I don't want to mess this up again."

"How about you be you, I'll be me, and when those two things don't match up, we say so. We talk about it instead of holding back all the time."

He brought her hand to his mouth and kissed the back of it. "Deal."

"I'm a little nervous," she admitted.

"Why?"

"With my past and what men think of me, the way I look, I feel like when it comes to sex there's an expectation . . ."

Noah shook his head. "Trust me, Roxy. Let go, and everything will be perfect." He leaned in and kissed her softly, sweetly. A kiss so filled with promise she couldn't help sinking into it and him. Noah didn't hold back. He let loose the reins on his need for her and took the kiss deeper, sliding his tongue along hers, keeping things slow but powerful. His hand cupped her face and held her trapped in his spell. She matched his moves, his sultry mood, and let go.

Noah kissed her long and deep for another moment, then softly brushed her lips with a light caress and pressed his forehead to hers. "I've been hoping for that for a long time."

"What?"

"You to stop thinking and just go with what makes you feel good."

She rubbed her hand along his jaw. "You make me feel good."

"That's all I want to do, sweetheart." He squeezed her hand. "Come with me."

They met at the front of the car. Noah took her hand as they walked up the porch steps and right through the front door.

Roxy's stomach fluttered. Not with apprehension like the first time she walked into the house, but anticipation. She and Noah had grown close these last weeks. She'd fallen in love with him. It felt a bit strange to admit that to herself. But as they walked up the stairs and Noah glanced over at her with hunger, need, and true happiness in his eyes, it seemed like the most natural thing in the world to feel. And to want to show him.

Noah led her up the stairs. At the top, they paused and listened to the quiet. Annabelle slept peacefully, unaware the two people charged with looking out for her happiness had found some of their own together.

Roxy appreciated Noah's patience as he held still, waiting to see if she changed her mind and sent him on to his room at the other end of the house. No way. Not now. Never again if she had her way.

She hooked her hand around his tie and tugged him toward her room as she stepped backward down the hall. He closed the distance, wrapped his arms around her waist, picked her up off her feet, and kissed her hard and deep. He walked her into her room with her feet dangling at his shins. She held him close, her breasts pressed to the solid wall of his chest. Tall, strong, handsome, Noah held her secure against him. Right where she wanted to be, but not quite close enough.

Noah set her back on her feet but didn't stop kissing her. She waited for his hands to slide the dress zipper down her back. His fingers squeezed gently and stroked her bare skin, but he didn't dive in and rush. He waited, took his time kissing her, his patience reigned.

Despite her nerves that his expectations might be more than she could fulfill, she wanted to snap his rigid control. She wanted to demolish her reservations that she wouldn't be enough. She wanted to be everything he wanted in a lover, but feared he'd think less of her if she gave in to the overwhelming desire sweeping through her.

Noah broke the searing kiss. He cupped her face and stared down at her. "It's just you and me. Whatever you want, whatever you need, it's the right thing. Even if you need more time."

"I want you, Noah. I want to be us without my past making me think something I do will make you think I'm like her."

Noah listened without taking his eyes off her. He swept his thumb over her kiss-swollen bottom lip. "What's the worst that can happen? We make love, you like it, I like it, we want to do it all the time. I want you to *love* it. I want you to want to be with me all the time. If you don't, *I'm* doing something wrong. And I want to do everything right, because I want you in my life. I want you and me to be us."

And just like that, all her inhibitions and reservations disappeared. She didn't second-guess herself, but allowed herself to do what she wanted. And what she wanted was to get her hands on the gorgeous man with the kind heart.

She slipped her hands up his chest and over his wide shoulders, pushing his suit jacket down his back and off his arms. He stood still, letting her do as she pleased as they eased back into the intimacy and growing need between them.

He'd loosened his tie on the ride home. She slipped the knot and pulled it off his neck, tossing it away with a smile she hoped conveyed her eagerness to get him naked. His gaze followed her deft fingers as she undid one button after the next down his shirt to his belt. She slid her hands inside, spread the crisp white cotton aside, and rubbed her hands over the wall of muscle that tensed and rippled beneath her roaming hands.

Noah pulled the shirt from his waistband and kicked off his shoes. She pulled the shirt down his arms. When it caught at his wrists and he had to wrestle it free, she took advantage and kissed her way from his neck, down over his hard pecs, and rippled abs to his belt buckle. His breath stopped the second she let loose his belt, unbuttoned his slacks, slid the zipper down, and slipped her hand inside and down the thick column pressed against his black boxer briefs.

She worked her palm down, then back up his hard length. Noah released his breath on a heavy sigh as his head fell back and the shirt dropped to the floor at his feet. She slid both hands over his hips, pushing his pants down his legs, then slipped her hands around to cup and squeeze his very fine ass. She pressed kisses to his hard chest and snuggled into all his warmth and strength.

Noah took advantage of having her close, unzipped her dress, and slid his fingers down her bare back and up her spine. He swept his fingertips across her shoulders, then dragged her dress down her arms. She freed her hands and removed her black lace bra revealing her bare breasts. The front of the dress hung at her hips.

She looked up at Noah and caught the awestruck look in his eyes.

"God, you're beautiful."

A shy smile tugged at her lips as her eyes roamed over every sculpted muscle in front of her. "When you smile at me, my stomach flutters with a thousand butterflies. When you touch me, your warmth spreads through me like a wave of heat that's a fire that doesn't burn. When you look at me, I see how much you want to be with me. But when you kiss me, I feel your patience and need and how much the moment means to you."

Noah cupped her face in one hand and leaned down close. "*You* mean everything to me."

The depth of how much he meant that warmed her heart. His kiss made the connection between them draw them closer.

Lost in the kiss, his strong body pressed to hers, her need to touch and give him everything, their remaining clothes disappeared along with her inhibitions. They ended up on the bed tangled around each other.

Noah kissed his way down her neck and chest and squeezed her breast, her tight nipple caught between his thumb and finger as he licked it. The contact startled her. Not because she didn't want him to touch her—she wanted a hell of a lot more of it—but because it brought to light the stark reality of how careful and restrained he'd been these last weeks. He'd kissed her. He'd held her. But he'd been the perfect gentleman.

He stilled and removed his hand. Her past had ruined so many potential friendships and relationships with men. She didn't want it to ruin what she had with Noah. He cared about her. He stuck up for her. He didn't want to use her.

He wanted to love her.

If only she'd let him.

She took his wrist and planted his hand over her breast. She placed her hand over his and squeezed. "Don't stop. I want more."

Noah leaned up, kissed her, and swept his thumb over her tight nipple. The sweet sensation rocked through her and made her sigh. Noah took the kiss deeper. Her tongue tangled with his as his hand squeezed and stroked her breast.

Emboldened by the amazing feeling sweeping through her, she rubbed her hands down his back and over his bare ass, rocking her hips against his hard length. He groaned and kissed his way back down her neck to her breast. He took her hard nipple in his mouth. His tongue slid over her sensitive skin and she raked her fingers through his thick hair and held him to her.

Roxy lost herself in the moment and wallowed in the exquisite and erotic sensations Noah evoked with every kiss, sweep of his tongue over her skin, and press of his body to hers. Aching for him, her body pulsed with a need so great she couldn't contain it. His fingers brushed over her soft folds. One sank deep into her slick core. His thumb rubbed her oversensitive nub. She rocked into his hand to the steady rhythm. The more she got into it, the more Noah gave her.

He held her right on the edge as he rolled on a condom.

They joined together with the need to be close so great that the slide of his body into hers, against hers wasn't enough. She held him close. Moved with him. Loved him with everything in her heart.

When he rose above her, her body locked around his, and the sweet friction turned to exquisite pleasure so intense she called his name and they both flew happily into the flames.

Chapter Thirty-Three

Noah woke up with a beautiful woman in his arms staring at him and his heart overflowing with happiness at the rightness of it all.

"He's not in his bed. He must be with Roxy," Annabelle whispered outside their door.

Roxy's eyes went wide with shock, then filled with fear that Annabelle would walk in on them in bed together.

His heart beat double time, too.

Last night, all he'd wanted was to be with Roxy and take things to the next level. He hadn't thought about anything else. The reality of how they'd do that slapped him in the face this morning. They lived together. They couldn't exactly hide. He wasn't about to start sneaking around in his own house.

"If he's with her, that's none of your business," Mary admonished.

"I just want them to know I'm happy they finally got together. It's about time," Annabelle added with that teenage outrage mixed with indignation. Impatience, and the excitement she couldn't hide.

Roxy smiled softly, her sexy-as-hell body pressed down the length of his. Warm. Inviting. Tempting.

"Do you think now is the time to tell them that?" Mary's question made him catch the laugh bubbling up inside him before he let it loose and Mary and Annabelle figured out he and Roxy were awake and listening. "If they want to sleep in, let them. Now come downstairs for breakfast."

"Fine." Annabelle's heavy sigh faded with their retreating footsteps.

Roxy rolled and sat on the edge of the bed and looked over her shoulder at him, her face and eyes filled with concern and an unease he didn't like seeing after they spent the night together.

He brushed her long hair across her back and over her shoulder, then traced his finger along the vine tattoo trailing from one shoulder, down her back, to the opposite hip. "Where are you going?"

"We should get up. Get to work."

He leaned up and kissed each rose along the vine. "Four roses. You and your sisters."

She smiled. "Yes. We all have one."

"It's beautiful. Like you."

He hooked his arm around her waist, pulled her back down beside him, and brushed the mussed hair away from her face. "We used both the condoms I had with me last night, but it's Sunday, and I intend to start my day in worship." He rolled on top of her and kissed her long and deep until she melted beneath him. He broke the kiss and stared down into her sultry gaze, her body already responding to his as she gently rocked against his aching cock. He put action to words and kissed his way down her neck to one pink nipple, puckered and begging for his mouth. She tasted just as good as last night. His need for her had grown to a living thing inside him that demanded to be fed. And so he lavished one breast and the other with his attention while the woman below him offered up herself to feed his growing desire. She didn't hesitate to slide her hands over his shoulders and down his arms. She raked her fingers through his hair and held him to her. Every moan and sigh encouraged him to, *go on, keep it coming.*

She wanted him.

She couldn't get enough of him.

It empowered him to love her with complete abandon.

He'd been so careful not to make her feel like an object, something to be used and cast aside. She'd had a lot of that in her life.

Her own parents treated her like something they could set on a shelf.

Not him. He wanted her to feel how much he wanted her in his life as a partner and lover. Important and needed and wanted and precious.

He wanted her to be happy. He wanted her to have everything good and wonderful. He didn't want her to hold back with him. He wanted her to trust that what they had was real. He didn't just want some fantasy come to life, though she was that for him. But that fantasy went far beyond sex. The brittle connection they'd shared before last night had become pliable. He no longer worried one careless word or misconstrued deed would snap it. Now, they shared a bond that allowed them to bend and compromise to meet each other's needs.

Making love to her didn't change that bond. It strengthened it.

Now she knew he'd never hurt her. He'd never betray her. He'd never turn his back on her.

He'd love her for the rest of his life.

He might not know how to tell her, but he could show her.

And he couldn't wait to show her again. In this way, when they were alone and as intimate as two people could be, she had his devotion.

He left her full breasts for a taste of the prize he wanted to sink into so bad his dick hurt. But this morning was about making *her* feel good. And showing her that the trust she'd given was worth the courage it took her to believe in him. So he headed south with soft kisses over the plains of her taut stomach to her curved hip around her toned thigh and down to her slick core weeping to be touched. He licked her soft folds and smiled at her sharp intake of breath and long exhale as he teased her soft folds with one slow sweep of his tongue.

"Noah," she sighed.

He draped her thighs over his shoulders, palmed one breast, her tight nipple between his fingers, and placed the other over her lower belly and swept his thumb across her sweet little nub. "I'm right here, sweetheart. Hold on."

She heeded the warning and slid her hands over his arms to his biceps and held tight as he took her from putty in his hands to a delectable treat on his tongue. Her pliant body rode the wave of pleasure to a crescendo that had her hips coming off the bed as he stroked her deep, making love to her with his mouth until she crashed over the edge.

Turned on to the point of release by her eager participation and her body quaking against his lips, he buried his face in the blankets between her legs and gripped the sheets trying to ride out the explosion of lust filling his system to the point he nearly came.

Roxy scooted back and gave him some room. Her fingers brushed over his hair. Even that sweet gesture nearly undid him.

"You're killing me, sweetheart."

"Noah, come here."

He looked up, knowing he'd be staring at the most gorgeous naked woman he'd ever seen. And there she was, sitting with her back against the headboard, her legs wide, knees up, breasts begging to be in his hands, and her sweet, seductive smile as she held up a condom.

His dick twitched. His mind screamed, *Get her.*

She sat there calm as could be, tore the condom open with her teeth, pulled it free, and held it out to him.

He took it, dove forward and onto his back beside her, and slid it on. She took advantage and straddled his lap. Hands free, he laid back, closed his eyes, and let out a long breath as she slowly sheathed him. Her hips rocked forward, then back in a slow roll that never stopped. He clamped his hands on her hips, held on, and just let her ride. Every slip and slide of her body over his was pure pleasure. She didn't rush or take her time but found a rhythm that made his need for her grow with every brush of her body against his.

He stared up at her, hair spilling down her back, breasts tipped with tight pink nipples and red abrasions from his beard stubble, her creamy skin soft against his. Head slightly back, eyes closed, she rocked her body over his, completely lost in the moment. She let herself go, finding the exact way that made her breath hitch and him respond to make it better for both of them.

Her head fell forward and her sultry gaze found his. "You feel so good."

He didn't have words to tell her what he felt. It had been dark last night. He'd mapped her body and committed it to memory, but seeing her loving him in the soft morning light filtering through the drapes and making her glow, highlighting her too sexy curves and the sweet smile on her lips did something to his heart. His chest ached with a tenderness he'd never felt.

One with her, he could feel her breathe. His heart beat with hers.

In the soft morning light, she leaned forward, pressed her breasts and body to his, and kissed him long and deep, the kiss an echo of their bodies' movements. He thrust into her, filled her, and at the same time, she filled him. All the dark and lonely places inside him disappeared, replaced by a light and warmth that came from her.

Her love filled him up and made his heart expand in his chest to the point there was no way to ignore or deny how much he loved her, how special she was to him.

The tempo changed because he'd changed. She'd given him something he'd wanted for a long time. She loved him in a way nothing could ever break.

He felt it in the slide of her hand over his head and down the side of his face as she held him with a tenderness that matched the soft kiss she pressed to his lips. It said, *I'm here and I'm not going anywhere.*

All of a sudden, close wasn't close enough. He thrust into her hard and deep, hooked his arm around her hips, held her close, and loved her until she was as desperate for release as him but so caught up in the moment neither of them wanted it to end. But her body locked around his and they both gave in and fell over the edge and into something neither of them would ever let go of.

She collapsed on his chest, her face pressed against his neck, her heart thrashing against his as her panting breaths washed over his heated skin.

"I love you." The words couldn't be contained when the feeling took up every cell in his heart, mind, body, and soul.

"I know. I love you, too."

He turned, her body slipping off his to settle beside him. He stared into her eyes and found nothing but the truth in them. "It's not just because we made love."

"I know."

"I don't know when it happened. I guess I knew I did, but I wasn't really sure what it was."

"I know."

"Is that all you have to say?"

She raked her fingers through his hair and held on. "I'll never leave you."

Stunned, he couldn't take his eyes off her. How did she . . . His father left his mother when he was a baby. His mother died, but it still felt like she'd left him. John's passing was still so fresh it made his heart ache just thinking about him.

Roxy got it. John had abandoned her. Candy had mistreated and left Roxy to her own devices her whole life. She had her sisters, but their lives were changing. They were all kind of going their separate ways now that they'd raised each other.

He and Roxy both longed for that sense of family and home. She'd never really had it. He'd had it and lost it more than once.

Roxy didn't say things she didn't mean. Her saying that meant far more than the simple statement implied. Because of John, she was committed to the ranch and Annabelle, but she wanted him to know that the promise she just made, and not lightly, meant that he'd never be alone again. For all the worries she harbored about being in a relationship, she'd made sure to ease his biggest unspoken and buried concern.

He wanted her to have that same promise. "I'll never leave you." He meant it all the way to his soul. And he meant to seal that promise with a preacher, a ring, and a kiss. Not necessarily in that order, or only once, so he kissed her now with tenderness and filled with the depth of emotion he had no idea how to express to her with words.

He kissed her one last time, then pulled her warm body against his and held her close. "You can trust me."

"I do."

She needed that promise from him. That he'd never break that bond. He'd never give her reason to question that he was on her side. Always.

Her easy acknowledgment and confident, I do, eased his mind considerably. They'd forged this bond. Now all they had to do was hold on to it.

Easier said than done. But he'd work hard every day to make sure she never regretted putting her faith in him.

Chapter Thirty-Four

Roxy stopped midway down the stable alley and stared at the gorgeous man carrying the heavy saddle to the tack room, one hand around the saddle horn as he carried it over his shoulder and down his strong back. Dark jeans covered his fine ass and long legs. He walked with purpose, no sign the added weight bothered him in the least.

She let out a catcall whistle. He jerked around at the high-pitched sound and smiled like he'd just gotten his biggest wish.

"Hey, sweetheart. This is a nice surprise."

She usually spent the morning in the office working straight to lunch. "Wanna go for a ride?"

She cocked her chin toward the saddle dangling down his back. "Looks like you're putting that away."

"I don't mind saddling up again if I get to spend time with you."

She closed the distance between them and stood close enough to smell the grass, wind, and horse clinging to his hard frame. "You're sweet, but I came down to tell you I'm headed out on an errand."

Noah took her hand and gave her a gentle tug to make her follow him into the tack room. "When will you be back? Annabelle is out with the vet going out on calls to some of the nearby ranches. I thought you and I could head into town for lunch."

"I'd love to, but there's something I want to do today before we fire Tom tomorrow."

Noah set the saddle on its stand and took a seat on the padded bench in front of the cubbies that stored horse blankets and riding helmets. He reached out and held her hips and stared up at her.

"Are you going to talk to a new lawyer?"

She bit her lip and hoped he understood why she wanted to do this on her own. "I'm going to see Austin."

He cocked his head and studied her. "Why?"

"I think there's something going on between him and his father and that land."

"His dad is a dick and fucking with Austin because Austin won't do what he wants."

"People always have a reason for the things they do."

"Sometimes it's just because they enjoy hurting other people and making them squirm."

She knew that all too well. "He wants that land, and I want to know why."

Noah frowned. "I'll go with you."

Roxy shook her head.

"Why not?" Noah's words had a bite.

"He won't talk to me with you there. He's refused your help out of pride."

Noah pressed his lips tight. "And you think he wants your help?"

"He's a man plummeting to rock bottom. I think I can offer him a lifeline that doesn't come across as a handout or obligation that feels like pity."

"Why? Why would you go out of your way to do this?"

To ease his mind and make him feel the connection they shared, she moved close, planted one knee by his hip, swung the other over his legs, straddled his lap, and sank down on his thighs. She cupped his face and made him look at her. "You love him like a brother. He's your best friend. You worry about him. I saw the concern you had for him at the funeral and again last night at dinner. He wants what you have here at the ranch, but he's had everything taken away for no other reason than spite that he holds on to the one thing no one can take from him."

"His father will take it. Eventually. Austin sold everything he owns to pay the property taxes. If he doesn't do something soon, he'll default on them and lose the property."

"Then let me try to convince him that I'm his best option." She hoped Noah agreed, but his gaze searched her eyes for some deeper meaning. "He won't accept your help because you're too close to him. He doesn't want to disappoint you. He doesn't want to lose your friendship. I'm nobody to him. If this doesn't work, or he screws it up, it's not personal."

"I'm his best friend. You're mine. Don't you think that if he fucks this up that I won't be mad as hell on your behalf?"

"I'm not saying it makes perfect sense, but I'm hoping that I'm separation enough from you that he might take the lifeline I'm offering him." She brushed her thumbs over his hard jaw. "It wasn't just the concern I saw in you when Austin showed up those two times, but the relief that he hadn't completely self-destructed. Please, Noah, let me try to do this for you. I hate seeing you upset."

Noah pulled her close and wrapped both arms around her. "You know what it's like to have nothing and have the one person in your life who should be holding out their hands to pick you up only slap you down. I've tried a dozen different ways to get through to Austin. You want to take a shot at him, okay, but don't be surprised when he turns you down flat."

To tease him out of his dark mood, she leaned back and smiled. "Do you think any man would turn me down?"

He let out a half-hearted laugh. "Lord knows I can't, which is why you're getting your way right now."

"Oh honey, I had my way with you last night. I'll have my way with you later, too."

Noah slid one hand into her hair and stared right at her. "Promise?"

"I'm looking forward to it."

His fingers rubbed against her head. "I like this, you, relaxed and flirting and at ease with things the way they are now." To let her know he meant the new intimacy between them, he tightened the hold he still had around her hips, making her center rub against his hard length.

Her heart fluttered and the warmth that glowed inside her whenever she was in his company flared. "When I'm alone with you, it's easy. But I'm still worried that others will see us together and make trouble for you."

"I don't care what anyone says or does. I just want to be with you."

She traced his jaw with her fingertips. "You say that, but I saw the annoyance and anger last night when people stared, whispered behind our backs, and outright made rude comments to my face."

"It did make me angry. But by the time we left, most of those whispers were about how beautiful and smart you are. Those who made rude comments to your face were stumbling over their words to get you to tell them more about training Houdini for the Olympics."

"That's not a done deal. He still needs some work."

"The fact you've got a shot at getting that misbehaving beast sold to an Olympic rider is amazing." Noah gripped her sides. His mouth dipped into a frustrated frown. "If John had just brought you here, raised you instead of hiding you away like some dirty little secret, everyone would know you the way I know you."

She kissed him softly and hugged him close. "It took me a long time to understand nothing is ever that simple."

"He should have fought for you." He meant every earnest word.

"You showed me last night, you fight for me now."

"You can count on that." He slid his hand to the back of her head and drew her in for a long kiss. "Can I talk you into ditching this humanitarian mission to come up to the house with me?" Noah squeezed her hips, eliciting a shiver of need that prompted her to roll her hips against his hard length.

Roxy wanted to stay and give in to her growing need for Noah's affection. No one had ever made her feel this wanted and desirable in a way that went far beyond her sex appeal.

Loving Noah, giving in to her need for him, expressing her love felt so natural and right, she didn't hesitate to wrap her arms around his neck and kiss him as answer to his question. If he wanted to be alone with her, everything else could wait.

She'd meet Austin later.

Nothing and no one was more important to her than Noah. And after their rocky start, she wanted to show him that her earlier reservations and inhibitions wouldn't carry through the rest of their relationship.

The freedom she felt with him made her euphoric and daring.

She liked it.

This is what she'd always wanted. What she'd seen others enjoy and wished for herself.

Her heart and life had never been this full.

Noah gripped her ass and stood. Feeling light as a feather in his arms, she kissed him again and again, not worried one bit he'd drop her.

Someone cleared their throat behind them. Noah growled his displeasure at the interruption. They broke the kiss and turned. Heat flushed her cheeks when she spotted Robby staring at his feet, avoiding looking at them.

"Uh, sorry to interrupt . . . didn't mean to walk in on . . . Garvin's here about the colt you talked about selling him. I'll get the colt and buy you ten-twenty minutes." Robby shuffled his feet, snuck a peek at them with a silly grin on his face, then darted back out the door into the main part of the stables.

Noah sighed.

Her cheeks burned, but she laughed.

"What's so funny?"

She smiled at him. "I've never seen Robby blush."

"The last time he caught me in the stables with a girl, I was a teenager, and got a talking to about respecting women."

"And do you respect me?" She didn't need to ask. She just wanted to see what he'd say, seeing as how they'd been caught. And she still had her legs wrapped around his waist.

"I tried to get you up to the house instead of slamming the door and having my way with you on the tack room bench."

She glanced over at the padded seat. "We've got at least ten minutes."

Noah hugged her close, his face tucked against her neck. "God, I love you. But I don't want anyone else catching us in here like this."

"Then you might want to take your hands off my ass and put me down."

"I don't want to do either of those things." Contrary to his words, he hugged her close, then set her on her feet. "How long will you be gone?"

"I'm not sure. Depends on how stubborn Austin wants to be."

Noah rolled his eyes. "Stubborn is Austin's default these days. Be home for dinner. You'll need the sustenance if you really want to have the stamina to get Austin to cooperate."

"Wish me luck."

Noah kissed her softly, then stared down at her with regret in his eyes and a longing to finish what they started. "I think I should wish Austin luck. He's got no shot against you. When you set your mind to something, you get it done." He smacked her lightly on the ass. "Go get him, honey. I can't stand to see him falling deeper and deeper into a bottle."

Roxy pressed her hand to Noah's chest over his heart to let him know she understood how much Austin meant to him. She headed out to her car and smiled when Noah apologized to Garvin for being late for their meeting and Garvin waved to her and said, "I won't hold it against you that you'd rather spend time with a beautiful woman than an old geezer like me."

Roxy blew the older gentleman a kiss before slipping into the front seat of her car.

Garvin smiled and tipped his cowboy hat.

Noah grabbed Garvin's shoulder and turned him away from Roxy and toward the colt in the corral.

Roxy headed out to Austin's place, knowing that some part of her needed to help Austin the way she'd tried to help her mother all these years. She didn't want to see Noah's best friend ruin his life and spend the rest of it trying to kill himself a little at a time. She hadn't saved her mother from that fate, but if she could help Austin, maybe that would assuage some of the guilt she felt for failing her mother.

To make Noah happy, and change the course of Austin's life, she had to try.

Chapter Thirty-Five

Roxy turned into the narrow driveway and took it slow, watching in the rearview mirror for the gray Accord that followed her from the ranch out here to Austin's place. Sure enough, the Accord stopped on the road. The driver stared at Roxy's bumper as she headed toward the weathered white house.

Roxy wasn't in the mood to play games and get caught up in whatever drama her mysterious stalker had planned.

She had work to do.

The unexpected neglect and abandonment of the house and property solidified her resolve even more. Austin's wealthy father had turned his back on his son and left him living in squalor. No wonder Austin had floundered this past year. If he grew up anything like Noah on a prospering ranch made even more successful by the Hubbards' thriving mining business, then Austin had been ill-equipped to face the hardship and struggle of turning this place into something with no money. When you've always had money and knew it solved most any problem, trying to do anything without it seemed like a daunting task. Add in that Austin's father had probably thwarted his efforts and degraded him for every attempt to change his circumstances and it's no wonder Austin gave up.

Sometimes parents sucked.

She parked in the driveway next to Austin's truck, the only thing in sight that the last decade and more hadn't deteriorated. The farmhouse and outbuildings had a corroded feel. They stood rotting in the sun.

And so was the man who stumbled out of the barn. Though his unsteady gait said he was also marinating in whiskey.

Roxy exited her car and walked toward Austin, hoping she didn't have to catch him if he lost his struggle against gravity.

One quick glance down the driveway confirmed her suspicions. Their unwelcome audience intended to stay for the show.

"Aren't you a pretty sight on this shitty morning?" Austin didn't stop in front of her like she expected but walked right into her and wrapped his arms around her in a hug that turned into her holding up his big frame. The stench coming off him wrinkled her nose. Whiskey and sweat. He needed a shower, coffee, and time to sober up.

"You're drunk."

"Truer words . . ." Austin's hands slipped down her back to her ass. It probably had more to do with his lack of coordination and the booze than him trying to cop a feel.

She pushed against his chest to get him standing up straight so she could see his face. "I need to talk to you. It's time to stop the self-pity and be happy again."

Austin frowned and shook his head, his eyes at half mast, bloodshot, and filled with misery. "Happy is for people who have something worth living for." He cupped her face and stared down at her. "Noah has you."

She appreciated the drunken admission laced with true appreciation and tinged with envy that Austin sincerely wanted Noah to be happy.

"I have this shithole that is worth less than spit." He glanced at the land and buildings around them. "Maybe I should just sell the place to my father, take the easy way out, and leave for good." Austin released her face, stepped back, turned toward the hills, flipped them off, then shouted, "Fuck him. Why the hell does he want this place? Just to take it from me. So I don't have anything." He took a step toward the hills. "I don't have anything, motherfucker!" He flung his arms wide to encompass the desolate land and shabby buildings that anyone passing by would assume had been abandoned long ago.

Roxy hooked her arm around Austin's waist and led him toward the porch. He draped his arm over her shoulders and leaned on her. Mostly so he didn't face-plant in the knee-high weeds.

It wasn't the first time she led a drunk where they needed to go. She hoped he'd let her lead him to a better sort of life. Back to the kind of life he'd had growing up. A life he didn't think he deserved anymore because Austin's father wanted him to think that without him, Austin was nothing but a worthless failure.

Roxy spotted the cot and sleeping bag on the porch with the mostly empty bottle of bourbon beside it. A stack of clothes, a pair of boots, miscellaneous bathroom supplies, and a two gallon jug of water made it appear Austin was living outside. The stench she'd mostly attributed to Austin got worse as they walked up the porch steps and approached the door.

"What the hell is that smell?"

Austin stopped in his tracks and tried to turn her back to the steps. "You should go. No one should be here."

Roxy tried to steer Austin to the door, but he held his ground, strong and determined despite his intoxication.

"We can't go in there."

"Why not?"

"Trust me, you don't want to see what's in there." Austin shuffled over to the cot and sat on it. He propped his elbows on his knees and raked his fingers through his hair and held his head between his hands.

She crouched beside him. "Austin, I'm here to help. Tell me what is going on."

"The kind of help I need . . ." He shook his head. "Even if I could make it work, the amount of money it would take . . ."

"If you had the money, what would you do with this place? What's the dream, Austin?"

He stared out across the porch and property. "A working ranch. Horses. Cattle. Life," he added on a whisper. "Grandpa talked about mining treasure. I'd like to see if that was just old west bedtime stories or if this land really has a hidden treasure." He glanced at her, his eyes filled with loving memories. "I see now why he told me wanting more than you need can lead a man to ruin. I certainly don't need this headache." He held his hands out to indicate the property he kept instead of selling it because it meant something to him despite the fact it cost him everything. "This place has ruined me."

"It doesn't have to be that way."

He shot her an incredulous look, then exploded. "I have a house that's a cemetery to rats, squirrels, and God knows what else. It's filled with every single thing my grandfather ever owned. To the rafters. The stables are falling apart. I wouldn't dare put a horse in there, but it's where I sleep when it's too damn cold to sit on my throne here and lord over my pile of rubble and rail at my grandfather for leaving me this mess, and my father for taking everything I ever had just so he can have this piece of shit property." Austin sighed out his frustration and anger and glared at everything around him. "You know what I want? To show him what this place could be. That I'm the better man because I turned this pile of shit into something worth having."

"Okay. Let's do that."

"Yeah, sure. I'll get right on it."

"We'll start with coffee and making a list of what needs to be done first." She headed for the front door.

"Where are you going?"

"To the kitchen to make coffee."

She opened the front door and took two quick steps back as the stench hit her like a tidal wave and the sight before her stunned her speechless.

Austin scrambled to the door and pulled it shut. "I warned you."

"Austin? How can you live in there?" Newspapers, books, shopping bags, boxes, Christmas and other holiday decorations, a colander, and dirty clothes filled the room from floor to ceiling, leaving only a foot-wide path from the front door into what could only be described as a junk heap on steroids.

"No one can live in there. My grandfather died because he couldn't let go of anything."

"What happened?"

"I came out here all the time to check on him. He always met me on the porch. This place shamed him, but he didn't have it in him to fix it. He refused to talk about it, let alone admit he had a problem."

"Why haven't you cleaned it out?"

Austin swung his hand out toward the door. "How the hell do I fix *that* when I can barely afford to feed myself? Garbage service picks up the recycling and garbage can each week that I fill to the brim and then some, but let's face it, it'll take me ten years to clear that place out." Austin went back to sitting on the pathetic cot. "I look at that house and see how easy it was for my father to manipulate him to do what he wanted. He made my mother believe he saved her from this place. That she should be grateful. Maybe she was. I don't know. But I do know she loved her father. I loved my grandfather. Even with all this," he pointed with his thumb at the house behind him, "he was still a better man than my father could ever hope to be."

"You're a better man than you've been this past year," she pointed out. "Which is why I'm here."

"Why the fuck do you care about me? Go home to Noah. He loves you. You guys have the ranch. A life together."

"I care because I know what it's like to have a parent turn their back on you. I know what it's like to feel worthless and useless and determined with no means to turn that determination into dreams that actually come true despite the nightmare of your life."

"I don't want your help," he snapped.

"Well, you've been having this pity party all by yourself for a long time. Now, I'm RSVP'ing and shutting down the blues."

Austin glared up at her, still not willing to even hope she could turn this party around and make his life a celebration and not a wake for all he'd wanted and never achieved.

"You and I are starting a business together. We'll start by getting this ranch up and running. I assume you know a few geologists and mining experts we can have come out and survey the land. Who knows, maybe you're sitting on a shitload of sapphires or a huge deposit of copper."

"I'm sitting on a lump of coal."

"I'm pretty sure it's shoved up your ass and making you a total jerk."

Austin pressed his lips together, holding back a grin he didn't want her to see. "Don't you have something better to do with your time and money?"

She copped a squat on the weathered porch boards in front of him and settled in to let him know she had no intention of letting him push her away. "Noah says you're worth the bet. I'm from Vegas, and willing to take a gamble on you. So what's it going to be, Austin? Can you turn this place into a winning hand if I stake you?"

Austin stared over her head at the land he so obviously loved. "If I had the money, I could make this place something."

She heard his unspoken, *I could make myself into something.*

"Let's get down to business." She pulled out a notebook from her purse and flipped it open.

"Roxy?"

She looked up and got caught in the sincerity in his eyes, the depth of gratitude she saw in them, and a hint of fear that she'd back out or disappoint him when he dared to hope. "It's going to be okay now, Austin. I promise."

To give Austin time to let it sink in and shift his focus to the job at hand, she clicked her pen and put it to paper. "Let's start with the house. What needs to be done?"

"Aside from bulldozing it to the ground?"

She laughed under her breath. "I think we can salvage it." A touch of relief lit his eyes. "This place means everything to you. You don't want to demolish it. You want to hold on to it and the fond memories you have of your grandfather. We'll keep the good and toss out the trash."

She began her list with ordering several large dumpster bins for trash and recycling.

"Thank you, Roxy."

She glanced up at him. "For what? We haven't even gotten started."

"For seeing what no one else but me seems to see in this place."

She nodded, acknowledging his attachment to the ranch, the house, the legacy his grandfather left him that may not be much, but it meant the world to him. It was a piece of his history, his family, and the mother he lost far too soon.

John left her a legacy. Maybe not the one she wanted, but she'd make the most of it and use what she earned to help her sisters and Austin. And on Speckled Horse Ranch, she'd found peace and love and a home.

Austin deserved that, too.

But it would take a lot of work to turn this place into a home again.

Austin needed help, and Sonya needed to set her numbers aside and live a little. They both needed this project.

Chapter Thirty-Six

Noah pulled his phone from his dusty jean pocket hoping Roxy sent the text. He stared at the picture of Austin embracing Roxy with his hands on her ass for a good ten seconds with his heart clenched tight in his chest cutting off his breath and turning the lead stone in his gut to a roiling ball of rage. A second text popped up.

CHERYL: Since Austin doesn't have any money she must be giving it away

His anger found the right target.

Another picture popped up. The second picture showed Roxy and Austin walking with their arms around each other up to Austin's house.

She swore last night in his arms that she'd never leave him. He believed that all the way to his soul.

Because he trusted her, he dismissed what the pictures implied.

He rode the mare he'd been training for the last hour back to the stables and handed her off to one of the stable hands who eyed him with alarm when he ran off. He jumped in his truck and tore out of the driveway.

The pictures of Roxy with Austin burned in his head. The reason they were sent roiled his gut. He expected Cheryl to be there when he arrived and he wasn't disappointed. She sat in her car at the end of the drive and stepped out when he slid the truck to a jarring halt behind her car and jumped out.

"You got here fast."

"Why the hell are you stalking my girlfriend?"

Taken aback, Cheryl retreated as he advanced on her. "Why are you mad at me? She's the one secretly meeting Austin. Your best friend."

"I know she's here. I know why she's here. Because she's a good person and wants to help him. Why are you here? Just to cause trouble? Make up more shit about her?"

"You saw the pictures. The way they were with each other."

"Neither Austin nor Roxy would ever do anything like what you're suggesting. I know that. But what does it say about you that you'd follow her here looking for any little thing you can spin into a sordid tale to get me to break up with her?"

"She's not good for you, Noah. She's the Madam of a notorious brothel at best. We all know what she really is."

"You and all the others you include in that *we* can all go to hell. Stop calling and leaving me messages. Stop texting me. We're over."

He turned to walk away, but stopped at her next words.

"I know you don't want to see Annabelle ordered to live with her mother. Send Roxy away, or that's exactly what will happen. Roxy doesn't belong here."

"No one will ever take Annabelle from me or her home."

"Playing house sounds like a good idea, but in the end, she'll get bored and she'll leave you. She'll go back to what she knows."

"What she knows?" He glanced up at the sky, thinking about what Roxy knew. "You want to know why she's here? To start a business with Austin. To help my friend dig himself out of the hole his father unfairly put him in."

"Buying off your friends," she suggested, her words filled with skepticism.

Noah shook his head, disheartened that Cheryl, someone he thought of as a friend, refused to see the truth or even give Roxy the benefit of the doubt.

Lisa's influence no doubt.

"Helping others, taking care of them, that's what Roxy knows. Annabelle has blossomed. She's found her confidence. She stands up for herself and others and doesn't fall to peer pressure. She's found a purpose that makes her happy. All of that because of Roxy's influence." Noah held up his hand to stop her from saying anything. "Before you turn even that into something ugly, you should ask yourself what you hope to accomplish by trashing Roxy, because I want nothing to do with you. Lots of good folks got an up close and eye-opening introduction to Roxy last night. They liked her. They learned about who she really is. Rumors and trash talk aren't going to be believed so easily anymore."

She gave him a snide smile. "A picture is worth a thousand words. It brought you here today."

"Only to stop you, not because I believe anything is going on with Roxy and Austin. What are you going to do, smear his name and mine just to get in a dig at her? People will see, just like I do, that it's petty and rooted in jealousy." He purposely looked her up and down and shook his head. "And why wouldn't they believe that, because she's beautiful inside and out and you've shown your true colors. Keep this up, you'll be the one ostracized and talked about behind your back."

The stricken look on her face tweaked his conscience. He didn't like hurting her, even though he spoke the truth. And because he had nothing left to say, he walked away and hoped this was the last time she interfered in his life under the misguided notion that she was helping him.

"Noah, it can't end this way," she called after him.

He held the door to his truck open and looked back at her. "It ended when you made it clear *I* didn't appeal to you as much as what you wanted from me."

"That's not true."

"Sure it is. That's why you showed up for the reading of the will under the guise of consoling me over John's death. But we both know you tried to use that as your way back in. It didn't work and it's made you desperate and bitter." He contained his anger and tried to remember that once he'd liked Cheryl. Once, they'd been happy together. "Let this go, Cheryl. Don't make me hate you."

This time, Noah jumped into the truck and sped down the driveway. Roxy and Austin walked out of the dilapidated stables, Roxy with her head down as she wrote something in a notebook. Austin tapped his elbow to her arm to get her attention. Roxy's head came up. Even from twenty feet away he saw the annoyance and anger flash in her eyes when she spotted him getting out of his truck and walking toward her.

He didn't stop until he stood right in front of her and took her beautiful face in his hands. "Are you okay? She didn't say or do anything to you, did she?"

Roxy leaned into his palm and the anger faded from her eyes and turned to resignation.

"Who was that woman?"

"My ex, Cheryl."

"Well, Cheryl wants *your* attention, not mine. Looks like she got it."

"Yeah, and me telling her *again* that we're over. There's a hard ex on that ex-girlfriend." He brushed his thumb over her cheek and held her gaze. "I love you."

Noah took a good look at his friend. "Are you drunk?"

Austin shrugged. "Only about eighty-two percent. Your woman won't leave me be. She's bossy and won't take 'no' for an answer." Austin stared at the ground for a moment, then tilted his head and glanced at Noah out of the corner of his eye. "What do you think about me partnering with her?"

"Best thing that ever happened to me. You'd be an idiot to turn her down."

"You're okay with me working with her, taking her money?"

"Roxy is smart and you're not an idiot."

Austin gave him a lopsided mock frown that only made Noah grin.

"Taking a helping hand isn't the same as taking a handout. You do your part, make this place into what you envision it to be, Roxy will make out just fine. She believes in you. So do I."

Austin hung his head and let out a heavy sigh. He closed the distance between them and gave Noah a bear hug and hearty pat on the back. "Thanks, man. You don't know what that means to me."

Noah had a pretty good idea how much it meant to Austin to have someone believe in him after his father had treated him so horribly.

"I'll get this list to Sonya. She'll be here soon."

Austin gave Roxy a tilted grin. "You don't trust me to do it on my own?"

"My reasons for wanting to bring Sonya here have more to do with her than you. But this is a big project, more than any one person can handle, especially if we want to get this place up and running as soon as possible. Even if you hate to admit it, you need the help, Austin. And yes, Sonya will be here to ensure my investment isn't wasted."

"On booze, you mean?"

Roxy smiled with a touch of mischief mixed with a threat. "Sonya won't put up with your shit, so I'd sober up and get your act together before she gets here."

"You didn't say, but is she from the ranch?" Austin's eyes lit up with interest.

Roxy got in Austin's face. "She's one of my sisters. She's family. She's an accountant, not a hooker. Anyone says otherwise, you better be the first to correct them."

Austin held his hands up like he was about to be arrested. "I swear, I'll be on my best behavior."

Noah took Roxy by the waist and pulled her away from Austin and into his chest. "Austin knows you and your sisters aren't like your mothers."

"I wish everyone, including your ex, got the message."

Noah kissed her on the head. "That's out of our hands, but you worked another miracle: Austin agreed to work with you."

"Work is the right word." Austin raked his hand through his hair. "We're going to need an army to whip this place into shape."

Roxy cuddled into Noah's chest. "Sonya is as good as a drill sergeant. I'll send the list to her when I get home. Be ready. When she gets here, she'll want to hit the ground running."

Austin leaned back and to the side, stretching his muscles. "I'm in no shape to run."

"Right now, you can't even walk a straight line," Roxy teased. "Fix that, so you can fix this place."

Austin took Roxy's hand and tugged, pulling her out of Noah's light embrace. He hugged her close and said into her ear, "Thank you."

Roxy tightened her hold. "You're welcome." She released Austin, turned to Noah, kissed him, then headed for her car. "See you back at the ranch, Noah. Austin, I'll be in touch."

Noah and Austin watched her drive away.

Austin tapped him in the gut with the back of his hand. "Does she ever stop?"

"No." Pride filled that tiny word to bursting.

"Don't let her go."

Noah turned and looked Austin in the eye. "I'm going to marry her."

"If you don't, I will." Austin smiled at Noah's glare. "Congrats, man."

"Keep it quiet. I still need a ring and to ask her."

"Details. Everyone who sees you together can see it's a forever kind of thing."

Noah rolled his eyes. "Tell Cheryl that."

"Do what Roxy does: drop the haters in your life."

"I think Cheryl got the message today. Tomorrow, Tom."

Chapter Thirty-Seven

Roxy held Noah's hand as they drove to town. She still felt the warmth and echoes of pleasure they shared last night. Waking up with Noah again this morning reinforced the connection they shared and helped knock down any fears that she'd lose this amazing thing they shared. Every day it felt stronger, more meaningful. If she felt this wonderful today, how would she feel months, years, decades from now? She didn't delude herself into believing it would be easy to keep their relationship this happy. She was prepared to put in the work, because she cared deeply for Noah and wanted what she never thought possible: a happy life with a man who loved her.

Noah reached over and brushed his hand down her hair. "You look happy."

She smiled over at him. "I am. More than I've ever been."

"I could live on your smile."

She leaned over and gave him a soft kiss, then fell back in her seat as her phone dinged with another text from Sonya.

"Is Sonya excited about moving here?"

Roxy sent off the last in a string of texts about Sonya temporarily moving and working in Whitefall.

"Getting a ranch and potentially a mining business up and running aren't exactly Sonya's dream jobs."

"Doing the accounting for the Ranch probably isn't her dream job either."

"Numbers are easy for Sonya. She needs a challenge. Whether she thinks she does or not."

"Austin is certainly a challenge."

Roxy eyed him. "How was he yesterday when you left him?"

"Stunned. Overwhelmed. But incredibly grateful for the opportunity. Though he also seemed to not believe it either."

"He'll believe it when the work starts."

Noah pulled the truck into the parking lot outside Tom's office and swore.

Roxy sat up straighter. "What's wrong?"

"That's Lisa's car. What the hell is she doing here?"

"Conspiring with the enemy."

Noah swore and swung the truck into a parking spot. "They're both our enemies."

"If you don't want to deal with this, I'll do it alone."

Noah glared at her. "We are both Annabelle's guardians. We both own the ranch. We're partners. Professionally and personally. We do things together, Roxy. Always." He took her hand and brought it to his mouth and kissed her palm, then laid it against his cheek. "Now let's go ruin this asshole's day."

"Looks like Tom and Lisa already ruined your day."

"With you beside me, every day is bright and sunny."

Roxy's heart melted over the love-drenched, sappy sentiment. "What am I going to do with you?"

"Keep me," he suggested.

"Always," she mimicked his earlier statement.

They exited the truck and met on the path leading up to the single-story building with flower boxes dripping ivy under the windows. Roxy assumed the gardening service or an eager assistant kept the flower beds filled with annuals appropriate for the season. Pink, yellow, and white blooms welcomed clients.

Tom was not going to be happy to see them. Losing their business would cost him money, but also other potential clients. Rumors were already circulating that Tom was the one who outed Roxy as the owner of the Wild Rose Ranch. Privileged information.

They'd see over the next days and weeks if Roxy's appearance at the rancher's dinner would turn the tide of gossip in her favor.

They entered the small reception area and stopped in front of the un-manned desk. Tom's office door stood ajar about six inches. Though they couldn't see Tom and Lisa, they heard them loud and clear.

"We need to do something now," Lisa whined.

"We're building a case. The pictures from Cheryl will help, but they aren't enough. Acting without caution could jeopardize everything."

So Cheryl had two reasons to take the pictures, to turn Noah against Roxy and to make a judge think Roxy had done something inappropriate.

"They cut me off. I need the money."

"Soon."

"Soon? You keep saying that while she digs her claws in deeper to what should rightfully belong to me. I married that old man. I gave him a daughter."

Noah and Roxy shared a look and raised eyebrows. Finished listen-ing to the two of them conspire, Roxy planted her hand on the door and pushed it open wide. She and Noah stared at the two wide-eyed traitors.

Roxy shook her head. "Did you even earn your law degree? Or do you just not have any regard for the law? Maybe you're too stupid to under-stand the concept of privilege and conflict of interest. Doesn't matter. You're fired. Noah and I will have our new lawyer file charges against you."

"You can't do that. You have no idea what is going on here. She just wanted to talk about the terms of the will and her daughter's welfare."

Noah glared down at Lisa. "If you cared one bit about Annabelle's welfare, you'd call her once in a while or come visit her."

"She won't take my calls."

"Do you blame her?" Roxy shot back.

"I want what's mine."

"You want the money, not Annabelle." Noah pressed his lips together, disheartened on Annabelle's behalf. "You won't get either. Ever."

Lisa practically shot lasers out her eyes as her white-hot anger boiled over. "You want me to go away, give me back what you took. Do the right thing."

Roxy held Lisa's hate-filled gaze. "We are. Annabelle has a home with people who love her and want the best for her. You think you know me. I haven't shown you half of what I'm capable of when it comes to protecting that girl. You push me, I'll push back, and believe me, you're not prepared for what's coming."

"You can't threaten me."

"That's a promise." She shifted her gaze to Tom. "You should have just done your job instead of making this personal. After all, it can't be the first time a woman shot you down. You should be used to it by now."

Tom's ears went red with rage.

Roxy smiled. "I told you not to fuck with me. You'll be hearing from our *new* lawyer."

Noah took her hand and they walked out together.

He stopped beside her on the path in front of the truck. "You're something else."

"I've got a lot of pent-up rage when it comes to mother's using and abusing their children and people conspiring to do bad things because they think less of you and you deserve it."

"I'm just glad I'm on your good side."

"You should be. I've got plans for those two."

"Oh yeah, like what?"

"Point your finger at someone, there are more pointing back at you. We know they're trying to undermine me. And they aren't even trying to hide it if they're meeting at his office. Digging up dirt on them shouldn't be difficult. I've already given Randal the information we have on Tom and what he's been doing, but I also gave him a directive to dig deeper and wider to see what else Tom and Lisa have planned to take Annabelle from us."

"You're going to make Randal earn that retainer."

"Damn right."

Noah chuckled. "Do you have time for lunch before you have to get back to work?"

She tapped him in the gut with her fist. "I'll make time for you."

Noah wrapped her in a hug and kissed her on the head.

"This isn't over, you know?" Lisa walked down the steps.

Roxy stepped back from Noah's embrace. "If you know what's good for you, you'll drop this now."

Lisa sauntered past them and said over her shoulder, "Honey, I haven't even gotten started."

Roxy wanted to dismiss Lisa's words as nothing but bluster, but she sounded as bitter and scornful as Roxy's mother ever had and Roxy had learned the hard way never to underestimate a selfish, self-centered bitch with a grudge.

Chapter Thirty-Eight

Roxy slipped into bed, tired to the bone, her brain ready to shut off. Lunch in town with Noah after the scene at Tom's office was well worth the extra hours at her computer and on the phone with Big Mama. No surprise, 90% of their phone conversation was about Candy's increasingly bad behavior and out of control drinking. Big Mama believed Candy was only acting out to get Roxy's attention and to make her come home. Not going to happen. The Ranch seemed a long way away. Especially when she had the one thing here that wasn't there: Noah.

The second her head hit the pillow, Noah rolled to his side, hooked his arm around her waist, and pulled her under him in a move so smooth and effortless, she wondered how he contained all that strength and touched her so gently she melted under him.

Naked, warm, and wanting her, Noah leaned down and kissed her softly again and again. Each kiss intensified and went deeper until she was rocking her hips against his hard length and clutching at him, wanting so badly for him to do something about the hot ache he'd built inside her.

Noah kept things sultry, letting her need for him burn like a living thing inside her begging for more, needing every brush of his hand, sweep of his tongue, and press of his body against hers.

Desperate for him, she gasped when his tongue flicked her peaked nipple and moaned when he sucked it into his mouth. She cried out with the intensity of her desire when he slipped two fingers deep into her core and swore when he pulled out. He slipped them back in with a chuckle that vibrated against her breast a second before his tongue circled her nipple then he suckled it again.

"Noah, baby, please."

He must have had the condom at the ready, because he thrust into her not five seconds later, filling her and easing and increasing her desperation for the inevitable climax all at once. Then a change came over him, an earnestness she'd sensed but he'd restrained until now. Each touch, every stroke of his body, each kiss seemed to mean more than the last. The connection they shared grew stronger as the intensity between them bloomed into an explosion of love that rocked both of them.

Noah found the strength and skill to roll them both over. She lay atop him, cuddled in his strong arms, his heartbeat and panting breath the only thing she heard besides his unspoken love for her. In the quiet contentment that surrounded them, she settled into the peace she'd only found in his arms.

"Is this home, Roxy?"

She squeezed his shoulders and snuggled her cheek against his chest. "This is the only place I want to be."

"So you see yourself living here long after the terms of the will?"

"If you're tired of me already, your actions say otherwise." She couldn't help the teasing smile that he couldn't see, but amped how good she felt in this moment.

"That's just it. I want you to want to be here. With me."

She stacked her hands on his chest and rested her chin on them, meeting his earnest gaze. "Noah, honey, of course I want to be here with you. Why would you think otherwise?"

"I don't. I'm not asking you this right."

"Then ask me what you want to know."

"You have the means to do anything and go anywhere you want. Do you see your future here with me? Do you want to build a life here with me?"

She leaned up and kissed him softly and looked him in the eyes. "There's nothing I want more than you."

His eyes darted away, then fixed on her again. "What about kids?"

"Can we enjoy this part first?"

"After all you've been through, growing up alone with your sisters, do you ever think about being a mom?"

"In the past, not so much. Now I think everything is possible."

"Are you going to keep working like this, Roxy? You have no time to yourself."

"Trying to take care of me again?"

He swept his hands up and down her back. "Always. You work two jobs, train Houdini, and now you've taken on this project with Austin."

"Sonya will work with Austin."

"With a heavy hand from you." Noah sighed. "I want more time with you, not just the ten or fifteen minutes you squeeze me in between every-thing else you have to do. After dinner, when I kick back and relax, you sit next to me, but your focus is on your laptop, not the movie I put on for us to watch. You spend more time with Annabelle than you do me. I know she needs you, but I do, too."

She had no idea he felt this way. And hadn't really considered that's exactly how things were between them. "Noah, I'm sorry. You're right. And I want to spend more time with you." She laid her cheek on his chest and let her body go completely limp. "I'm tired."

"You put in sixteen-to-eighteen-hour days. Why, Roxy? You don't need the money. I know you like your job and it's important to you, but you need to give yourself a break. You need to decide what is most important in your life." His fingers brushed through her hair again and again, the sweet gesture hypnotizing her into a deeper relaxation.

"You. Always you. Even when it doesn't seem like it." She yawned, falling faster into sleep. "I don't want to end up like my mother with no one to love. No one who loves me."

"I love you, Roxy. I want you to be happy. You work so much, I'm afraid you're going to burn yourself out. Or find yourself working through one task after the next and not really living. Life has been so hard for you. It doesn't have to be that way anymore."

"Life is better with you," she mumbled and fell asleep with the next stroke of his fingers down the length of her hair.

ROXY MISSED NOAH. After the night they shared, the words they spoke to each other, she'd rather be home with him having dinner with the family than running around town on errands. She should have sent one of the ranch hands to pick up their order at the feed store and the medicine for a sick foal at the veterinary office. Since she was headed into town, Mary gave her the grocery list. She had enough on her plate and another late night ahead of her. But all she really wanted to do was curl up on the sofa, watch a movie, and make out with Noah cuddled under a blanket together.

She hadn't stopped thinking about what he really asked her last night: did she want to be his wife? It felt like a secret whispered in the dark, too precious and fragile to hold up in the light of day. But that was the old Roxy who didn't believe dreams come true.

Now those whispered words in the dark felt like a promise. She knew he wanted more time with her. She wanted more of him.

Which meant she needed to get her priorities in order.

Maybe she'd pick up a sweet treat at the bakery and take a night off. She'd have to make it up later, but making Noah happy was worth it.

She didn't expect Noah to ask her to marry him any time soon, but it was coming. And that lovely thought made her belly flutter with anticipation and her heart soar higher than she ever thought possible. She could see herself so easily as his wife. And though she'd never thought about children past the initial thought of, *yes, I want them*, she now pictured herself with mini Noah's in her arms.

Noah would be an amazing father. Annabelle a wonderfully caring and fun aunt. Adria, Juliana, and Sonya would spoil a niece or nephew rotten.

All that love and family for her children. Everything she never had but wanted.

It was hers now because Noah loved her, and her father left her a family of her own.

She never thought she'd be this lucky, or her heart could feel this full.

She couldn't wait to get home to Noah.

She pulled into the grocery store lot and parked right in front. Her high spirits plummeted with one look at the woman walking out of the store, heading right for her as Roxy made her way to the door.

"Roxy, can we talk?" Lisa hefted the shopping bag strap up her shoulder. She looked around, but they seemed to be alone on the sidewalk in front of the store.

"It's been a long day. I'm not really in the mood for a fight."

"You and Noah are always harpin' on me about taking an interest in Annabelle. Can't you spare a few minutes to talk about *my* daughter?"

Roxy bit back her irritation and the notion that this was a waste of time.

"Please." Lisa seemed earnest, even if Roxy didn't believe her intentions were good.

Roxy crossed her arms and cocked a hip, settling in for another futile conversation. "Fine. What about Annabelle?"

Lisa glanced over to the café next to the store. "Let me buy you a cup of coffee and we'll chat."

Roxy gave in, wondering why she felt the need to be nice to a woman who had been sneaking around with Tom plotting God knows what to get control of Annabelle's inheritance.

She followed Lisa, who dropped her bag in a chair at an outdoor table. "What can I get you? My treat."

Somehow she'd pay for this, but Roxy gave her order. "Small caramel macchiato."

Lisa rushed inside, leaving Roxy to take a seat and wait. Instead of leaving like she wanted to, she reminded herself this was for Annabelle. To kill time, she checked her email.

Roxy hit send on a particularly technical reply to a business email, then looked up surprised to see Lisa had deposited her coffee in front of her and sat down across the table. "Sorry. Work." Roxy held up the phone, then dropped it back in her purse.

"I find it funny that John was your mother's John."

Roxy didn't even crack a smile at the absurd attempt at a joke. "What does that have to do with Annabelle?"

"Everything."

Roxy stood to leave.

Lisa grabbed her hand. "Sit down. Drink your coffee. Let me have my say."

Roxy dropped back into her seat, picked up the coffee she really needed if she planned to stay up late with Noah, and took a sip. The sweet, hot treat helped calm her simmering anger, so she drank more and waited for Lisa to say whatever the hell was on her mind. She'd hear her out and leave. Nothing she said would change anything.

Roxy could rest easy knowing she'd given Lisa a chance for Annabelle's sake.

"Good, huh?" Lisa held up her own coffee.

"Yes. Thank you. Now, what do you want?"

"How is Annabelle?"

Roxy sighed and took another sip. "She's fine. She works part-time for our vet."

"She's rich. Why the hell are you making her work?"

"I'm not *making* her do anything. It's a chance for her to explore being a vet before she applies to college."

Lisa shook her head. "That's two years away."

"Which is why she needs to decide. If she hates working for the veterinary clinic and working with the animals, she'll figure that out on the job. As it stands right now, she loves it. But she's young and might change her mind next week and want to do something else." Roxy shrugged, then rubbed her forehead, trying to clear her vision. She wrote off the blurriness as too many hours on the computer and focused on her conversation with Lisa. "If she wants to try something else, I'll help her with that."

"By making her work."

"How else will she learn? She needs to . . ." Roxy took another gulp of coffee, hoping it would wake her up. All of a sudden, she felt very tired. "Annabelle is happy. She likes the job and working with the horses."

"What about boys? I've heard you've had a string of high schoolers in and out of that house. Not to mention your friends."

Roxy shook her head and blinked her eyes. "Uh . . . Annabelle's got a handle on her curious friends. She's set them straight about me. My sister is coming back in a few days."

Lisa leaned forward. "Are you okay?"

Roxy grabbed hold of her purse. "I'm not feeling that great."

"Drugs." Lisa gave her a knowing look.

"I don't do drugs." Roxy stood, but had to grab the table to steady herself.

"No one will believe that when I'm done with you." Lisa tossed both coffee cups in the garbage.

Roxy could barely make out Lisa's face or take a step. No way could she drive. She reached for her purse to call Noah. Her heart raced along with the thoughts she was having trouble holding on to longer than it took one to form and disappear from her mind.

Lisa yanked Roxy's purse away. "You think you're so smart. Who's the one in charge now?" Lisa took her by the arm and helped her across the lot to Roxy's car where she shoved Roxy into the passenger seat. Roxy tried to grab her purse. The only thought she could hold on to now was to call Noah. He'd come get her. He'd help her. She needed help.

Lisa tossed the purse in the backseat and slammed the door. Moments later she slid behind the wheel and started the car.

"Call Noah."

"Fuck Noah. That self-righteous asshole. He thinks he can have everything and I get nothing. You're making crazy money off that place and you deny me my alimony. I earned it, bitch: on my back, fucking your old man. So Annabelle wasn't his. Big fucking deal. He got the child he wanted. He loved her. The least he could do is pay me."

Roxy rolled her head toward Lisa and tried to focus on her because the outside world looked like it was racing past in a bizarre haze that left trails of color. "You sound just like my mother."

"I bet she fucking got paid."

"If . . . if you want . . . money . . . fine. I'll pay . . . you. T-take. Me. Home."

"You live at a fucking whorehouse."

No. Noah was home. She needed to get to Noah.

"I've got plans for you, bitch. I told you this wasn't over."

She should have known Lisa was just biding her time, waiting for her opportunity to strike. Candy had mastered that tactic, always waiting for the best moment to make the greatest impact to mess up Roxy's life.

Lisa shoved Roxy's shoulder, sending her crashing into the passenger door. Roxy knocked her head against the glass and came awake with a startled cry. For a moment, she had no idea what happened. Then Lisa dragged her out of the car. Stumbling toward a door and a place she didn't recognize, terror seized her throat and sent her heart pounding into overdrive.

Roxy did not want to go through that door.

In a desperate attempt to get away, she pulled free of Lisa and swung, hitting Lisa in the face with a satisfying smack. Lisa stumbled back, holding her hand to her cheek. Roxy tripped and fell to her knees. Pain radiated up her legs.

Lisa fisted her hands in Roxy's shirt and hauled Roxy up on her wobbly legs. "You're going to regret that, bitch."

Her body lacked the strength and coordination she desperately needed to flee. Her mind seemed to take an inordinate amount of time to process a single thought, if she could even hold on to it with the fear masking everything with the overwhelming need to run.

Lisa unlocked the door and shoved her into a dark room that smelled of stale cigarette smoke and pine cleaner. Roxy staggered and bounced off the edge of the bed and landed on her butt on the floor. She turned and backed into the end of the bed. Shag carpet brushed between her fingers. She tried to focus on the dirt-brown floor, hoping to stop the room spinning.

Time seemed to stop and go with one horrible snippet of reality or dream that all felt like a horrible nightmare.

Lisa pinching Roxy's nose and dumping water down her throat. It drizzled and dripped on her chest.

Lisa pulling Roxy's shirt over her head.

Things getting even fuzzier.

The door opening, letting in a dark figure that chuckled like some canned laughter in an amusement park funhouse echoing in her head.

She wanted off this ride.

Lisa telling the dark figure to, "Put her in the chair."

He dropped Roxy into the seat. She stared down at the glass of whiskey and several pills lying on the table. Several flashes went off. She blinked against the blinding light.

True to her word, Lisa set her up to look like a drunk, drugged-out whore and there was nothing she could do about it.

"Move her to the bed."

The shot of adrenaline those words unleashed gave her a blast of strength, but it didn't help her escape the hands grabbing at her or the heavy body that pinned her down.

"Get off her."

A knee wedged between her thighs and roughly pushed against her center. The friction made her realize she still had her jeans on. Thank God.

But she couldn't move. At this point, she could barely open her eyes.

A hand clamped onto her jaw and someone leaned close. "How's it feel to have my knee in your crotch?" He jammed it into her again hurting the soft, sensitive flesh. Not as badly as she'd hurt him.

Tom.

It had to be him, though she couldn't make out his hazy face.

If he wanted his revenge, he certainly had her right where he wanted her. Which made the room make sense. They had her stashed in a seedy motel.

And she couldn't get out of here on her own.

Terror squeezed her heart and choked her throat. What did they really want?

Her mind didn't work enough to even conjure one nightmare beyond the obvious.

And though she feared what they would do to her and she tried desperately to stay alert, her eyelids fell closed like thousand-pound weights.

Chapter Thirty-Nine

Noah had a bad feeling. Roxy never turned off her phone. She was never late. She always left word about where she was going and she'd never miss dinner and not call. Something happened. He wished he knew what, because he was going stir-crazy in the house.

He wasn't doing any good standing in the foyer watching the road. He went back into the office. He'd given her desk a cursory look, but now he went through her papers, looking for anything, a note, an itinerary, something that said where she'd gone and why.

Nothing jumped out at him or hinted to an appointment or errand she needed to run. All the papers told him was that she had too much to do and worked too hard. Her laptop and tablet were both password protected. If she kept an electronic schedule, he couldn't get to it.

"Noah, what are you doing?" Mary asked from the doorway.

He shoved his hands against the piles of folders on the desk and stood straight. "Nothing. I can't find a damn thing that tells me where she went."

"She never made it to the store."

"What?"

"I called and asked the manager to check with the cashiers. None of them checked her out."

"Maybe they forgot?"

"Forgot a woman who looks like Roxy?" Mary shook her head.

Annabelle walked in behind Mary. "Have you heard from her? Where is she?" Her eyes glassed over.

He held his arms out. Annabelle rushed into them and he held her to his chest, trying to keep his emotions in check as his mind conjured one reason after the other, one worse than the last for why Roxy hadn't come home. Why she couldn't call.

Because if she could, she would.

"Call the Ranch. See if she's there," Annabelle suggested.

Mary nodded, thinking it a good idea, too.

He thought about it earlier, but hesitated to reach out to anyone at the Ranch because Roxy tried so hard to keep that part of her life separate from them.

He released Annabelle and pulled out his phone to see if an emergency sent her back there. He had to Google up the number. Mary and Annabelle stared intently at him as he made the call.

"Thank you for calling the Wild Rose Ranch. How may I help you?" Seemed like a normal way to answer a business call, but the husky, sultry voice made him believe she'd do anything to "help" him.

"Hi, this is Noah Cordero. Is Roxy there?"

"I'm sorry, Mr. Cordero, Roxy isn't on staff, but we have a lot of other beautiful women ready and willing to satisfy your every need."

"No. You don't understand. I'm Roxy's boyfriend. She owns the Ranch. Candy is her mother."

"Please hold."

Noah didn't want to wait. He wanted answers now. He should have called Roxy's sisters but he didn't know their numbers or even their last names. When Roxy got home, he was going to make her write down all the information for the people in her life so this never happened again.

"Hello, sugar. I have to say, it's a real surprise you're calling me."

"Candy?" He never expected to talk to her.

"The one and only."

"Is Roxy there? I can't find her."

"Lover's spat?"

"No. She went out to run errands this afternoon and never came home."

The long pause unsettled him. "She's not here, but let me check the girls' house and see if she's with Adria and Juliana."

"Can you give them my number and tell them to call me if they hear from her?" Noah rattled off his phone number.

"I'll call you back as soon as I talk to them. It's not like Roxy to disappear without a word. She'd never make anyone worry about her."

"No, she wouldn't."

"Why would you think she came here? Last I talked to her she said she wouldn't be back until next month because she used up her days she's allowed away from your ranch. Do you want her piece of the ranch so bad you've done something to my girl?" The intensity in that question knocked him back.

He didn't expect Candy to be so ferocious on Roxy's behalf.

Noah hadn't thought about the will's stipulations. If Roxy didn't come home soon, she would in fact be in violation of the terms.

"I would never do anything to hurt Roxy."

"We'll see. I've never known a man to stick around long."

"Maybe they're not the problem," he shot back, pissed she'd question his dedication to Roxy and their relationship.

"Touchy. Maybe she needed a break from you."

"Candy, I don't have time for this. Roxy and I are great together. She's happy. If she wasn't, I'd do anything to fix it because we belong together."

Another long pause frayed his nerves. "I overheard her tell Sonya about some trouble with others in town. Close-minded hypocrites. You know they're all smokin', drinkin', and having sex like the rest of us. And if they're not, they're probably doing a lot worse."

Noah rolled his eyes. "Please ask Adria and Juliana if they've talked to or seen Roxy."

"If someone hurt my girl, you better make sure they hurt worse."

"Count on it. And that goes for you, too."

Candy giggled. "I like you."

"Great." He couldn't give a shit. "Call me back."

Noah hung up and bit back a string of swear words.

"Was that Roxy's mom?" Annabelle asked.

"Yeah. She's not there, but Candy is going to check with Roxy's sisters."

"So we still don't know anything." Annabelle hung her head.

"Candy said something that makes sense. If Roxy doesn't come home tonight, she violates the terms of the will."

"She'd never do that. No." Annabelle shook her head. "She loves it here. She loves us."

Noah hugged Annabelle to his side. "Yes, she does. So there's only one other person who would benefit and who would do something underhanded to make sure you and I got Roxy's share of the ranch."

Annabelle's eyes flooded with tears that cascaded down her cheeks when she looked up at him. "My mother."

Noah nodded. "I don't know anything for sure, but Lisa and Tom were talking about needing to do something because Lisa's running out of money now that she doesn't get anything from the ranch."

"This is all my fault. If they hurt Roxy . . ."

Noah tipped Annabelle's face up and stared down into her grief-stricken, guilty eyes. "You didn't do anything wrong. We'll find her."

His phone dinged with a text.

His heart leaped with joy when he saw that it was from Roxy, then stopped when he read the message.

ROXY: I hate it here
ROXY: I'm leaving you and going back to Vegas
ROXY: Time to move on

None of that sounded like Roxy. She loved Montana and hated the Nevada desert. If she wanted to move on, she'd say it to his face.

A picture came up that sent a bolt of rage through his system.

Roxy lay in a bed, her hair a tousled mess, her eyes barely open, shirt off, breasts spilling over a black bra, a man's chest pressed against the side of her, his hand on her stomach.

"That's not right." Annabelle stared at the picture. "She'd never cheat on you."

No, she wouldn't. And whoever took the picture and sent the texts would regret treating Roxy like some . . . whore. That's what they wanted her to look like. As if she'd pick up some random guy, have sex with him, cheat on Noah, all without a thought to hurting him.

Not Roxy.

Whoever did this, didn't know Roxy.

They didn't know she swore she'd never leave him.

NOAH: When I find you you'll wish you never laid a hand on Roxy

Annabelle grabbed his arm. "I need my cell phone."

"This isn't the time. You'll get it back at the end of the month just like we told you when we took it from you."

Annabelle shook his arm. "No. I need it to find her." Annabelle ran around the desk and pulled her cell out of the top drawer, plugged it into the charger connected to Roxy's computer, and turned it on. It felt like an hour waiting for it to come on. She tapped an app and held up the phone with a map and a blinking red dot. "She's at the Mountainside Motel."

Shocked, Noah held Annabelle's wrist and stared at the map. "How do you know that?"

"She put a tracking app on my phone so she can find me in case of emergency. Or I don't answer," Annabelle added under her breath. "It works both ways."

Noah remembered Roxy adding it to his phone, too, but he'd never used it. "Why didn't you do this earlier?"

She scrunched her mouth. "I snuck in here and tried, but her phone has to be on. Duh!"

Noah didn't even bother to ask how many other times she'd snuck in here to use her phone. He headed for the door, not surprised whoever sent the text from Roxy's phone didn't respond to his reply.

Annabelle caught up to him.

"You're not coming."

Her eyes held a desperate plea. "Noah, she's my sister. If my mother has her . . ."

Noah stopped, though he wanted to run to Roxy. He held Annabelle back with a hand on her shoulder. "Stay here. Let me handle it."

Annabelle's lips trembled. "I want to help."

"It could be dangerous. If they're willing to kidnap her, who knows what else they'll do?"

Mary wrapped Annabelle in a light hug and nodded for him to go. "I'll give you a head start, then call the police."

Noah jumped into his truck and sped away with Mary and Annabelle in his rearview mirror as worried and scared as him about what he'd find when he got to that motel. If Roxy was hurt, he'd kill them. As it was, they'd be lucky to live through his wrath.

His phone rang as his tires ate up the miles to the outskirts of town where Tom had told Roxy he had a private place picked out where they could meet and fuck. If he caught Tom there, he'd be wishing the only thing Noah did to him was knee him in the nuts.

"Hello."

"She's not here. The girls haven't heard from her." Candy's words came out fast and filled with worry he wanted to believe was genuine.

"I found her. I'm on my way to her now."

"So she's okay?"

"I don't know. My best guess is that someone took her and is holding her against her will so she forfeits the ranch to me and Annabelle."

"If her father hadn't put those stupid stipulations on the will, none of this would be happening."

"He had his reasons." *To get her away from you.*

"Everybody's got a reason. Doesn't mean it's right."

"Agreed. John wanted her and you wouldn't give her up so she could have a better life, because you wanted to keep cashing in."

"She had a good life."

Noah rolled his eyes at Candy's false optimism that was true.

"She does now. And I'm going to make sure she's happy and loved every day. Anyone gets in the way of that is going to deal with me."

"Then deal with this and tell her to call me. I want to know she'll be all right."

"She will be with me."

"For what it's worth, I believe that. She deserves it." The sincerity in those words made him believe she meant it.

"She deserves a hell of a lot more, and I aim to give it to her."

"You better, or you'll get a visit from me."

"God help me."

Candy laughed, then hung up on him.

He pressed the gas pedal to the floor and sped the rest of the way to the motel where he skidded to a stop behind Roxy's Camaro and Tom's Subaru. He jumped out of the truck, ran to the door in front of Roxy's car, and kicked it in with a splintering crash of wood.

He stood in the doorway and stared in disbelief at Tom and Lisa naked in bed. Lisa straddled Tom who had his hands out wide and tied to the bedpost with red scarves.

"Shit, Noah, what the hell are you doing here?" Lisa pulled a corner of the sheet up and tried to cover her breasts but didn't bother to get up.

Tom's eyes were wide as saucers as he glanced from Noah to the door and back. Looking for a way out? Hoping no one else came in and saw him splayed out and naked? Noah didn't give a shit.

"Where is she?"

Lisa glanced around the room, one eye red and swollen, and lied through her teeth. "We're the only one's here, you maniac."

"Why is Roxy's car out front?"

Lisa's face paled, the first sign she knew she'd been caught.

Noah walked to the closet and threw open the door. Empty.

"You can't just bust in here and . . . No! Get out!" Lisa scrambled off Tom's lap and came after him.

Noah turned the bathroom doorknob and shoved it open, nearly falling forward when Lisa attacked him from behind and tried to close the door again. Too late. He caught a glimpse of Roxy lying like a limp ragdoll half naked in the tub, pale and out cold.

"Get out!" Lisa pounded on his back.

He didn't usually hit girls, but he planted one hand on her chest and shoved her back. She fell on her bare bottom on the ugly carpet and stared up at him with tears shimmering in her eyes. "You ruin everything."

"You do that all on your own."

Sirens sounded in the distance.

"Untie me. Let me go." Tom struggled against his bonds. "She made me do it. She's crazy. Look at this. She tied me up and did things to me."

"Shut up, you idiot." Lisa grabbed her clothes off the chair by the window and started putting them on.

With the cops closing in, Noah left the two of them and went into the bathroom. He kneeled by the tub and gently touched Roxy's face. He pulled his fingers away, shocked by her too cold skin. He slipped his hands under her and pulled her up and to his chest. He carried her back into the room and laid her on the end of the bed.

Lisa had some mercy in her and had untied Tom. He leaned over and reached for Roxy's arm.

Noah punched him right in the face, breaking his nose. "Don't you fucking touch her again."

Noah grabbed a blanket out of the closet, hoping it was cleaner than the one pulled off the bed and dumped on the floor. He laid it over Roxy and tucked it in, hoping to warm her up. He needed to do something because she hadn't moved or shown any sign of waking up.

"What did you give her?"

Tom held out one bloody hand. "I didn't give her anything." The sheet he held against his nose turned red as blood continued to flow down his mouth and chin.

Noah turned to Lisa, who grabbed her purse and draped the strap over her shoulder. She turned for the door, but he snatched the strap and pulled her back and around to face him.

"Let me go."

"You're not going anywhere."

"I didn't know she was in there. He invited me here to have some fun. You saw him. He likes things a little wild. I have no idea what he did with that whore before I got here."

"Bullshit," Tom mumbled behind the bloody sheet. "She tricked Roxy into having coffee with her. She roofied her and brought her here."

Noah held up his phone with the picture they'd sent. "And what did you do to her?"

Tom flinched away. "Nothing. Just took the picture and put her in the bathroom."

Lisa snorted. "Not before he put his hands all over her." Lisa sneered at Noah. "Without me here to stop him, who knows how far he would have gone."

"She's still got her clothes on."

Noah went after Tom, who backed himself into the wall, nothing but the sheet hanging from his hand at his nose as protection. Noah grabbed him at the throat, squeezed, pulled him forward, then shoved him back. His head thumped against the fake wood paneling. Tom winced and tried to suck in a breath that wouldn't come.

"Do you think it's okay to touch an unconscious woman, clothes on or off?"

Tom sputtered, but couldn't answer with Noah holding his throat closed. Noah shoved him against the wall again.

"No. The answer to that question is *always* no." Noah sidestepped and brought Tom around and shoved him backward. Tom scrambled to keep up, his eyes wide and scared, then surprised when the cop standing in the open door took hold of Tom's arm. "Did you get all that?" Noah asked the cop.

"Heard every word. Ambulance is two minutes out." The cop passed Tom off to another officer and walked toward Lisa.

Lisa backed up two steps, hands held up to ward off the officer. "What do you think you're doing?"

"Arresting you."

Lisa pointed at Tom. "He did it. Not me."

Noah scooped up Roxy, turned, and sat on the bed with her in his arms. "At the very least, you kidnapped and drugged her."

"I heard something about pornographic pictures taken while she was unconscious," the cop added. "You're in a lot of trouble." He clamped the handcuffs on Lisa's hands at her back.

"Noah, you can't let this happen. What about Annabelle? I'm her mother."

"She's better off without you." Noah spotted the ambulance pulling in outside. He stood and carried Roxy to the door.

"Noah, please, Annabelle needs me."

He glanced over his shoulder. "No, she doesn't. She's got Roxy." He walked right out and into the back of the waiting ambulance and laid Roxy on the gurney. He tossed the motel blanket out the back and took the one the paramedic handed him before getting to work on Roxy.

"Do we know what she was given?"

Noah brushed his hand over Roxy's hair. "A roofie."

The paramedic put a needle in Roxy's arm and started an IV line. Roxy didn't even flinch when the needle went in. She didn't acknowledge Noah's soft touch on her forehead. She didn't kiss him back when he pressed his lips to hers.

The cop appeared at the back of the ambulance. "Mr. Cordero, you need to move your truck."

Noah pat his pocket then glanced back at the cop. "Keys are still in the ignition. I'm not leaving her."

The officer nodded to another officer to move the truck. "How's she doing?"

The paramedic looked up from writing something on a chart. "The IV will help flush the drug from her system. She'll sleep for a few more hours. When she wakes up, she probably won't remember what happened."

"Maybe that's a good thing," the cop said.

Noah wished he could erase this day from Roxy's life. Even if she didn't remember, she'd hear all about it. No way he kept this quiet. Lisa and Tom weren't going down without a fight.

Noah needed evidence. "Can you take a blood sample and confirm she's been drugged?"

"They'll do that first thing at the hospital."

The cop tossed Noah back his keys. "I'll be in touch." He closed the ambulance doors and they left for the hospital.

Noah pulled out his phone and called the house.

"Hello."

"Hey, Sprite. I've got her."

"Let me talk to her."

"She's unconscious, but she'll be okay."

"Is she hurt?" Annabelle's voice trembled.

"No, Sprite. She's been drugged. She's just sleeping it off. We're on the way to the hospital."

"Did my mom do it?"

He gave her the hard truth. "She and Tom were working together. We'll talk about it later."

"She's going to hate me."

"Never, Sprite. Roxy loves you. She'd go through this a thousand times to spare you one moment of hurt from your mother."

"She has to be all right."

"She will be. I'll make sure of it." His phone buzzed with another incoming call. He checked the screen and saw that he'd missed three others. "I gotta go, Sprite. Roxy's sisters are calling me. I'll call you in the morning when Roxy wakes up."

"You better. Love you."

"Love you, too." He accepted the incoming call before it went to voicemail. "She's okay. I found her."

"Thank God. This is Adria and Juliana. We tried to reach you earlier."

"I had to get her back from her kidnappers." It took him ten minutes to fill them in, especially with the twins talking over each other and asking him questions. By the time he and Roxy reached the hospital, he'd assured them he'd take care of Roxy and have her call them tomorrow when she was feeling better.

He was in for a very long night but he didn't care because Roxy was safe and back with him where she belonged.

Chapter Forty

Roxy woke disoriented and in a panic. She didn't know why or what happened that put her in the hospital. She lay still, breathing hard, then found a smile for the group gathered around her, staring in disbelief.

Noah practically fell on top of her and held her close, his cheek pressed to hers. "Finally, you're awake."

"I told you, she can't handle her drugs," Juliana teased.

Roxy hugged Noah, needing his strength and love. He pulled up, but she grabbed hold of his shirt and held him still. "What happened?" She narrowed her eyes, trying to remember, but most of what came to her was snippets of hazy images that didn't make a lot of sense.

"As far as we've pieced together, Lisa kidnapped you at the grocery store."

"I think she drugged my coffee."

"You got roofied," Juliana supplied.

Roxy focused on Juliana and Adria standing on the other side of the bed from Noah. "What are you doing here?"

Adria squeezed her thigh. "Noah called last night looking for you. When we found out what happened, we came to make sure you're okay."

"We thought you might need your sisters," Juliana added.

"It's so good to see you." She turned back to Noah. "Who found me?"

"Annabelle did. On that phone app you put on her phone. Something your mother said made me think Lisa and Tom were involved."

Roxy tried to keep up. "You talked to Candy?"

"Yeah. I'm still not a fan." He brushed his fingers over her cheek. "Your phone had been off for hours, but then Lisa sent me a text pretending to be you, saying you were leaving me."

"I'd never leave you. Or break up with you by text."

"That's how I knew it was a lie."

Roxy touched her hand to her chest, remembering someone touching her.

Noah placed his hand over hers. "They sent me a picture of you with a man. Turned out to be Tom. The doctor checked you out and confirmed Tom's assertion that nothing happened." Noah let out a frustrated sigh. "He put his hands on you, but nothing more. You were still in your bra and jeans when I found you. They just wanted the picture to rile me."

"It did." Adria's smile reflected the admiration in her eyes. "Noah busted Tom's nose, nearly choked him out, and left him with a mild concussion."

"It's better than he deserved," Noah bit out. "You got your shot at Lisa. She had a black eye when I found you."

"I take it they're in jail."

"They should be six feet under," Noah grumbled. He leaned down and kissed her. His lips pressed to hers for a long moment, then he broke the kiss and pressed his forehead to hers. His intense gaze softened. "Don't ever scare me like that again."

She held his face in her hands. "Thank you for coming to get me."

"For a moment there, I thought I might have lost you. You were really out of it when I found you."

"The coffee made me groggy, but at one point Lisa forced me to drink some water. It must have been dosed, too."

Adria patted her thigh. "After what you'd been through, the doctors decided to just let you sleep it off."

She kissed Noah again, then turned to her sisters and held out her arms. "Come here."

It was something they did all the time at home when one or more of them was having a hard time. Juliana and Adria crawled up on the bed, lay on each side of her, and held her close.

Roxy kissed both of them on the head. "I'm so glad you guys are here."

The door opened and Sonya walked in with Annabelle following her. "You're awake." Sonya wasted no time climbing up the end of the bed and snuggling in between Roxy's legs and Adria and Juliana.

Surrounded by her sisters, Noah beside the bed holding her hand, Roxy's heart filled to overflowing with love. What she'd been through the night before seemed insignificant to everything good and wonderful she had in her life.

But one face in the crowd dimmed Roxy's growing sense that every-thing was going to be okay. "Annabelle, what's wrong?"

Tears immediately streamed down her cheeks and her head fell for-ward. "It's all my fault."

Everyone turned to Annabelle, which only made her cry harder. Noah hugged her to his side, trying to console her.

"None of this is your fault, Annabelle. Lisa did this. Don't take on her guilt, her flaws, her inadequacies and make them your own."

"Trust us," Adria added, "you take on her stuff along with your own, it's a load too heavy to carry. You are not your mother."

Annabelle's head came up. Her eyes scanned Roxy, Adria, Juliana, and Sonya. Roxy saw understanding dawn in her eyes.

Sonya held her arm out wide. "Come here, little sister."

Annabelle didn't hesitate. The look in her eyes said she wanted to be included. She wanted to belong.

Annabelle climbed on the bed and fell between Sonya and Juliana.

Roxy brushed her fingers through Annabelle's hair. "You're one of us."

Noah leaned down and kissed her on the forehead. It felt good to have everyone she loved surrounding her and know that Annabelle may have a selfish mother just like theirs, but now she also had people who under-stood her, loved her, and who would be there for her always.

She loved her sisters for understanding that Annabelle needed them just as they'd needed each other all these years.

Annabelle traced the wild rose vine twining up Juliana's arm. "This is really cool."

Juliana glanced at the tattoo. "We all have one."

Roxy remembered Noah's fascination and the way he'd kissed his way along her tattoo. "They're all a little different, but the same. Like us," Roxy confirmed.

"Can I get one?"

Roxy smiled because that right there was confirmation enough that Annabelle wanted to be one of them. "Are you sure you want to be a Wild Rose?"

"I want to be just like you."

"Roxy's the best of us," Sonya confirmed.

Adria and Juliana nodded their agreement.

"I'll take her," Juliana volunteered.

"Not until she's older," Noah said, leaving the door open and not crushing Annabelle's hopes that she'd get the tattoo that for her would solidify her as part of the group.

"Roxy?" Annabelle hoped for a different answer.

"You heard your brother."

Annabelle rolled her eyes and everything felt like it was back to normal.

Noah stared down at her lying beneath a pile of sisters. His smile melted her heart just like it always did. She smiled back, letting him know everything was okay. The love that passed between them made it so easy for her to know their future together was as solid as the connection binding them together.

Chapter Forty-One

Noah led Roxy up to the rise and stopped his horse at the top. Roxy walked her mount up next to his. Her and Noah's legs rubbed together as the horses stood close to each other. Just the way she always wanted to be close to Noah now.

He'd made it clear he didn't want to be without her. Ever.

Which is why they started taking these long rides before dinner. She'd found a better balance in her life, working part time as a designer because she loved it and it fulfilled her need to have something of her own. But the shorter hours gave her more time to spend with Noah.

She stared at the amazing view and sighed with sheer pleasure and contentment. "It's beautiful up here."

They stared out across hills and pastures to the ranch house and buildings spread out over the vast valley below them.

"This is where John and I used to come to talk about the ranch, family stuff, and nothing at all. We'd both come up here alone sometimes. It's a great place to think and make decisions without all the distractions down there."

She caught a note of nostalgia and something else in his voice. "This is where you were when he collapsed."

"That day changed my life. It brought you here. He brought you to me."

"He changed my life, too. *You* made it even better."

"Things haven't been easy," he admitted.

"I had a rocky start. I expected it. But this past month, people have been more welcoming."

She didn't feel like John's dirty little secret anymore. People were starting to know her.

And she had the last person she'd ever expected in the world to help her make people see she wasn't the whore everyone assumed she was because of Cheryl, Lisa, and Tom's accusations. Lisa's horrible stunt turned the town against them and put nearly everyone on Roxy's side.

Lisa and Tom made a deal with the DA. Tom got six months' house arrest and six months of probation. He'd never practice law again. Lisa got three years in jail. She'd probably get out in eighteen months. Noah wanted a harsher sentence. Roxy accepted the DA's recommendation to put the matter behind them, so they could move on for Annabelle's sake.

Roxy sighed, letting the past go. "I love it here."

Noah stared out at their land, a look of belonging in his eyes.

He took her hand, looked at their linked fingers, then back at her, his eyes filled with earnest intent. "I love you. Whatever happens in your life, I want to be there. I want to share all your hopes and dreams and the day-to-day good and bad." He gently squeezed her hand again. "You need me, I'm there. You want me, I'm there. Anything, everything, I'm there."

Tears shimmered in her eyes as she stared at him in wonder. She'd hoped this day would come. She wanted this, him, for the rest of her life.

With his free hand, he pulled a black velvet box from his shirt pocket, flipped the lid open, and showed her the ring.

Roxy gasped at the diamond solitaire. Her heart pounded in her chest and the one word she wanted to shout lodged in her throat when he spoke again.

"John gave my mother this ring. He truly, deeply loved her. The way I love you. Be my partner, my lover, my wife. You're *my* everything. I want to be yours. Will you marry me?"

Tears spilled down her cheeks. "Yes. Oh God, yes." His tense body relaxed the second she said "yes." He shouldn't be surprised at all she agreed to be his wife. She loved him. He loved her. It was meant to be this way.

She reached for his face as he leaned down to kiss her. Her hand slid along his jaw and settled there as he kissed her long and deep.

He stopped kissing her long enough to slide the ring on her finger.

Roxy held her hand up and admired the sparkling diamond. "I don't think I've ever been this happy."

"John brought you here to give you a better life. It kind of feels like John wanted us to be together. He wanted his Cordero blood to live on, on the ranch. And it will with our children. His last wish was for me to take care of you. I intend to do so for the rest of my life, not out of obligation, but because you make my life so full. I'm a better man because of you. My life is better because of you." Noah kissed her again. "I'll spend the rest of my life making sure you feel the same way about me."

Roxy cupped his jaw and brushed her thumb over his cheek. "I already do. We're going to have such a good life. We'll be a real family."

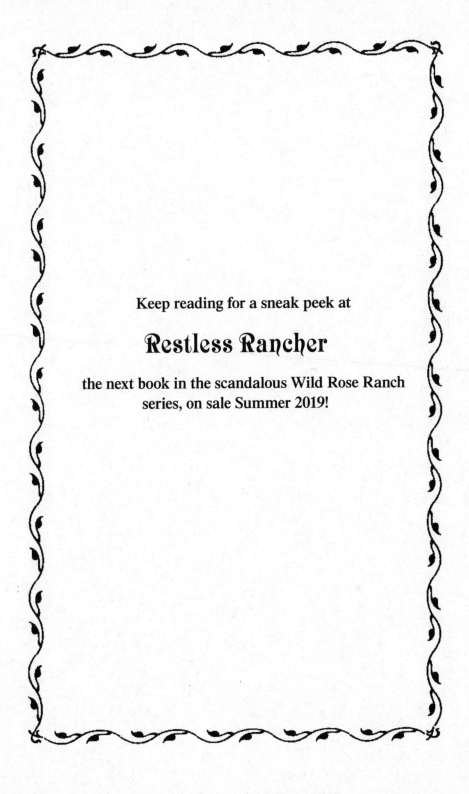

Keep reading for a sneak peek at

Restless Rancher

the next book in the scandalous Wild Rose Ranch series, on sale Summer 2019!

Chapter One

Austin stood in front of the small mirror he'd hung on the wall in the stables and drew the razor down his jaw, scraping away shaving cream and two days' worth of whiskers. He rinsed the blade in a bowl of lukewarm water, ran it down the last section, then wiped his face clean with a damp towel. His hair could use a trim. A comb would do it a hell of a lot of good. Eye drops would erase the red from his eyes. But not even the four ibuprofen he'd taken an hour ago could eradicate the headache raging through his skull because he'd been too anxious to sleep.

Most of his sleepless nights occurred courtesy of a bottle of whiskey. But he'd put the bottle down two weeks ago and was on the cusp of piecing his shattered life back together again.

One of those broken pieces from his past walked in through the barn door that hung off kilter on one hinge like a drunk propped against a bar.

He'd been that guy. But not anymore.

"Lookin' good, Austin, honey." Kelly's voice evoked a lot of memories. Not all of them good.

Her gaze swept over his chest, down his abs, and landed on the button on his jeans, which sagged dangerously close to dropping to his ankles. "You are a sight to behold." Her tongue swept over her red painted lips. For a split second, he remembered how those lips used to wrap around his cock.

But not anymore.

Lust turned to resentment and set his back teeth to grinding.

Wearing a pair of worn jeans barely hanging on his skinny hips and nothing else, he felt naked under her lascivious gaze. He'd lost some weight these last many months drinking and living hand to mouth, hoping he came up with enough money to pay the bills let alone groceries.

Yes, he'd been humbled going from living large with money in his pockets and overflowing his bank account to scraping by on any odd job he could find without his father finding out and retaliating against the person who'd graciously hired him. Most everyone in these parts wouldn't dare cross Walter Hubbard. Not when most of them did business with Hubbard Ranch or worked for Blue Mining. If they didn't, they knew someone who did. Those few brave souls who hired him paid shit because they were desperate and some of them wanted to take Austin down a peg or two.

Just like his old man.

After his grandfather died and left him this ranch, Austin's father fired him from the family business and kicked him out of his home because his father wanted the land with a passion and vengeance Austin never saw coming.

He held on to the one thing that was his even after the money ran out and so did Kelly. This dump wasn't the home Kelly imagined they'd live in after getting married—though she left before he ever asked her—and raise their babies. Not after she'd seen the life he'd lived at Hubbard Ranch, where the good life and their future seemed so easy to imagine.

Here on his grandfather's dilapidated ranch, you needed a fantastical imagination to see its potential.

And in his case, an investor willing to take a chance on someone who'd hit rock bottom but dreamed big.

Unlike Kelly, his best friend Noah's girlfriend, Roxy, believed he could make this place great again. She was an amazing woman with a huge heart and an even bigger bank account. He didn't know what he'd done to deserve it, but Roxy wanted to partner with him and turn this pile of dirt and rotten wood back into a modern working ranch.

Kelly walked away because she didn't believe in the dream or him.

She never gave him a chance to turn this place into what she wanted. What he'd promised her. Abandoned by his girlfriend and disowned by his father in a matter of weeks, beaten down by his father sabotaging his chances for work, yeah, he'd given up and slowly drowned in a bottle and his going-nowhere life.

"What are you doing here? Last time we spoke, you said you'd never step foot on this shit pile again."

Kelly pasted on a pretty pout, not an ounce of regret in her eyes about what she'd said to him. "I wanted to see how you're doing. Can't I come by to check on a friend?"

"You think we're friends?" When he'd lost everything, he'd found out just how many friends he truly had, and she wasn't one of the few who'd stuck by him.

"Don't be like that. How can you still be angry at me? I wanted you. I wanted a ranch and family of our own. You refused to see that this place wasn't going to be our place. All I wanted you to do was sell it and give your father what he wanted. Put a stop to your feud. We could have bought a new home, got married, and had the life we wanted. It was stupid to hold onto this place out of spite and nostalgia. It's just a piece of land."

That last part struck him like a gut punch. "To you. Not to me." They'd had this same argument dozens upon dozens of times. "My father took away everything from me because he wanted to take the one thing that actually belongs to me. This land belonged to my mother's father, and his father before him. I won't sell it."

"Everyone knows you don't have the money to hold onto it." The pity look pissed him off.

"He's made sure of that." Bitterness filled his words and every fiber of his being.

"So you lose it to him anyway. It's useless and stubborn to keep holding onto something when it's already lost."

He didn't want her or his father to know about his new partnership with Roxy. Let them find out when the work finally began and he had his operation up and running. He'd show Kelly, his father, everyone, that he could rise from the ashes and rebuild this place. He had the skill, the drive, and the money if Roxy came through the way she'd promised.

"Did you get dressed up and come all the way out here just to call me names and tell me how stupid I am again?"

He appreciated her sexy legs sticking out the bottom of that flouncy white skirt and the way her breasts rose above the low cut dark blue top. He'd bought her the brown boots with the embossed roses on the sides when he'd had money to burn. Her blond hair was curled into fat rings and tousled to look like she'd just been tumbled good in bed.

He'd messed up her perfectly styled hair and wrinkled her clothes in numerous ways when they were together. He wondered if she'd come here to rekindle the old fire. Before his brain had time to process what a bad idea that was, she stepped up close, wrapped her arms around his neck, pressed her soft breasts against his bare chest, and kissed him with a slow, sexy sweep of her tongue along his bottom lip.

She knew how to tempt him. He'd been living in a sexual drought for a good long while now. So he didn't move and enjoyed the brief moment of feeling desirable and wanted.

She'd burned him in the past, so had many others, and a subtle alert went off in his mind.

She kept her body plastered to his and leaned back to look at him. "What's wrong, honey? You never used to hesitate to take what you wanted." She nudged her belly against his neglected but eagerly growing dick.

He was always ready to bed a beautiful woman, but something didn't feel right.

Kelly had never been this . . . calculated.

Why come back now?

Nothing had changed in his life or with his circumstances.

Unless she'd found out about Roxy partnering with him and thought he had money and means now. But he hadn't told anyone, and Roxy wanted to keep things quiet. She didn't need everyone else in town gossiping about her and the fact that her money came from the notorious Wild Rose Ranch brothel she owned outside of Vegas.

The business was legal, but that didn't matter to folks in Whitefall. When she first came to town, people believed she was a prostitute. Noah and he had made it their mission to change people's minds when they introduced her around at the last ranchers' dinner. That's where Roxy got an up-close view of his relationship with his father and decided she wanted to help him.

"Why are you here now? I'm still broke and you still don't want to live here."

She leaned in and kissed him again. He tried not to get sucked in by her familiar scent and lush curves pressed against him.

"This hasn't changed. I want you. You want me."

His body wanted the release and relief, but the passion and need he once felt for her didn't rise up and drive him to fill his hands with her soft breasts and thrust his aching cock into her welcoming heat.

Her hand slid over his hard stomach, dipped into his jeans, and ran down the length of him. She gripped him in her hand and stroked up and down, her mouth planting hot, wet, open-mouthed kisses down his neck and over his chest. "You know you want more."

She hooked her leg around his hip and used her free hand to take his and slide it up her thigh and under her skirt to her bare bottom. All that silky skin at his fingertips made him grab a handful of ass and press her closer.

She undid his jeans and freed him. "That's it. Give it to me."

His body wanted to give her a good, hard fucking right here, standing up in the dusty barn. But his mind started adding things up. One and one still equaled two, but her and him doing this right here, right now, didn't add up to anything good happening after the deed was done.

She never showed up to any of their dates with no panties and I-can-paint-your-dick-red lips. She flirted but never took an aggressive lead with him for sex. He'd had to talk her into making love on a picnic blanket under a tree on a secluded spot on the ranch. She'd been afraid someone would see them, though the possibility had been near im-possible where he'd taken her. She'd preferred tame public displays of affection and the privacy of a bedroom.

All this shot through his mind and his hands went to her hips as one final thought blasted through his mind. She always, always, insisted on a condom because she didn't want to have children until they were good and married. So a split second before she encased him in her slick core, he set her away and zipped his jeans.

"What the hell is going on here?" His mind identified the clues, but he didn't see the whole picture.

"Why did you stop?" Her cheeks flushed pink. She took a step toward him, her hand reaching for his neck.

He sidestepped before she backed him into the wall and faced her, standing just out of her reach.

Her gaze dropped to his thick erection, then back up to his face. "You still want me."

"My dick's not broke the way I am. I don't have a dime to my name. Seems to me you cared more about that than fucking me anymore, so why don't you tell me why you're all of a sudden all hot and bothered over me to the point you haven't insisted I wear a condom?"

"I'm on the pill."

"Bullshit. We had this talk a long time ago. You can't use the pill because it messes up your system so bad. Try again."

She huffed out a breath and flipped her long blond hair over her shoulder with a careless flick of her hand. "I can't believe you remember that."

"Important talks like that kind of stick with you, especially when *you* made it clear no kids before marriage."

She pressed her lips together and eyed him before the stiffness left her shoulders and they slumped. "I want to get pregnant." Her lips tilted into a lopsided frown. "We want a baby."

"We." For the first time, he saw the diamond ring on her finger. How he'd missed the dime-sized rock, he didn't know. He'd been too stunned to see her and distracted by her attempted seduction to take in the details that had helped set off that alarm in his mind.

"I've been seeing someone. He's good to me. He loves me and wants to give me everything I ever wanted." Her eyes pleaded with him to understand. Like it wasn't personal she loved someone else now.

Despite what happened between them, he wanted her to be happy. "If that's the case, why the hell are you here cheating on your fiancé?" His stomach soured with the thought of touching someone else's woman. He didn't do those kinds of things. He believed in being faithful and telling the truth even when it hurt and meant the end if you wanted out.

"He wants another child, but he had a vasectomy years ago. He had it reversed but the doctors told him his low sperm count would make it difficult to conceive a baby. We talked about alternative ways to get pregnant and he encouraged me to see you."

IVF. Surrogacy. Sperm donor. Adoption. Take your pick of available options. But send your fiancé to another man?

No man who truly loved his woman would share her with another man.

That alert he got earlier turned into a full-on alarm in his head. Acid ate away at his gut and his chest tightened with a weight he didn't want to carry because he suspected where this was going and he didn't want to believe it. It couldn't be true.

"Why me?"

"*We* have a history. I always thought we'd make beautiful babies. We're not together, and things for you haven't exactly worked out the way you wanted. I'm ovulating. I thought we'd have one last good time."

"And what? You'd never tell me about the baby?" His stomach soured and his chest tightened to the point that every breath ached.

"With the way your life is now, you can't take on that responsibility or financial burden."

He didn't know this callous, calculated woman.

"My fiancé and I would love and care for the baby. He'd want for nothing." She moved closer and put her hand on his chest. "Please, Austin. You know how much I want this."

He slapped her hand away. His heart thrashed in his chest and his mind screamed, *no*. This could not be happening. It couldn't be as bad as it appeared. But he had to know the full truth and what she'd planned to keep from him as long as she could before it all came out. Because secrets like this always come out.

"Who put that ring on your finger?" His mind screamed, *you don't want to know.*

Her gaze dropped to his boots. "We've kept our relationship quiet."

He pointed to her hand. "Astronauts can see that ring from space. You really think you're being discreet?"

"Austin, who I'm with doesn't change the fact this is what I want. You don't have to take responsibility for the child. Ten minutes and your work is done." A plea filled her eyes. "I know that sounds insensitive, but men get women pregnant all the time and don't have anything to do with the child."

She sounded like a lunatic.

"And you think I'm that kind of man." It hurt that someone would believe that about him.

"I want a baby, Austin. This is the most expedient way to get one. You and I care about each other, which makes this easier. You're a good guy. You want me to be happy. So please, help me have a baby."

Despite what she thought of him and the hurtful words, though she really had no idea how much they stung, he did want her to have everything. Maybe some guys would see the upside of having sex with a beautiful woman and walking away. But he would never turn his back on a child the way his father turned his back on him. That she didn't see that hurt more.

"No."

Surprise filled her eyes, but his rejection didn't squash her determination. "I'll pay you."

The desperate words slammed into him with the force of a knife plunging into his chest. "Not only no, but fuck you. I'm not some stud for hire." The thought sickened him.

For the first time, he understood how Roxy felt when people accused her of being a prostitute.

"Ten thousand dollars." She clasped her hands in front of her like she prayed he'd accept. But her desperation spoke of more than her desire to have a child.

She *needed* him to say yes.

He wouldn't play Kelly's whore for any amount of money. And he wondered, like the ring, where she got that kind of cash. "Who is your fiancé?"

She shook her head and backed up a step, too afraid to tell him.

And that's when the rage exploded inside him as fast as the truth lit up his mind.

He shot forward, tilted her chin up with the tip of his finger, and made her look at him. "Who is it? Say it," he dared her.

Tears filled her eyes. Her gaze strayed over his shoulder and she whispered, "Your father." Those two words blasted through his mind and constricted his chest. He couldn't breathe for trying to contain the fury burning inside him.

Before he lost his head, he released Kelly and turned his back on her.

His own father had taken up with his ex-girlfriend and wanted Austin to sire a child that he'd raise. The thought turned his stomach and sent bile to the back of his throat.

Over my dead body.

"He wants *my* child." He spit out the vile words.

"You two are so stubborn. You won't sell. He refuses to leave his estate or the companies to anyone but family."

"So long as that family isn't me."

"Do you blame him?"

Austin spun around to face her. "Yes! Why do I have to bend and give up what's mine? Why do I have to do what he says because he demands it? Why can't I have what's mine and make something of it? I busted my ass working for him. I did everything he wanted from the time I was a child to running the operations. But this one thing he can't let go of. Why?"

Kelly held her hands out and let them drop to the sides of her thighs. "I don't know. I tried to change his mind, but he won't let it go."

"Instead, he doubles down on humiliating me by seducing my ex-girlfriend, then sends her here to fuck me for my baby. He hasn't taken enough, he wants my child, too!" Anger stung his throat as those ridiculous words burst out his mouth.

"The child would be his grandson. He'd get everything."

"And that's all that matters. You get what you want. He gets what he wants. What about what I fucking want?" He yelled so loudly he was sure the rickety rafters overhead vibrated with his rage the way his whole body shook with it. "I would never—EVER!—give up my child. Anyone who thinks that of me doesn't know the real me. And that includes you." He took a menacing step toward her, his body rigid and begging for a fight it wouldn't get. "How could you come here with his ring on your finger and think I'd ever want to touch you, let alone have a baby with you? I don't even want to look at you. Get out."

She reached for him again, but he stepped back. The thought of her ever touching him again sent a shiver of revulsion through him.

"Get out!"

This time he was sure his fury would bring down the roof.

She spun on the heels of the boots he'd bought her, her skirt flaring out, showing off a lot of thigh. She'd come here hoping he'd knock her up without a second thought and she'd walk out with his child and raise it with his father.

He didn't think Kelly or his father could hurt him more than they had when they abandoned him, but this twisted deception they'd tried to pull over on him hit hard and cut deep.

He waited for the sound of her car to fade before he walked out of the barn and headed for his pathetic bed on the porch of the hoarder house he couldn't stand to go in and the bottle he'd left under the cot and hadn't touched in two weeks.

He needed a drink.

Or ten.

There might not be enough whiskey in Montana to make him forget what just happened.

His life couldn't get any worse than this. Right?